The Ho

Phillip Strang

BOOKS BY PHILLIP STRANG

DCI Isaac Cook Series
MURDER IS A TRICKY BUSINESS
MURDER HOUSE
MURDER IS ONLY A NUMBER
MURDER IN LITTLE VENICE
MURDER IS THE ONLY OPTION
MURDER IN NOTTING HILL
MURDER IN ROOM 346
MURDER OF A SILENT MAN
MURDER HAS NO GUILT
MURDER IN HYDE PARK
SIX YEARS TOO LATE
GRAVE PASSION
MURDER WITHOUT REASON

DI Keith Tremayne Series
DEATH UNHOLY
DEATH AND THE ASSASSIN'S BLADE
DEATH AND THE LUCKY MAN
DEATH AT COOMBE FARM
DEATH BY A DEAD MAN'S HAND
DEATH IN THE VILLAGE
BURIAL MOUND
THE BODY IN THE DITCH
THE HORSE'S MOUTH

Steve Case Series
HOSTAGE OF ISLAM
THE HABERMAN VIRUS
PRELUDE TO WAR

Standalone Books
MALIKA'S REVENGE

Copyright Page

Copyright © 2020 Phillip Strang

Cover Design by Phillip Strang

All rights reserved. No part of this book may be reproduced, stored in a retrieval system, or transmitted in any form or by any means (electronic, mechanical, photocopying, recording or otherwise) without the prior written permission of the publisher, except by a reviewer who may quote brief passages in a review to be printed by a newspaper, magazine, or journal.

All characters appearing in this work are fictitious. Any resemblance to actual events, locales, or persons, living or dead, is coincidental.

All Rights Reserved.

This work is registered with the UK Copyright Service

ISBN: 9798669760939

Dedication

For Elli and Tais who both had the perseverance to make me sit down and write.

The Horse's Mouth

Chapter 1

It was a Saturday, the first meeting of the season at Salisbury Racecourse, Red Rose out in front, the third race of the day, and Detective Inspector Tremayne of Homicide enjoying a day away from the office, twenty pounds to win on the horse.

'He can't lose. The horse is in great form; the going's firm. I've got a couple of hundred pounds on it to win, no messing around with each way, not today,' Les Daniels, the stable hand who had prepared the horse, had said. 'Straight from the horse's mouth, that what it is. You were right to put twenty pounds on it.'

'And then, what are your plans for the future?' Tremayne said as the two men drank their pints of beer.

'Who knows? I want to be a trainer, get a couple of horses under me, a few wins,' Daniels, a small and wiry-thin man in his forties, said. A former jockey, he had ridden in the Grand National once, the premier horse race over fences in England, came in second.

Les Daniels was, as Tremayne knew, a man who had been on the cusp of greatness as a jockey, only to have it ruined by the jockey's curse, alcohol. Tremayne liked the man, and even if he didn't get out to the races that often, he made sure to have a drink with him, reminisce about horses Daniels had known, and Tremayne had lost money on.

Red Rose, a horse with a moderate record, only winning once on its last ten starts, won at Salisbury that day, to cheers from those who had made good money on the horse, a look of disbelief and criticism from those who hadn't.

It was, as was soon known, contrary to the expected outcome of the race. The result subject to investigation, no bets to be paid out until the win was confirmed.

Daniels, made aware of what was happening, downed his pint, shook Tremayne's hand and dashed off. 'Sour grapes, not allowing a great horse to show its promise,' he said.

Tremayne went back to his beer, confident he would be returning home that night with a full wallet instead of his pockets hanging out, and Jean telling him what a fool he was.

It was, however, a pleasant early summer's day, the sort of day when the English countryside is at its best, the picture-postcard image that adorns tourist brochures.

Tremayne stayed long enough to finish his beer and then left the bar. He found Honest Joe Blakely, his bookmaker, hustling. Over the tannoy, the announcement of a steward's enquiry into Red Rose's win.

Tremayne didn't give much credence to the delay, as disputed results weren't unheard of, but this was a good win for the police inspector, a chance to prove that those who criticised him, mainly in a whispered aside, would be proved wrong.

The Horse's Mouth

'You'll have to wait, Tremayne,' Blakely said. The punter's friend, that was how the bald man with a shiny head, an even shinier nose, a twisted mouth and a pronounced lisp, saw himself. Tremayne, nobody ever called him Keith, not even his wife, knew that Blakely was a friend of no one. He lived in a large house on the edge of the New Forest, proclaimed a royal forest in 1079 by William the Conqueror. It was once the haunt of kings for hunting, but now it is the largest contiguous area of unsown vegetation in lowland Britain, a National Park, and no hunting is allowed.

Even so, Tremayne would afford Blakely the epithet of 'Honest' as he had always paid out the winnings, kept the money from those that had lost, which meant in Tremayne's case that Blakely was in profit. But not today, not if the stewards came out in favour of Red Rose.

'Good day?' Tremayne said.

'Could have been better. I could be out of pocket.'

Tremayne knew that Blakely never left a racecourse without a profit.

Blakely was an anachronism, able to switch from hot to cold, from agreeable to miserable. Even so, Tremayne had to admit that the man was a colourful character, the type of person that racecourses draw.

Another announcement from the tannoy. The runner up in the race had been declared the winner.

Tremayne symbolically tore up his betting slip and threw it into a bin.

'Better luck next time,' Blakely said.

'There'll not be one,' Tremayne's reply.

Both men knew that one did not rely on luck to make his money, and the other would be back.

***

Les Daniels found Tremayne standing next to Blakely, and beckoned him over, insisted that he came with him.

Tremayne followed Daniels down a path away from where the bookmakers conducted their business. It wasn't like Daniels to be furtive, Tremayne thought but didn't dwell on it. After all, Les Daniels, when half-drunk, was a strange man.

Some remembered Daniels' racing career. He had shown great promise and won a couple of prestigious races, but he had been a careless rider, cutting in where he shouldn't have, whipping the horse more than the regulations allowed. In the end, it wasn't his riding that doomed him. It was his drinking, how he and other jockeys, starving to keep the weight down, relaxed at the end of the day, and especially at the end of the racing season.

'It's Red Rose,' Daniels said, grabbing Tremayne by his arm. 'I've not told anyone. I want you to see.'

Daniels undid the lock on the stable. Inside four stalls, three unoccupied, the one remaining occupied by Red Rose.

Daniels grabbed hold of Tremayne by his collar, a not altogether easy action, as Daniels was short, barely up to Tremayne's shoulder, and pulled him forward into the stall.

'There,' Daniels pointed.

On the ground, Red Rose. Tremayne knew death when he saw it. The animal had run its race literally, on the track and off.

'What do you want me to do?' Tremayne said, transfixed by the sight.

The Horse's Mouth

'They'll blame me, say that I nobbled the horse, made him run fast, and then, a dead racehorse. If he had gone out to stud, assuming he could have won a few more races, he could have made money for the owners, but now, he's worthless, and it's my fault.'

'Is it?' Tremayne asked. 'Can they blame you?'

'They can, and they will.'

Tremayne knew the truth: blame the messenger, or in racing circles, if not the trainer, then the stable hand who had worked the horse too hard, not fed him correctly, not allowed him to cool down after a race. The reasons for shifting the blame were infinite, Tremayne knew, having experienced it at the police station.

'An autopsy?' Tremayne said.

'They'll want to know the reason for its death.'

'Insurance?'

'I'd not know,' Daniels said. 'I only ride the horses on track work and look after them, paid a pittance for the privilege.'

'A vocation?'

'I love the animals, and Red Rose, well, he could be cantankerous, but he had spirit, a personality. Always pleased to see me.'

Tremayne had noticed that before. An expert at judging the potential of a horse before he had placed money on it, he had seen how some horses warmed to a particular jockey, not to others. Not that it ever helped him to place a winning bet. However, a dead horse wasn't a pleasant sight, and Daniels was emotional as the animal lay in its stall.

'Any reason?' Tremayne said.

'None that I'd know off. Red Rose was always in good physical condition. I suppose his heart must have failed.'

Tremayne left Daniels grieving at the body and walked around the stable, not sure why.

In the other three stalls, there was straw on the floor, a pungent smell that reminded him of his childhood in a small village in Somerset. He had never felt affection for the rural life, although the odour brought back memories of a cheerful mother and a stern father, a man not averse to taking his belt to the wayward Tremayne in his youth.

It hadn't done him any harm, Tremayne mulled. As a junior policeman, new in the force, a swift kick up the rear end, a clenched fist in the stomach, had waylaid a few hooligans on their way to crime, a few criminals who had felt his wrath, learnt some respect.

Time had moved on, and policing was now political correctness and a softly-softly approach. Tremayne wondered if his time as a police officer was up, whether he should accept a retirement package, and spend time with his wife, travelling the world as she wanted to. He took stock of himself, stored the melancholic thoughts where they belonged – in the back of his mind.

'Over here,' Daniels shouted.

'What is it?' Tremayne asked.

'It's the horse. Look at the hind legs. Red Rose's white markings.'

'I can't see anything wrong.'

'It's paint, white paint. This horse isn't Red Rose.'

'You led the horse out.'

'It was Red Rose that I prepared this morning, but it wasn't me that took him out.'

'Who did?'

'Sally Kirkland, the owner's daughter. I handed the horse over to her.'

The Horse's Mouth

'Has she done it before?'

'Red Rose always liked her, and yes, a couple of times, never any problem.'

'But today the horse was substituted?'

Tremayne's interest was piqued. Nobbling a horse was one thing, switching it for another indicated something else, and why use paint when peroxide would have been more effective. But he knew that peroxide took time to take effect, and paint was quicker.

Tremayne could see professional intent, amateurish resolve.

'How could the switch be made?' Tremayne asked.

'Not so easy. From the stable, the horse is visible, apart from when it goes between another couple of stables.'

'Show me.'

Daniels made a phone call, informed the owner of what he knew so far. 'He can deal with the stewards. We need to find my horse,' he said.

Tremayne followed as best he could behind the agitated little man. Yet Daniels was fast, almost running, calling out the horse's name.

Inside the first stable, three horses; none were Red Rose. At the second stable, Daniels entered gingerly, Tremayne waited outside. A group of men were heading his way, a red-faced rotund man wearing tweeds at the front. Tremayne knew him by sight, Barton Kirkland, the owner of the missing horse.

From inside the stables, there was a shriek. 'In here.'

'I want a word with him,' Kirkland said to the stewards who were behind him. 'I want to know what's going on.'

Tremayne stood in the man's way. 'You'll have to wait,' he said.

'And who do you think you are, blocking my way?'

'Detective Inspector Tremayne, Salisbury Police.'

'It's not a police matter.'

'I'm not saying it is, but Daniels just let out a shout. It's up to me to check, seeing I'm here.'

'Very well. It's my horse I want, not that snivelling little man. My best horse, subject to an enquiry.'

'Foul play?'

'That's not proven, not yet,' one of the stewards, a neatly dressed man, said.

'Daniels told you the horse that ran was a substitute?' Tremayne said.

'He has,' Kirkland said.

Tremayne left the fuming Kirkland and the befuddled stewards outside.

'What is it?' Tremayne said to Daniels, who was leaning up against a far wall inside the stable.

'In there, in there,' he said.

Tremayne walked over, took hold of Daniels by the shoulder. 'Take a grip of yourself. Kirkland's outside spitting blood. I can't help you if you act like a headless chicken.'

'In there,' Daniels said again.

Tremayne released Daniels' shoulder and looked to where the distraught man pointed.

It was strange, Tremayne thought, that a dead horse upset him, but a dead body did not. There was no need to approach: the rope around her neck, the colour of the woman's skin, the look of death.

How long she had been there, he couldn't be sure, but it would have been more than an hour.

'It's Sally, Kirkland's daughter,' Daniels blurted out. 'Somebody has killed her.'

Tremayne took stock of the situation, phoned his sergeant, gave her a brief update. He knew that she'd call Jim Hughes, the chief crime scene investigator, as well as organise for the uniforms to secure the crime scene. For him, the task of breaking the news to the woman's father.

Chapter 2

Barton Kirkland initially reacted with bluster and anger as Tremayne came out from the stable, followed by the visibly shaken Daniels.

'Mr Kirkland,' Tremayne said as he took hold of the man's arm and pulled him to one side, away from the stewards, 'unfortunately your daughter has died.'

Kirkland stood rooted to the spot, his red face turning ashen, his body shrinking.

'It can't be, not Sally,' he finally said with a trembling voice.

'Subject to confirmation by you, I'm afraid it is. Daniels has identified the woman.'

'And the horse?'

'It's not your horse,' Tremayne said.

'I want to see my daughter.'

'I'm sorry, I can't allow that, not yet. It's a crime scene, and I don't want you and anyone else destroying vital evidence.'

'I hold you responsible for her death,' Kirkland said as he stretched out a beefy hand and grabbed Daniels, causing the man to grimace.

'For the horse, maybe,' Tremayne said. 'But his alibi's cast-iron for your daughter. Mr Kirkland, I don't think you fully understood what I was saying, or maybe I wasn't clear. It's a homicide.'

'Sally? Murdered?'

'That's up to the crime scene investigators and pathology to confirm, but yes, that's what it is.'

The Horse's Mouth

'I understood you clear enough the first time. We've met before, you and I, haven't we, Inspector Tremayne?'

Tremayne took a long hard look at the man, imagined him younger, a lot less weight, a healthy complexion. 'That wasn't the name you used back then,' Tremayne said.

'You weren't in Homicide then,' Kirkland said.

'Over thirty years ago, a constable back then, wet behind the ears.'

'Five years I got, out in two.'

'You deserved it. Although we never got you for the other crime.'

'Robbery with menace, I'll not deny it, but I used my time well in prison, educated myself. I'd appreciate it if you kept it in confidence.'

'And now, wealthy,' Tremayne said.

'My daughter?'

Tremayne looked over at the stewards who were standing apart, huddled in a group. 'Anyone of you a doctor?' he said.

'I am,' a man, ginger-haired, his hair parted in the middle, said.

'Mr Kirkland will probably need a sedative. He's just received bad news. Mrs Kirkland?'

'There is no Mrs Kirkland,' Kirkland said. 'She died five years ago, cancer. It was just Sally and me.'

How quickly the verb tense changes, Tremayne thought. Sally Kirkland now referred to in the past tense.

'It's not Red Rose,' Daniels said. Some colour had come back to his face, and he had procured a bottle of water from somewhere.

'Then who or what is it?' a tall, imperious man with skeletal features said. He introduced himself as Colin

Branson. Tremayne could see him with a pince-nez perched on the end of his beak-like nose, a quill in his hand, entering the figures into a voluminous ledger, a character out of a Charles Dickens novel.

'I don't know. Whatever the horse was, it wasn't the animal I handed over to Sally.'

'Sally?' Kirkland said.

'She sometimes took the horse from the stable up to the parade ring, as you well know.'

'Was she killed for this?' Kirkland looked over at Tremayne.

'That seems to be why we're here, although I was initially more interested in the horse, had money on it.'

'I can update you on that,' Branson said. 'Excessive use of the whip, suspension of the jockey if upheld.'

'Not a reason to dispute the race's outcome.'

'If it's only the whip, but we needed a full report, a veterinary examination of the animal for maltreatment, administration of stimulants. It's winning time wasn't expected, not on the firm going.'

'How long before you make a decision?'

'That, Inspector, is up to you. If it's murder, then it's safe to presume that whoever committed the heinous crime is also responsible for substituting horses, and for the death of one of them.'

'I don't presume anything,' Tremayne said. 'Homicide I know; horse substitution I don't. Although, no doubt, I will become an expert soon enough. As for you, Mr Kirkland, your daughter, any enemies?'

'None at all. Sally was a lovely person, admired by many, a large circle of friends.'

The Horse's Mouth

Tremayne had heard it before, too many times, how the dead person was almost saintly, cared for by all, wouldn't harm a butterfly, ad infinitum.

Everyone had skeletons in the cupboard, enemies, some visible, some not, and somewhere someone would have their nose out of joint, a financial deal that went wrong, a jilted lover. Sally Kirkland's past and present would be examined in close detail, as would her father's.

Tremayne cast a glance over at the father; he could see that the realisation was starting to impact on him. In the distance, the ginger-haired steward, a doctor's bag in one hand, was ready to dispense medicine to calm the man, but not to quieten him, not totally. It was a murder, and the father and Les Daniels were prime suspects. The two of them were in for a long day and most of the night, as were Tremayne and his sergeant.

***

'Whoever killed her wrapped a cord around her neck and hoisted her up,' Jim Hughes, the senior crime scene investigator, said to Tremayne as they stood next to the body.

Inured to death, the two men discussed the murder with a professional detachment. Hughes sucked on a cough tablet; Tremayne fumbled for a pack of cigarettes in his pocket.

'It doesn't make any sense,' Tremayne said. 'Fixing a race, I can understand. That's just criminal, but killing someone, especially here under everyone's noses, just raises the curiosity of many, the interest of the police.'

'I'll leave that to you. Does your man's alibi stand?'

'He was with me. He didn't kill her, and besides, the woman would have been a lot stronger than Daniels. I'd say he's not the healthiest, too much time spent drinking and smoking.'

'The same as you.'

'I'd say so, but I've got a bit more flesh on me than he has. He's a strong contender for substituting the horse, may even know where Red Rose is, but he's not a murderer.'

'He's not off the hook?'

'Far from it, nor is Barton Kirkland, not that he would have killed his daughter. Although the man's hardly a saint.'

'Committing a crime so close to his home makes no sense,' Hughes said.

'What else on the body?'

'She had been pulled up. One person, not two, which would have seemed more logical considering that the deceased wasn't a small woman.'

'A preliminary report?' Tremayne asked. Hughes would give him the salient facts. After all, the woman had died no more than three hours previously, the body still warm, and murder was not in dispute.

'One person, strong enough to have hoisted her. The time of death, from when she left the horse in the parade ring and the time Daniels discovered the body. Rigour Mortis begins approximately three hours after death, and the body shows some signs, although the ambient temperature in the stable has slowed the decrease in the body temperature. Her fingernails are clean, which tends to rule out farm work, and if she rode or worked with the horses, it's unlikely she cleaned out the stables.'

'Over here,' one of the CSIs shouted out, too loud for Hughes, given they were near a dead body, and

The Horse's Mouth

some dignity was appropriate. But then Gwyneth Dexter was a boisterous individual, a little too fond of alcohol and a dubious taste in men. Hughes had warned her a couple of times about her out-of-work behaviour, only for the woman to state that her private and personal life were two parts of her, and that one was Jim Hughes's concern, and the other was her business and for him to keep his nose out of it.

Hughes knew she was right, and whereas he would gladly dispense with her services, she was a brilliant and perceptive investigator, diligent, and her reports were of the highest quality. On another investigation five months earlier, she had found a diamond stud in a drainpipe at a house, the one piece of evidence that linked the tenant to the robbery of a jewellery store in Salisbury.

Hughes looked down at a small shard of glass that Gwyneth Dexter had found.

'Easy to miss,' she said.

'Your opinion?' Hughes asked.

'Why would there be glass in a stable with valuable horses? It makes no sense.'

Hughes knew she was right. It would have been a deduction he would have made, although some of the other investigators, more experienced than Dexter, would not have.

'What sort of glass?' Tremayne asked.

'A wine glass,' the woman replied. 'Someone's been in here celebrating.'

'Any sign of another person in here?'

Gwyneth Dexter went over to where the glass had been and sniffed close to the ground.

'Chardonnay, Australian,' she said.

'How can you be so sure?' Hughes asked.

'My father runs a pub, grew up around alcohol and drunks, the reason I don't drink,' the woman's standard response to questions about her sobriety or lack of.

'Your father?'

'Occasionally he'd drink too much. No violence or abuse from him, so I'm not laying my abstinence at his feet. It's just that I don't like it, nor the people who can't handle it. But it's a Chardonnay; I'll guarantee that.'

'How long since the glass contained wine?' Hughes asked.

'It's recent.'

'Sally Kirkland, recent sexual activity?' Tremayne said.

'The pathologist would be able to tell you,' Hughes said.

Chapter 3

Les Daniels sat in the interview room at the police station. He needed to give a statement, although he hadn't killed the woman, his alibi the best there was, in the company of a police inspector when she died.

'Les, your take on this,' Tremayne said. 'What do you reckon? Why kill Sally Kirkland and substitute a horse?'

'Kirkland?'

'He's at his house. After here, we'll be out to see him. Sad, which is understandable under the circumstances. Sally, the daughter, your impression of her.'

'She understood horses, and even if she had her nose in the air, she was friendly to me, a mutual love of horses, especially Red Rose.'

'Nose in the air?' Clare Yarwood asked. Thirty-nine years of age, almost as tall as Tremayne, taller than most men, she had been with Tremayne for more than a decade.

The relationship between the recalcitrant inspector and his younger sergeant came with great affection. However, Tremayne would not say it out aloud nor show it. Although, in the quiet of the family home, Tremayne would admit to Jean, his wife, how fond he was of his sergeant.

He had stood up at Clare's wedding the previous year and spoken of their time together as a team, how she and Jean had helped him through his illness, exacerbated by drink and cigarettes, and how they had solved cases together, each playing off the other's strengths.

Clare had shed a tear as he spoke, and her husband Clive Grantley had firmly shaken the man's hand afterwards.

'I remember Kirkland when he first started buying horses,' Daniels said. 'Back then, he didn't know much, and he wasn't as polished as you see him now, not as wealthy. The first horse he bought, a sad-looking eight-year-old gelding, only fit for a riding school.'

'You helped him with the purchase?'

'I did.'

'Why buy a dud?'

'Kirkland was interested in horse racing, but he didn't have the money. As I saw it, if we kept to racecourses where the horses weren't necessarily the best, then we could learn the trade, and slowly upgrade.'

'The same as buying an old car, fixing it up and buying another,' Tremayne said.

'More or less. Salisbury Racecourse wasn't a place to run the horse, but we found other racecourses, made a few bets, and the horse, even if it was sad-looking, perked up with good food and attention. It even won a few races.'

'The horse?' Clare asked.

'We sold it, bought another. By that time, Barton's got more money. The next horse, similar to Red Rose, lasted a couple of years before we sold it.'

Which to Clare meant that it went to another buyer or the slaughterhouse, destined for pet food. She didn't want to think about it, having been an avid rider in her younger years back in Norfolk.

'You've not explained about Sally Kirkland's nose in the air,' Tremayne reminded Daniels.

'Kirkland wasn't anything special, just an average knockabout guy, scraping by, trying to better himself, eventually succeeding. As his wealth improved, so did his social circle; no place for a past-his-prime jockey.'

'You were friends?'

'It was our mutual interest, a love of horses, that formed the friendship, although we had known each other since childhood. But then he's going about with the affluent and the landed gentry, anyone with a title.'

The murder was the reason for Tremayne's and Clare Yarwood's interest. Still, illegal gambling, altering the outcome of a horse race, were powerful motives for violence and ultimately death.

'Sally Kirkland?' Clare asked for the third time.

Daniels looked over at Tremayne and Clare, readjusted his position on his chair and rested his elbows on the table. 'It was like this. As Kirkland changed, so did his daughter. It was the best schools for her, and then her easy association with those of the social standing he aspired to.'

'And reached,' Tremayne said.

'He thought so, but I could see them sometimes, sniggering behind his back. If you want friends, get a dog, or someone like me. They only pretend that he is one of them, but Kirkland was nouveau riche, an upstart.'

'And Sally?'

'Second generation, and besides, she carried it well. The manner about her, the ease with which she integrated. She was accepted; her father was tolerated.'

'Did you like her?'

'She loved the horses, the same as I did. And yes, I liked her very much, even her father. Good people, treated me well.'

'But you've stayed poor, whereas he became rich.'

'Not everyone wants the trappings of wealth. As long as I was around horses, I had a place to sleep, a few pints of beer in my belly and good food, what more should anyone want?'

It was a reasonable outlook on life, Clare thought, but she wondered if it was true. After all, Kirkland's attitude towards Daniels had been anything but friendly or even respectful at the murder scene.

'Let's come back to when you handed the horse over to Sally,' Tremayne said.

'It was ten, fifteen minutes before I met up with you,' Daniels said. 'Usually, I'd lead the horse out, but Sally did today.'

'And you had no problem?'

'As I said before, it wasn't the first time, and besides, it's her father's horse, and if she wanted the fame and glory, who am I to stop her?'

'Fame and glory? That's a sweeping statement,' Clare said.

'She liked to show off. No doubt some of her friends were at the course.'

'You don't approve?'

'Fair-weather friends, not the sort you could rely on when you're down and out.'

'Were they?'

'Kirkland knew them for what they were worth. He confided that much in me, but Sally was still young, not experienced in life or reality. Age brings wisdom, and one day, she would have found out the hard way.'

'Do you blame her for her naivete?' Clare asked.

'It's just an observation. If you spend enough time with animals, especially horses, smart that they are, you get to know a thing or two. Look into a horse's eyes, observe how it stands, how it moves, and you can tell if

The Horse's Mouth

it's got the right spirit. If it's an animal that will run fast because of a whip and the jockey pushing it, or whether it runs because it wants to, whether it wants to win.'

'Red Rose?' Tremayne said.

'Middle of the road. The same as the first horse that Kirkland bought. He had his heart in the right place, and sometimes he produced great results, but what you need is consistency, the natural ability, the desire to want to win, to respond to the jockey. Not many have got that, but when they do, they're unassailable.'

'Kirkland's looking for that?'

'We all are. Red Rose could have bred that winner, who knows? But now, the horse is missing. What are you doing about it?' Daniels asked.

'Sally Kirkland is our primary focus.'

'She left with the horse. You can ask me more questions, but I can't give you an answer as to what happened to her, or how the substitution occurred. But whoever did it, wasn't an amateur, although the paint on the hind legs was. Find that person or persons, and you'll find your murderer.'

Tremayne agreed in part with Daniels' summation as to the crimes committed, but it was conjecture, unsupported by fact. Barton Kirkland would be the next interviewed, and his testimony would hopefully be more telling than Daniels.

***

Barton Kirkland said little when Tremayne and Clare met him at his house on the outskirts of Salisbury, just off the Amesbury Road, close to Old Sarum, an Anglo-Saxon fort, the site of a previous murder they had investigated.

'We have a few questions,' Tremayne said as the three of them sat down at a table in the kitchen.

Clare could see the tiredness in the man's eyes, the redness. She remembered a brash, full-of-himself man whom her husband tolerated, but didn't like, and she had met at a function two months previously.

'Not as many as I have for you,' Kirkland's response. He was, Clare could see, shrunken in stature, his shoulders hunched, his back curved, his face looking down at the floor. In front of him, a half-empty bottle of whisky. Judging by the smell of the man's breath, it had been full a few hours before.

Clare couldn't blame the man; she knew the hurt when a loved one died, felt a twinge as if she were unfaithful to her husband when she thought back to her first love in Salisbury, Harry Holchester, but he was long dead.

'That's as may be, and Kirkland, I'm sorry for your loss, but it's a murder enquiry. There are questions that we need to ask.'

'Ask them and leave. I need time to myself.'

'Your daughter? Her relationship with Les Daniels and Red Rose?'

'There was no relationship. Daniels has been with me for a long time. A good jockey in his day. He could have done better, but the man hadn't the self-discipline, too easily swayed by the bottle and the good life.'

'He's not got that now,' Clare said.

'It takes effort to rise above the crowd. Daniels never had it.'

'But you do?'

'Until today, I did.'

'Tell us about Sally.'

'She loved horses, would have fancied herself as a jockey, but she didn't have the physique, too heavy boned, too much weight.'

The Horse's Mouth

'That's an unusual statement, almost critical,' Tremayne said.

'I don't see how,' Kirkland said. He lifted his head, looked at Tremayne and Clare. 'It's not only the horse that wins the race; it's the jockey. Sally could have never got down to the weight, and she knew that. No amount of starving would have let her. Now her mother, rest her soul, she could have made the weight. A small woman, petite, but Sally, she took after me.'

'We need to put the pieces together. We've got a missing horse to deal with, not that its fate is necessarily our concern, but we have to assume that those who took the horse and killed your daughter are the same.'

'But why swap horses?' Kirkland said. 'It doesn't make sense, not to me. Red Rose was in good fettle. He would have won the race.'

'Would or should?' Clare said, remembering that Tremayne was a master of knowing which horse should have won the race; afterwards, equally astute, why it hadn't.

'Okay, I'll admit that a couple of other horses would have given him a run for his money, but I had faith in the animal.'

'Did you have money on the horse?' Tremayne asked.

'I never bet on my horses,' Kirkland said.

'Why?'

'I always thought it was bad luck, somehow jinxing the horse.'

'Superstitious?' Clare asked.

'It's just the way it is. I do have the occasional bet on races where one of my horses isn't running, never on my own.'

'And sometimes you bet on a horse that's running against Red Rose?'

'Just a flutter, a couple of hundred pounds each way. If you know the odds, and the horse you've put your money on comes in in the first three, then you're ahead. It's just an interest, the thrill of cheering on a horse. Tremayne would understand.'

Tremayne did, but the most he ever placed on a horse was twenty pounds, sufficient to ensure a good return if the horse won, not enough to leave him out of pocket if it didn't.

'I'll be honest with you,' Tremayne said. 'You, Barton Kirkland, have done well, bringing yourself up from minor crime to a person of note. Commendable, we'd all agree, but how have you done this? What skills do you have that others don't?'

'Tenacity, a need to make each day worthwhile, not to languish in a pub, waste my time on frivolous pursuits.'

Tremayne thought the man's comments might have been an aside to him, but dismissed them as just a sad man speaking without conscious intent to offend or otherwise.

'Your daughter?'

'The same drive, and now she's dead.'

'No doubt you want to solve your daughter's murder, the same as we do,' Tremayne said.

'I do.'

'Then level with me. Is your affluence a result of crime? Did you swap horses, affect the odds, the chance of a horse winning or losing? Not so difficult these days, you'd have to admit.'

Kirkland sat still, a pause as he thought through what Tremayne was saying. Clare was sure that the man wasn't squeaky clean, but a criminal act that inadvertently resulted in the death of his daughter was too hard to contemplate.

'No.'

A one-word reply, but it wasn't true, Tremayne knew that.

Outside the house, Tremayne lit up a cigarette. Kirkland, he knew, would take the law into his own hands. As he had said, he was tenacious, determined. Wherever his horse was, so were guilty men, men who would kill; and in the house they had just left, a man who would have his vengeance.

It was an awkward situation, and it was only going to get worse.

Chapter 4

It was strange, Tremayne knew, that after the initial flurry of activity in a new murder investigation came the inevitable anti-climax when the leads start to dry and the ideas of how to proceed dull. It was a time he did not like.

'I reckon that Kirkland was involved in the death of a man over thirty years ago, not that I could ever prove it,' Tremayne said to his sergeant.

Clare Yarwood, a long time with her senior, knew full well that Tremayne held on to bits of information and suspicions about people and crimes that he knew of or suspected. And if he believed that Kirkland, grieving or not, was a murderer, then he was.

As for herself, married life with Clive Grantley, a man admired in the city after the truth of his brother's death had been revealed and who was still the mayor of the market town, had settled into a pleasant routine. A private man, Clive had not reacted to the criticism when a young and attractive woman spent the night in his house, not willing to state that she was his daughter, Kim, the result of an earlier romance. One parent had preferred academia, and the other was ensconced in Salisbury. Even though they had separated, they maintained the emotional tie of a shared child, brought up by her mother but spending time with her father, joint holidays in the summer, his presence at Christmas and birthdays and school functions. The truth had reluctantly been divulged during the investigation into Grantley's brother, and now Kim was Clare's closest friend.

The Horse's Mouth

Clare's dilemma about whether to have a child still weighed on her; after all, she was approaching forty. Her position was secure in the police, but Tremayne was still heading towards retirement, not that he wanted it.

If anyone else was in the office, he'd be there, animated and in control, but when the lights were low, at night, or if writing up a report, the eyes would close. Sometimes, he would stand up with a start, look out of the window, take a deep breath. Clare, like Tremayne's wife, Jean, knew the truth. Jean would happily have him at home to fuss over, but she knew that without a focus her husband, a man devoid of hobbies, not interested in golf, and not bothered with gardening, would slowly pine away, dying earlier than he should. Policing was the man's vocation, his joy; it was what gave him stress levels too high for his age and his physical condition. It was a Catch-22, and he knew it, as did the two women who worried about him.

However, tiredness on Tremayne's part and a dilemma on Clare's did not help in resolving the murder of Kirkland's daughter, nor the reason for the substitution of a horse. A horse didn't figure in a murder enquiry usually, but the death of an animal, no matter how unfortunate, how loved, and how valuable, did this time appear to be very relevant.

Barry Vincent, Kirkland's vet, was initially insulted when Tremayne told him that he would not be conducting the autopsy of the dead horse, a London-based veterinarian surgeon would be responsible, a man accredited by the police.

The dead horse, now identified as Scarlet Soleil, a three-year-old from a stable in the north of the country, had never raced at Salisbury before. However, it had won at three other regional racecourses.

'You never picked up the switch?' Tremayne had asked as he and Vincent stood close to the horse.

'I never saw Red Rose before the race. To be honest, I'm not too keen on them.'

'Horses?'

'I trained to specialise in small animals, household pets.'

'Why horses now?' Tremayne asked. Apart from a dog that used to chew his slippers when Jean lived with him, the first time they were married, and which she took with her when she had left, he hadn't had much time for pets of any description.

'I was here in Salisbury for a couple of years, came up from Southampton, partnership in a veterinary surgery on Bemerton Road. A steady number, enough to pay the bills, slap down a deposit on a small semi-detached on Windlesham Road. It suited me, but I came to the races one day. Something different, the chance for a meal, a few drinks, a couple of pounds each way on a race, but there was a problem. A horse collapsed on the course just in front of me, the jockey pinned underneath it.'

'The jockey?'

'Apart from a broken leg and a dented ego, he was alright. The horse wasn't, barely breathing, close to expiring. Horses, after all, aren't that much different to other animals, people included. I prised open its mouth, grabbed its tongue, pulled it to one side and thrust my hand down its throat, came up against a restriction and pushed. The stable hand kept a watch out for me, and a few days later, he presented me with a child's plastic toy that somehow the horse had swallowed.'

'You were the man of the moment?'

The Horse's Mouth

'The horse was worth money, and the owner, not Kirkland, was delighted, took me on as his preferred vet, paid me five times as much as if it had been one of the small animals that I usually dealt with.'

'You took the money?'

'How could I say no? After that, other horse owners were phoning me. The money was better, so I sold out of the partnership and turned my speciality to horses.'

'Good money?'

'Great money if you fix them; if you don't, then it's another matter.'

'Could you have fixed Scarlet Soleil?'

'A plastic toy is one thing; a bowel obstruction, a breech birth, maybe. But from what I can see, the horse here, apart from someone's handiwork with a can of paint, has been poisoned.'

'Any reason for the diagnosis?' Tremayne asked.

'How long before your expert arrives?'

'An hour. You're too close to the investigation, and besides, two experts are better than one.'

'My temper used to get me in trouble. Sorry about my earlier outburst.'

'Don't worry,' Tremayne said. 'Why poison?'

'It wasn't here, another racecourse close to Bristol. The owner was livid, blaming the jockey, the stable hand, the condition of the course.'

'Prime horse flesh?' Tremayne asked.

'Middle of the road. At one meeting, the horse is out in front from the start, another day, and it's barely able to make the distance.'

'Suspicious?'

'Not with this horse. This horse, it ran for itself, not for anyone else. It's not often that people dislike an animal, but they did this one.'

'Then why run it?'

'A couple more races, a burst of speed, and its price went up. The owner knew this, and no doubt, so did the horse. Look into its eyes, though, and there was a coldness.'

'What did you find?'

'When?'

'The horse you've just been speaking about.'

'It was in the stable, resting against the side of the stall. It was listless, so I took a blood sample, managed to get some urine out of it, and sent them to a laboratory for testing. Drugged, just enough to take the edge off its performance.'

'Similarities with the dead horse we have now?'

'A heavier dose, but yes, it's poison. It makes your job harder, and no doubt, its death is tied in with Sally Kirkland's death.'

'It's a logical conclusion,' Tremayne said.

Outside the stable, two uniforms stood upright when Tremayne and Barry Vincent came out. The day was turning cold, and Tremayne was feeling out of sorts, in part due to the beer he had drunk earlier, in part because he was not well, a not altogether uncommon occurrence.

Chapter 5

'Tremayne had received clear dictate. 'Come with me, and we can talk, but for now, I've got business to conduct, another horse to check on, and hopefully this time it'll have the decency to win. If not, it's for the knacker's yard.'

There was a bluster about Kirkland that Tremayne found unsettling on his second visit to the house. He was as much a lover of horse racing as Tremayne was, and he found it hard to come to terms with what to him should have been a distraught father.

He could have insisted that the man had stayed at his house, or had accompanied him to the police station, but either option could have proven counterproductive. And besides, a cooperative witness or suspect or father was preferable to someone hostile.

The day after Sally Kirkland's death, the pathologist had conducted the autopsy, concluding that she had died from strangulation, that she had eaten curry in the preceding hours, that her general physical condition had been good, and that she snorted cocaine. The only addition that Stuart Collins, the pathologist, had come up with, and which was important, was that in the stable Sally Kirkland had had sexual intercourse, and it had been voluntary. The bruising was from the rope, not the violence of rape.

At the racecourse, not Salisbury but a forty-five-minute drive away, Kirkland first checked on his horse, then spoke to another stable hand, not Les Daniels, who was not in favour and no longer in his employ.

The horse placed second in the fourth race of the day, netting the man a small amount of prize money, as well as a lot more from betting on the horse that won.

During the day, Tremayne questioned Kirkland about his treatment of Daniels, his daughter's death, her probable lover, the cocaine.

To each question, a one- or two-word dismissive reply. It was only the mention of Red Rose that caused the man to falter, to discuss the animal.

'It doesn't make sense,' Tremayne said, 'that whoever Sally was with would have hung around the racecourse if he was involved in the horse's disappearance.'

It was late in the day, and the two men were sitting on the rear deck of Kirkland's Range Rover. A sombreness had settled over the previously ebullient man, tears forming in his eyes.

'Tremayne, a person rises above their problems, their sadness, or at least, a successful person does. Of course, I cared about Sally. But I'm damned if I'm going to let anyone know it.'

'You're showing it to me.'

The two men, each with a bottle of beer in their hand, reminisced. Tremayne spoke about his life, how he had met Jean one drunken night, their first marriage, and then the divorce, her marriage to another man and the two children she had with him. How, in time, after Jean's husband had died, they had reconnected and married for a second time. He even told Kirkland about the time when he and his sergeant had nearly died, the result of a murderous cult bent on making sacrificial offerings to malevolent gods, and how it was that Clare's fiancé had died saving her. It was an old story, known by many in the area, but never spoken of by Clare.

The Horse's Mouth

Kirkland opened up about his childhood, a tenement in the north of the country, an education that was rudimentary and bored him. How he had pulled himself up by his bootstraps, read a great deal, studied some more, educated himself.

'I'm not a criminal, and that's the gospel truth,' Kirkland said as he took a swig of his beer.

'You're a suspect.'

'Not for my daughter's death. I spoilt her, and sometimes her taste in men was dubious, and as for cocaine, I knew about that.'

'You approved?'

'Not totally, but she was over the age of twenty-one, a liberated woman. She made mistakes, the same as we all do, but we rise above them. You've had a few knockdowns in your life, so have I, and as for your sergeant, she's had more than both of us. We've all prospered, found ourselves in a better position, or at least you and your sergeant have. For me, I've got to deal with the loss of a daughter, but time's a great healer. No need to prolong it, no point in depression or negative thoughts.'

'Your nonchalance about her death leads to suspicion.'

'No doubt a few men have swung on the gallows just because they didn't break down when their wives or lovers had died at the hand of another. Guilt by behaviour isn't a good way to condemn a person. I hope you're not going to condemn me out of hand.'

'I'll do my job. I'll not hold you for the murder of your daughter, not yet. It seems that your alibi is strong, although cast-iron is not a word I'd use, not now.'

'Red Rose?'

'We're looking, but you'd be a better bet to help us with our enquiries.'

'How? I may have placed a bet on another horse, made sure one of my horses lost a few races, improved the odds and then bet heavily when I gave the jockey the word to push hard.'

'How do you get a horse to lose?'

'Nothing as drastic as you suspect,' Kirkland said. 'Exercise the horse too vigorously before the meeting, ensure it's not fed the best oats, insufficient vitamins. This idea of steroids or another drug is fanciful. Premium horses, the same as elite athletes, are subjected to drug testing. And if a horse is to lose, it can't be by much, raises suspicion. A skilled jockey can subtly hold it back; another one can get that bit extra on the day. That's why Jack Doyle was on Red Rose in Salisbury; he's only young, but the man's a master with a horse, an empathy, able to sense the animal's mood.'

'And he didn't suspect?'

'Probably not. Red Rose was a complex animal, subject to mood swings. One day as sweet as pie, another day, rearing up if you went near him.'

'Sally used to ride it,' Tremayne said.

'Similar temperaments. Horses are smart. If Red was down, it would be Sally that would cheer him up and vice versa.'

'I have the occasional flutter, lose more often than not.'

'Everyone loses. A horse has good days and bad, the track conditions, the weather, humidity in the air, rain. You can't compute all the variables, and then the odds are a reflection of the punters' beliefs, not the reality.'

'Why would someone swap Red Rose? After all, Scarlet Soleil still won.'

'Red Rose would have won. He was a good horse, worth decent money, but he wasn't worth in the millions, maybe thirty to forty thousand pounds.'

'That's still a lot of money.'

'It is, and I don't have it now. All I've got is a dead daughter and you for company. It's not what I'd call a fair trade.'

Tremayne realised that the conversation had gone on for too long, and Kirkland was heading into melancholy. And besides, Tremayne didn't believe that he was innocent in the switching of Red Rose, although why remained unknown for the present. But he was tenacious; he would find out.

'We'll find the horse, but what we need for now is your daughter's lover. Who was he, the man in the stable?'

'A liberated woman, as I told you.'

'She had more than one?'

'We didn't speak about it. It's not the sort of thing fathers discuss with their children, especially the females, that is. You'd know that.'

'I never had children.'

'At least you've been spared the heartache. Sally was keen on one man a few years back; he treated her well.'

'What happened?'

'The romance withered, but he's been around recently, took her out a few times, a weekend away a few weeks back. He's one that I know of.'

'His name?'

'Ian Swift.'

'I know him,' Tremayne said.

'The other?'

'Andrew Fortescue. I assume you've heard of him?'

'I have, the Honourable if I'm not mistaken.'

'He was keen on her, spent two weeks in the Caribbean with him. Swift was more her style.'

'For you?'

'Fortescue was wet behind the ears. Even so, Sally should have grabbed him in a rush, raced him down the aisle.'

***

Clare stood with Barry Vincent, Kirkland's vet, and Doctor Herbert Houghton, a supercilious man in his early fifties, who had arrived at Salisbury Racecourse the morning after the horse had died. A graduate of the Royal Veterinary College in London, as was Vincent, but that was where the similarities ended. Vincent was agreeable and affable; Houghton was not. On Houghton's business card, a string of abbreviated qualifications; on Vincent's, only one, DVM (Doctor of Veterinary Medicine). Clare could feel confidence in Houghton's ability, not in his attitude.

'Sergeant Yarwood, my investigation will be thorough,' Houghton said, looking over at Vincent in a condescending manner.

'We will do whatever we can to assist,' Clare replied. 'Mr Vincent will assist you.'

'I understand that Vincent resents my presence.'

'It's been explained that you have accreditation with the police that I do not. I will assist you to the best of my abilities, rest assured,' Vincent said.

'As long as that is understood,' Houghton said. 'Have you examined the animal?'

'Only rudimentary.'

'The samples you took? Have they been sent for analysis?'

'They have,' Vincent said.

'Will you conduct a full autopsy?' Clare asked.

'I don't think that's necessary. I will, with Vincent's assistance, conduct a detailed examination, but I don't intend to open the horse up. At least not at this juncture. Why it died is important, and Vincent's acted appropriately,' Houghton said.

'Corroboration of my work?' Vincent said.

'Hopefully, that's what it is.'

The man was professional, Clare had to admit, and not quick to make a comment or to criticise.

'The body after the examination?'

'Cold storage. It might not be there for long, but I'll need a sign off before disposal,' Clare said.

'There'll not be much to gain if poison is proven. But why kill the horse?'

'There must be a reason.'

The smell close to the horse was pungent, stale urine and faeces, and combined with the heat was starting to attract horseflies. Clare, a keen rider in her younger days, remembered that they bit, and the resulting red and itchy swollen bump could be painful.

Houghton opened up the case he had brought with him, put on a pair of white coveralls and nitrile gloves and moved over to the horse. Clare left the stable, took a breath of fresh air, and opened the boot of her car.

Inside the stable, on her return, she handed Vincent a set of police-issue protective gear.

'Not necessary,' Houghton said. 'I just didn't want to get my clothes dirty.'

It was a gentle putdown of Vincent's attire, a pair of denim jeans, an open-necked shirt and an old jacket. Clare wasn't confident that he had picked up on the jibe, but Vincent said nothing, only thanked Clare for her kindness and put on the coveralls and gloves.

Houghton walked around the horse, taking photos, dictating into his smartphone. Vincent followed, observing the man in action, but saying nothing.

Clare walked outside, found Les Daniels sitting forlornly on a bale of hay.

'Rough day?' she said.

'I've had better. Sometimes I like animals more than I like people,' Daniels said.

'Today, one of those days?'

'Why kill it? After all, it's not going to talk, is it?'

'If it had, once in its life, it wouldn't be running around a track, would it,' Clare said. It was a flippant comment, she knew that, but humour, even in bad taste, often became a staple of a murder investigation. There was only so much negativity that any one person could take, and an opportunity to defuse the situation, no matter how momentary, was always worthwhile.

'Red Rose could have given it a run for its money. Why switch horses?'

Clare noticed a hesitation in the man's speech. After all, where there's a surfeit of money, there's always crime.

'Les, let's be honest here. You were a jockey, and gambling on the outcome of a race is big money. Weren't you tempted to alter the outcome of a race?'

'I was, and yes, they tried it on me, but I resisted…'

Another pause, longer than the first time.

'What is it?' Clare said.

The Horse's Mouth

'I'm a suspect, aren't I?' Daniels stood up, looked down at Clare.

'You are, even Barton Kirkland and Barry Vincent.'

'Sally?'

'Men in her life? Were you one of them?'

'Not me. You should read up on me, the accident where the horse I was riding fell; and how I was trampled on by another that was coming up fast from behind—a couple of ribs, a broken jaw, a hoof to the groin. I wasn't much for the ladies, but after that, even if I'd wanted, nothing was going to happen, crushed testicles. It still makes me wince to think about it, and Sally, even though she put it about, was classy, and the men she went with were decent enough.'

'Sorry about the accident,' Clare said.

'So am I. What you're asking is whether Sally could have known about the substitution, isn't it?'

'Yes. What do you reckon?'

'I don't see it. Sally loved horses, especially Red Rose. If she was involved, and I'd not believe it for a moment, then the horse is safe and secure, and she would have been keeping an eye on him.'

'Yet, she's dead, and the horse is missing. Her relationship with her father?'

'I would have said good, but Kirkland's a dark horse, sorry for the pun. A tough man, but he had a weak spot for his daughter, and she took advantage of it. No need for her to do much, other than what she liked. He gave her money, a fancy car to drive, holidays if she wanted one, although if you do nothing, I can't see the point.'

'Do you have holidays?'

'With the money he paid me? Not a chance, and besides, what use are they? Sure, a few drinks, sit in the sun, but at the end of the day, a lonely bed, looking up at the ceiling.'

The more that Clare talked to Daniels, the more obvious it was that behind the façade of agreeability there was a darker side, anger and frustration at the accident that had robbed him of his manhood.

If Kirkland didn't pay much and Sally was enjoying the good life, and there was every possibility that he had fancied her, maybe even loved her, then how would his pent-up sexual and financial frustration have expressed itself?

Clare was glad of Tremayne and his inappropriate humour on occasions. Daniels' hard-luck story wasn't to be the last she was going to hear during the current murder investigation, probably not the last murder either. She could feel the buzz, the adrenalin that came as the pace of the chase intensified.

***

Whatever had transpired inside the stable, it had a marked effect on Herbert Houghton. He and Barry Vincent were both smiling.

'I used to lecture occasionally at the Royal Veterinary College,' Houghton said. 'Vincent was one of my students. He reminded me in there as we were checking out the horse. I couldn't have been that bad as Vincent knows his way around an animal.'

It was refreshing to see two professionals working in unison, Clare thought, but paramount was the dead horse. 'Scarlet Soleil?' she said.

The Horse's Mouth

'I'll concur with Vincent's initial observation. If the toxicology tests come back negative, then we'll need to investigate further. But there's a puncture mark, a needle. It's not easy to see.'

'The injection? In the stable after the race or before?'

'Impossible to tell. The toxicology report will clarify. If it were before, a stimulant, it would make the heart beat faster, the muscles work harder. If it was to kill the animal, then another poison.'

'Sally died because she didn't agree with what had happened,' Vincent said.

'Blackmail, conspiracy, the possibilities open up before us,' Clare said. 'The horse?'

'A freezer van,' Houghton said. 'Vincent will stay with you to assist. Moving a dead horse is not that easy, and I'm sure you want to preserve the evidence intact for the time being.'

'We do. Thank you for your time.'

'Vincent had some amusing anecdotes about the college.'

The outcome from the previously haughty Houghton had been zero, apart from the discovered puncture mark. The horse was dead, and Les Daniels had an underlying layer to him, and Sally Kirkland had had knowledge of foul deeds.

Clare pulled Vincent off to one side.

'How long have you known Sally Kirkland?'

'As long as I've known the father,' Vincent's reply. 'Why?'

'According to Daniels, she had a few boyfriends, easy with her favours.'

'Did he say that?'

'Not in as many words, but she's dead, and I've put two and two together.'

'And come up with the wrong answer. I took her out a couple of times, but that was four years back.'

'Lovers?'

'I'm not sure that it's pertinent or any of your business.'

'The woman's dead. Any question, no matter how insignificant or intrusive, is justified. Just answer the question. Did you and her sleep together?'

'Why ask such a question? You're my age. What do you think?'

'Thinking is not for me to do here. What's the truth?'

'Yes, we made love. She was a good person, and I don't want to speak ill of the dead.'

'The romance?'

'It was transitory, just two people out for a bit of fun. No love from either side, just a friendship. Satisfied?'

'For now,' Clare said. It was going to be a long night. Firstly, she had to arrange for the horse to be placed in a refrigerated van, and then the CSIs would check where it had lain. Clare knew that Clive would understand.

Chapter 6

Les Daniels had raised an interesting point, Tremayne realised after Clare had spoken to him. Why switch horses when there was no apparent advantage?

It was late in the evening in the office, the usual modus operandi for the inspector and his sergeant. It was the time when they had a chance to reflect on the day's activities, who said what, what seemingly unimportant piece of information slipped out, the time to plan for the next day, to ponder the imponderable.

'Red Rose would have won that race,' Tremayne said. 'That's why I had my money on it.'

Clare was a cynic when it came to her senior's expertise in picking a winner, due to his less than impressive record.

'You checked his form?' she said, feeling the exhaustion of a long day, and ready to go home to Clive and their house in Cathedral Close; her small house in Stratford-sub-Castle rented out to a young couple with a child. The ageing cat that had stayed there after she had married was with her and Clive now. Its movements were restricted by arthritis, and it moved only a short distance, preferring to remain curled up in the far corner of the kitchen, a blanket over it. Clare knew that one day she would have to take it to the vet to be put down. On that day, she would be sad.

'In part, but it was Daniels who reckoned it was a sure bet. If you get a tip from the horse's mouth, it's best to follow through.'

'Which works in his favour.'

'I don't see how,' Tremayne said, although he could see where his sergeant's logic was heading. But it was her experience speaking, and even though she was much younger than him, he felt pride in how he had guided her over the years. Fresh-faced and idealistic when she had joined him, and now, almost fourteen years later, as good a homicide detective as any. He knew she should be an inspector, the same rank as him, and that her promotion had been curtailed by him standing in her way. If she transferred out of Homicide, a promotion would be a foregone conclusion. It had been suggested on several occasions by Superintendent Moulton, but she had always turned down the opportunity. And Tremayne knew that without her as his partner, policing would not be as pleasurable. Two people, unlike in many ways; he a plain-talking man with a West Country accent; she with an educated accent, the result of an affluent Norfolk upbringing. But regardless, an unspoken affection existed between the two, and when Clare's fiancé had died saving her life, it had been Tremayne who had pushed her hard on her return to work. No words of sorrow from him, and she had gained from it.

Clare's relationship with her father was excellent; her mother not so good. Tremayne and her mother did not see eye to eye, and whenever she visited Salisbury, which was not often, he would keep his distance.

Before her marriage, Clare's mother had been opposed to it, as Clive Grantley was sixteen years older than his intended. However, a son-in-law who was the mayor of Salisbury soon won her around.

'If Les Daniels tells you to bet on Red Rose, then he's not likely to do that knowing you're a police officer, not if the race was fixed.'

The Horse's Mouth

'Unless he lined me up as a stooge, the perfect alibi.'

'Daniels is not the greatest intellect,' Clare said. 'Sure, he can tell you all about a horse, but what else? Subtlety would have been needed to set up the switching of two horses and guide you to be where you were needed. I don't reckon he's capable.'

'Nor do I,' Tremayne concurred. 'Which means the man was acting on instructions.'

'Kirkland's?'

'It was his daughter that died. I can't see how.'

'She led out the horse. She must have noticed that it wasn't Red Rose.'

'Would she?'

'When was the switch made? In the stable with Les Daniels, with Sally Kirkland, or before arriving at the racecourse?'

'We don't know. Daniels reckons it was after it left him, but that's working on the premise that he's telling the truth.'

'Yet, the horse comes back from the race, and it's in his charge. Surely he would have known before seeing the paint on the leg?'

'Unless he'd had a few too many pints of beer,' Clare said, casting a wary eye over at Daniels' drinking pal.

'He could have, but a lot of jockeys drink too much,' Tremayne's reply. Clare's logic was valid. He wondered if he was the stooge, past his prime, long in the tooth. A losing horse would end up in a field to see out its days or else in the knacker's yard; a police inspector who started to lose cases would be retired—an ignominious end to a career, hoodwinked by a villain.

Maybe Moulton was right and his time was up. Tremayne hoped not, but he couldn't dismiss the possibility.

'Jockeys burn off the drink, but stable hands?'

His sergeant was taking the investigation down a road that did not bode well for him, Tremayne thought.

'Extrapolate where this is heading,' Tremayne said. 'If Daniels is involved, why tell us about the paint? And why kill the horse?'

'I'm not sure I have the answer. Unless–'

'Unless what!' Tremayne snapped.

'Unless it was part of the plan. It was beyond Daniels' capabilities to set this up, but there could be someone telling him what to do.'

'And if it was, then where does that place me? Fool of the week, that's where.'

'I'm hypothesising here, not pointing the finger,' Clare said. She wasn't used to her senior losing his temper with her. It wasn't a reaction she had expected, and she worried for him. If she were right then, it would be a black mark on a blameless career. It was not something she wanted.

Tremayne picked up the cup of tea on his desk, took one sip, and put it down. 'It's cold.'

'I'll get you another, one for myself,' Clare said. 'And then we can try and reason through what we've got.'

'I shouldn't have barked at you.'

'Don't worry. It's not often you blow your cool, but we need to keep an open mind. Besides, it's early in the investigation.'

'More deaths?'

'But who and why? And yes, why not? The death of a horse, another one missing, a dead woman,' Clare said.

The Horse's Mouth

For ten minutes, no more was said. Clare went to get a couple of teas and Tremayne looked out of the window at a cloudless night. The city was quiet, and the police station had taken on a sleepy feel, infrequently disturbed by a printer churning out more paperwork. Someone else was burning the midnight oil in the building. The ancillary staff in Homicide had long since departed, aware that a new murder investigation would take up more of their time, enjoying the interlude before the pace quickened. To Tremayne, some of them were premature in leaving, as case files needed to be prepared, the evidence collated, someone needed to follow up with Forensics. It was, he knew, his sergeant and him who would be doing the legwork, driving the investigation.

'I still reckon Daniels is involved,' Clare said.

'And, by default, me,' Tremayne replied calmly.

'Not necessarily. If Daniels had handed Red Rose over to Sally Kirkland, and the switch had occurred after that, then he's done his job. He's free to give you a tip, to have a few drinks.'

'He had a few, but he wasn't drunk.'

'How many?'

'Four pints, no more.'

'And you?'

'I matched him pint for pint.'

'The limit is two, and you know that,' Clare said.

'No lectures, not now, not with a murder investigation, and if Jean finds out, then you know what she'll say.'

'The same as I should. But yes, focus on Sally Kirkland's death.'

'Red Rose is at the meeting; the horse is led off by Sally, who then takes it where?'

'The parade ring, a chance for the punters to see what they're betting on.'

'Do we have video of Red Rose after Daniels had handed it over?'

'It's a regional race meeting. Someone may have taken photos or a video with a smartphone.'

'Then we need to find if someone has. We need to know when the switch occurred.'

'I'll get a couple of constables out to the racecourse in the morning to see what they can find,' Clare said.

'Hypothesising,' Tremayne said, 'to use your terminology, we're working on the belief that Sally Kirkland's death and the horses are related.'

'It seems logical.'

'Logical, but not certain.'

'Then we treat Sally Kirkland's murder as unrelated for now,' Clare said.

'I don't believe it is, but we have a couple of people to talk to.'

'Three. Barry Vincent's a former lover. He may know something about her, still carrying a flame.'

***

Ian Swift, one of Sally Kirkland's paramours, did not react kindly to two police officers marching into his office out on the Southampton Road. The genial financial adviser, often seen on regional television and heard on the radio, was also a car dealer, specialising in second-hand luxury vehicles. He was a successful man, admired by many, not liked by Clare's husband, Clive.

To Clare, her husband's invective about Swift seemed out of proportion for the sins he had committed.

The Horse's Mouth

A Salisbury city councillor, he had temporarily occupied Clive's position as mayor when Clive had stood down during the investigation into his brother's murder.

Clare knew the man, having met him at official functions; Tremayne knew him in passing.

'Clare, I don't appreciate this,' Swift, an unattractive man with dark eyes, a crooked nose and a lopsided mouth, said. He was in his forties, unmarried, but with a charisma that attracted women. He was a man about town, full of charm, long on spending on women that interested him, quick to discard when he had tired of them, and short on outlaying more money than necessary on a financial deal.

'Ian, it's official,' Clare said. 'You know Inspector Tremayne?'

'I do.'

'Sally Kirkland, we've got a few questions,' Tremayne said. Important man or not, Tremayne was not willing to grant the belligerent man any more civility than was necessary. After all, Swift was one of the two men known to have taken out the dead woman in the last few months.

'I was sorry to hear about her,' Swift said. 'Tragic, so young.'

'It sounds as though you're ambivalent about her death.'

Clare could see that Tremayne was baiting the man. She had to agree it was a viable tactic. Men such as Swift are careful in what they say, weighing up the pros and cons. Anger, not feigned, but genuine, often loosened the tongue, caused people to say things that otherwise would remain hidden.

'Inspector, if you are looking for a heartfelt response from me, then you will be disappointed,' Swift said as he swivelled in the chair behind his desk. Up on the walls of the room, some photos of him with happy customers, others with minor celebrities.

To Clive, Swift was a usurper, a sycophant who would use a person when they were needed, ignore them when they were not.

'Your relationship with Sally Kirkland?' Tremayne asked.

'Casual,' Swift replied.

'A roll in the hay or something more?'

'It appears, Inspector Tremayne, that your questioning is antagonistic. If you wish to proceed in this manner, then I will take legal advice before proceeding further.'

'And you'll be down the police station if you don't answer.'

Clare thought that Tremayne was losing control, and that, coupled with the previous night's snapping at her, concerned her. After all, she respected him more than any other man apart from her husband, although she had known the inspector for a lot more years. She hoped he wasn't coming to the end of his policing career.

'Gentlemen, please,' Clare said. 'Ian, one day ago, we saw Sally Kirkland dead, a rope around her neck. Inspector Tremayne, I suggest we let Mr Swift speak.'

Tremayne, unsure how to react, not used to criticism from his sergeant, acquiesced. 'Yes, you're right. Ambivalence towards a death irritates me.'

'I'm sure it does, Inspector,' Swift said. 'Let me reiterate, my relationship with Sally was casual, and I hadn't seen her for five, maybe six weeks.'

'Why?'

The Horse's Mouth

'I'm a busy man, and women come easily. I'm sorry to say this, and I'm sure that Clare wouldn't like me to be so open, but it appears I must be.'

'The truth is always best, regardless if it offends,' Clare said.

'Then I'll be honest. No doubt I'm a suspect.'

'You're on our list,' Tremayne said. 'Did Sally understand the ground rules?'

'She said that she did. I wasn't the only one who spent time with her. You're aware of that?'

'We are. Any names?'

'Fortescue is one of them.'

'And you weren't concerned?'

'Sally was a free spirit. We were similar in many ways. If she was capable of love, I'm not sure; or maybe she was wronged at some time, jilted by a man she cared for, but I don't know. We went out, a good meal, a few drinks, sometimes a weekend in Paris or London, take in a show, and that was it. No harm done.'

'Were you at the racecourse on the day she died?' Clare asked.

'It was Sally who was interested in horses, not me.'

'Is that a no?' Tremayne asked.

'It is. Why?'

'On the day she died, Sally had sexual intercourse before her death,' Clare said.

'It wasn't me.'

'If you've lied, we'll be back,' Tremayne said.

'I've not lied.'

'One last question before we leave.'

'What is it?'

'Substituting a horse, a disputed result, has all the marks of substantive betting. I'm not accusing you of

51

involvement, but would smart operators make a lot of money?'

'You're baiting me again, Inspector. It's not my area of expertise, but yes, a lot of money.'

'Sally Kirkland's murder could be related, or it is unconnected. We're not sure,' Clare said.

'She loved horses. She'd not agree to a horse suffering, and to hear her speak about Red Rose, she loved the animal. If she's involved, and I don't think she is for a moment, the horse is safe somewhere.'

'The somewhere would help us a lot,' Tremayne said.

'Barton Kirkland?' Clare asked.

'He understands the value of money,' Swift said. 'A soft spot for his daughter, but not for much else. I can respect the man, but I wouldn't want to be involved in a business venture with him.'

'Why?'

'He runs too close to the wind, keeps dubious company at times.'

'Criminal?'

'Too smart to be caught, but nefarious activities.'

Outside, Tremayne looked in the window of a Bentley Continental for sale and then up at the price tag. 'Too expensive for me,' he said.

'Ian Swift?' What do you reckon?' Clare said.

'At this time, we'll regard what he said as the truth.'

'He could still be involved.'

'Check him out, see if there are hidden compartments that he doesn't want to be opened.'

'You don't trust him?'

'He was obliging, aiming to portray himself as a decent man, hardworking, ambitious. And get your constables to check the video and photos at the racecourse, not only for Red Rose but for Ian Swift and Andrew Fortescue,' Tremayne said.

Chapter 7

Death came quickly according to the gardener at Lord Fortescue's stately home to the north of Salisbury. It wasn't the first time for Clare at the house: a Saturday afternoon visit to walk around the garden, the money paid donated to charity.

Tremayne had not been to the Fortescue estate before. His and Clare's visit seemed to be an omen of things to come.

Three days since Sally Kirkland's murder, one day after meeting with Ian Swift, one of her lovers, another one was dead. Andrew Fortescue had fallen from the open full-height window of his room on the third floor at the Georgian mansion; his body was lying askew between the carnations and the roses, his head smashed on a concrete ornament. It wasn't how Clare remembered the garden, splendid as it had been on the day she had visited.

Even Tremayne, hardened by years of dealing with death and despair, and not troubled by the sight of a body, no matter its condition, couldn't help but feel a sadness at the scene. On the ground, Andrew's body; to one side, Lord Fortescue and his wife, clutching each other. Clare was solemn but maintained her dignity, and the gardener, a cockney born and bred by his accent, appeared insensitive.

The gardens may have been immaculate, and the man might have been a craftsman tending to the neatly trimmed hedges, mowing the lawns and ensuring that the flowers bloomed, but his manner was not helpful.

The Horse's Mouth

The Fortescue title was hereditary, awarded for services to a king two hundred and sixty years previously. Andrew Fortescue would have inherited the title on the death of his father, which judging by the wheelchair the father sat in and his sallow face and consumptive cough wouldn't have been long. But now, the title would remain vacant, the last of the Fortescue line dead on the ground.

'I saw him fall,' the gardener said.

Tremayne pulled him away from the parents while his sergeant went to find a sheet to place over the body. Jim Hughes and his investigators were on the way, and Hughes would understand why Clare Yarwood had taken the action of covering the body.

'Why? Why?' Lady Fortescue sobbed.

She was a good-looking woman in her late fifties, whereas her husband was over seventy. A one-time socialite in London, she had recognised a good deal when the Honourable Bernard Fortescue had proposed to her thirty-six years previously. One child had resulted, and contrary to the predictions of his parents and her friends, the marriage had endured.

Clare took hold of the grieving parents just as the village constable arrived. He would take responsibility for the body, while Clare would settle the parents in the house.

'Are you the head gardener?' Tremayne asked as they walked around a hedge and out of the sight of the main house.

'The name's Upton, and yes, it's my responsibility.'

Tremayne didn't warm to the man. Initial impressions meant a lot to him, and the man didn't read right to him.

'We divide the gardens up into three. Front of the house is mine, and then there are two other gardeners.

One looks after the garden at the rear, and another person is in the greenhouse nurturing new plants.'

'Where the body fell, that's yours?'

'It is.'

'Good people, the Fortescues?'

'I've had worse.'

'That's not an answer. Upton, let me remind you that this is a crime scene. Your being obstructive won't help.'

'I didn't kill him.'

'No one said you did, but he's the second death now, and the first one was murder.'

'Lord Fortescue can be difficult; always reckoned he knew better than anyone else on any subject.'

'Gardening?'

'Always lecturing me on my job. We didn't agree on a lot of subjects, but he loved the garden, the same as I do.'

'You've been here for a long time?'

'Twelve years now. Before that, I worked at Kew Gardens, but the job came with a house on the estate, and the wife is happy. And if she's happy, so am I. The Fortescues can have the fancy house and all the money, not that it's been good for them.'

'What does that mean?'

'Him, the dead one…'

'Andrew Fortescue,' Tremayne said.

'Yes, Andrew. He used to argue with his father something dreadful.'

'About what?'

'I don't keep my ear to the keyhole.'

Tremayne knew an untruth when he heard it. The staff of the wealthy always knew all the details, no matter how trivial.

The Horse's Mouth

'I'm not saying you did, and no doubt there are staff in the house that would tell me.'

'There are. Mrs Jenkins, she's down in the kitchen, she knows all. It must be awful having people listening, making idle gossip. I don't know how they put up with it.'

'It's not a problem you and I have, is it?'

'No, I suppose not.'

'Upton, level with me. I don't want to waste your time or mine, and you know the reasons for the arguments. Hostile witnesses, no matter how justified their discretion is, only bring attention to themselves. The father wouldn't have killed him, and it's unlikely that the mother did.'

'Her, tough as nails.'

'Did you like her?'

'I liked his lordship, always a bonus at Christmas. Enough for a fortnight in Majorca last year, the wife and myself.'

'His wife?'

'She was devoted to her husband, and she loved her son, but she ruled the household.'

'Andrew Fortescue, what can you tell me about him?' Tremayne said.

'I saw him up high, leaning out of a window. It's one of those that come down to the floor, dangerous, easy to fall out. There wasn't much I could do.'

'Fell or pushed?'

'Fell. I saw him there. He killed himself.'

'Describe him to me.'

'Personable, not stuck-up like his father. He used to come down into the garden sometimes, light up a cigarette and give me one. He liked to talk about this and that, no snobbery in him, not at all. A regular gentleman, have a drink down the pub, buy me one if I was there.'

'The arguments with the father? What were they about?'

'The son, he realises that the upkeep of this place is draining the bank accounts. The money the family had is slowly being whittled away, and the returns on their investments are not keeping pace with inflation. At some stage, the bailiffs will be knocking on the door, demanding their pound of flesh.'

'Lord Fortescue must have realised this.'

'It's not for me to be telling you this, and if he finds out, I'll be out on my ear,' Upton said.

'I'll be discreet,' Tremayne said, 'but this is a murder investigation.'

'His lordship is a believer in the class system, stiff upper lip, muddle through regardless. He might be right, I'd not know that, and his aristocratic friends could have helped out.'

'A lot of them are in the same sort of trouble.'

'One or two occasionally turn up looking for free accommodation.'

'Andrew?'

'He wanted to put the place on a commercial footing.'

'It's not big enough for a lion park, and besides, that's passé.'

'Andrew wanted to convert one of the barns into upmarket weekend accommodation for people down from the city, allow weddings in the house. It wouldn't be the same if it happened, but when the money ceases to come in the front door, the lifestyle soon goes out the back.'

'Sally Kirkland? Does the name ring a bell?'
'Andrew was keen on her.'
'She was murdered. Did you know that?'

The Horse's Mouth

'I heard something about it. Do you think that's why he jumped?'

'You tell me.'

'If he was keen on her, he could have been distraught, but it's no point asking a gardener. That would need a psychologist.'

'I am asking you. You knew the man, what do you reckon?'

'He suffered from depression at times, confined to his room, the curtains drawn. Who knows what goes through the mind of people when someone they loved dies?'

'Did he love Sally Kirkland?'

'If he were taking her out, he would have.'

***

The crime scene investigators checked the window ledge from where Andrew Fortescue had fallen. Either he had been a lovesick fool unable to deal with Sally Kirkland's death, or he had killed her. Whichever it was, Tremayne was perplexed, and if he was, then his sergeant was under pressure. Another late night, another meal sent over from the Chinese restaurant on the other side of the road.

Clare, with an appreciation for good food, the legacy of her parents' hotel and her mother's fastidiousness for serving only the best, knew that the restaurant's food was less than spectacular. In short, it was an awful meal, although Tremayne, not cultivated in the finer things in life, ate his food heartily while Clare picked at hers.

'The numbers are going up,' Tremayne said as he finished his meal and threw the plastic plate into a bin.

'Scarlet Soleil died of barbiturate poisoning,' Clare said. 'The horse was euthanised.'

'Why kill a perfectly fit horse? What's the point?' Tremayne said.

'And without a sedative. But you're right, and a dead horse doesn't tell tales.'

Tremayne leant back in his chair, a sure sign to Clare that he had had a revelation, something that would set the investigation down another route of enquiry.

'In your own time,' Clare said.

'Red Rose has won a race, but it's got a congenital problem, something that will diminish its breeding potential, another pot of gold at the end of the rainbow.'

'How does this help us?'

'Insurance fraud. Phone up Vincent, ask him if such a thing exists.'

'Or I could switch on my laptop.'

'You and your damn technology. Vincent would be quicker, but then again, where does he stand? If I'm right, then he could be involved.'

Clare left Tremayne's office, went over to her laptop and entered racehorse insurance into the search bar. Tremayne's eyes were closed when she returned.

'Equine insurance is big business. If a horse dies then insurance will pay. It will also pay if there's a congenital issue, unable to breed.'

'If a congenital issue is discovered while it's still racing?' Tremayne asked.

'A complex question, but an insurance company will be looking for loopholes not to pay.'

'An investigation by an independent vet on contract to the insurance company might look deeper than Barry Vincent into Red Roses' death, for instance.'

'He never found the puncture mark, whereas Herbert Houghton did.'

'It still doesn't explain Sally Kirkland.'

'Solve one, resolve the other,' Clare said. Another line of enquiry and one that had potential. Insurance fraud was big business and big money, and Barton Kirkland would profit if Red Rose, the winner of the race at Salisbury, died. And to all intents and purposes, it had, until Les Daniels found the paint.

'If Kirkland's on the fiddle and Vincent's not doing his job, then those two are in trouble. It still doesn't explain what's happened to the real horse.'

'Killing two birds with one stone,' Clare said.

'Or two horses,' Tremayne's said.

'Only the one. Red Rose, wherever it is, is alive.'

'It'll not race again in the UK.'

'If we find it, so much the better, but some of the guilty parties are here in Salisbury. Vincent must have known, so would Kirkland, and if Sally had suspected, then who knows to what extent people will go.'

'Not her father,' Tremayne said.

'He wouldn't, but he might be frightened. If he's committing fraud, then in all likelihood it's not the first time.'

'Les Daniels?'

'He's a minor player, certainly not Sally's murderer.'

'Any luck with faces at the racecourse?'

'Not yet. The constables are following up on a couple of leads, enthusiastic punters who are always taking photos. We should find something.'

'Let's not forget,' Tremayne said, 'insurance fraud, the death of a horse, the disappearance of another are only of interest to us in solving the murder of Sally Kirkland.'

'I won't,' Clare said as the two of them walked out of the office. From Homicide's point of view, it had been a good day, but others out at the Fortescue mansion were suffering, and others elsewhere were worrying.

Chapter 8

Herbert Houghton was not pleased to be back in Salisbury, and the idea of opening up a dead horse that had been in the freezer did not excite him. However, circumstances dictated. For this check of the horse, Barry Vincent would not be present.

Samples from Fortescue and Swift, the latter reluctantly forced to comply, had shown that neither man had been with Sally Kirkland in the stable just before her death. Vincent had taken umbrage at his exclusion from the full autopsy on Scarlet Soleil until Tremayne had taken him to one side, told him that he was treading on thin ice, and he was lucky to be still free.

It was, Clare knew, a Tremayne tactic to frighten the man into doing something foolish, such as making a phone call or visiting someone. After all, as Tremayne reasoned, Vincent didn't have the necessary skill or the contacts to pull off such a deception, and besides, what was the man's angle? Vincent did not display overt signs of wealth; he drove a modest car, lived in a small house, and dressed comfortably, but with no designer labels, not as Andrew Fortescue had.

The investigation by the CSIs at the Fortescue residence had completed, a report sent to Tremayne and Clare. Hughes's professional opinion was that Andrew Fortescue had taken his own life; the reason why remained unknown. Clare had revisited the family mansion, spoken to the grieving mother, the type of person who holds the tears back, acts with the civility required of a person of her social standing.

'He was always highly strung,' Lady Fortescue, the former Marjorie Buxton, good-time girl and socialite, said.

'I'm sorry,' Clare's response. Dealing with the parent of a deceased person was always the most challenging part of a police officer's lot. At least this time she hadn't had to tell them that their son had plummeted to his death as they had been at the scene when she and Tremayne had arrived.

'It's Bernard. His health isn't the best, and now he's feeling guilty.'

The two women sat in the main room of the house. It had been impressive, with its walls festooned with oil paintings, a deer's head and a collection of swords, but as with the general condition of the rest of the building, an aura of decay pervaded.

'Your husband, his lordship?'

'In his bed. It's the shock, don't you see? His only son, the heir to the title and the estate, and he kills himself. Why would he do that?'

'Lady Fortescue, I appreciate this is not the most opportune time, but I need to ask you about your son, his state of mind, his relationships, his financial status.'

'The Fortescues don't shirk their responsibilities, nor do they cower.'

Clare had checked on the former Marjorie Buxton before sitting down with her; she had been notorious for her outrageous behaviour, her lovers, her minor brushes with the law, stealing a policeman's helmet on one occasion. Yet now she was a woman full of the proprieties of her position.

'The relationship between father and son?' Clare asked.

'Strained. Bernard, my husband, is a conservative man, not inclined to rash decisions. In contrast, Andrew was of a different generation, a generation that places little value on assets and investments, preferring the immediacy of a good time. Not that he was foolish with his money, and he did put money to one side, it's just that Bernard is sombre and takes his responsibilities as a lord seriously.'

'Suicide is often the result of emotional distress.'

'Often? I would have thought always, and Andrew was an emotionally-charged man. Either he was up or down, in love or getting over another failed love affair.'

'Sally Kirkland, did you know her?' Clare asked.

'I knew of her, but I never met her.'

'Andrew was, we believe, keen on her.'

'It's a big house. Andrew used to bring her here sometimes, spend the night with her, but we never met, only saw him drive in and out with her.'

'You disapproved?'

'The daughter of Barton Kirkland. What do you think?'

'I've spoken to him, and it's his daughter that's dead. It's your opinion that's needed.'

'Barton Kirkland is a rogue. Of course, he conceals it well, but his history reveals that his wealth is ill-founded.'

'His daughter, is she tarred with the same brush?' Clare asked, realising that the snobbery that her mother concealed from others was present in Lady Fortescue. It was a side of her mother that Clare did not like.

A dead son, and yet the stiff upper lip, the air of superiority remained. The reaction of most women would be gushing tears, a doctor administering a strong sedative, a gaggle of relations nearby to console. At the Fortescues, apart from his lordship taking to his bed, nothing had changed.

'A fling with the woman, that's fine, but Andrew would have seen it as something more.'

'Did he speak to you about it?'

'She was easy with her favours. Did you know that?'

'It has been mentioned.'

'Promiscuous, unable to control her carnal desires,' her ladyship said.

Clare thought it was the pot calling the kettle black. Sally Kirkland, even if she was easier than most, belonged to a generation more condoning of such behaviour. If the newspaper clippings from Marjorie Buxton's era were correct, then it was her that was the more promiscuous of the two women.

'He would have married her?'

'Probably. Andrew was besotted. But dying the way she did, then his mind disturbed from arguing with his father, and Andrew's mental condition must have suffered a meltdown.'

'The arguments with the father. You didn't elucidate,' Clare said.

'Bernard wanted Andrew to take his responsibilities seriously, to act as the future lord.'

'A penniless lord by all accounts. From what we know, you have financial difficulties, and Andrew wanted to commercialise the place.'

'Turn it into a theme park.'

'Weddings, weekend accommodation for those that could afford it hardly constitutes a theme park.'

'If you think, as he did, that I would sully myself and the good name of the Fortescues by standing behind

The Horse's Mouth

the counter of a craft shop selling homemade honey and lemon curd, you've got another think coming.'

'Would Sally Kirkland have married Andrew?'

'For the title, so would a myriad of other women.'

'You did,' Clare said. A Tremayne tactic, bait the woman, look for the reaction.

'I upheld my end of the bargain. I did my duty, but Andrew and the Kirkland woman – over my dead body,' Lady Fortescue said.

Or someone else's, Clare thought.

***

Houghton, kitted out in coveralls and nitrile gloves, stood to one side of the animal. Tremayne had spoken to his assistant, another accredited equine vet.

Also present were a representative of Kirkland's equine insurance company and two students from the Royal Veterinary College who were there to gain work experience. As far as Tremayne could see, all they were to gain was how to mop up the blood and guts from the floor and to store the dead animal's organs if required.

Even Tremayne had to admit to feeling queasy as Houghton made the first cut on the animal's body. He left and went outside. Les Daniels was leaning up against a wall, and although no longer in the employ of Barton Kirkland, his interest in the dead horse and Red Rose remained.

'Kirkland?' Tremayne asked Daniels.

'He's holding me responsible.'

'For what? The horse or his daughter?'

'Both. I should have picked up on the substitution, and as for Sally, he says that I shouldn't have let her take the horse, seeing it was an important race for him.'

'I thought it was just another regional meeting, or am I missing something?'

Inside the stable, the sound of men at work, the teeth-grating noise of an angle grinder. The smell where Tremayne and Daniels stood was unpleasant. They moved away and sat down on a couple of wooden boxes.

'Kirkland has a chequered past, and you know that,' Tremayne said.

'I'll not hold that against the man. He played fair by me, and I'm hopeful that once this blows over, he'll take me back. I'm good with the animals; I care about them, and they know it. Some of the younger stable hands and the trainers, they come here with their university degrees, but they don't understand how to deal with temperamental horses, not like I do. They think knowledge comes out of a book, but it's experience that matters.'

Tremayne had to concur. Some of the newer officers at the police station never left the cosy surrounds of the building, believing that policing was conducted from a computer. But Tremayne knew the racecourse was where he would find out hitherto hidden facts, and the one that concerned him and Clare the most was who had been in the stable with Sally Kirkland before her death and during it. The CSIs had not found conclusive evidence, only footprints inside the stable on a concrete floor.

'You're aware that Sally Kirkland had a man with her before she died?'

'I am, but it wasn't me.'

The Horse's Mouth

'Then who? We know she was spending time with Ian Swift and Andrew Fortescue, but it wasn't either of them, although one's committed suicide since.'

'Swift wouldn't, tough man.'

'You know him?'

'I do. Not that I like him.'

Tremayne enjoyed Daniels' company, even though he wasn't sure of the man's innocence. He wasn't a murderer, that alibi was firm, but he could have injected the horse, and Tremayne remembered five minutes when Daniels had excused himself that day. The two men had been near the stable at the time, and it might have been long enough to commit the act.

Houghton walked out from the stable, removed his protective gear and placed it into a large plastic bag which he sealed. He then looked over at Tremayne. 'Messy business,' he said.

'Anything?' Tremayne asked.

'Not yet. We'll take the organs and check them out. But I'd say we'll not find much, and if the animal had a problem, how would anyone else know? Modesty aside, I know horses, and if I can't pick up on the visible, I'm not sure anyone else could.'

'If it was alive, someone could have checked it on a treadmill, figured out something, checked its heart, respiration. That's possible, isn't it?'

'It is, but it would need specialised equipment. And besides, it's the missing horse that concerns you, not the one we just examined.'

'Big business, equine insurance fraud?'

'Not that I'd know. My people will clean up, wrap what remains and put it back into the freezer.'

'Any reason to keep what's left?' Tremayne asked.

'None that I know of. We may be back, but I hope not.'

After Houghton had driven off in his Jaguar, Daniels looked over at Tremayne. 'He'll be upset later,' he said.

'Why?' Tremayne asked.

'He didn't see it, but there was a patch of blood on the back of his trousers, and he sat on the seat in his car wearing them. It'll be hell to clean afterwards.'

'Why didn't you tell him?'

'None of my business.'

Chapter 9

Clare sat with Tremayne as the photos and a video of the race, but more importantly, the horses in the parade ring, were displayed on a large monitor plugged into Clare's laptop. The constables she had assigned to the racecourse had done their job well.

'What do you reckon?' Tremayne said after they had finished watching.

'I can't tell. We need someone to work with us on this,' Clare said.

'I'd trust Les Daniels before Kirkland and his vet.'

'It doesn't matter either way. We show the photos to two of the three. If there's consensus, then we can accept the result, for now, subject to certain provisos. If there's a disparity, then we bring in the third member of the triumvirate. Whoever dissembles or gives a false answer brings suspicion onto himself, and I don't think any of them are that stupid.'

'What about Swift and Fortescue at the racecourse? Any luck there?'

'Fortescue was there. The constables showed his photo around the place.'

'Yet it wasn't him with Kirkland's daughter, not in the events leading up to her death.'

'He could have killed her.'

'Too neat, too easy. We'll not be that lucky in this case. Fortescue might have killed himself, but it's unlikely he would be capable of murdering someone in cold blood, and especially Sally if as his mother said, he was in love with her. It goes against the grain of what we know about him.'

'Apart from a distant father and a social-climbing mother, not a lot, although Upton, the gardener, reckoned he was a good person.'

'Being thwarted in love is a strong motivator,' Tremayne said.

'With no proof, that angle's going nowhere. What we need is the man she had been with in the stable, someone callous.'

'Swift could be callous, thrusting women away when he's finished with them.'

'The man's too intelligent to do it. He values his life more highly than that.'

'Your constables, anything else?'

'They were looking for a horse, or either Swift or Fortescue. Apart from that, what did you expect?' Clare said.

'A miracle, but you're right. There are a mystery man and a four-legged absconder. We need them both.'

It was the banter of two people, the chance to let off a little steam and to relax, although neither downplayed the seriousness of the situation. Sally Kirkland's body was at the mortuary, a formerly valuable horse had had its vital organs removed, and a highly strung, infatuated man had taken a jump from the third storey of the family's mansion.

'Which is the most important, the man or the horse?' Clare asked.

'How do we find a missing horse? It's not as if you could file it away in a cabinet. This premise of Barton Kirkland's that someone has taken his horse unbeknown to him still doesn't ring true. And what's been said about

The Horse's Mouth

the woman? Was she screwing around with two, possibly three men at the same time?'

'Women are wired differently to men; they want romance, an emotional attachment,' Clare said. 'But, of course, she could be predisposed to the need for physical love.'

'What does that mean?'

'Could it have been a random stranger, an employee at the racecourse?' Clare said.

'Her father would be able to fill in the blanks. A father's love might try to put on a brave face for us and others, but to himself, he might have read her differently, blamed himself.'

'Or hated her for what she was.'

'I don't like complicated theories,' Tremayne said. 'They're the first to collapse. I still hold with the lover and the murderer being the same.'

***

Tremayne left the office that night perplexed. Was it him, he wondered, was it right what they were saying, that he had lost his edge? He had seen the sideways glances in the corridors at the police station, the whispered comments after he had passed. He knew what they were saying: the oldest person in the station, the man who wouldn't accept the inevitable.

Jean had gently nudged him towards retirement, spoken of taking a trip somewhere, a cruise possibly, the chance to visit her brother in Australia, to visit New Zealand. But Tremayne, although feigning interest, had no great desire to travel. Sure, he had enjoyed the trip to Singapore during the hunt for the murderer of Richard Grantley. It had been good to take Jean back to the city-state a few months later, but now, the thought of another long-distance flight did not appeal, certainly not in economy, and he could not afford business class. And as for a cruise, sitting in a deck chair, sipping at a drink that came with an umbrella in it, that he couldn't take.

He knew he would have another sleepless night, a not uncommon occurrence. He was worried.

At home, a meal and Jean with a bottle of beer for him. Seeing her always cheered him up, and even though pub lunches and a few pints were behind him unless they were the only option, the comforts of a warm house, a loving wife, did have their benefits.

As he lay in bed, sleep eluding him, the phone rang. It was after two in the morning. At his side, Jean was fast asleep.

Tremayne picked up the phone and went into the other room. It was Yarwood. Strange, he thought, that in all their years together, he had never called her Clare, only referring to her by her first name when he had given a speech at her wedding.

'It's two in the morning. What do you want, waking the dead?' Tremayne acted annoyed. The habit of a lifetime; he wasn't going to break it, although, he knew his sergeant wouldn't phone unless it was necessary.

'You're not dead,' Clare said in reply. It was she who had been fast asleep when the phone call had come, not Tremayne.

'Okay, I'll give you that, but what is it? A development?'

'I'll pick you up at 6 a.m. sharp. They've found Red Rose.'

'Nearby?'

The Horse's Mouth

'In Devon. A two-hour drive, maybe three. I've phoned Houghton, and he didn't shout at me. He's coming down.'

'Any more?'

'Not a lot. A local sergeant spotted the horse in a paddock down there. It seems he's an avid admirer of horses, recognised the markings.'

'Good work. Now let me get back to sleep,' Tremayne said, although he knew that he would not. The doubts, the aches and pains, they were all gone. He was a man fired up again, a man who was going to solve a murder. He realised though that he had complimented Yarwood for a job well done; he'd have to watch that. Compliments and Yarwood were not mutually compatible; sarcasm worked better.

As Tremayne settled back into his bed, Jean leant over. 'six in the morning?'

'You heard?'

'Clare?'

'They've found the horse,' Tremayne said. 'In Devon.'

'A full breakfast, bacon and eggs, toast?'

'That would be good.'

'I'll message Clare, tell her to be here twenty minutes earlier. I'll make breakfast for the two of you,' Jean said.

Tremayne allowed himself a little smile. He wasn't that old, not yet.

***

Barton Kirkland looked out the window of his six-bedroom house. He knew he had done well.

Two negatives disturbed his idyllic lifestyle: the death of his wife and now, his daughter, Sally. He knew that both women were flawed, and it was easy to love one, his wife, to dislike another, his daughter. But that wasn't the emotion he could feel towards Sally. He knew that she was wild, but she always remembered his birthdays, and she did care for him.

After all, it had been the two of them for many years. The years from her mother's death until puberty, him and her against the world; the world hadn't had a chance. But puberty had hit Sally with a vengeance. The pretty girl blossomed out into a woman, and the hormonal instincts went into overdrive as she found that men, no more than boys really, were infinitely more intriguing than a father. Even so, they had remained close, and no matter how much he disliked what she had become, he continued to pamper her, hope that with time she would quieten down, find herself a good man.

Andrew Fortescue had been such a man, but he was weak. Ian Swift had the determination and the drive, but he was a philanderer. And as for Barry Vincent, a competent vet, but lacking in Fortescue's aristocracy or Swift's financial acumen.

To have heard that Sally had met a man in the stable did not surprise him. But why she had died, he didn't know.

In the corner, largely ignored, even though his presence had been requested, sat Les Daniels. He would not speak until Kirkland was ready.

After what seemed like an eternity, Kirkland took a seat opposite Daniels and spoke. 'Who was the man with Sally that day?'

'I don't know,' Daniels replied. It was a conversation he had not wanted to have with his former

The Horse's Mouth

boss and long-time friend. The two men, separated by wealth and education, but joined by a mutual love for horses and Sally, although Daniels would never reveal the latter to Kirkland.

'As for the other matter, it's not important, and I don't want to know or discuss it. You do understand that.'

Daniels had to admit to trepidation. Even though it wasn't widely known, Barton Kirkland had killed a man in the past, and he, Les Daniels, knew the details, not that he would ever reveal them to anyone, no matter how indifferent or dismissive the man was to him.

'I do,' Daniels said. He sat upright on his chair; Kirkland was leaning back on his.

'The man, who was it?'

'I wasn't there.'

'I know that. You were with Tremayne. If you hadn't spent your time with him, who knows what might have happened. My daughter might be still alive.'

'You don't think I haven't thought the same?'

'That's not what worries me now.'

'You have the wealth to outrun whatever happens. I don't.'

'I'll see you right. After all, we have a lot of water under the bridge.'

'Past histories that I would never reveal,' Daniels said.

'The name?'

'As I said I wasn't there.'

'Sally wouldn't open up to me. She knew what I thought and who I would have chosen for her.'

'Fortescue?'

'A weak, ineffectual man, but he had the title, the breeding. What could the others offer?'

'Passion, love?'

'And when they wane, then what? Nothing, only an empty heart and an even emptier bed.'

'Barton, it is uncharacteristic of you to talk to me about such matters.'

'You will never reveal our conversation; I know that.'

'True, but what advice can I give you? Talk to me about horses, and I can help, but with Sally, I am mute.'

'I need to know who the man was. Sally used to spend time with you, maybe even seduced you…'

'She didn't,' Daniels replied.

'But you wouldn't have objected.'

'I would have wanted more.'

'Another soft lily-livered dreamer.'

'I am, but Sally was a good person.'

'I knew about Fortescue. She liked him, but she was keener on Swift, although she knew him for what he was,' Kirkland said.

'Sally and love were fickle.'

'And he may have killed her. He owes me.'

'You're not a young man anymore. Don't do anything rash.'

'Daniels, don't offer me advice, not in this matter. Tell me about horses and what I should do, how much they should be fed and exercised, and I'll listen, but don't talk to me about my daughter.'

'I would have been a good trainer,' Daniels said.

'After this is over, I'll give you a couple of horses to train, but you were unstable in the past.'

'Admittedly, but not now.'

'I need that name.'

'She never mentioned a name. All I know is that he had been in the army. A man's man, Sally reckoned.'

'Someone suitable, possibly as suitable as Fortescue. Why did he have to kill her?'

'That I don't know,' Daniels said. 'We both miss her for different reasons.'

'I know,' Kirkland said as he lowered his head.

Daniels got up from his seat and left the house.

Chapter 10

'We never knew,' Sue Nixon, a ruddy complexion and smelling of horses, said, 'otherwise we would have refused to take the horse.'

It was still early, just after 9 a.m., and at the stables in Devon, there had been activity since before five in the morning. Both Tremayne and Clare had enjoyed Jean's breakfast, and Tremayne had slept on the way down, Clare driving as always when it was the two of them.

Clare recognised Sue Nixon's type from her formative years in Norfolk. The healthy glow from fresh air and the physical exertion of riding the horses, rubbing them down afterwards, mucking out the stables.

'The full story,' Clare said in the comfort of the house that adjoined the paddock where Red Rose stood, oblivious of the part it was playing in a murder enquiry. Even from a distance, both of the police officers could see the similarity to Scarlet Soleil.

The three main protagonists, Kirkland, Daniels and Vincent, believed the horse that ran was Scarlet Soleil as was the horse in the parade ring, which meant that the switch happened between the stable and the parade ring.

Whatever way it was looked at, it was evident that the dead woman was implicit in either a crime or a conspiracy. It had been a damning conclusion about a woman to whom both of the police officers were willing to give a degree of latitude. After all, the instinct was to think the best of a dead person.

'We received three horses in the last week, two for training and the horse you're interested in, for spelling, to have a rest,' Sue Nixon said.

Clare, who had ridden horses, knew what the word meant, so did Tremayne.

'How long is it here for?' Tremayne said.

'Six weeks.'

'Have you seen the horse before?'

'Never. We received the money upfront for the six weeks, but after that, who pays?'

'We'll worry about that later,' Tremayne said, although he was sure it wouldn't be the police. Whoever did, one thing was certain; Sue Nixon would be responsible for it until a decision was made.

'You didn't believe anything was untoward?' Tremayne said. Sue Nixon was, to him, culpable until proven innocent.

'No reason. Horses, especially if they've had a hard season or suffered an injury, often spend time with us, to allow them to spell. We don't only prepare them for races, although that's the main part of our business.'

'A heavy responsibility.'

'Inspector Tremayne, are you an admirer of horses?'

'I am, although they don't always return the affection.'

'They won't if you spend money on them.'

Clare thought it was an ideal opportunity for a comment, and she knew Tremayne would enjoy it if it were just the two of them, but not in front of a third person. However, she still had an internal chuckle to herself.

'You've been told the history of the horse out there in the paddock?' Clare asked.

'After I found out its name, I did some checking. It appears that if that horse could talk, it would have some telling to do.'

'Straight from the horse's mouth, literally,' Tremayne said, 'but, unfortunately, it's not about to do that. What can you tell us? Who brought the horse down here?'

'It came down in a horse transporter. As to who paid for the horse, I can't be sure.'

'Why? Thoroughbred horses are valuable, registered, their pedigree documented.'

'They are, and as far as I'm concerned, the paperwork was correct.'

A car pulled up outside, and Herbert Houghton got out. He walked over to where Clare stood, having left the house to meet him.

'Over in the paddock,' Clare said.

'I'll give it a check, and then I'd like someone to stress it on the training track. Is this possible?'

'It can be arranged. I'll talk to the owner of the stables.'

Houghton entered the house, accepted a mug of tea, nodded to Tremayne and kissed Sue Nixon on the cheek. 'Sorry that you're mixed up in this,' he said.

'You've met before?' Clare said.

'We were at college together, kept in touch over the years, met up occasionally.'

Tremayne didn't like coincidences, not in a murder investigation. Another piece of the jigsaw, albeit small.

Houghton went over to the horse. Sue Nixon and Clare were with him as he checked the animal, taking notes.

The Horse's Mouth

Tremayne, at a loose end, wandered around the stables, looked at the horses and the facilities. He had to admit to being impressed.

After twenty-five minutes, with Red Rose saddled, Clare took the opportunity to ride the horse around one of the paddocks. If Tremayne asked, she'd say she was working on instructions to warm the horse up before a more exhaustive test of its physical stamina.

Tremayne returned and watched the horse run, first at a gentle gallop, and then faster, and finally, a short sprint at high speed.

'Not bad,' Sue Nixon said.

'Good enough to win at a meeting in Salisbury?' Tremayne asked.

'It depends on the competition.'

Houghton went over to the horse, took note that it was panting, walked around the horse, checked its breathing, listened to its heartbeat, and walked over to his car.

Tremayne followed and waited for the man to close the boot lid before asking, 'Red Rose?'

'A little out of condition, but apart from that, I'm not sure there's much wrong with it.'

'Good enough to have won in Salisbury?'

'Probably. But then so was the other horse. I've not found anything wrong with that horse either. If it's insurance fraud, it doesn't make sense to me.'

'Any ideas?'

'None that I can think of,' Houghton said.

***

Barton Kirkland knew one thing. Whoever had killed his daughter was answerable to him. He didn't know why he had thought of Exodus 21:24, an eye for an eye, a tooth for a tooth.

Only one man could be trusted to help him. He made a phone call. 'I need you to work with me, find this man.'

'Not if you intend to kill him,' Daniels said, although pleased to be in favour again. Even though Kirkland had not always treated him well over the years, he had still looked out for him.

'Not yet, and besides, you'll be out of the country if it comes to that.'

'I've always had a craving for the Caribbean.'

'Then that's where you'll be. Find this man.'

'Reluctantly, but don't do anything foolish. You can't be protected the same as before, and you know that.'

'I know.'

It wasn't that Daniels didn't know, but he had promised Sally that he wouldn't tell her father about the man that she loved. After all, if he knew, then he would either be gushing over the man or pushing him away, spending money if needed.

Daniels, a man who had been close enough to Kirkland and his wife and daughter over the years, but not an intimate acquaintance, had seen them close up. Kirkland's wife, a frail and timid woman with a strong sense of right and wrong, loyally supporting her husband on all matters, acceding to his every request, had adored the man, as he had her. And then there was Sally, a pretty child, but tough-willed as her father, not easily controlled but loving him.

Yet, for some reason, when Sally had matured into her twenties, she would come and talk to him. That was when Les Daniels had started to fall in love with her. Only once had he told her of his feelings, and she had put him down gently. And now she was dead, and he grieved for her as much as her father did. He resolved to tell the father what he knew; it seemed to be the right thing to do, what Sally would have wanted.

Chapter 11

Another day, another early start in Homicide, although it was mid-morning by the time Tremayne and Clare arrived at the Fortescue mansion, the lord having passed away in the night.

They had held back from visiting Lady Fortescue until later in the day at her request. On their arrival, a servant opened the door and led them through to what had been the dining room, now devoid of furniture apart from a large formal dining table. On it rested a coffin; inside it the body of Lord Fortescue.

'It's tradition,' her ladyship said.

'The body should be down the mortuary. Your husband is part of a criminal investigation, no matter how peripheral he is to the murder of Sally Kirkland,' Tremayne said. Sensitivity was not his strong point.

'I've agreed, and yes, his body will be going to the mortuary soon. I needed to talk to you.'

'In here?' Clare said.

'With my husband, yes. Unless you're squeamish.'

'No, that's fine.'

'Andrew was obsessed with Sally Kirkland, but that's not why he committed suicide.'

'Then why?'

'It was my husband. He disapproved of the match. To him, breeding was all-important, and Sally wasn't suitable.'

'Barton Kirkland?' Tremayne said.

'When Andrew told us that he intended to ask Kirkland's daughter to marry him, my husband was incensed. He hired an investigator to check out the woman.'

'What did he find?' Clare asked.

'What you probably know. Sally Kirkland was well-educated, intelligent and capable.'

'Her father?' Tremayne said.

'Barton Kirkland was an upstart who through hard work and the right attitude raised himself from the gutter.'

'That's better than inherited wealth,' Clare said. 'It proves that the man has a backbone.'

'I could handle it, and I've never forgotten my roots. Barton Kirkland and I are from the same stock. People who've strived for better, fought for it hammer and tongs, and once we've got it, will do anything to keep it.'

'I'm not sure where this is heading,' Tremayne said.

'Kirkland had been a criminal, up before the courts.'

'We know this.'

'Do you know a man died, murdered by Barton Kirkland?'

'I do, but it's unprovable, and not necessarily relevant.'

'It is, or it was to my late husband. It was proof that beneath the surface, the veneer that Kirkland affects, there is a ruthless and violent man who will stop at nothing to achieve what he wants.'

'If you don't mind me saying, Lady Fortescue,' Clare said, 'the Fortescue history and how the first lord gained his title are documented. Is it so different from Barton Kirkland?'

'It was a crueller time, and the first lord, George Fortescue, was a man of his time. He had protected the king, had become a trusted adviser to the man, killed a few or had them killed to protect the king.

'My husband was concerned with the present; he saw the past as colourful, nothing more. I don't believe that you can use our family's history against my husband's attitude or his dislike of Barton Kirkland.'

'Sally Kirkland had no intention of marrying your son,' Tremayne said.

'Why do you say that? Because she was sleeping with other men, Ian Swift, for one.'

'There's another man, someone we don't know.'

'Someone she might have loved, but she would have married my son.'

'You seem certain,' Clare said.

Four men dressed in black entered the room, nodded at her ladyship and took hold of the coffin by its four corners. They then left the room.

'Before she died, Sally had sexual intercourse with an unknown person.'

'The man she loved, but she would have still married my son.'

'Did he know she was playing around?'

'My husband told him, gave him proof, photos.'

'Your son's reaction?'

'Distraught, a frightful argument, my husband was saying that if he sullied the house with Kirkland's daughter, he'd disinherit him.'

'When was this?'

'The morning of the day she died.'

'Are you telling us that Andrew didn't know about Sally's lifestyle?'

The Horse's Mouth

'He knew, but he wouldn't have believed it, and then if he had been at the racecourse and seen her with that other man…'

'Are you implying that your son could have murdered Sally?'

'It's not what a mother wants to believe, but I must have the truth.'

'Why?'

'Sally was me. She would have married Andrew, done the right thing, and never looked at another man again.'

'But she was in love,' Clare said.

'Love is transient. An aristocratic title, a position in society, both are permanent. I upheld my part of the bargain with my husband, and he never needed to regret our marriage. Nor would have Andrew, and if he hadn't been at the racecourse, hadn't seen the proof that he had so long denied, then he would be alive and Sally, as soon as she married, would have become Lady Fortescue, and I would have been the dowager.'

'It's a tragic tale,' Tremayne said. 'Although I'm not convinced he murdered Sally.'

'Why?'

'It's logical, but Andrew was a fractured, emotionally lovesick man. A man who would have left evidence of murder, but we found none. I might be wrong on this, but I believe we're looking for someone cold and emotionless.'

'I would prefer it not to be my son.'

'The man that Sally would have left behind if she had married your son?' Clare asked.

Lady Fortescue was tiring, and the stiff aristocratic upper lip was slipping, so much so that under the cultured accent there was the occasional lapse to the working-class voice that she had had in her younger days.

'Do you have proof of who it was, the man that day in the stable?' Tremayne persisted with Clare's original question.

'I know who she would have given up if she married Andrew. If he were in the stable with Sally on that day, I'd not know, and Andrew never spoke to me about what he saw.'

'But you know he saw something?'

'The man you want is Jeremy Liston.'

'The Jeremy Liston?' Clare said. 'I've met him.'

'Who hasn't,' Tremayne said. 'A Victoria Cross, a collection of medals, a colonel before he retired, became an estate agent in Salisbury.'

'That's your mystery man. It seems my husband was ahead of you in obtaining that name.'

'And what now for you, Lady Fortescue?' Clare asked.

'The title died with my husband. Andrew was right in his approach, but I couldn't have dealt with it, all those people tramping around the place. I'll sell up, get what I can, travel the world and in time, find myself another man. There are over thirty years of pent-up frustration to deal with, but today is not the day to talk of such matters.'

Chapter 12

Jeremy Liston, a man who single-handedly and with a total disregard for his safety had stormed an enemy position, killing two fundamentalists with machine guns, saving the lives of five on his patrol in Helmand Province, Afghanistan, was a marked man.

Tall, muscular and popular in Salisbury due to his gallantry – a local lad made good – Liston had taken the goodwill and transposed it into a successful business selling property in the area.

It was late in the afternoon when Liston arrived at the police station and parked his Range Rover next to Tremayne's run-of-the-mill Toyota.

'You have a few questions for me,' Liston said as he sat down across the table from Tremayne and Clare.

'Thanks for coming in,' Clare said.

'Any time, Clare,' Liston said.

Clare had already told Tremayne she knew Liston through her husband and his mayoral duties, and that Liston had put forward his name to be a councillor in the city.

'Inspector Tremayne, does this relate to Sally Kirkland?' Liston looked over at the detective inspector.

'It does. You were a friend of hers.'

Tremayne, confident of some facts, unsure of others, allowed Liston to talk.

'She was someone whose company I enjoyed.'

'Jeremy, is that it?' Clare asked.

'I know she's dead,' Liston said.

'You don't appear to be upset,' Tremayne said.

'I'm not, Inspector.'

'A callous remark.'

'Is it? I've seen death on too many occasions, knelt by the side of a colleague, his head blown half-off, seen friends with their innards splayed out, killed a few, maimed some others.'

'Your heroism is not in question, nor the trauma of what you went through.'

'I'm accustomed to people dying. And yes, we were lovers.'

'Did she love you?'

'It's probable.'

'That's not a convincing statement,' Clare said. Whereas she knew the man, she had never fathomed him, a distance about him, hidden depths, a coldness belied by his charm.

'You ask me to comment on an emotion I cannot feel,' Liston said. There was a soulful look on the man's face as though he was plumbing the depths of his psyche.

'What does that mean?' Tremayne asked.

'Inspector, you have seen deaths, some of them gruesome, the sort of things that give people nightmares.'

'I have.'

'But you've not been there when those deaths have occurred, nor have you been responsible for causing them. I have, and whereas it was my duty to kill for my country, something I did with pride, it doesn't affect the fact that base emotions are exposed. After a time, killing becomes mechanical and gratifying.'

'You're painting yourself into a corner.'

'I am innocent of the crime you would label me with, but if you are asking me whether I would have been capable of killing someone in cold blood, then the answer is yes.'

The Horse's Mouth

'Is that a confession?' Clare asked.

'It is not. Sally professed to love, and even though I admit to a certain fondness for the woman, the emotion that she wanted from me in return I could not give, not to her, not to any woman.'

'You left the military, distanced yourself from it,' Tremayne said. 'What's the reason?'

'I just told you. Killing became easy, too easy. It wasn't as if I liked what I was doing, but without a feeling of something, it was wrong.'

'Post-traumatic stress disorder?'

'No, just a muted emotional response. Sally was a good person, a little frivolous, but she wanted me, I know that.'

'It was you at the racecourse,' Tremayne said.

'I saw her just before she died.'

'We'll need a sample, proof that you had sex with her on the day,' Clare said.

'Let me be clear on this,' Liston said. 'I did not kill her. It was a release of pent-up needs, from her and me.'

'Are you as easy as she apparently was?' Tremayne asked.

'If you're asking, do I put it about, then the answer is an unequivocal yes. But I don't mistreat the women, profess love at the moment of intimacy, nor do I kill them.'

'Do they understand that you only want them for mutual pleasure?' Clare asked.

'They should, but some don't. Sally wanted to, but love is stronger than reason. As for the others, it seems that I have the aura of a brave man. I can understand, although the concept of bravery is overrated. I wasn't heroic in Afghanistan, only instinctive in my reaction in a dangerous situation. I never gave any thought when I killed those Afghans, nor did I think about those whose lives I supposedly saved.'

'But if it makes you successful with women, you'll use it.'

'The intimacy, but not the emotion.'

***

Sue Nixon phoned. She was alarmed, and her voice was breaking up. 'Someone's been down here, attempted to kill Red Rose,' she said.

'Speak slower,' Clare said. It had been an early night for her and Tremayne, and she was at home with Clive, enjoying a peaceful interlude. Near to the heater, the old cat was curled up, and Clive was reading a book on politics. Clare was savouring the moment, a glass of red wine in her hand, the ambience of her surroundings, the love of a good man.

'We had put the horse into the stable last night, and normally we keep a watch on them through the night. They're valuable, highly strung animals, and sometimes one of them rears up in its stable, and the risk of damage to our cost would be frightening.'

'The salient facts,' Clare said.

'One of the stable hands was down by the horse, taking a stroll around the place when he saw someone in the shadows. He shouted out, but the person bolted over the fence at the back.'

'Why do you believe it was Red Rose this person was after?'

'Why would someone be walking around late at night? Besides, there's a driveway at the front, and at the back, it's a wooded area, a stream running high on account of the recent rain.'

The Horse's Mouth

'Is that it?'

'As this person took off, they dropped a bag.'

'What was in it?'

'You'd better get down here and see for yourself.'

'In the meantime, what can you tell me?'

'I've not opened it up, not fully, only peeked. The stable hand was smart enough not to touch it, only to take hold of the handle with a piece of plastic and to bring it to me.'

'Good man. You've both acted correctly, but what do you reckon is in it?'

'A syringe, sedatives, barbiturates. They were going to kill Red Rose, but why?'

'The local police?'

'I've not contacted them, only you.'

'I'll phone them as a courtesy,' Clare said. 'But I don't want you to give the bag to them, just put it somewhere safe. I'll bring someone from our crime investigation team to check the back of your stables and what you found.'

It was late in the evening by the time Clare had roused Jim Hughes, arranged a CSI to accompany her, and told Tremayne what had happened.

***

'You've found my horse,' Kirkland said as he set eyes on the inspector. It was race day, and Tremayne thought he'd achieve more by being there, talking to people, trying to figure out how the substitution occurred.

'No thanks to you,' Tremayne's reply.

'I didn't know where it was.'

'Barton had no idea, nor did I,' Les Daniels, who was standing close to his boss, said.

Tremayne, perceptive, said nothing about the restored friendship of the two men. To him, a person's change in character either meant a change for the better or a turn for something more sinister. Whatever it was, he'd play along for the time being.

'Someone tried to kill it last night,' Tremayne said. 'Any comment?'

'Only one. When can I get the animal back? I'm out of pocket until he's returned,' Kirkland said.

'Why? You're not paying for its upkeep, or are you?'

'I'll not let it suffer at Sue Nixon's.'

'The money was paid upfront.'

Tremayne was not willing to fall in with the camaraderie of Kirkland and Daniels, preferring to maintain a slightly cynical, penetrative style of questioning. To him, it was odd, the two men, boss and long-standing employee acting as though something bonded them.

'How come Sally never noticed it wasn't Red Rose?' Tremayne asked the two men.

'It was Red Rose when it left me,' Daniels said.

'Maybe it was, maybe it wasn't, but Sally knew the horse.'

'Barton believes me, why won't you?'

'I deal with facts, with indisputable proof, and from where I'm standing, someone had to have switched the horse and got it off the racecourse.'

'Getting it off isn't that difficult,' Kirkland said. 'Put it into a transporter and close the doors.'

'Sue Nixon here on the day?'

'One of her vehicles was,' Daniels said.

Tremayne felt that more would be gained by spending time alone with Les Daniels, but as Kirkland was buying and he was insisting, the police inspector joined the two men at the owners and trainers bar. He kept to the one beer, whereas Daniels downed two pints in as many minutes, and Kirkland had a double whisky.

Daniels was fond of a drink; it wouldn't be long before he would be unsteady on his feet.

'Tremayne,' Kirkland said, 'you might think me an uncaring man, but that's far from the truth. I did love my daughter, and I indulged her.'

'I'm not holding you for that. But the man in the stable, who was he?'

'I don't know. If I did…'

'You would deal with him?'

'He would be answerable to me, but that's not what I'm saying.'

'You killed once,' Tremayne said.

'Inspector, we're here having a quiet drink. Why bring up the past? Besides, I didn't kill anyone.'

'I can make an aspersion without proof. You were a vicious man in your day, before you made good, attained airs and graces, left Daniels in the gutter.'

'Hardly the gutter,' Daniels said.

'You were there, weren't you?' Tremayne said although he had no proof or knowledge of the fact. But over a few drinks, tongues loosen, and Daniels wasn't the sharpest intellect.

'Raking over old coals only shows the inadequacy of the current police investigation,' Kirkland said. 'Les and I have been colleagues for many years; a bond forms, a bond that is challenged in times of difficulty but remains resolute. Are you attempting to coerce either of us into an indiscretion? You are here as my guest, enjoying my hospitality.'

'The man in the stable with Sally? Who was he? Do you know?'

'I don't. Do you?'

'We have identified him. We have no reason to doubt the veracity of what he told us. However, he is not Sally's murderer.'

'His name?' Kirkland asked.

'Not yet. I need to know your reaction. Why was Sally with another man when she intended to marry Andrew Fortescue?'

'Who told you?'

'His mother,' Tremayne said.

'His lordship wouldn't have approved, cut him off without a penny.'

'For how long? The man was old, barely able to move, and besides, he's dead. Andrew Fortescue would be Lord Fortescue now. If only your daughter hadn't screwed another man in that stable.'

'Are you saying Andrew Fortescue saw her in there?'

'He was at the racecourse, in the vicinity of the stables, and he left soon after. He saw it, and then he jumped out of a window.'

'What a fool my daughter was. Of course, she wanted the title, the same as Marjorie Buxton,' Kirkland said.

'You knew of her before she married Lord Fortescue?'

'No, but I found out they were in debt up to their eyeballs. Andrew had great plans for the place, a way out of debt.'

'He told you?'

'He knew he couldn't do it on his own. But with Sally at his side, breeding the next lord, and me dealing with the finance and the management of his plans, then I would have made plenty, so would he. Not bad for a working-class lad, I thought. And now, what do we have? Nothing.'

Daniels downed his pint, called over to the barman for another. Kirkland sat down. After what seemed an eternity, he looked over at Tremayne. 'Sorry, it got to me. We'll talk again, but for now, I'm off home.'

After Kirkland had left, Daniels said. 'The man's heartbroken, but he's stoic, never lets you and I see his grieving.'

'This man in the stable. Do you know who it is?'

'Yes.'

'Then why didn't you tell him or me?'

'Because he didn't kill her and I knew what Kirkland's reaction would be.'

'Is that because you know what he had done in the past?'

Daniels took his beer from the barman, held it up to his mouth and drank it down in one go. He said nothing, only to excuse himself, leaving Tremayne looking at an empty seat and an empty glass. He stood up, walked over to the bar. 'Another pint,' he said.

Chapter 13

At Sue Nixon's house, the woman waited with a cup of tea for Clare; it was just after 8.30 a.m. 'A cold morning,' she said.

Two people from Jim Hughes's crime scene investigation team were due at the site within twenty minutes.

There was something about horses and cold weather, Clare remembered from when she had been younger, riding every week. The cold air, the horse's exhaled hot breath visible. Out on the training track, a couple of horses were pacing it out, not stretched to their limits.

'Red Rose is down in the stable,' Sue Nixon said. 'He's not on his own.'

Clare walked down to the stable with her and over to where a horse stood, unaware of its importance.

'Young Bob has stayed close to the horse,' Sue said.

'Why someone would want to kill a horse, I don't know,' Young Bob, a short, balding man with a sad face, said.

One thing that Clare knew, Young Bob was anything but young. He had to be over sixty and bent low.

'Nor do we,' Clare said after she had shaken the man's hand. 'The bag that was dropped?'

'It's safe,' Sue Nixon said.

'What's the story? Why is the horse here?' Young Bob asked.

'A murder in Salisbury, another dead horse. Red Rose listed to run, but Scarlet Soleil substituted. It's important, but we don't know why,' Clare said.

'Were they both in good condition?'

'It appears so. There may be a genetic defect with Red Rose, an exhaustive autopsy conducted on the other horse, a vet from the Royal Veterinary College, Herbert Houghton.'

'He's a good man,' Young Bob said.

'You know him?'

'He's been here on a couple of occasions, a friend of Sue's.'

'He is, but Sergeant Yarwood knows that already.'

'Not that he's a friend, I didn't,' Clare's response.

'Young Bob's a little strong with his estimation of my relationship with the man,' Sue Nixon said.

'He's not the most sociable,' Clare said.

'Not like Young Bob, talk the hind legs off a donkey.'

Clare looked back over at the stable hand. 'You asked before why the horse was here,' she said.

'It's just unusual, that's all. Red Rose is not a bad horse, a little out of condition, but no obvious injuries, and I've watched him run around our track. The gait is not perfect, and I'm not sure he's got the necessary competitive streak, but at regional races, a modest performer, win a few races, then out to stud.'

'Your opinion of why two horses would be swapped, and then why they would want them dead.'

'Who knows what goes on behind the scenes, the men who own these animals. Red Rose's owner, you know him?'

'I do. Barton Kirkland. His daughter died.'

'I read about it.'

'Nobody substitutes a horse then kills it,' Sue Nixon said.

'Crime? An act of revenge?' Clare said.

Two people walked into the stable: Gwyneth Dexter, one of Jim Hughes's CSIs, although a woman whose personal life was on the wild side, and another woman.

'This is Cathy, Cathy Appleton,' Gwyneth said.

'Pleased to meet you all,' Cathy said as she shook the hand of everyone in turn. To Clare, the young woman and Gwyneth Dexter, although a similar age, were as chalk and cheese. One was buxom and wore tight-fitting clothes, the other was as short as Young Bob and dressed in modest attire, a crucifix around her neck.

The wanton woman and the vestal virgin, Clare imagined. What conversation the two women had had on the way down to Devon, she could only imagine.

Back in the house, Sue Nixon opened the safe and showed the women the bag that had been left by the intruder. Cathy Appleton opened it carefully, wearing nitrile gloves, and withdrew the contents: two syringes and three bottles. All of the items were placed separately into evidence bags.

'Forensics will check them out,' Gwyneth said. 'Where was the intruder?'

'Back at the stables. I can show you,' Sue said.

The four women walked down past the stable, stopped where the bag had been dropped. Cathy Appleton remained to check in the immediate vicinity. Clare and Gwyneth climbed over a fence at the far end of the stables, Clare catching her skirt at the top, whereas Gwyneth climbed over with ease. Sue Nixon, not as agile as the two younger women, walked up the slight incline for twenty-five yards and opened a gate and walked through. She rejoined them soon enough.

'Did the intruder use the gate?' Clare said.

'He climbed the fence.'

'It was dark, and maybe he didn't know it was there.'

'Or he could have been in a hurry.'

'Are you certain it's a man?' Gwyneth asked.

'I'm not, but it's hard to imagine a woman killing an animal.'

'A logical conclusion,' Clare agreed.

'I can see where the person walked, but it doesn't tell us much, only a footprint in the mud. I'll take a cast, see if it helps,' Gwyneth said.

'If they came this way, then where would they have parked a car, assuming they drove?'

'There's a road at the rear,' Sue said.

'Then I suggest we go there. There's nothing to be gained traipsing through long wet grass.'

'I will, see if I can find anything else,' Gwyneth said. 'And pick up Cathy on the way.'

'A good friend?' Clare asked.

'Not likely. Pure and chaste and boring. Don't expect her down the pub of a night, kicking up her heels.'

***

Tremayne sat in his office. It was seven in the evening, and without his sergeant, although he had a report to prepare, he was lost as to what to do next. If he went home, Jean would pick up on the fact that he had drunk more than his stipulated two pints of beer at the racecourse.

After Kirkland and Daniels had left, he had sat at the bar chatting and drinking, and even though he had gained no further insight into Sally Kirkland's murder, he had enjoyed himself.

The sight of Barry Vincent in his office came as a shock.

'We need to talk,' Vincent said.

'On the record?' Tremayne said.

'You'll record it, no matter what I say.'

'Is this a confession? Do we need the interview room?'

'Not for me,' Vincent said. The man was agitated. 'It's Les Daniels. He knows something.'

'He told you?'

'It was after he had fallen out with Kirkland. The man had had a few drinks and he was sounding off, sour grapes. The usual "What I've done for that man. He'll fall flat on his face without me to look after his horses". I'm sure you've heard similar before.'

Tremayne had.

'A natural reaction. And besides, the two are back together, friendlier than ever.'

'That's the problem. I was out at the racecourse a couple of days ago. There was a horse that had been training, a jockey gently easing it back to racing after it had pulled a tendon. The trainer wanted me to watch it run.'

'All in a day's work for you.'

'It was. Anyway, I'd finished with the horse. It was fine, and it should be racing in another couple of months. A similar horse to Red Rose, good for regional meetings, not for the premier races, certainly no chance in the Epsom Derby.'

The Horse's Mouth

'That's for three-year-old colts and fillies,' Tremayne said. He had picked last year's winner, taken Jean to her favourite restaurant to celebrate, even though the winnings were less than the price of their meals.

'The horse was a three-year-old colt. The owner has great hopes for it.'

'You know your horses?'

'I never bet on them. You're a fan of the sport, what do you reckon to putting money on a horse?'

'I take into account the course, whether it's firm or not, wet or dry, and the horse's form, as well as the jockey, at the distance, how many wins, how many losses, the odds.'

'And it works?' Vincent asked.

'I like to think it does.'

'It's the same with a marathon runner, the lead up to the race, the increased distances, the measured food intake, the right type of vitamins. Get it wrong, and there's no chance. It's a fine art, and I'm good at it, but it's not a perfect science.'

'Was Red Rose in peak condition to win that day?'

'I detected blood at the nose the day before.'

'You didn't mention this before.'

'I told Kirkland that it was a possible exercise-induced pulmonary haemorrhage, an exercise-induced condition. It's not uncommon in racing thoroughbreds. The stewards would have banned it from racing for three months if they had known.'

'Would the condition have affected its performance?'

'It's a hereditary precondition left over from when they were wild and vulnerable to predators. The horse would have run to the best of its ability. Spell the horse for a while, and it'll recover, but Kirkland didn't want to know, and Daniels argued with him over it.'

'Why would Kirkland have continued to race a horse that was not fit to race?'

'According to Daniels, and remember he was bitter and drunk when he spoke to me, Kirkland's a man who lives on the edge; the next deal, the next horse race.'

'The man's in debt?'

'According to Daniels, but that's not all of it. He starts rambling on about how he and Kirkland had known each other for a long time, and that the man had killed someone.'

'He must have been very drunk.'

'He was, but I don't want to get involved. And if Kirkland wanted to race the horse, then that was a decision for him to make. As I said, it's not uncommon for a racehorse to suffer the condition and it's not generally fatal if they take the vet's advice.'

'Which Kirkland didn't,' Tremayne said.

'He didn't.'

'Why now? Why tell me now, knowing full well that withholding vital information in a murder enquiry is a crime?'

'I suppose I was scared, and what with Sally dying, I wasn't sure of what to do.'

'Who killed her?'

'I don't know.'

'Who switched the horse?'

'It had to be Sally, but why?'

'Would she have acted contrary to her father's wishes, a concern about the horse?'

'EIPH is rarely fatal, and the horse would have survived the race, win or no win.'

The Horse's Mouth

'Houghton found nothing wrong with the horse in Devon.'

'It's had time to recuperate, and unless it's exercised strenuously, he wouldn't have seen it.'

***

Clare left Sue Nixon's place at around the time Tremayne left his office. She updated him as she drove along, and the two decided they would meet in the office at six-thirty the next morning. She was tired after a long day, and the time spent investigating the attempted killing of Red Rose.

The revelation from Vincent that Kirkland was in financial trouble provided a motive. After all, homicides were statistically more likely to be related to love and money than any other cause, and alarmingly the murderer was more often than not associated with the deceased.

Jeremy Liston wasn't off the hook, not yet. The tyre tracks found at the side of the small road at the rear of Sue Nixon's were from an SUV. Gwyneth Dexter took an imprint for analysis by Forensics. The possibility remained that the vehicle was a Range Rover, the same model that Liston had, the same as Barton Kirkland. However, Liston had managed to sneak to within fifteen feet of a Taliban machine-gun emplacement before shooting two men in cold blood, and as he had said, death and killing raised no emotions, good or bad, so a horse's death wouldn't have fazed him. His vehicle would be the subject of a thorough examination in the morning.

Clare phoned her husband after talking to Tremayne, to let him know that she would be home in the hour. He seemed distracted, and on her arrival, she found out that his position as mayor was at stake.

Clare's initial reaction was of dismay, but secretly she hoped that the robes of office that Clive wore proudly would eventually be handed on. On several occasions during a recent murder investigation, being the wife of a prominent citizen had impacted on her function as a police officer. In that investigation, she had asked Clive to perform the opening ceremony at the refurbished pub restaurant when Maria, the licensee, reopened it. That never happened as the woman's husband had admitted to the murder, and she had not had the heart to continue. It was a tragic tale and one which still made Clare sad.

That was the problem, Clare saw, in that murderers and their spouses and relatives were often decent people placed in impossible situations, reacting in a way out of character. People you came to like, then to arrest, later to be questioned about in court when they're on trial, only to see them convicted.

Was that to be the case again? Was there another person in clear sight, yet their involvement not known? Was Marjorie Fortescue involved, and was Jeremy Liston, the great hero, a murderer? Would she be arresting him? An up-and-coming future councillor, a potential rival to her husband. How would people react? Would it be her husband's position impinging on hers, or would it be her doing her duty that rallied the conspiracy theorists, the mayor using the law and his wife to remove a foe?

It was how certain people thought, and Clive, if toppled, would take it with dignity, not once allow his disappointment to show through, although in the quiet moments that she was privy to, she'd know how sad he was.

Chapter 14

Jeremy Liston was acting irrationally. The man, out of character, had got drunk the previous night, causing an affray, and with the help of two other men, the pub's landlord had evicted him from the premises.

It was a sore-headed man that Tremayne and Clare sat down with at the police station. Cautioned and asked whether he wanted to confess, Liston declined.

'It's circumstantial,' Liston said. 'Okay, you've got me as the last person who saw her alive.' Results back from a laboratory had confirmed that he had been in the stable with Sally just before she died.

Clare realised that if the man's behaviour of the previous night continued, then he would be no threat to Clive, as his chances of being elected a councillor would be doomed.

'You made a fool of yourself,' Tremayne said. 'What's the reason? Feeling the heat?'

'I am. Not only have you taken my car, but I was with Sally.'

'Why didn't you come forward after her death,' Clare asked.

'No reason. And, besides, I was incommunicado for thirty-six hours afterwards. It was when I got back to Salisbury that I found out, and by then you would have been grasping at straws, looking for the slightest reason to pull me in, charge me with her murder.'

'That's not how we work,' Tremayne said. It wasn't the first time he had heard the excuse, but Liston was supposed to be a notch above the average, a man who should have known that was not how the British police operated.

'Where were you?'

'A cottage down by the sea.'

'Another woman?' Tremayne asked.

'It was.'

'You make love to Sally, then take off with someone else. Hardly the act of a gentleman,' Clare said, disgusted by Liston.

'I told you before. I like women, and Sally was a decent person, but she was never under any illusion, or she shouldn't have been.'

'But you knew she was.'

'So was the one I took to the cottage. It starts as an innocent romance, but then they want it to be something more.'

'Who was this woman?'

'Does it matter? You know when Sally died, and I was not at the cottage then, probably either at the racecourse or on my way to meet the other woman.'

'Did this other woman know about Sally?'

'I tell them up front that if it's marriage and love they're looking for, then I'm not the man for them.'

'Which makes them even keener,' Clare said. 'You become a challenge, the chance to tame a wild man.'

'I'm just a man who in dangerous situations acted without thought, risked my life, saved others.'

He was, Clare had to acknowledge, an impressive man. Tall, attractive in an earthy way, and charismatic. She could see why certain women were attracted to him.

Her husband was cerebral and not a demonstrably passionate man, whereas Jeremy Liston was neither of the two. She judged Liston to be of above-average intellect, capable of taking a position of authority, and no doubt physically animated in his lovemaking, whereas Clive was considerate and less demanding.

'Let us come back to the Fortescues,' Tremayne said.

'What's to say?' Liston said.

'With Andrew dead and the Fortescue land under his mother's authority, the decision to subdivide it hers.'

'It is, but that's not what she wants.'

'You've spoken to her.'

'I have. Andrew had wanted to try and put the place on a commercial footing, a waste of time in my estimation, and then he would have had the title and Sally…'

'She told you of her intent?'

'That's why I was in the stable with her, a fond farewell. The reason I had taken a couple of glasses and a bottle of chardonnay. Two lovers, one was going to war, the other staying behind.'

'Was it a war for you?'

'Not me, Sally. She knew that Andrew's father was adamantly opposed to his son marrying her.'

'But why worry? We saw Lord Fortescue on the day Andrew died. The man hadn't long for this world. Sally could have waited a few months, and then there would have been no problem.'

'It was Marjorie; she was the vixen.'

'That's not the impression we got,' Clare said.

'Butter wouldn't melt in her mouth, off to the see the world, that sort of thing?' Liston said.

'Are you saying it was an act?'

'The former good-time girl, the socialite who screwed her way through London society.'

'Her past is well known,' Clare said.

'As for the former Marjorie Buxton, you'd better talk to her, ask her about her control of her son, her subtle domination, the submissive and incompetent, dribbling man that her husband had become.'

'He was coherent when we met him.'

'Coherent, unable to move unless someone pushed the wheelchair. His lordship was a vegetable with a mouth that gave utterances, but were they his?'

'It doesn't let you off the hook,' Tremayne said.

'You'll not find any proof against me. Sally understood the situation, although she wanted me. Andrew didn't understand very much, a mindless nonentity who would get what he wanted, not because of his endearing personality, but because of a title and the prestige of his position. Sally, very much her father's daughter, knew the value of respectability, something her father had strived for all his life.'

'Lady Fortescue?'

'Sally could have the title, but not the money. Marjorie would have dealt with that, somehow. And besides, she has a plan to sell off some of the estate, deal with the financial difficulties.'

'Will you handle the sale?'

'I've already commenced. It'll be an easy sale.'

'Will it?' Clare said.

'As you can see, I had no reason to kill Sally; on the contrary, she was part of the plan, a suitable diversion while Marjorie dealt with wresting control from her son.'

'Are you and Marjorie, lovers?' She's a lot older than you.'

'She's still in her fifties. There's life in the woman.'

'Is that a yes or a no?' Tremayne asked.

'Ask her.'

The Horse's Mouth

***

Another week had passed, and Superintendent Moulton was in Tremayne's office. It was a ritual the two men indulged in: the older inspector, the younger degree-educated superintendent. An uneasy truce existed, a mutual and grudgingly won respect for each other.

Moulton, performance-oriented, focussing on key performance indicators, the need to reduce the budget, to utilise the internet further and the databases for investigation, not fully cognisant as to how valuable it was to be out and about, talking to people, keeping a watchful eye, reading the body language.

Moulton's primary reason for trying to lever Tremayne out of Homicide and into retirement was the need to lower the average age of the personnel. Tremayne's age, although still shy of compulsory retirement, concerned Moulton, so much so that the retirement package on offer was generous, and Jean, initially keen for him to take it, had mellowed about the benefit of the money compared with the well-being of her husband.

Clare had the qualifications and the experience to take Tremayne's position as the senior investigating officer if he ever retired. But it was a prestigious position and others in the station would want it as well. Tremayne knew them, did not approve of any. To him, one was chauvinistic, another was a man who delegated and then claimed all the glory, and another rarely left the police station, preferring to write reports and to involve himself in office politics. The only time the man was animated was when he was off to visit his mistress, even though he was married with three children.

Tremayne was certain that Moulton, a moral man, didn't know about the mistress, but Tremayne had no intention of reporting it, not now, and probably never.

As far as Tremayne was concerned, the measure of a police officer was in the number of convictions, how many cases assigned to that person were unsolved, and whether he or she was capable of mentoring a new generation of officers. And in that aspect, he knew that he had mentored well.

'A difficult investigation?' Moulton said.

'The usual,' Tremayne said. 'Dig deep, and the skeletons are exposed.'

'Is Jeremy Liston one of them?'

'Of interest to you?'

'We bought a house through him.'

'He's got hidden depths. I'm not sure he can be trusted.'

'Have you considered the latest offer?'

'Not yet. I've got a murder to solve, and besides, even if I did agree,' Tremayne said, knowing that he would never accept, but he wanted the man off his back, 'I'd need an assurance that Yarwood would get the position and the appropriate rank.'

'I can't give you that, and she'd be an inspector now if you and she weren't so pally.'

'That would mean a transfer to another department, and I'd not agree to that.'

'You're fond of the woman. It's clouding your judgement.'

'Whether I am or not, and I'm not saying I am, it's her decision. And besides, she's the mayor's wife. That's enough of a position for her.'

'She's a seasoned police officer, the future.'

'Whereas I'm not, just an antique.'

'I've kept a watch out for you, even when you were in the hospital, and believe me, you're not getting any younger.'

'None of us is,' Tremayne said. He was tired of the conversation. He needed time to think; he needed to smoke one of the two cigarettes that he was allowed a day.

Clare walked into the office, exchanged pleasantries with the superintendent.

'He's holding out on me,' Moulton said.

'We need him,' Clare said.

'I need this case wrapped up if I'm to defend him.'

'It will be soon.'

Tremayne looked over at Clare. He could see she had something to say to him, something she didn't want the superintendent to know, aware that the man would start asking questions. As far as Tremayne and his sergeant were concerned, it was the two of them. They didn't want or need additional help.

The superintendent left the office; Clare took his seat.

'What is it, Yarwood?' Tremayne said.

'The two constables that I had out at the racecourse.'

'They did a good job.'

'I checked with them. Lady Fortescue was there on the day that Sally Kirkland died.'

'Could she have killed Sally?'

'She could have, but we've no proof, but if what Jeremy Liston was saying is true, it doesn't place her in a favourable light.'

'Liston concerns me,' Tremayne said. 'The great hero may be as he said, just a man who acted instinctively.'

'He still made colonel,' Clare said.

'Before or after receiving the VC?'

'He was a captain in Afghanistan. The promotion came later.'

'This emotional vacuum, I don't hold with it.'

'No one is emotionally dead, not unless they're a sociopath.'

'Define a sociopath?'

'A superficial charm, manipulative and cunning, grandiose sense of self, pathological lying, lack of remorse, shame or guilt, shallow emotions, incapacity for love, a need for stimulation,' Clare said.

'It sounds like Liston, which means he could be lying about that last meeting with Sally Kirkland, the fond farewell, and that Lady Fortescue is a devious woman, as well as Liston's lover.'

'Not proven, not yet. And the need for stimulation, a possible reason for his apparent bravery, over the top and confronting the enemy, killing two at close quarters.'

'If Liston or her ladyship are involved in deceit and shady dealings, that's one thing, but it's still a homicide. Liston didn't kill her…'

'Are you sure?'

'He could have, and as the description says, he wouldn't have cared, not about her. He'll not want to be in prison, regardless. But he could be playing us for fools.'

'And doing a good job of it. Clive doesn't trust him.'

'Your husband is astute.'

'I know. If we evaluate all those involved, it's only Liston who displays the necessary capacity for murder and deceit. Psychologically, he's a mess, probably why after becoming a colonel and receiving the VC at Buckingham Palace, he left the army.'

'Lady Fortescue?'

'We need to put Liston's allegations to her. And if she was at the racecourse, a seething hatred could exist under the surface, a deep-rooted concern that Sally Kirkland could have severed her control of her son.

'She admitted that with her husband's and her son's deaths, she intended to sell out and make up for lost time. Underneath the façade of respectability, who knows what she is thinking, what she might be capable of?'

As for the superintendent, he would have to wait for an arrest, and as for his inspector's retirement, it was a wait that would tire him before it would Tremayne.

Chapter 15

A light frost covered the expansive grounds of the Fortescue estate as Clare drove along the winding road up to the front door of the mansion.

It was a sensitive subject, and whereas Tremayne would usually have accompanied her, she decided to go on her own. Liston had made a statement about him and her ladyship. It needed checking, to be either denied or confirmed.

It was Lady Fortescue who opened the door and asked her in. The house was cold.

'Your son?' Clare asked.

'He'll be placed in the family vault this Sunday, along with his father.'

'United in death.'

'But not in life.'

'I have a few questions, but first I must clarify one thing.'

'Jeremy phoned. I know what the question is.'

'You're still a young woman, a few years younger than your husband. Jeremy Liston is a charming man.'

Lady Fortescue laughed. 'Charm? Jeremy?'

'You've not answered the question.'

'Not yet, I haven't. If he has it, it doesn't work on me.'

'He exhibits sociopathic traits,' Clare said.

'If that means he's out for number one, and he doesn't care who gets in his way.'

'You've had dealings with him. What do you reckon?'

The Horse's Mouth

'I wouldn't trust him for a minute.'

'Did he use his charm to seduce you?'

'Not with me, but with Sally. Poor Andrew, such a clod. He was desperate for her, unable to see her for what she was.'

'That's what Liston said. What we know of you, what we had deduced on our previous meetings, you acting out a part.'

'I cared for my husband; I loved my son. That doesn't mean I didn't see each of them for what they were. My husband was a modest man, a believer in his birthright; Andrew was a lovesick puppy, in and out of love, yet he had chosen Sally. I did not have to like her, but I couldn't let Andrew run this place on his own with her in his ear. My husband did not have long for this world, and Andrew's suicide ensured it was less than more.

'But now, I'm left with this place and their burials. Not for me, not any longer, and once the two are in their resting places, I will leave here, give a proxy to a lawyer I trust, and the sale to Jeremy.'

'You've not answered the question,' Clare reminded her.

'For the record, I have not considered him suitable, not at this time.'

'You've not slept with him?'

'No, not yet.'

'But you would do so under the right circumstances.'

'As you said, I'm still young enough to enjoy life, and I told you before that I intended to make up for the years gone by.'

'With Jeremy?'

'That's up to him. If he's there, maybe, otherwise there are others.'

***

Even though Tremayne had reservations, Red Rose returned to the stable close to Kirkland's house. Kirkland had obtained a court order reclaiming his horse, and as the man was not under suspicion for murder, it was granted.

Sue Nixon had expressed relief to Tremayne when he had phoned her. 'It's not over, is it?' she said.

'No,' Tremayne's reply.

'That's what I thought. Anyone who can kill a horse has to be sick.'

'A dumb animal, is that it?'

'I'd dispute the dumb, but yes. An animal bears no malice; it doesn't connive or cheat. If you treat it well, it will aim to please, and Red Rose isn't a bad horse.'

'It's been treated well?'

'By us, yes, he has. Barton Kirkland made sure of that.'

'What now for the horse?'

'That's up to the man, but there's no reason he can't race again.'

It had not been a long phone conversation, and as Tremayne sat back in his office chair, he wondered where the case was heading. So far, no leads had firmed up. The main players all had secret depths to them, yet only two of them had killed a man; one in battle and under orders of his government, the other in crime. One gets a medal, the other, if proven, a lengthy prison term.

Tremayne could see the injustice; as to how, Liston receives a medal for killing illiterate tribesmen who believed in a cause, but not criminal, just disillusioned and ignorant. In contrast, Barton Kirkland had rid the world of the most innocuous piece of slime that had ever walked the streets.

It was in the north of England that Kirkland had started to carve out a career for himself. Still inexperienced and wild after a heavy night of drinking, he had met with Billy Shripton around the back of the pub, down a secluded lane sometimes used by lovers.

Kirkland had been brought in, questioned at length, held in the cells for twenty-four hours, and then released. He had killed the man, yet on the street nobody was talking, and at the crime scene, a zealous inspector had attempted to falsify the evidence. The planted evidence was enough to ensure there was no charge for murder.

Tremayne decided to put Kirkland's slaying of another to one side and to go and see the man.

Kirkland was pleased to see him. 'Red Rose is back,' he said.

'Your daughter? You seem to have moved on from her death.'

'I've not. But I'll not give you the satisfaction of seeing me down.'

'It would make sense for you to be distraught. Have you found out the name of the other man yet?'

'Not yet. Did he kill Sally?'

'We can't be sure, but it's unlikely. No valid reason. The man's not strong on emotions, either way, love or hate, and I doubt if anger or jealousy are of any interest to him.'

'Would I know it if I met him?'

'He conceals it well, and besides, don't do anything rash. I know all about Billy Shripton. It could still prejudice a trial if it came out.'

'Tremayne, I've no intention of doing anything, regardless of what you think and I might have said.'

'Sally had intended to marry Fortescue. That would have pleased you.'

'Sally would have done her mother and me proud.'

'Your wife was the reason that Shripton got into an argument with you, isn't that the truth?'

'That was his nature. A street brawler, a nasty piece of work. The world's a better place without him, but I didn't kill him.'

'No great loss to society.'

'It's a long time in the past, and I'd appreciate it if you don't mention it,' Kirkland said.

'Level with me. What would anyone gain by substitution of the horses? It makes no sense.'

'Let's have a look at the horse. Daniels is looking after it.'

'Do you intend to answer my question?'

'On the way over.'

The two men walked out of the front door of the house and headed over to Red Rose. It wasn't far, just a five-minute walk, but there was a cold breeze. Tremayne turned up the collar of his jacket and shrugged his shoulders; Kirkland left his jacket unbuttoned, and the top button of his shirt undone. The age difference was only five years, Tremayne the older, and he knew he was not in as good a physical condition as Kirkland, and his was marginal. It worried him.

Chapter 16

A relative calm descended on Homicide for two days, only to shattered on the morning of the third day by the death of Les Daniels.

As his landlady, a small grey-haired woman in her eighties, said, 'He kept himself to himself, never any visitors, not that I hold with this modern view of sleeping around.'

'If he had snuck the occasional woman in?' Clare asked, amused by someone who seemed to have missed the last fifty years, dressed conservatively in black, a scarf tied around her head.

'My Bert, when he was alive, he was dead against it.'

Upstairs in the house, Jim Hughes and his team were conducting their investigation. Downstairs in the front room, Tremayne and Clare sat with the woman.

'But then my Bert, he was a drinker, so I suppose it balances out. Anyway, Les never caused any trouble, paid his rent on time.'

'Daniels was a drinker,' Tremayne said.

'He was, but harmless.'

Clare didn't need it spelling out. Behind the façade of respectability, a woman who had been abused by a violent husband, but unable to admit it even to herself, holding cherished memories of a better man. It didn't alter the fact that upstairs a man who had been loyal to Kirkland and a good man to have around horses had died.

Hughes came into the room. The landlady, always considerate of others, not comfortable unless everyone had the solution to all of life's problems, a cup of tea, left the room to heat the pot and to bring another cup.

'What can you tell us?' Tremayne asked.

'A knife to the heart and his face had been covered with a cushion. He wouldn't have known much about it, not for long, that is.'

'A tussle? Did he put up a fight?'

'Not much of a fight, and besides, he was a small man and judging by a bottle nearby, either unconscious drunk or incapacitated.'

'He died in his room?' Clare asked, aware that the landlady had been adamant that no one had been in the house, but then, the woman had lied about her dear departed, a picture of the two of them on the mantelpiece, ice creams in their hands, a beach in the background. The image was old, a honeymoon scene. Two young lovers setting out on life's journey together, although when she had married Clive, they had flown to Italy and spent two weeks travelling around Tuscany.

For them, there was no ice cream, but the landlady, Salisbury-born, would regard a day trip to London as a significant event.

Happiness was a construct, Clare realised, and the small woman with her cup of tea and her jaundiced outlook on the world was the embodiment of contentment, with the ability to remove emotionally and mentally the trials and tribulations of life.

'Downstairs, the landlady,' Tremayne said. 'Would she have heard?'

'Not if she had the television on.'

'Any idea who killed him?' Clare asked.

'A taller person, but as I said, Daniels wouldn't have put up much of a fight.'

'According to the woman, she wasn't partial to visitors.'

'It was a man,' Hughes said.

'Can you be certain?'

'As certain as I can be. The evidence is scant, and there's no sign that the murderer spent longer than necessary up there, in and out quickly.'

'Forensics?'

'We're checking for fingerprints, but it's unlikely we'll find any. Whoever it was, they knew what they were doing.'

'Professional?'

'Skilled,' Hughes said.

Both of the officers knew of only one person who would have been capable – the reluctant hero, Jeremy Liston.

The landlady returned, this time carrying a tray with four cups, another teapot and a plate of small cakes. 'Oh, I am enjoying myself,' she said. 'So many people here at the same time.'

The landlady was forgetful, Clare could see. It was probably early-onset Alzheimer's, although the woman may not have been conscious of the fact. Even if she had seen or heard whoever had visited Daniels, she might not remember, not now, not ever.

'How long has he been dead?' Tremayne asked Hughes.

'I checked his phone. I took a time from when he last made a call as to when he had definitely been alive, extrapolated it forward, taking into account the body's temperature. He died between two to three hours ago.'

'Are you certain?'

'I made a call to the number, got a reply.'

'Who from?'

'Jeremy Liston.'

'Did you tell him why you were using Daniels' phone?'

'I used my phone. I just apologised, said it was a wrong number.'

'Why would Liston have risked coming here with the landlady in the house?' Clare said.

'It's still that damn horse,' Tremayne said.

'Even so, we need to find out why Daniels phoned him.'

The teas and the cakes were left on the tray as Tremayne and Clare made their excuses and Hughes returned upstairs.

***

The one man who may have been able to fill in the blanks if he had been willing or not afraid was dead. Tremayne knew that Daniels' murder was a critical turning point.

'Yes, I spoke to Daniels,' Liston said. 'No law against it.'

Tremayne and Clare had met with the man in the Pheasant Inn in Salisbury. It was four in the afternoon, but Liston had been adamant, and that if the police felt the need to enter his estate agency, unsettling the staff and frightening off potential customers, then it had better be for a good reason. He'd make sure his lawyer was present.

Tremayne sat there with a half-pint of beer. Liston drank a whisky and Clare kept to orange juice. It was too early for her, and besides, she was a moderate drinker.

'Liston, you're a man who cares little for others,' Tremayne said.

'I've not denied that, but don't try to portray me as evil or murderous.'

'I'm not, only we've got to speak to those who knew the man, and you were the last person to speak to him.'

'On the phone, and as for not caring about people, that's ambivalence, not a crime. It's also brutally honest. The world is full of politicians preaching how much they care for the common man, especially when they're up for election; businessmen who claim they are there for the customers' benefit when they're only interested in their money.'

'And police officers?' Tremayne said. Clare could see that her senior didn't like him.

'Interested in a conviction, although Tremayne, you're old school. You might be honest.'

'I am. Do you know some who aren't?'

'Not in this country.'

'What does that mean?'

'Have you been overseas, had to deal with the authorities?'

'Singapore,' Tremayne said.

'I don't mean there. I mean the third world, those bigoted countries where life is cheap and corruption is rife.'

'You didn't like them?' Clare asked.

'I've seen them close up. They're not worth it.'

Tremayne, who did not think about such matters, could see that Liston was racist, and if he was emotionally void with women, he was not in his political views.

'Daniels? Worth it?'

'If he knows a horse that can't lose, and the odds are good, he'll phone me up.'

'Often?'

'Rarely.'

'How much do you bet?' Clare asked.

'If Daniels phones, five hundred pounds.'

'Do they always win?'

'Not always, but I've made good money from the man, given him ten per cent.'

'How much profit in total?'

'Close to twenty thousand pounds.'

'And to Daniels?'

'Ten per cent as I said, two thousand pounds, and he must have put some of his own money on the horses as well.'

Tremayne looked over at Clare. 'How much money did Daniels have?'

'Judging by his accommodation, not much.'

'Don't judge a book by its cover,' Liston said. 'Daniels wasn't interested in fancy cars or big houses, and certainly not classy women.'

'Are you saying he had more money than he let on?'

'I don't know, not really. He used to have a few drinks at a pub I go to occasionally. Not with me, over the other side of the bar, downing beers as fast as he can go.'

'He came over and spoke to you?'

'I was with Sally. He was slurring, not making a lot of sense, telling her how much he liked her. He made a fool of himself, but the next day, he probably didn't remember.'

'As you were saying,' Tremayne said. He eyed his half-pint, realised that his best intentions had been in vain. Clare took the hint and went over to the bar and ordered him a pint.

On her return, Liston looked up from reading messages on his phone. 'We waited for you,' he said.

Clare took a seat, passed over the beer to Tremayne who held it up to his mouth and took a drink.

'Liston, what were you about to say?' Tremayne said.

'Daniels, drunk as a lord, although Sally was about to marry one.'

'You're rambling.'

'Daniels tells Sally that he's got more than she thinks.'

'What do you think he meant?'

'It wasn't to do with his sexual prowess. Sally knew about that, as did almost everyone. He used to tell the story, too often for my liking.'

'It upset you?'

'Not at all, but a man's not a man if he can't…'

'He can't satisfy a woman,' Clare said.

'I didn't want to say it, but yes.'

'You thought he was talking about money?'

'I did. Whether he's got more money than he showed, then it could have been criminal, or just betting on the horses. After all, if it's poverty you want, get married. That drains the bank account more than anything.'

'Have you ever been married?' Clare asked.

'It never interested me. I told you before; I don't get emotional.'

'But you can get angry. That's an emotion.'

'A negative emotion. Love is supposedly positive and harmonious, something that doesn't exist for me.'

'A troubled soul?'

'It's why I was let go by the army after I had received the medal.'

'Killing comes easily,' Tremayne said.

'It was no more to me than squashing a fly.'

'Daniels, if you had killed him, it wouldn't have worried you. You could have met with us today, sat here as you are now, and denied it.'

'I could,' Liston said. 'There's only one problem.'

'You didn't do it.'

'If I had wanted him dead, I wouldn't have killed Daniels at his place. A quiet location, the back of a stable, somewhere I'd not be seen.'

Tremayne thought of a stable, a woman dead with a rope around her neck. Liston had described the place where Sally Kirkland had died.

***

Joe Blakely, Tremayne's bookmaker at Salisbury Racecourse, and a man who had taken more than his fair share of the inspector's money over the years, sat calmly in the interview room at the police station.

'What am I being charged with?' Blakely asked.

'You're assisting with our enquiries at this time,' Tremayne said.

'Then why the police car to bring me here?'

'Considering the seriousness of what we believe you to be involved in, you should be thankful it wasn't in handcuffs.'

'I've committed no crime,' Blakely said as he shifted uneasily on his chair.

Tremayne cautioned the man as required. Blakely's lawyer, Hector Blair, sat to the side of his client. He was a plain-looking man, wearing a dated pinstripe suit, his hair slicked back.

'Les Daniels died yesterday,' Tremayne said.

'He was a good man around horses.' Blakely said.

'A business partner of yours?'

'Hardly. The man drifted along, and if it hadn't been for Kirkland, he would have been labouring somewhere or other.'

'Your lawyer has the details, so have you. Let me put it to you again. Why was there in Daniels' bank account a substantial amount of money deposited by you? Why was there a smaller amount debited from him to your account?'

'He liked to bet occasionally. No law against it.'

'We're not talking about twenty pounds each way on the last race of the day,' Tremayne said.

Blair felt the need to intervene. 'Inspector, speculation serves no useful purpose. Either you have evidence of criminal activity against my client, or you don't.'

'I'd say that twelve thousand pounds into Daniels' bank account four weeks ago is a damning indictment.'

'My client can explain.'

Clare waited for the response, knowing full well it would be long on rhetoric, short on substance.

'Les Daniels was a shrewd man. He preferred to be seen as a hard-luck case, laid low by injury and never the great jockey that he could have been,' Blakely said.

'According to others, the man didn't have the necessary determination,' Tremayne said.

'It served him well to continue with his story. And yes, determination wasn't his strong suit, more willing to muddle through.'

'He could pick a winner though,' Tremayne said.

'On the day better than anyone else.'

'He had the ear of the jockey, a few pounds here and there to make sure of the race's outcome.'

'Inspector, I wouldn't know. I'm a bookmaker, take the bets, pay out the winnings, keep the rest. If one man wins big, that's his good luck, my loss.'

'It's not only that one payment. What about the others. We've totalled close to one hundred and thirty thousand pounds to Daniels' account, payment of eight thousand to yours.'

'As I said, his good luck.'

'Mr Blakely, we've seen your house, your lifestyle. You make a good living, but losing over one hundred thousand pounds would have hurt,' Clare said.

'I honour my debts,' Blakely said.

'This is conjecture,' Blair said. 'Whether my client is unwise in allowing Daniels to bet to the extent that you've mentioned, it still doesn't form the basis of a criminal investigation.'

'It does,' Tremayne said. He had Blakely on edge. A little more and the man would crack.

'If Daniels bets once and wins a lot of money, wouldn't you have refused any further bets from him?' Clare asked.

Blair looked momentarily lost, unable to advise his client. The inference was damning. Tremayne could read the body language, Blair distancing himself from his client. Blakely was on the ropes.

'Blakely, I've known you for a long time. Daniels places a substantial bet with you. You then bet heavily through an intermediary, using Daniels' money and some of yours,' Tremayne said.

'It's not illegal,' Blakely said.

'How would your competitors feel about you taking unfair advantage?'

'Envious.'

'Or angry that you hadn't cut them in, but taken them for a financial ride.'

Blakely looked over at Blair. 'I've not broken any law here, but Tremayne's right.'

Blair raised his hand as if to say to his client, 'Shut up.'

Blakely looked over at Tremayne and Clare. 'Okay, Daniels would give me a tip, and I'd bet heavily, offset my cost to Daniels. Not every horse that we bet on won. Some lost miserably, and as for Red Rose, that was a disaster.'

'How? Why?'

'I don't know. As far as I was concerned, it was Red Rose. Only Daniels could have substituted the horse. No one else could have pulled it off.'

'A dead man, easy to lay the blame,' Tremayne said.

'He was an odd character. A great skill in picking a winner, and with him alive, I could have made a lot more money.'

'What happens when the other bookmakers, the online bookies, find out how you've been cheating them?'

'No reason to, not unless you tell them.'

'But if I do? How much have you taken from them?'

'Somewhere north of six hundred thousand pounds.'

'If you were betting heavily with them, they would have been placing bets with their competitors. A regular round-robin, profit for one, cheat another.'

'It could be,' Blakely said.

'If their profits have been impacted by you or by others, they'll want retribution.'

'They're all doing it, playing the game, out gambling each other.'

'Why was Sally Kirkland killed? Was she the first to die? Someone who got in the way? A warning?'

'I don't know.'

'Are you scared?'

'I am,' Blakely said.

'An innocent woman could have died because of what you and Daniels were involved in. Doesn't that concern you?'

'Life's tough. I know that, although Daniels didn't.'

'I've no further questions. You're free to go,' Tremayne said.

'Go where? To Salisbury Racecourse? To my home? To my death?' Blakely said.

'Let's hope you survive,' Tremayne said. 'Give me a chance to get some of my money back.' It was an attempt at levity, but it was ill-founded and inappropriate. Tremayne knew that Blakely had played dangerous people for fools, and whether it was illegal or not, was not the issue.

Chapter 17

Barton Kirkland took the news of Les Daniels' death philosophically.

At the time, Tremayne had given little thought to Kirkland's reaction; after all, he hadn't killed the man, as Daniels' murder had required a deft hand and the ability to enter the house, climb the stairs, kill him and then leave the house, all unseen.

Even though the evidence at the crime scene was sparse, Barton Kirkland was a large man, heavy-footed, incapable of the necessary finesse.

Tremayne and Clare sat with him at his house. Kirkland sat in a chair, leaning back, a glass of whisky in his hand.

'It's strange how things turn out,' he said.

'What do you mean?' Clare asked.

'Life. Look at me, raised myself from a nobody to where I am today.'

'Financially secure,' Tremayne said.

'That's not what I meant. When I was down there scratching to making a living, one day I knew that the house on the hill, the money in the bank, would be all mine.'

'That's what you have now.'

'And yet,' Kirkland sat up and leant forward, 'was it all worth it?'

'Are you melancholic for what was?' Clare asked.

'I miss Sally, that's all. And if it hadn't been the pursuit of money, then she would still be alive.'

'Life's a journey, not a destination,' Clare said, quoting Ralph Waldo Emerson, a nineteenth-century essayist and philosopher.

'What does that mean?' Tremayne asked. He knew his sergeant was more academic than him, prone to come up with the occasional comment that sailed straight over his head.

'Mr Kirkland is sad for his daughter, but who knows what life brings us. In life, there are defining moments, when we should have turned left instead of right, when we should not have driven down that road, but another. If Richard Grantley had not died, I wouldn't have met his brother, Clive.'

'Understood,' Tremayne said. He had first met Jean on a drunken night with others, and they could have easily gone into another pub than the one where she was. And if he hadn't been so pig-headed and determined to pursue every criminal, she wouldn't have left him and taken the family dog, but now she was back, and if it wasn't life's destination, it suited him fine.

'Your sergeant is right,' Kirkland said. 'She was the best thing in my life, even though I despaired sometimes.'

'The drugs?'

'The men. Sally was too fond of them.'

'She intended to marry Andrew Fortescue.'

'She knew the value of respectability, and what Fortescue could have brought to us.'

'Did it matter that much?' Clare said. 'An antiquated title of privilege?'

'It did to me, to Sally,' Kirkland said. 'Sally had grown up with their offspring, the children of captains of industry, politicians, church luminaries. One of her friends was a bishop's daughter, not that it meant anything to Sally.'

'Not religious?'

'Not in my family, and certainly not from my parents. The bishop was a pious fool. I met him on a couple of occasions, and he'd be spouting from the bible. No problem with that, per se, but he seemed to use it to deal with every situation.'

'His daughter?'

'Dead. Drug overdose.'

'Joe Blakely, what do you know of him?'

'He knows his trade, but apart from an acknowledgement when we pass each other, I don't believe I've spoken to him for any length of time.'

'Les Daniels? Did he have money?'

'A hand-to-mouth existence, that was Les.'

'Would you be surprised to know that he had over one hundred thousand pounds in his bank account?' Clare said.

'If he did, then he didn't flash it about,' Kirkland said.

'The question needs to be asked,' Tremayne said. 'How did he come to have it?'

'I didn't pay him much, and he frittered away whatever he made as a jockey, too much drink, too many women.'

'Women? We've never heard that he was interested in women.'

'I suppose I was just flippant. But why are you here? A man's entitled to mourn his daughter.'

'It's not apparent when you're at the racecourse.'

'If people think I'm a hard man, so much the better.'

'Les Daniels was fond of your daughter,' Clare said.

'I know that, and she liked the little man, not as anything more than a friend. Compared to the others she ran with; he was a better bet.'

'Why?'

'Dependable, decent and, until you mentioned the money he had, honest.'

'He was working with Blakely, giving the man the nod as to which horse to bet heavily on, which one to steer clear of.'

'Fixing races?' Kirkland said.

'It's a line of enquiry.'

'You think this has something to do with Red Rose?'

'Here's what we reckon. Daniels switched the horses, handed over Scarlet Soleil to your daughter.'

'She would have known,' Kirkland said.

'Would she? It's important.'

'It's always possible she didn't. After all, there was nothing distinctive about Red Rose, plenty of horses similar.'

'She has the horse, leads it out to the parade ring, hands it over to the jockey. She comes back to the stable, meets up with someone–'

'Someone?'

'We know who he is,' Clare said.

'He murdered her?'

'We don't believe that, not yet.'

'Were you also involved in race-fixing?' Tremayne asked.

'I wouldn't have switched Red Rose out, would I?' Kirkland said.

'Barry Vincent?' Tremayne said.

'She went out with him on a couple of occasions, but she wasn't too keen.'

'Did it worry you?'

'It wasn't recent. Fortescue was the man she had chosen, and then she's murdered, and he jumps out of a window.'

'We believe that Fortescue saw your daughter in the stable with another man,' Clare said.

'Murdered her?' Kirkland said.

'That's a possible reason for his suicide.'

'It makes no sense. After all, Fortescue had his mother as an example. Once she had married, she went cold turkey. Fortescue must have known that Sally would have been the same,' Kirkland said.

'Andrew Fortescue had a weak personality; his father did not, and his mother definitely doesn't.'

'I'll not mourn Daniels or Fortescue. My daughter, I will.'

'As for Les Daniels, murdered for what he had known or done is probable. And if Blakely had benefited by over six hundred thousand pounds, that meant that others had benefited or lost too, but who were they? Were they hiding in plain sight? Would they kill again and who?' Tremayne said. 'Are you involved?'

Kirkland said nothing, only got up from his chair and opened the door for the two police officers to leave.

***

A torrential downpour overnight didn't prevent the racing the next day. Tremayne was there, and even though there were rain clouds up above, a blue sky was visible.

It was rare for the inspector to visit Salisbury Racecourse three meetings in a row, but of those, only one had been social; the other two, official business.

Joe Blakely was in his usual position, touting for the punters to place their bets, the punters checking their form guides, seeing what odds he was offering, checking if another bookmaker offered better.

'What do you fancy?' a voice said from behind him.

Tremayne looked around. The previously despondent Barton Kirkland, father of a dead woman, dressed in a dark blue suit and a bright red tie, was back to his usual ebullient self.

'I'm here on official business. Trying to understand if Blakely's more involved than he says he is,' Tremayne's reply.

'Or if I am?'

'That goes without saying.'

'A drink?'

'I'll be asking you questions.'

'That's fine. There's something I need to tell you.'

The two men settled down in the owners and trainers bar. Tremayne had hold of a pint of beer; Kirkland kept to whisky. The bar was full, but Kirkland had found an alcove away from the loud sounds of hilarity on the other side of the room.

'A few will write themselves off,' Kirkland said.

'Not you.'

'I know my limit.'

'I do now, doctor's orders,' Tremayne said.

'Isn't it about time you gave up policing? It can't be much fun, not now.'

'Why now?'

'Your health.'

'I take it easy, and besides, this is my life. What would I do if I wasn't here investigating a murder?'

'Two murders, although I can't see that my daughter's is related to Daniels'.'

'You wanted a word,' Tremayne reminded him as he finished his pint. It was his favourite brew, and he wanted another.

'You caught me at a bad time the other day. I wasn't totally truthful.'

'You switched the horse.'

'You're fixating on the wrong issue.'

'It's the only issue we have,' Tremayne said. 'Are you saying there's something else?'

'I knew that Les Daniels had money in his bank account.'

'How?'

'Daniels was the most astute judge. He would know better than anyone else whether a horse was capable or not of winning.'

'Fixing races? You're skirting around what you intended to tell me,' Tremayne reminded Kirkland. 'You've met Ian Swift?'

'I have. Sally was involved with him.'

'An unimpressive man on first meeting, but wise once you get to know him.'

'I admire a man who takes what God's given him, which in his case wasn't much, and makes something out of it,' Kirkland said.

'He's charismatic.'

'A natural gift, but other than that, fat, short, of poor physical stock.'

'Yet a hit with the ladies.'

'With Sally, yes, but she never knew what it is to be poor or to worry where the next meal is coming from.'

'Was Swift involved?'

'I believe so.'

'How?'

'I overheard Daniels speaking to him once on the phone. I didn't get the full conversation, only one side of it.'

'Blakely?'

'He'd know where to put the money. Daniels was only part of the operation and not the smartest part. Blakely knows where to place bets, but big money would require someone smarter.'

'Criminal?'

'Opportunists, the same as Blakely and Swift. How big do you reckon online gambling is?'

'I've no idea,' Tremayne said.

'Upwards of fifty billion dollars annually. Enough for people who know how to manipulate the margins. Skim ten or twenty million off the top, and nobody would notice.'

'They must have systems in place to trigger alarms.'

'It depends on who's watching the alarms.'

'Are you saying that the online gambling companies are skimming off the top?'

'It can't be proven, but Swift is a genius. He'd know how to do it. He could have a financial stake in one of these companies, and nobody would know.'

'Offshore? The Cayman Islands, Seychelles, Panama?'

'Precisely,' Kirkland said.

'It would be impossible to prove.'

'If Swift is playing with the big boys. not keeping his eye on the game, or he's advising them incorrectly, then…'

'They'll be after him. Daniels?'
'It could be a warning,' Kirkland said.
'How about you?'
'I'm not guilty of any crime. They have no reason to come after me, but that's supposition. Whoever is behind Daniels' death and my daughter's, they are dangerous.'
'In Salisbury?'
'Unlikely. And it's too big for Swift on his own.'
'Fortescue?'
'Andrew, not a chance. He would have given credibility to a legit company, his name as a director, but not as an active participant, and publicity is not what these people would want.'
'How do you know so much about this?'
'Whispers, rumours, racecourse gossip.'
'That's not good enough for me,' Tremayne said.
'It's all I'm going to give you.'
'Blakely?'
'Not him. Try Swift,' Kirkland said.

Chapter 18

Ian Swift took umbrage at the suggestion that he was involved in nefarious criminal activity. It was ten in the morning; the setting was the interview room at the police station. Swift, declining legal representation, had been duly cautioned.

'The assertion that I'm involved in fixing horse races for profit is ludicrous,' Swift said.

Clare thought the man was a picture of sartorial elegance, and what he lacked in looks, he made up for in his bearing, the timbre of his voice, the confidence he exuded.

Swift, known for his financial skills, did not fit the mould of a criminal. Still, both of the officers knew that this was a white-collar crime, committed from a laptop, Daniels out doing the spadework, fixing the results, handing out cash incentives to the occasional jockey, Blakely placing the bets.

'Even if I was involved, which I categorically deny, how do you think I did it?' Swift said.

'That's for you to tell us,' Tremayne said.

'It's for you to prove.'

'An admission of guilt?'

'Not at all, but it gives room for thought. Firstly, there are the races to be fixed, not so difficult probably.'

'That was Daniels' responsibility, although he was in Salisbury, and this may have been international.'

'Fixing races around the world?' Swift laughed. 'How do you think that happens? And even if it did, why bother? There are enough mug punters in this country.'

Tremayne knew he was right about the punters; he was one, but his betting was in the tens of pounds. He'd seen it at the racecourse – respectable people in business, middle-aged housewives, young and very drunk youths, placing bets in the hundreds of pounds. Money that most of them could ill afford to lose. But then, Tremayne was not a problem gambler, no more than he was a problem beer drinker. It was just that he enjoyed both in equal measure.

'You've got the talent and the ability to pull this off,' Clare said.

'If I devoted myself to it, but why would I?' Swift said.

'The intellectual challenge,' Tremayne said. 'You've enough money, enough fame; you could have become bored with the mundanity of it.'

'I work best when challenged, I'd agree to that, but what you're suggesting is criminal, and I don't see myself behind bars,' Swift said as he looked over at Clare, gave her a brief smile.

If he thinks I'm susceptible to his charms, Clare thought, then the man is in for a rude shock.

Tremayne knew they had no evidence to hold the man, only Kirkland's passing comment that Joe Blakely wouldn't have been the mastermind and Swift was the person they should talk to. And now, the man was sitting across from him, and the detective inspector was floundering, worried that he was losing his edge. He'd dealt with villains in his time, white-collar and blue, and he had never been tongue-tied, not once. Yet with Swift, the man had stumped him. He looked over at his sergeant for help.

'Ian,' Clare, sensing her senior's despair, took over from him, 'you knew Les Daniels and Joe Blakely.'

'Daniels, I did, but only in the pub. He was good company, if not too smart.'

'Blakely?'

'I've met him. I can't say I liked him, too smarmy for me.'

'Explain what you mean,' Tremayne said, glad of the chance to regroup his thoughts.

'I'd see him around the city, and once or twice up at the racecourse. He always wanted to stand close, and sometimes his lack of dental hygiene was disturbing.'

'Bad breath?' Clare said. 'I can't say I've noticed it.'

'He's a secret drinker, and fond of garlic.'

'Why so close?' Tremayne asked.

'He's not the only one. It's the way people flock to celebrities, hopeful that their life will rub off on them.'

'It doesn't.'

'We know that, but the fawning fans don't.'

'Are you saying that Blakely was a fan?'

'The man had aspirations. Middle-class, done well for himself, but he wanted more.'

'That's everyone's prerogative,' Clare said.

'It is, and Blakely might have been good enough for a bookmaker, but as a financier, he didn't have it in him.'

'What would he have gained from you?'

'Not a lot. Maybe he's read too many self-help books about positive thinking and associating with like-minded souls.'

'Has that been your secret?' Tremayne asked.

'Blakely wasn't going to use me to help him, and as for working with the man, fixing horses, why bother?'

'Money.'

'I've enough.'

The Horse's Mouth

'A rich man never has enough,' Clare said.

Clare knew that if Swift were guilty of any crime, it would need the threatening environment of a police station and her senior's persistence to break him.

'Never. But prison, that's another issue.'

'Is it?' Tremayne said. 'Surely a motivated person, one who's read all the books on positive thinking, reciting their affirmations each morning, can't allow themselves negativity?'

'You've read them?'

'I did when I was younger. That's why I'm an inspector.'

'You didn't read enough,' Swift said. It was a cutting remark, beautifully delivered. Clare wanted to laugh, but did not; Tremayne wouldn't have appreciated the humour, not in the interview room.

The door opened: a young constable, two weeks in the station, entered.

'If you've got a moment, Inspector,' the sheepish constable said.

With the interview interrupted, Tremayne ended it, thanked Swift for his time, and escorted him off the premises. Outside, on the street, both men lit up cigarettes.

'You're wrong,' Swift said.

'About the fixing of races, large sums of money changing hands?' Tremayne said as he exhaled the smoke from his second cigarette of the day.

'No. I mean Daniels' death.'

'How?'

'Daniels may have been fixing races and in league with Blakely, but it doesn't end there.'

'I'll level with you, Swift,' Tremayne said. 'I don't believe anyone is innocent.'

'Barton Kirkland?'

'In financial trouble.'

'Marjorie Fortescue?'

'A husband and a son dead, yet if you met her, you'd not believe it.'

'Stiff upper lip, never show your emotions to the proletariat. You've met her type before,' Swift said.

'I have, but a son who takes a step out into space… that would take a remarkable person to remain emotionally calm.'

A cold wind blew, and Tremayne wanted to return inside the station, but Swift was saying more than he had said in the interview room.

'Kirkland expected his daughter to marry the fool.'

'How do you know this?'

'I took her out a few times,' Swift said as he lit another cigarette. 'Her father was an embarrassment to her.'

'Was she ashamed of him?'

'It wasn't something she talked about, but I believe she was.'

'Anger?'

'Ambivalence. The man had spoilt her, given her everything she wanted.'

'She should have been grateful.'

'The indulged children of wealthy parents often aren't. Sally thought she should be more, but since leaving school, what had she done?'

'Partied, got laid, drunk and drugged,' Tremayne said.

'And she knew it. She would have made a go of it with Fortescue, revelled in the title for a few years, bred a couple of children, and then got bored. Done what Marjorie Fortescue has.'

'Secret lovers?'

'You need to raise your mind out of the gutter, Inspector.'

'That's where most of the murders are solved.'

'What I meant was charity work, putting on an act, pretending to be the loyal and loving wife.'

'Was she?'

'I'd not know.'

'You've not weaved your charm there?' Tremayne said.

'Why? Lord Fortescue, before he ended up in a wheelchair, was not a man to wrong.'

'He was broke,' Swift said.

'How could a family who had so much end up in financial trouble? Andrew Fortescue was a fool. He could have had Sally and enough money to live in the main house, but what does he do? Jumps out of a window.'

'What if he had seen Liston with his intended in that stable, killed her?'

'You're the police officer, but from what I know, emotionally disturbed people are unpredictable, capable of the most heinous actions,' Swift said.

Tremayne stubbed out the cigarette under his shoe, kicked the stub into a nearby bush and walked back into the police station.

***

Barton Kirkland sat on the floor of the stable, his head in his hands, tears rolling down his face.

That's how I found him,' Trevor Lawless, a tall, gangly and heavily tattooed individual, said. 'I phoned Barry first; he told me to phone you.'

'Vincent was right,' Clare said.

On the other side of the stable from where Kirkland was sitting, Red Rose on his side, almost motionless.

'Is it?' Tremayne asked the vet.

'Someone got in here last night, injected the animal, the same as Scarlet Soleil, the same as they tried down in Devon.'

'Will he live?' Clare asked.

'I don't know,' Vincent said. 'All I can do is to try and reverse the effects of the sedative and barbiturates, but I think it's too late.'

'Do what you can,' Kirkland murmured. 'My best horse, the one that could have made it, and look at him now, on his side, half-dead.'

After ten minutes, Barry Vincent got up from where he had been kneeling, packed his case, patted Kirkland on the shoulder as he walked past him and out into the fresh air. 'I'm sorry, Barton. I did what I could,' he said.

'He never cried over his daughter,' Clare said outside the stable.

'I can't say that I know him, not really,' Vincent said.

'Generous?'

'He knew the value of money. A steady resolve about the man, enough to make you know not to cheat him.'

'He was upset when his daughter's body was discovered. What about Trevor Lawless?'

'Kirkland took him on a couple of years back. He does a good job, keeps the horses in good condition, and then at night, he's into heavy metal.'

'Your alibi?' Clare said.

'It depends on the time. It could have occurred two hours ago, maybe six.'

'How do we find out?'

'If I take a sample of blood and urine from the animal. There's the possibility I could have been responsible, and that I'm covering my tracks.'

'An independent person would be best. Herbert Houghton?'

'I've already phoned him,' Vincent said. 'He'll be here in thirty minutes.'

'You expected the horse to die?'

'I tried to keep him alive, but yes. I phoned Houghton for advice, and to let him know that I'd value his expertise.'

'Are you as good as him?'

'I'm a practical everyday vet. He's not. A clever man and thorough, but he wouldn't have been able to save the horse any more than I could have.'

'He looks good,' Clare said.

'Looking good doesn't mean he's the best, no matter how many initials after his name.'

Tremayne came out of the stable, his arm around Kirkland's shoulder. 'I'll take Barton up to the house, get a stiff drink into him.'

'Barry's called Houghton. He'll be here soon.'

A feeble thank you from Kirkland to Vincent.

'At least he doesn't believe I'm responsible,' Vincent said. 'You're still not sure about my involvement in Sally's death, are you?'

'We've no proof, for or against.'

'That's not an answer.'

'It is.'

'I was alone and in Salisbury. I could have killed the horse, but I didn't,' Vincent said.

Chapter 19

Clare came over, clutching a pint of beer for Tremayne, a glass of red wine for her. It was nine in the evening, and she would have preferred to be at home with Clive. However, when Tremayne wanted to mull over the case, it was for her to be with him, and she knew that a casual chat often revealed another facet to the murder investigation.

'Yarwood,' Tremayne said, 'are we going about this the wrong way?'

'I don't see how.'

'But what if it's more regional?'

'If it's regional,' Clare said, 'where's the profit?'

'You can bet on any race in the world, even watch it on streaming video.'

'Which means that punters from anywhere in the world could bet on the races at Salisbury.'

'They could, and if someone was letting them know which horse, they could spread the bets out across online gambling websites, placing large bets, placing small, winning a few, losing more, but maintaining a profit.'

'Which over time and with enough money would still amount to a fortune.'

'Enough to make it worthwhile, but it would require a smart individual.'

'There's only one person we know with the ability,' Clare said.

'Ian Swift has the financial credentials, and he'd be capable of pulling it off.'

'Swift, could he do that?'

'Not on his own. He'd need someone who knows his way around a computer.'

'That rules me out,' Tremayne said.

'And me.'

'If the online gambling companies are as smart as you say they are, they'll soon find out what's going on.'

'Not necessarily. What if this person has hacked them, immobilised the warnings, falsified the payouts?'

'Why work if you can do that?'

'If a person can, they're neither motivated by money nor assets. The challenge is what's important.'

'Ian Swift appreciates money.'

'He wouldn't have the necessary skills. We need someone under the radar, not so visible. A person more at home with a computer than people.'

'Who do we have?'

'Chris Fairweather.'

'Light-fingered Chris?' Tremayne said.

'Apart from his kleptomania, he hides away for weeks on end.'

'A friend of Ian Swift?'

'Fairweather? He's not the type of person to have friends, not unless they're online.'

***

Fairweather had not changed for the better since Tremayne and Clare had first encountered him six years previously, a witness to a murder in a store where he bought copious quantities of carbonated drinks and microwave meals.

A short, squat body, barely any neck, with dank, stringy, dirty hair hanging from the rear of his head almost down to his waist, the bald patch on top having increased over the years.

Clare could only imagine how long it was since he had changed his clothes, a tee-shirt with Guns N' Roses emblazoned across the front of it, a pair of blue jeans. The man was bare-footed, and his feet were a delicate shade of mouldy grey. He smelt.

'What do you know about gambling?' Tremayne asked.

'What's this about?' Fairweather asked. 'I've not broken any laws.'

Only the law of personal hygiene, Clare thought.

'We need your help,' Tremayne said. The friendly approach was preferable to a more interrogatory style.

'For what? I don't steal anymore.'

'I thought it was a compulsion,' Clare said.

'It was, and besides, time away from here is time lost.'

'An impressive array of equipment,' Tremayne said.

They were in a room at the back of the house, the only window looking out to the world hidden by a black curtain.

Clare counted four large monitors, a couple of desktop computers and at least six laptops. On one of the monitors, a video game; on another, a couple of women writhing; and on the third, a YouTube video. The fourth was not on, nor were the laptops, apart from one. Elsewhere in the room, a metal-framed bed, the sheets ruffled, the white pillowcase marked with the grease from Fairweather's hair.

'If you could turn off the second monitor, it would be appreciated,' Clare said.

'Homicide, you must have seen it all,' Fairweather said.

'Seen, yes. That doesn't mean I want to watch it here. We need your help, not your taste in viewing.'

'Free to download if you've got the password.'

'You do?'

'I didn't pay. I don't pay for much.'

The house, built in the late nineteenth century, was a ramshackle rabbit warren. Clare could see that once it had been the pride and joy of a successful man and his family, but Fairweather, who had inherited it, gained no pleasure from it, and the house was dark, apart from the room where he played and slept and ate, a microwave on top of a small fridge in one corner.

'Still hacking?' Tremayne asked.

'You'd be surprised. Nowadays, I receive money to do it legally.'

'Why?'

'Who better to advise on security? I've got an insurance company in France. They've paid me twenty thousand euros to try and break through their firewalls and their security software protection and for me to remove a test file they've placed there for me.'

'If you can do it, so could someone else,' Clare said.

'Someone? In the UK, only five or six would have a chance.'

'Will you succeed?' Tremayne asked.

'It may take a couple of weeks, but I'll crack it.'

'And then they'll take action?'

'If it takes me a day, they will. A couple of weeks, it's secure. All they will need to do is to change the passwords, implement another line of defence.'

'Which you could hack again?'

The Horse's Mouth

'If I've done it once, what's the point of doing it twice? No satisfaction in that.'

'You could take money from their accounts,' Clare said.

Fairweather shifted in his seat, it creaking beneath him. 'If I wanted money, there are easier ways of getting it.'

'How?'

'The banks are vulnerable, but if they found out who it was, then that's criminal.'

'This house?' Tremayne asked.

'My parents, but you know that. There's enough money for me to live my life the way I want.'

'The temptation to use your skills for a crime must be there.'

'As long as I've got my games, and I get paid to hack, then why break the law?'

'You've got your women to keep you company,' Clare said.

'Harmless fun. You'd not believe what you see.'

Clare did, only she didn't want to see it.

'Here's a challenge for you,' Tremayne said. 'A hypothetical scenario.'

'Okay, I'll give you advice if that's what you want,' Fairweather said. 'Just make it more difficult than the insurance company in France.'

'We don't have twenty thousand euros.'

'It's not the money. It's the challenge.'

'I asked you before about gambling.'

'And I didn't answer.'

'Why?' Clare asked as she shifted further away from Fairweather. The room was hot, and the door was closed. The smell from the man was rotten, and she wanted to leave, but couldn't.

'I only deal in certainties. No point to gambling. If I wanted money, and I told you before that I don't, I'd hack a bank or a building society.'

'Easy to do?'

'Not easy, but who knows; with time I reckon I could do it.'

'Online gambling sites, could you hack them?'

'It would take time. They would soon discover an intrusion into their server.'

'Would they? What if you placed a script in there, something that would alert you if they were about to find out, able to delete your information?'

'As I said, complex. One or two companies it might be possible.'

'It would be criminal,' Tremayne said.

'Why risk it? A prison cell and no internet connection.'

'If you're as smart as you believe you are, why should anyone ever know?' Tremayne said.

'Is someone doing this?'

'Two people murdered; another has committed suicide.'

'Is that an answer?'

'It's the outcome. Someone's involved in switching horses, fixing races. No one would go to the trouble unless there was money in it.'

'You never mentioned the dead horses,' Fairweather said.

'How do you know about them?' Clare asked.

'The monitor that's not switched on. I use it to watch the news. Sally Kirkland was the first person to die.'

'You knew her?'

'We were in the same class in school, until about the age of ten.'

'Then what happened?'

'Her father happened. The man became wealthy, sent her off to a fancy school.'

'Did you keep in touch?'

'It was the same class, that's all.'

'Ian Swift?'

'I know the man. If you're inquiring about my social life, you're wasting your time. I don't have one.'

'A girlfriend?' Clare asked.

'Apart from the two on the monitor, no one else.'

Clare wasn't sure whether Fairweather was aiming to make her feel uncomfortable or if it was his sense of humour. Either way, the man did little for her. And as for Sally Kirkland barely talking to him when they were children, it was clear that she was not alone, and even as an adult, nobody spoke to him.

'Swift's a clever man,' Tremayne said. 'However, if he's committed a crime, he'd need you to set it up.'

'Then he'd be sorely disappointed. That's not my game, and besides, he's not contacted me.'

Outside the house, Tremayne spoke. 'We need proof of our theory.'

'Fleecing the fleecer, poetic justice.'

'Yarwood, I wonder about you. You have a criminal bent.'

'Not me. Just an appreciation of man's ingenuity,' Clare said.

Chapter 20

Barton Kirkland was calm when he sat down with Jeremy Liston, knowing full well that initially, he had considered violence against the man.

'Kirkland, believe me, it wasn't me,' Liston said.

In the restaurant where they met, the other diners were going about their business, indulging in idle gossip, discussing the day's activities or what they had bought on sale that day. In one corner, a couple of young lovers played footsie under the table. At the table next to Kirkland and Liston, an elderly couple were complaining about the attitude of their daughter.

'After all we did,' the woman said. 'Sent her to the best school, always made sure she was dressed nicely, and did we ever object when she brought home her friends when she was younger, the occasional boyfriend?'

Kirkland hadn't wanted to listen, but couldn't avoid it. Was that how he had been with Sally? Letting her do what she wanted, not once critical or putting his foot down firmly? Was that why he was meeting with one of her lovers?

'And then she swears at us,' the grey-haired man said across the table to his wife.

'She's bad, that's all I know,' the woman said.

'You can't ignore your children.'

From what Kirkland could see, the daughter was probably decent, but of a different generation, a generation of taking, not giving. It was the same with him. His parents had given him nothing, not even if they had wanted to, as life was tough in his youth, and most

The Horse's Mouth

people got by on a week-to-week basis, going hungry at times.

Nowadays, if a child wanted a laptop, the parent bought it, or if it was a weekend away with friends in France, the parent put his or her hand in their pocket and paid. And what did the parent get, Kirkland thought. A warm embrace, a kiss on the cheek? Not from Sally, and the one time he had put his foot down and said no, a tantrum. It was the only time he had stood in the way of her pleasure.

Kirkland had to admit that Liston was a fine figure of a man, even if his face showed the effects of war. He would have been a man fitting for Sally, but she had planned to marry Andrew Fortescue.

'Sally told me she was going to marry Fortescue,' Liston said.

'It was you in that stable, wasn't it?' Kirkland said.
'It wasn't as if she loved Fortescue.'
'Did she love you?'
'I believe so, but she's the same as Marjorie Fortescue.'

'That woman was a tart in her day,' Kirkland said sharply. 'My Sally never was.'

'Marjorie's behaviour back then wouldn't raise a comment today.'

Kirkland knew that Liston was right. Sally had been way too liberal with her favours, expelled from one school at fifteen for sneaking in local boys to her dormitory.

'You're involved with her ladyship?'
'We are involved in a commercial transaction.'
'That's not what I meant.'
'I know.'
'You're a bastard,' Kirkland said.

'If it hadn't been Sally, you would be slapping me on the back, buying me drinks.'

'But it was.'

Behind Kirkland, the elderly couple had reached the stage of accusing each other.

'It was you, too soft,' the woman said.

'She's the same as that layabout brother of yours. Her bad blood comes from you,' the man said.

Kirkland remembered his wife, and how close they had been, rarely arguing.

How many have raised their children well, only to have it thrown back in their faces when the children reach puberty, he thought. And then you get an exceptional individual who is the child of a drug-riddled couple. The genetic throwback, good or bad, played a vital part in how the adult developed. Sally had not once sworn at him but was predisposed to recreational drugs and men, some good, some bad.

'I wished her well, left her there in the stable,' Liston said.

'And went off with another woman.'

'Sally would have understood.'

'Someone killed her, and you were with her last.'

'Why would I murder her? I don't kill people, not anymore.'

'And received medals for doing it.'

'I don't know who killed Sally and Daniels.'

'My daughter. Daniels doesn't concern me.'

'It could be the same person. What if he's after you?'

'I've done nothing wrong.'

'Nor had Sally, or was she involved in substituting your horse?'

Kirkland felt he should be angry at the man's aspersion, but he couldn't be.

'Sally wouldn't have done anything to harm Red Rose.'

'With me, she was fine, her usual self,' Liston said.

Was Jeremy Liston putting on an act, an Oscar-winning portrayal of an emotionally-detached man, playing the field with a collection of females? Was the man a latent gay, covering up an inner turmoil? Was he dangerous? Kirkland didn't know.

***

Marjorie Fortescue walked out of the front of her house. She was in a strange mood, she knew, even for her.

A recent visit by her late husband's sister had got her thinking about whether selling the Fortescue property was the right move.

The sister was a middle-aged matronly woman with her hair severely pulled back in a bun, an unusual walk – Marjorie thought it was due to the woman's life-long horse riding – and her clipped speech. Perfectly acceptable for royalty and BBC newsreaders, out of context for a woman who dressed cheaply, spent her time with horses and smelt of them. She wasn't, to Marjorie, a fitting example of the aristocracy, whereas she had always carried herself well, maintained a discreet distance from those of a lower class.

'My brother wouldn't have approved,' Bunty Fortescue had said. That was another thing that irritated Marjorie, the woman insisted on using a childhood nickname, a term of endearment from friends due to her plumpness.

'If Andrew had had his way, this place would have become an amusement park,' Marjorie had said.

'Your son was a fool, totally incapable of making it work, but he had the right idea. What about the Kirkland woman?'

'He would have married her.'

'Capable woman.'

'She would have made him a good wife, but…'

'Frivolous, a weakness for men, the same as you,' Bunty Fortescue had said scathingly.

Even though the two women were related through marriage, there wasn't much affection.

'My past remained where it belonged.'

'You doubted the Kirkland woman? Or was it something more?'

'I believed that she would be a fitting Fortescue.'

'Or was it that she would usurp your position? Did you want Andrew all to yourself, the power behind the throne?'

The comment had hit a raw nerve.

'Fine day, your ladyship,' Ted Upton called out from where he was planting a small bush after Bunty had just left.

'It is. How are you, Ted?'

'The cold mornings are playing hell with the flowers, but a couple of warm nights and they should be better.'

It was, she realised, the longest conversation that she had had with the gardener for a long time. Bernard had spent time talking to the man, and Andrew regarded him as a friend. But then, Andrew had not deemed rank and privilege as estimable qualities.

Was that it? Marjorie thought. Is that why I can't mourn my son the way I should?

The Horse's Mouth

'I hope you're right,' she said.

'If you don't mind me asking,' Upton said, 'what are your plans for this place. After all, my wife and I, we've been here a long time, and we don't want to go, but if we have to, then we must.'

'It was clear in my mind. Lord Fortescue wanted to act as if nothing was wrong, but it's no longer possible to hide behind a title and thumb your nose at the world. Andrew had plans for the place.'

'What do you want?'

'I want to get out and enjoy life.'

'You enjoyed it here. We're not so different, are we?'

Marjorie Fortescue couldn't see how. One was a gardener of limited education and even less ambition; the other always keeping close to those who could better her, eventually scoring the jackpot with the Honourable Bernard Fortescue, the incumbent to the title of Lord, the squire of the manor, a stately home.

'Are we?'

'We're happy here.'

'I was, but with my husband and son dead, I'm not sure I can be again.'

'Time heals. It's the same with plants. One day they're wilting, but the rays of the sun and they soon perk up.'

'And some compost as well,' Marjorie said. 'That's what I've received of late. I'm not sure how I can perk up, not here.'

'These are your roots. You're a part of this place as much as Lord Fortescue and Andrew were, as much as I am. Whatever you do, and if that's following through with Andrew's plan, then do it. It'll be his legacy to you, to all of us.'

'Not on my own, I couldn't.'

'Then find someone you can trust.'

'You know, Ted, you're a wiser man than I gave you credit for.'

'This place gets in the blood. And besides, it's selfish on my part. My wife is happy here, and that means I am.'

'You're right; I was happy here. Maybe I can be again.'

Upton walked away, a smile on his face. He had heard the stories about the woman, even checked up on her past on his wife's iPad, found out about her lovers and the chequered lifestyle she had led, but he wasn't a man to judge a person by past actions. To him, Lady Fortescue had always been polite, a credit to the name, a decent mother and a good wife.

In his youth, he had been an ardent banner-waving socialist, with no fondness for the unentitled privileged, but his advancing years had mellowed him. Ted Upton knew a good thing, and seeing out his remaining years with the Fortescues suited him fine. And he did like Lady Fortescue, a decent and surprisingly open woman on that one day. He knew that the next time they met, it would be more formal, and she would be reticent in her conversation.

And that suited him fine, although he was glad of that shared intimacy in the garden.

***

Daniels' murder seemed more logical to Tremayne. After all, the man had proven to him on several occasions that he had a talent for picking a winner, although how much of that was down to skill or fixing the race, he couldn't be sure.

If, as Tremayne surmised, the switching of two horses and the murders of two people were related, it indicated someone psychotic or seriously disturbed, or it was professional.

Tremayne didn't hold with conspiracy theories, felt they were an easy way out of an investigation, clutching at straws, stating that it was persons unseen and unknown from out of the area attempting to enter Salisbury and its racecourse.

He knew horseracing, and there were hundreds if not thousands of racecourses around the world, more prestigious Salisbury, bookmakers who would accept more than twenty pounds each way.

It concerned him, the belief that he and his sergeant were looking for shadows that weren't there.

Ian Swift sat bolt upright at the police station. His second visit in as many days. Even though the man was not pleased to be there, he wasn't about to show it.

'Mr Swift,' Tremayne said. 'A hypothesis.'

'Another one? How many is that? Or is it that you want to put forward a scenario, which by default is an oblique accusation of me, or that you want genuine advice?'

'All of what you've just said.'

'Ian,' Clare said, 'the sooner we start, the sooner you'll be out of here.'

'Very well. What is it you believe that I've done?' Swift said.

'Do you know Chris Fairweather?'

'As it happens, I do.'

'May I ask how?'

'You've met his sister?'

'Not yet. Should we?'

'Fairweather is a repugnant individual,' Swift said. 'His sister is not.'

'We would agree with your estimation of the man,' Tremayne said. 'It doesn't explain his sister.'

'You were in my office the other day.'

'We were.'

'The lady outside, dark hair, pale complexion, attractive in a homely way, my personal assistant.'

'We remember her,' Clare said.

'She's Chris Fairweather's sister.'

Tremayne smelt a rat.

'How long has she worked for you?'

'Eleven years. I trust Gwen totally.'

'Her brother?'

'He comes around from time to time. However, I don't like him in the office. If she sees him before he reaches the door, she takes him to a café or somewhere else.'

'He never mentioned a sister.'

'I'm not sure they're close, although Gwen looks out for him.'

'The man needs someone,' Clare said.

'He's borderline genius, or maybe he's just plain mad, I'd not know.'

'Do you use him?'

'If I have a financial model that needs programming, a webinar to set up, I'll call him on one condition.'

'He doesn't come near you.'

'I don't want him in the office, but I've been to that squalid little room that he calls home.'

'Who came first? Gwen or Chris?'

'Gwen. I needed someone to set up a computer server for me; she recommended her brother.'

'He came to your office?'

'The first time during the day. After that, if he had to visit, it was after hours, enough time for the smell to go.'

'How do you communicate?'

'By email or over the phone. Video conferencing sometimes. Besides, Chris doesn't like to move away from his games and his women.'

'I've seen both,' Clare said.

'He doesn't care who he offends.'

'He didn't say that his sister worked for you.'

'Don't hold that against him. As I said, if you're asking him, don't be sure you hear the right answer.'

'Are you curious as to why we mentioned your name?' Tremayne said.

'Personally, I'm not,' Swift said. 'But you'll be telling me soon enough.'

'Online gambling.'

'What about it?'

'You've heard of it?'

'Of course.'

'It's us trying to figure out the angle on Sally Kirkland's and Les Daniels' murders.'

'And you think that it's gambling?'

'The question is, why would a regional meeting, a minor racecourse, attract so much attention? Why would people and horses die?'

'You're about to tell me.'

'Heavy betting worldwide on the outcome of a race, even in Salisbury, could involve large amounts of money.'

'Up to a million is possible.'

'You know?'

'Not personally, but I read.'

'That's why we were with Chris Fairweather. He's the acknowledged computer nerd, the most skilled person we know.'

'Did he say that?'

'He reckoned that his hacking skills placed him in the top five or six in the country. He's now paid to hack companies, check out whether he can get in, advise them on preventative measures.'

'Good for him. No doubt he's paid well.'

'Twenty thousand euros from a French insurance company,' Clare said.

'He's selling himself cheap. I would have charged fifty,' Swift said.

'If someone has found a way to hack an online gambling company or to have set one up, Fairweather would be the best man for the job.'

'He would, but what's this got to do with me?'

'Fairweather might have the skills, but he's neither got the motivation nor the organisational skills to make it work.'

'And you think I have?'

'Interesting, isn't it?' Tremayne said. 'We come up with a possible set of circumstances which lead to a motive, and you and Fairweather are bonded through his sister.'

'Ludicrous,' Swift said. 'And if that's why I'm here, then I'll bid you farewell. I've better things to do with my time than sit here and listen to this nonsense.'

Swift rose from his seat and left the room, angrily slamming the door shut behind him.

'An interesting reaction,' Tremayne said to Clare.

'Damning. Either he's angry because we hit the nail on the head, or he's regretful that he didn't come up with the idea.'

'The former,' Tremayne said.

Chapter 21

Tremayne found the day hard. Early in the morning, it was his aching back and another visit from Superintendent Moulton, purportedly interested in an update on the current murder investigation.

If it weren't that Tremayne was so singularly minded on policing, he would have taken Moulton's offer and walked out of the police station.

The afternoon wasn't much better. It was the afternoon that Barton Kirkland died.

Standing in the man's house, Clare to one side, Jim Hughes to the other, Tremayne in the middle, the three of them looked down at the body.

'There goes one theory down the drain,' Tremayne said.

'What theory?' Clare said. She had seen death too many times now, but even so, she still felt a pang of regret. Tremayne was impassive, not concerned that the man lying face down in a pool of blood had purchased him a drink on a couple of occasions.

'How long?' Tremayne asked.

'Three to four hours,' Hughes said.

'The knife?'

'Stiletto, six-inch blade.'

'Anything unique about his death?'

'Whoever it was left a print from a shoe outside the window.'

'Male or female?' Clare asked.

'Judging by the print, I'd say it was a man. We'll conduct compaction tests of the soil. That should give us an approximate weight of the person.'

'Are you certain it's the murderer's?' Tremayne asked.

'At this time. Unless someone else had come in through the door. Kirkland had an open bottle of whisky on the table. Logically, he would have offered one to his guest.'

'Assuming the visit was cordial,' Tremayne said.

'If it was murder, then why come in the front door? It's too visible, and there's always the probability of touching something, leaving a fingerprint, a strand of hair,' Hughes said.

'Not if he wore gloves,' Clare said.

'He would have shaken hands with Kirkland,' Tremayne said.

'You two can debate it, but I'm telling you someone came in through the window,' Hughes said. 'There's a clear sign the latch had been lifted, no broken glass, and he would have been in the room before Kirkland came in.'

'Hiding behind a curtain? A touch of the melodramatic.'

'Facts are facts. Whoever it was, skill was required to open the window, although Kirkland's security wasn't the best.'

'What was the man doing?' Clare asked as she once again looked down at the body. A rambunctious person in life, a man who would have made more enemies than friends, a man with a murdered daughter. Even so, it was an ignominious end to a life, repeatedly stabbed with a thin knife.

'Waste of a good whisky,' Tremayne said.

'The bottle was smashed in the struggle,' Hughes said.

'I don't see any sign of a struggle.'

'We believe that Kirkland didn't see the person before the first thrust, but then had reacted.'

'A fight?'

'Short-lived.'

'One knife wound wouldn't have slowed him much,' Tremayne said.

'Look at the body. Heavy, out of condition, more than one glass of whisky. I'd say Kirkland was drunk,' Hughes said.

'In this room? How long would that take? Surely no one was going to wait that long behind the curtain?'

'If not in here, then Kirkland brought the glass and the bottle from another room.'

'Which means that whoever killed him knew that he would eventually come in.'

'Unless murder wasn't on the intruder's agenda.' Clare said. 'What if he was looking for something, and then Kirkland's there, and the person, tired of waiting for him to leave, stabs him in the back?'

'Why kill him?' Tremayne asked.

'' As Jim just said, Kirkland confronted his attacker. The man panics.'

'Which means a confused individual.'

'Someone who might just come forward and confess,' Clare said.

'What was the person after?' Hughes said.

'I might have read it wrong,' Tremayne said. 'I had Swift pegged as Mr Big, but it could have been Kirkland.'

'He wouldn't risk Red Rose,' Clare said.

'What if he was protecting the horse? He's playing with the big boys, betting heavily, taking money, distributing it, all the while conscious some individuals would have no hesitation in taking revenge if they felt cheated.'

'The horse's head in the bed, that's already been done,' Hughes said.

'Why not?'

'It makes sense,' Clare said. 'What if Kirkland was in too far, and we know he was in financial difficulties?'

'The horse was his stake. If it won, he would keep it. If it lost, then he would sign it over to someone else. Scarlet Soleil was expendable.'

'It was still a valuable animal.'

'Daniels painting the horse's hind leg, Sally leading it out, Daniels putting Red Rose into a horse transporter.'

'Or it wasn't even at the racecourse,' Clare said.

'Three people who could corroborate or deny it – all dead,' Tremayne said.

'Two horses, as well. Innocents doomed due to greed.'

'But which men? And why kill Sally?'

'She didn't want to be involved in a scandal, and after the horse had won, was prepared to go to the police, convince them that her father and she were merely pawns in a bigger game.'

'I don't like it,' Tremayne said. 'Too many holes in your argument.'

'You've got a better one?' Hughes said.

'Not yet. It's what is in this house that's important. Was the intruder looking for something? Did he find it? Will it lead us to Daniels' and Sally Kirkland's murderer?'

'Or murderers?' Clare said.

'Three murders, three murderers, I can believe that.'

'When you've finished,' Clare said to Hughes, 'we would like to check the place.'

'Three hours and it's all yours.'

'Long enough for a cigarette and a coffee,' Tremayne said.

'How about lunch at the pub and a pint of beer?' Clare said.

'If you're treating.'

'I am.'

It was either a cigarette or a beer, Clare knew. Tremayne was going to commit one sin, regardless. Beer was the lesser of two evils.

***

Jeremy Liston listened as Marjorie Fortescue outlined her plans for the future of the Fortescue estate. He was neither enamoured nor dismissive.

'If I take Andrew's ideas, put them in the hand of a partner, then it could work,' her ladyship said.

Liston looked at the woman. Even though she was fifteen years older than him, he liked what he saw. A personal and professional partnership appealed to him.

'There are a couple of cottages we can rent, and then we can offer horse riding and walks in the country, and converted stables used as accommodation.'

'It's all very well, Marjorie,' Liston said. He felt that there was no need to keep calling the woman 'My Lady'.

'If we're to be partners, then I suppose we can drop the formality,' Marjorie Fortescue said.

'What you're suggesting is wedding receptions, a night in the house with you, candlelit dinners, the butler and the servants.'

'What's wrong with that?'

'Nothing in itself, but you're missing the main point.'

'Which is?'

'How much land here?'

'You know that.'

'I do. The house and the gardens you can keep. But at the rear of the property, behind a wooded area, out of sight to you, you've enough land to build twenty to twenty-five houses.'

'Selling off part of the estate to unscrupulous developers seems to be sacrilege, an insult to my husband and my son.'

'Marjorie, you're a member of the Fortescue legacy. Ruthlessness is required.'

'My husband was a good man; he wouldn't have sold off part of the estate.'

'That's why you're in a financial dilemma. His old-fashioned belief that it would be alright in the end, money or no money, means nothing. The title might be good for getting a good seat in a restaurant and the locals tipping their hats when they see you.'

'Or touching me for a donation to fix the church roof.'

'Marjorie, your husband was wrong, and Andrew, not that I've got anything against him, was a child in a man's body. Sally would have moulded him to her way of thinking, probably distancing him from you.'

'Bernard had a stronger personality, and I never exerted total control over him, nor did I want to. I loved him; you know.'

'Lay off the rhetoric,' Liston said.

Marjorie Fortescue felt the conversation was getting too personal. And whereas she had decided to leave the place, find a lover or two, Liston was there with her in the house, and they were alone. He was physically attractive, but an intimate relationship with the man would put her at a disadvantage.

'Very well. I was fond of him.'

'Good. Let me be honest with you,' Liston said. 'You're an attractive woman, but if this is to work, you and I have to keep our hands to ourselves.'

It wasn't what she had heard of the man, and she felt a pang of regret, almost an insult. 'I agree,' she said.

'What I need from you is the authority to deal with rezoning the land to low-density residential. That way, you can sell it off, either to one developer or to individual purchasers.'

'Will that be expensive?'

'If permission is granted, then the land has value. The bank will finance the cost of preparing it for sale.'

'What cost?'

'That's why I'll do it for you.'

'What do you want?'

'Twenty-five per cent of the profit.'

'In writing.'

'Your lawyer can draft the document setting out the terms. Do you trust him?'

'He's a Fortescue, the poor side of the family.'

'He'll do. I don't intend to cheat you on this, no reason to. There's plenty of money for both of us. You'll be financially unencumbered, and then if you want guests in the house and tramping over the place with their grubby children, that's up to you.'

'If I have enough money, they won't be coming.'

'You're more Fortescue than your husband ever was. You are, Marjorie, if you don't mind me saying, a person with an inflated opinion of self.'

'And you, Jeremy Liston, are a rogue. I don't trust you one bit, but my husband's cousin is no fool. He'll hold you accountable for your actions.'

'I'm what your husband should have been. Forget the meek who shall inherit the earth. With us two, it will be the aristocrat and the hero.'

'Reluctantly, from what I've heard.'

'That's for public consumption. I did what I had to, and I enjoyed it.'

'Killing comes easily,' Marjorie said.

'As screwing did for you when you were younger.'

'But I found Bernard. What have you got?'

'It's a shame. You and I, we would have made a great couple. Plenty of arguing, no doubt; plenty of making up.'

'I'll not drop my guard, not for you now. Secure the deal, make sure I've got the money, and then, maybe.'

Chapter 22

To Bunty Fortescue, a strait-laced woman of strict morals and stringent control over her husband, Marjorie Buxton was a woman of loose morals with a talent for bedding the right man, eventually securing her brother.

Her brother, Bernard, was a person who had shown promise in his youth, yet had succumbed to the charms of a good-time girl, the type of person who was hopping from bed to bed, aiming to better herself, eventually settling on the son of an ailing lord.

And what now? Bunty Fortescue pondered. What of the land and the mansion? Who would inherit if Marjorie was dead? It had to be her, the sister of the dead lord, the only direct descendent of a noble line.

It was an interesting thought, but she dismissed it as nonsense. After all, it would involve a death, Marjorie's, and with the intense interest in her nephew's death and the murder of the woman he intended to marry, the police were too close, too ready to make an arrest.

However, although rejecting the previous foolish notion, Bunty Fortescue realised that her sister-in-law was only one of two people who could turn the Fortescues' fortunes around: she was the other one.

She had been told of the plan to develop the land at the far extreme of the estate, a project she approved of wholeheartedly, but for which she would receive no money.

Bunty was determined to amend that discrepancy. With a stout heart and the determination to turn the situation to her favour, she got into her car and drove to Salisbury, and up to the council chambers.

'Grantley,' she bellowed in her deep voice, the legacy of smoking two packs of cigarettes a day. 'A word in your ear.'

Clive, Clare's husband, recognised the bearing of someone who believed that life owed them, attempted to distance himself from the woman.

'Grantley, it's no use. You and I are going to have a little chat.'

Cornered, unable to avoid the inevitable, Clive Grantley stopped, turned and shook the woman's hand. 'Not here,' he said. 'In my office, if you want.'

'Not in front of the staff, is that it?' Bunty said, looking around at two women sheltered by their computer screens, a man who was looking aimlessly out of the window.

'It's an open office,' Grantley said. 'No secrets in here, but your visit does not seem cordial.'

'It will be if you give the right response.'

Grantley said no more and opened the door to his office. It was too sparse, too modern, for the old-fashioned and severe woman, but she did not comment.

'A coffee? Tea?' Grantley said.

'Tea, white, two sugars,' the curt response.

'What can I do for you?'

'It's what that woman and Jeremy Liston are up to.'

'I don't see what I can do. You do realise that my wife is a police officer investigating the murder of people known to your sister-in-law, to you?'

'I'm not here about a homicide; it's a criminal travesty that concerns me.'

'Then it is a matter for the police.'

'It's a crime in the making.'

Bunty Fortescue sipped at her tea. 'Lady Fortescue intends to sell off part of the land,' she said.

'That's her prerogative. It will be subject to approval by our planning department.'

'That's what I want.'

'Is that it?'

'I want it refused.'

'At the appropriate juncture, you will be able to register your disapproval of your sister-in-law's intention, as long as you have a legal stake in the land, or you live within the area affected.'

'I don't qualify on both counts. You, Clive Grantley, understand. I want her and Liston's plans scuttled, thrown to the wind.'

'You want me to use my influence to intercede in a family matter?'

'It's more than that, don't you see? The Fortescues used to represent something. We provided stability in a troubled world. If she sells one part of the place, then what next? Hell, she could sell the place to, heaven forbid, a singer of jingles.'

'Change is inevitable,' Grantley said. He wasn't enjoying the conversation, the woman even less.

'A person needs to know their place in life. Marjorie Fortescue is not of my blood. She's common, and she's going to destroy my heritage.'

'This is a conversation that you should have with her.'

'What would be the point? You support the local heritage council, don't you?'

'I do.'

'Then protect the Fortescue estate from that woman.'

'A planning proposal would be subjected to appraisal by the heritage council. But I should tell you that land would not usually be an issue, not unless it's close to a site or place of interest.'

'Fortescue House?'

'The house, an example of Georgian architecture, is subject to restrictions on what can or cannot be done, I would agree, but the land, if it is sufficiently remote from the building, will have little bearing.'

'Clive, we're of the same class,' the woman said.

'Are we?'

'Our fathers were friends.'

'Yes, I remember him. A tall, strong man. I was young, though, and I can't say I ever spoke more than a few words to him.'

'Nor did I, shuffled off to boarding school as soon as he could manage it. But our father was strong-willed, and Bernard used to be. Andrew was a wimp, falling for Kirkland's daughter, another Marjorie. He was never going to be able to fix the Fortescue fortunes.'

'His mother could.'

'And so could I. I want what she and Liston are plotting stopped.'

'I can't intervene.'

'Are you a champagne socialist?'

'If you're inferring that I am financially comfortable with an abiding interest in the less fortunate, then yes I am. However, neither you nor Lady Fortescue nor Jeremy Liston qualifies. You were born with a silver spoon in the mouth; her ladyship married into the aristocracy, and, as for Liston, his heroics and his estate agency serve him well.'

'Refuse, give me time to strike a deal with Marjorie. I'll make it worth your while.'

'I believe this conversation has gone too far,' Clive said. 'Offering me a sweetener to be a party to your conniving is offensive in the extreme.'

Bunty Fortescue slammed her cup down on the table, got up and walked out of the door. From the sanctity of the other room, and in full view of the three in there, she shouted out, 'I'll get what I want. With your help or without.'

Clive calmly closed his door and phoned Clare. He felt that she should know what had just transpired.

***

Barton Kirkland's death, unexpected as it was, provided more impetus to the investigation into his daughter's murder. Clues at the scene of Sally's demise were inconclusive, and though it had been Liston in the stable with her, his time there had been amorous, not violent. However, Tremayne hadn't as yet ruled out the man, although he still didn't believe he had murdered the woman.

'Why not?' Clare said when Tremayne had mentioned his thoughts about Liston.

It was the time that Clare liked best, late at night in the office; one of the few times that Tremayne let his guard down, showed himself to be agreeable and caring, instead of the gruff and taciturn that he portrayed outside.

'Too easy. No evidence.'

'It's often the most obvious,' Clare said, not that she believed Liston was the murderer either.

It had been a busy day; Clare at Barton Kirkland's autopsy in the morning. She always tried to avoid attending, but it could sometimes prove beneficial to the case, although with the obese man it had been less than pleasant, and she had left the room with a throbbing headache and a nauseous taste in her mouth. Tremayne had spent time at Les Daniels' murder scene, walking around the area, speaking to a few locals, some that he knew, some that he didn't.

The only interesting fact was that Jeremy Liston had been in the house next door on the day of the murder. On checking, Liston verified that the house was for sale and he had received an offer from a middle-aged couple, the husband transferring to a civilian post at Boscombe Down, the aircraft research facility to the north of the city. And his wife had secured a position teaching at a primary school within walking distance of the house.

On the one hand, Liston was selling a modestly priced house and then, on the other, he was involved in a multi-million-pound development with Marjorie Fortescue. There was an inconsistency, Tremayne thought, but he couldn't see if or how it was relevant.

Clive Grantley's conversation with the bombastic Bunty Fortescue, a woman who had kept her maiden name after marrying into a minor branch of the family, hadn't been discussed as yet.

Clare broached the subject with Tremayne. 'Is Bunty Fortescue relevant?'

'It's another piece to the jigsaw,' Tremayne replied. 'We've not given her much thought before.'

'None. We've not met her.'

'And if we do, how do we protect your husband? She'll smell a rat if we bring her into the station, and if we go out to her place, you're likely to get the door slammed in your face.'

'It wouldn't be the first time.'

'It might be best if I go alone,' Tremayne said. 'It's going to cause problems for your husband.'

'I'm sure he knows that. Bunty Fortescue will go on the defensive, and Liston wants to be a councillor. He'll use it to his advantage if he can.'

'Is Clive ready for what's coming?'

'He went through it with his brother. He'll ride the storm.'

'Put on a brave face, remain stoic in public, less than cheerful in private.'

'Inspector, there is a sensitive side to my husband, I'd have you know,' Clare said.

'I'm sure there is; after all, you're his consort.'

'I thought you were about to be more direct.'

'I was, but thought better of it.'

'Old age, it's not what it's cracked up to be, is it?'

'In my dotage, I've found a subtlety, is that what you think? A need to be more caring, not to offend or cause embarrassment.'

'It could be,' Clare said with a smile. Late-night humour never went amiss.

'Bunty Fortescue may regard your husband's indiscretion in telling you as slanderous.'

'She could cause trouble. How you handle it, I'm not sure, but could she be involved?' Clare said.

'In Sally's murder? It makes no sense.'

'Think about it. Sally dies; Andrew is devastated and commits suicide. Lord Fortescue, virtually on his death bed, dies early.'

'Too many variables, too much left to chance.' Tremayne said.

'It's Andrew that's the weak link. Murder is murder, the death of an old and infirm man is a certainty, but suicide is not. Even if Andrew had killed Sally or

Bunty had, and Andrew had seen it happen, why didn't he go to the police? And if Bunty had done it, and she'd have had the strength, then why?'

'I don't know. I'm only postulating. With Andrew and her brother out of the way, there's only Marjorie Fortescue. After that, who gets the money and the estate?'

'And death duty and financial headaches.'

'Yarwood, check with her ladyship. I'll deal with the errant sister.'

'Errant?'

'I'd say so. If she hadn't visited Clive, we wouldn't be focussing on her. And if she had orchestrated Sally's death, or given Andrew a mental nudge, then where do we stand? The investigation's done a one-eighty, brought us back to where we started.'

'Andrew's suicide, how could that have been arranged?' Clare asked. Clive had told her to be careful with what he had told her about Bunty Fortescue.

The die was cast, tensions were to rise, people were to be offended, and someone was to be arrested.

Chapter 23

Bunty Fortescue, a pretentious woman who held an old-fashioned view of the world, in that breeding mattered, and those titled were deserving of respect, did not appreciate the tone that Tremayne was taking with her.

'It sounds like an accusation of something underhanded to me,' she said as she stood up, her back to an open wood fire in the rundown four-bedroom house, she shared with Claude, her third cousin and husband.

'Your husband is Lady Fortescue's lawyer. Isn't that a conflict of interest?' Tremayne said.

It was a house his wife would have loved, an old-world charm, the smell of leather and damp. However, his days of climbing ladders, precariously balancing a pot of paint at the top, were behind him, behind Jean as well, not that he had ever been a home handyman, and even less a gardener.

'My discussions with Marjorie are personal. I bear the woman no malice. And as for Claude, he'll do his duty, act professionally.'

'An unusual term for a lawyer, Mrs Fortescue.'

'What is?'

'Duty. What does it mean? Does it refer to you in a personal capacity, or to Lady Fortescue professionally?'

'I only wish to appeal to Marjorie's good nature. After all, she's not one of us, only there by luck and a lithe body.'

'An interloper?'

'Not when Andrew was alive, but what does she have now?'

'A big house, a lot of land, and a title,' Tremayne said.

The woman, for all her belief in her God-given right, was careless in her conversation, inclined to say what she didn't mean to, and then backtracking to cover it up.

Claude Fortescue, a beanpole of a man, had an imperious look about him. Tremayne had met him briefly and recognised the country lawyer in him, relegated to conveyancing, dealing with the local courts on occasion, complacent with the quiet life.

Tremayne believed the man would do the right thing by Marjorie, up to a point. And that point would be dictated by Bunty. He was hen-pecked, confirmed by Bunty checking his tie before he left the house, putting a couple of sandwiches wrapped in cellophane into the briefcase he carried.

'If Andrew hadn't died, it would have been his,' Bunty said.

'The land and the house?'

'The right of inheritance follows the male line. Marjorie would have become the dowager, and the Kirkland woman would have become the lady of the manor.'

'Marjorie would still be titled, and she would have somewhere to live, money of her own.'

'Andrew would have made the decisions, but yes.'

'Or Sally Kirkland. Did you ever meet her?' Tremayne asked.

'On two occasions.'

'What was your impression of her?'

'She was the same as Marjorie. Those two would not have found it easy to coexist in the same house.'

'It's large enough,' Tremayne said.

'Marjorie's a strong-willed woman. She wouldn't have been able to stand by and see Andrew ruin the place.'

'Sally Kirkland would have taken control.'

'Marjorie tried to control my brother, but he remained firm, up until…'

'Until what?'

'He became old and infirm. In those last few weeks, he was barely articulate.'

For a couple of minutes, Tremayne said nothing. He went over the case in his mind, realised that even if Bunty and Marjorie disagreed on many points, they were still united in preserving the Fortescue legacy.

'Mrs Fortescue, what we have here is a Catch-22,' he said.

'How?'

'If Andrew were alive, then the decisions would be his to make, good or bad. And if Sally were, he would have married her.'

'No solution was ideal, I'd agree.'

'But you would never be allowed to take control, not unless Marjorie is dead.'

'I'd be the only one to gain from her death, but yes, I would inherit.'

'Your husband? Is this what he has arranged?'

'The inheritance is enshrined in documents drawn up in the past. Even if Marjorie has a long-lost relative, they won't get a penny.'

'If that's the case, then let's examine the situation. You get nothing, other than what you can coax out of Marjorie, as long as she is alive.'

'Coax is an insulting term.'

'What you can arrange with the woman, is that correct?'

'It is.'

'Then, Sally's death ensured that she wouldn't take control, and Andrew's subsequent suicide brought you closer to the prize.'

'The prize, as you so elegantly put it, was not that important.'

'Then what was?'

'The Fortescues are a noble family with a rich history. That was what was important, and now with the death of Andrew, it will wither and die.'

'As much as you dislike Marjorie and Sally, one had ensured the title through the birth of a son; the other would have produced an heir.'

'Fortescue men are drawn to such women, their birthright to play the field: actresses, shop assistants, the maids.'

'You would have preferred them not to have?'

'Buying them trinkets, I've no problem with that, but my brother went and married one of them. If he had kept her as a mistress, married someone else more suitable, bred a son with a backbone, then the family would still be strong. Instead, he marries a well-known woman of loose morals and questionable breeding, sires a weak-willed equalitarian.'

'A man without the noblesse to keep the peasants in their place?'

'You're scathing terminology is treacherous. It may not be important to you, Inspector, but once the British Empire meant something, not a collection of stray islands and foolish notions of independence. Britain was at its best when families such as the Fortescues ruled.'

'And criminals were less sophisticated,' Tremayne said. 'I might agree with you on some of what you've just said, but it doesn't preclude the fact that with Marjorie dead, you would have a lot to gain, and at the moment your husband is the meat in the sandwich, able to play one of you off against the other. Which one will he choose?'

'He'll choose his wife, rest assured of that.'

'If Marjorie gives you a percentage, what then?'

'That's all I want.'

'If she doesn't? She's using Jeremy Liston to deal with the subdivision, the planning permissions.'

'That's her decision.'

'Marjorie intends to use your husband. Can he be trusted?'

'He can. As for Marjorie and me, we'll agree. If she wasn't so common…'

'You would have liked her.'

'But I do.'

'Are you interested in horseracing?'

'Horses, yes. Racing is barbaric.'

'Kirkland treated his horses well.'

'Did he?'

'What are you inferring?' Tremayne said.

'I only know that the man had pulled himself up from the gutter, affected the airs and graces of a country gentleman.'

'Isn't that admirable?'

'Once a mongrel, always a mongrel. A thoroughbred requires generations of careful breeding, the same as with a noble family. One bad seed and it starts to go downhill; two and the rot has set in.'

'Marjorie was the first?'

'Not the first, but now she's the last.'

'Whatever happens, you've gained.'

'A dilapidated house, an impotent third cousin for a husband? I've gained nothing, would lose everything if I had killed any of those people.'

Tremayne knew that wasn't correct. To Bunty Fortescue, breeding was all-important, and even if her husband was an ineffectual man and from a minor branch of the family, he was still a Fortescue. He left the house, not sure what to make of the woman.

***

'I'm under no illusion,' Marjorie Fortescue said. While Tremayne was with the woman's sister-in-law, Clare was ensconced in a conservatory at the back of the Fortescue mansion. It was the first time she had seen it, and she was impressed. The coldness of the main house transfused into a bright and warm place full of plants that had no right to grow in an English climate.

In front of Clare, a bottle of red wine, not a restaurant's house wine tasting of tannin, but a vintage that she would not buy due to its cost.

'It's magnificent,' Clare said.

'Are you a connoisseur?' her ladyship said.

'An enthusiastic amateur.'

'Your husband is a good man.'

'He is, but I'm not here as his wife. I'm here investigating a homicide, two in fact, hopeful there's not to be a third.'

'What do you mean?'

'Sally died due to her knowing about Red Rose and the substitution, either that or it's more convoluted.'

'This place?'

'That's it. You didn't want her, no more than your sister-in-law.'

'Bunty's opinion is of no importance.'

'Legally, it's not. But she's a Fortescue. The family name is all that matters to her, preserving the legacy.'

'It is for me too.'

'If Andrew had been alive?'

'He would have made the decisions, guided by a strong and resolute woman.'

'You or Sally Kirkland? That's an ambiguous statement, almost condemns you.'

'Either. It's strange, isn't it? I was of inferior stock when I married Bernard, but with time, I became accepted, seen as one of them.'

'Not by Bunty.'

'Bunty was not close to my husband. He couldn't stand her, told her once to leave the house, never come back.'

'How many years ago?'

'I hadn't seen her here for close on twenty-five years when she knocked on the door after Bernard died.'

'She didn't come here when Andrew died?'

'She phoned, that's all.'

'Salisbury is a small place; surely, you must have bumped into her from time to time.'

'Not often, but sometimes. We'd make small talk, have a coffee together, but nothing more, nothing mentioned about Bernard.'

'And now she wants money from you?'

'Yes.'

'Jeremy Liston?'

'People don't concern him, only money.'

'He would be interested in you. Has he made that clear?'

'He has, but I said something about not leaving your rubbish in your backyard.'

The Horse's Mouth

'Are you saying you wouldn't sleep with him?'

'Not entirely relevant,' Marjorie Fortescue said as she topped up Clare's glass.

'We've got to know Liston over the last few weeks. He's been honest, telling us that he's attractive to women and he enjoys their company. He would have mistreated you.'

'Sergeant, my past may have been chequered, but I'll do nothing to disgrace the name of Fortescue. If, as they would say, I wanted to screw around, I'd check into a hotel in the Caribbean or the Maldives, put out the welcome mat.'

Clare laughed. It was two glasses now, and she was only a one glass person, but the wine was like velvet and easy to drink, more alcoholic than a cheap bottle of Beaujolais.

'Do you trust Jeremy Liston?' Clare said, resolving to drink less.

'Claude Fortescue, I trust.'

'That's not an answer.'

'It is. Claude will deal with the legal side of it. I'll deal with Liston and Claude's wife.'

'You could seduce him.'

'If Jeremy was emotional, but he isn't. That won't occur. I've made that clear to him.'

'He'll keep trying.'

'As long as I keep the bait dangling. It will give me an advantage. You must know that.'

Clare hadn't indulged in such behaviour, but yes, she did.

'Bunty Fortescue?'

'I'm going over the figures with Jeremy. How much I'll give her depends on what the result is.'

'For doing nothing.'

'Apart from me, she's the only one of the Fortescues with any claim, however tenuous. Poor Claude, a country lawyer, struggling to get by. Bunty sees it as all-important, so do I.'

'Could she cause trouble?'

'She knows this place as well as I do. She could bring in the heritage council, lobby the city council, including your husband.'

'She already has.' Clare regretted mentioning the woman's acrimonious visit to Clive.

'That's Bunty. What with the council and then the heritage council, and petitioning the villages near here, she could slow us down for a long time. Better just to let her have a percentage. And besides, I'm considering one of the cottages on the estate for her to live in.'

'Would she want it?'

'More than anything. It's the sweetener to seal the deal. And besides, I intend to take long and lazy trips overseas. She'll keep Liston on his toes, look after the house.'

'You trust her?'

'The family name, enough money, living on the estate, something denied by Bernard. Yes, I would trust her.'

'While you're travelling the world, welcome mat under your arm.'

'Not there, but yes.'

Both women laughed, both a little drunk.

Clare thought she was not acting professionally, but it did not worry her. After all, Lady Fortescue's honesty was refreshing.

'If you died, your sister-in-law would inherit?'

'She would.'

'Doesn't that bring in a complication?'

The Horse's Mouth

'How? If I died, you'd have a motive.'

'Your husband died soon after Andrew's death. Was it grief?'

'Check with his doctor, but he had only a few months at the most. He was fifteen years older than me, and not in good health for several years. A heavy smoker when he was younger, a secret drinker late at night in his study.'

'My husband is sixteen years older than me,' Clare said.

'The age difference can be a problem, the waning libido.'

There was an earthiness about Marjorie Fortescue's conversation that Clare would have found unsettling had she not been drinking.

'We're fine,' Clare said, hoping that that would be the last mentioned on the subject.

'You're not the type to talk about such things, are you?'

Clare ignored the question. 'If your husband had not been so ill, what would he have done after Andrew's death?'

'He would have become introspective, rarely leaving his study. Similar to Sherlock Holmes on hearing of the death of Irene Adler.'

'Morphine?'

'It was whisky with Bernard.'

'He was dying, didn't he try to put his affairs in order?'

'Bernard believed in his position in society and his title. It was not for him to sully himself with the unpleasant business of dealing with tradesman and concerning himself about the bailiff at the door. Unfortunately, he wasn't a realist.'

'It's been left to you to deal with the mess.'

'It's not a mess, just an annoyance. If he had maintained us on a sound financial basis, you and I wouldn't be here drinking wine.'

'You've always seemed unaffected by your son's passing,' Clare said.

'If a man shows no emotion, that's fine. But a woman is meant to break down, cry endlessly.'

'Supposedly.'

'That's what men want, but women can pretend when they have to. I loved my son, and Sally would have looked after him, but neither are here now, nor is my husband. Life goes on regardless, and I intend to keep going.'

'The welcome mat at your side.'

'For a while. Then I'll come back here, open the occasional village fete, go to the theatre, walk the dogs in the garden.'

'And seduce Jeremy Liston.'

'Who knows,' Lady Fortescue said.

Chapter 24

Tremayne and Clare had spoken briefly to Gwen Fairweather at Ian Swift's office. In contrast to her brother, Chris, she was neatly dressed, in a floral dress, and pleasant company.

'Chris was always that way, even when he was young,' Gwen said. 'I'm older than him, almost eight years.'

'It's about your boss,' Tremayne said.

'He's been good to Chris and me.'

'Loyalty's an admirable quality,' Clare said. She found the woman endearing, a kindly disposition about her. The three were sitting in a café across from where Gwen worked.

'I always come here, every day,' Gwen said.

Tremayne, not predisposed to idle chat and a place that didn't serve beer, ate his sandwich. And besides, his sergeant was the best person to engage with the woman.

'Your brother and Swift?' Clare said as she put down her second cup of coffee. Her head still throbbed and her voice had a harshness about it after drinking a bottle of wine with Marjorie Fortescue the previous day.

'Our parents died young, a car accident. Chris was fourteen, doing well at school, although he was a little eccentric, fussing over this and that, not communicative, not in the normal sense. None of the usual schoolyard banter, no bringing a friend home for the night, he was otherwise—'

'Clean?' Tremayne interjected.

Gwen laughed out loud, almost spilt the cup of tea she was holding. 'Strange, isn't it? That was Ian's first comment when he met Chris or his lack of cleanliness.'

'His second?' Clare asked. She thought that Tremayne had spoken inappropriately, but Gwen had brushed it off, seen the humour.

'Next time he comes in here, make sure he has a shower first.'

'Did he?'

'His idea of a shower. Soap on the face, a dab under the arms.'

'Yours?'

'Not mine, but our father had a phobia about washing, something to do with the idea that people in the past believed that a clean skin opens up the pores to disease. Nonsense, I know, but he worked on the land, and rarely came into contact with people, a reclusive personality.'

'If he did?'

'Our mother would stand over him while he got in the bath, bubbles as well. You should have heard his comment about how he smelled afterwards.'

'Smelling like a tart out of a French bordello?'

'Worse than that, but more or less correct. Our father had a colourful turn of phrase, and he was devoted to our mother, to us. Chris adored him, so did I, but when they died, Chris became worse, truanting from school.'

'How about you? It must have affected you?'

'I was twenty-one. I had a steady boyfriend, and he helped me through it.'

'Where is he now?'

'Long gone. There's no man in my life. None of them wants the burden of Chris.'

'Should he be in an institution for his own sake?' Tremayne said.

'I know to other people he's weird, and maybe he is, but he's my brother, and if it hadn't been for our parents dying while he was so young, who knows what he might have achieved,' Gwen said.

'Clever?' Clare said.

'Exceptionally bright, IQ off the scale.'

'You're aware of our interest in your boss and Chris?'

'You'd not be the first. Ian's a hardworking and decent man, very smart, personable. He brings out admiration in some, loathing in others, disbelief from a few.'

'The disbelief interests us more,' Tremayne said.

'People can be cruel. Ian, he's no oil painting, and he knows it, but money and women are attracted to him like a fly is to flypaper.'

'Including you?' Clare asked. After all, Gwen Fairweather was closer to Swift's age, and she had a cherubic round face, the look of a woman that would have been married.

'Ian likes them younger. And besides, his charm doesn't work on me.'

'Why?' Tremayne asked. 'It seems to work on others with no problem.'

'Ian is a man to take in short doses. Work with him, and you'd understand.'

'I would,' Clare said.

'If you want to be wined and dined, weekends away, then Ian's your man. However, if you want a ring on the finger, he's not for you.'

'You want the ring?'

'More than anything, but with Ian, that's not going to happen.'

'We're digressing,' Tremayne said. 'Our problem is that we believe someone very savvy with computers is using them for criminal purposes.'

'Chris wouldn't do something like that.'

'He would if it was a challenge. Would he be skilled enough?'

'Have you asked him?'

'Not in as many words. To be honest, Sergeant Yarwood and I are out of our depth on this one,' Tremayne said.

'Do you believe Ian is using Chris for something illegal?' Gwen said.

'We've considered the probability. If he has committed a crime, it may be unintentional on Chris's part, not cognisant of the fact.'

'Sally Kirkland? Is this to do with her?'

'She's one that has died.'

'Ian took her out a few times, and she came into the office once or twice.'

'His reaction?' Clare asked.

'Polite.'

'He didn't like the women in his office?'

'He used to talk to me about it. The fun of the chase, the conquest and then the slow decline into nothingness.'

'A cold fish?'

'He never mistreated them, nor did he profess unrequited love. But that's how women are wired, including your sergeant.'

'That's true with Yarwood,' Tremayne said, 'but she found someone, you haven't. It must upset you.'

'Not as much as it once did,' Gwen said.

The Horse's Mouth

'Disregarding what you've said, if Ian asked you out, would you go?' Clare could see a sad woman who professed contentment where there was none.

'I wouldn't go as one of his floozies.'

'If he was serious, asked you to marry him?' Tremayne asked.

'I would say yes.'

'Do you love him?' Clare asked.

'Not the teenage notion of endless passion, but two people sharing a journey through life, then yes.'

'You make it sound like a Mills and Boon novel.'

'Or straight from the mouth of Barbara Cartland,' Tremayne said.

'She was sugary and sweet,' Gwen said. 'One day, Ian will settle down. I hope I'm there when he does.'

'Then work with us. If Ian's involved, or Chris is, we'll find out the truth. We always do,' Clare said.

'I can't believe it. I spend too much time with both to be fooled.'

'Your brother first. Talk to him, ask him what he's been up to.'

'I'm not an expert, and I'm certainly not as smart as Chris. I may not understand what he tells me.'

'Do what you can. It's up to you to prove their innocence.'

'Or their guilt.'

'Gwen, if you have faith in them, you have to help us,' Tremayne said.

'The sooner this is wrapped up, the sooner we'll all sleep easy.' Clare said.

'I won't, not tonight,' Ian Swift's PA said as she got up from her chair and walked back to her office.

Clare felt sadness for the woman, burdened with her brother, in love with a man who did not love her in return.

***

Two days passed; two days in the office, making phone calls, researching on the internet, and dealing with the paperwork.

Gwen Fairweather had phoned Clare twice; the first time to express her concern, the second time to let her know she had met with her brother and it would take time to get him to talk. Clare understood why.

After all, Gwen's brother was brilliant, and prying and probing, asking questions which would have been out of character for his sister, would have made him clam up. The fear that she had an ulterior motive, a possible move to a mental institution, a talk with a psychiatrist, anything to get him out of the house.

As Gwen had told Clare, the house had belonged to their parents, and she had gladly left him there, while she found a small place nearer to her workplace. But Chris was not always the easiest to deal with, and sometimes she was a little frightened of him, even though he had never harmed her.

The visit to Lady Fortescue hadn't been planned. It was late in the evening, sixteen minutes after ten, when Tremayne and Clare pulled up in front of the house.

'I'm not sure how to say this,' Marjorie Fortescue said.

'Say what?' Clare asked.

The three stood at the bottom of an impressive staircase up to the first floor, her ladyship wrapped in a fur coat.

The Horse's Mouth

'I'm not certain that Andrew committed suicide.'

'We had the crime scene investigators check out his room, found no evidence of foul play,' Tremayne said.

'You'll need to be more specific,' Clare said.

'It was Bunty, she was here, and so was Jeremy Liston.'

'When?'

'They left just before I phoned you.'

'An agreed meeting?'

'I wanted to be open with Bunty, so I invited her. Jeremy didn't know before she turned up at the door.'

'Angry?'

'More than I expected. I'm not sure if I've made the right decision. I don't know if I can trust Jeremy.'

'You were leaving it to Claude Fortescue to keep him under control.'

'Can I trust him? Can I trust Bunty? Who can I trust?'

For a woman in control of her emotions and self-aware, Tremayne thought she was giving a good impression of a dithering personality.

'We can't help you there,' Clare said. 'We're here because you believe Andrew didn't commit suicide, but the gardener saw him in the window, saw him jump.'

'Upton's eyesight's not the best, not that he'd tell you.'

'We're inclined to hold to suicide,' Tremayne said, 'not because we don't want another murder to deal with, but the CSIs are thorough. If someone had pushed him, that's one thing, but he was standing in the window.'

'You've seen the room, seen the size of the window, how it opens full length, down to the floor apart from a small rise of six inches.'

'He was standing on that rise.'

'Was he?'

'If he wasn't, the CSIs should have found evidence of tripping, scuff marks.'

'Andrew was going to marry Sally. Maybe Jeremy wanted to marry her instead.'

'That makes no sense,' Clare said.

'He can still get angry. Isn't that an emotion?' Marjorie said.

'A negative emotion, short duration,' Tremayne said. 'I'm not a psychiatrist, but most people will swear if they drop a weight on their foot. I don't see how we can believe Liston was in love with Sally Kirkland.'

'After all, we know Sally wasn't going to marry Andrew for love,' Clare said.

'Andrew always knew she was not in love with him.'

'Was he in love with her?'

'A weak man needs a strong woman.'

'That's not an answer.'

'Andrew loved her, but no more than Bernard loved me or I loved him.'

'It hardly leads to an enduring relationship,' Clare said.

'Maintaining the bloodline, retaining a strategic advantage, marrying for prestige and wealth, they're all important.'

'Not marrying the riff-raff,' Tremayne said.

'My background was hardly upper class or aristocratic,' Marjorie said.

The three climbed the stairs, her ladyship leading the way. She strode up two steps at a time, Tremayne kept to one and held on to the railing.

The Horse's Mouth

'It's here,' Marjorie Fortescue said as she went over to the bookcase in one corner of Andrew's bedroom.

On the third shelf, two books in, she grabbed the top of a book, pulled it back; a metallic sound could be heard. Taking hold of the right-hand side of the bookcase, she pulled it forward.

Tremayne peered into the space revealed, saw a door and behind it a narrow staircase.

'Why?' Clare asked.

'Intrigue, a place where the mistress could enter, or a disreputable character could meet with the lord,' Marjorie said. 'Or maybe it was just a fashion, the same as people want a swimming pool.'

'Not in this climate,' Tremayne said.

'There's one at the back of the house, covered and heated.'

The woman was a contradiction, Tremayne knew. On the one hand, she was willing to discuss her lowly background, and then in the next breath, boast about the title and the house and the prestige they both gave. She was, he decided, a snob who looked down on them, or at least him. After all, his sergeant was married to the mayor of Salisbury, and with that came prestige. The CSIs would be making a return visit, and the narrow and uninviting staircase would be checked.

'How long have you known about this?' Clare said as she peered down the hidden staircase.

'Bernard snuck me in a few times before we were married.'

'Where does it lead to?'

'There's a hidden door close to the servants' entry.'

'You didn't think it important to mention it when Andrew died?'

'I thought it was suicide, but it was Bunty who caused Jeremy to mention it.'

'Why her?'

'She was arguing with Jeremy, called him a son of a bitch, only interested in sleeping with me, using the land as a pretence.'

'Nothing she said, so far, that's not true to some extent,' Clare said.

'Bunty knew of the hidden staircase, but I didn't know that Jeremy did.'

'Did he mention it?'

'In the heat of the moment, "what do you take me for, sneaking into the house, up to Marjorie's room through that hidden staircase".'

'What did she say? What did you say?'

'Bunty was too angry for it to register, and as for me, I didn't overthink it at the time, but after they had left I did, and then I phoned you.'

Chapter 25

Claude Fortescue checked through the legal agreement he had prepared for Marjorie. It had been typed up by his legal secretary, a woman who had worked for him the last twenty-five years, although he still addressed her as Mrs Ruxton. She lived with her husband in a small bungalow close to the river that flowed through the village. Apart from the smell of carbolic soap, and that she always wore a blue jacket and skirt with a white blouse, he knew little about her.

She was discreet, almost invisible in the outer office, hidden behind a pile of papers and photos of her children and grandchildren, and Fortescue knew she would never disclose the contents of the document she had just typed.

Fortescue ran his finger slowly down each page, highlighting anomalies, ambiguities that might be open to interpretation, an area of dispute if anything soured in the business relationship or the development failed, or did not attain the profit expected.

He knew he was a supercilious man. To him, the development was ambitious, but then, Marjorie, his sister-in-law, was a woman of character, and apart from her humble beginnings, was a welcome addition to the family, or what remained of it.

Claude had grown up with Bernard, spent holidays at the mansion, loathed him, first as a child and then as a man. One was privileged; the other was the offspring of a minor branch of the family. They had even shared a dormitory at the endless schools they had attended – Bernard, the dullard; Claude, the academically gifted.

It was he that deserved the title, but he was only the third cousin: a worthy friend, but no more.

That was why he and Bernard rarely met over the years, although twice in the week leading up to his lordship's death. He should have told Bunty, but she'd not understand.

He struck out a line on the document, no reason to leave it there. Mrs Ruxton would take it from him after he had finished, retype it, add a file number, and present it to him. The document was twenty-one pages long and likely to get longer.

Bunty had wanted to look at it before Marjorie and the obnoxious Liston. He was a lawyer in the office, a husband at home. What she wanted; she wasn't going to get.

He didn't trust Liston, no more than Bernard.

A week before Andrew had died, the ailing lord had made a final and fateful decision. He was to remove the right of ownership from his son, allow his wife to take control of the estate. Andrew could have the title and sufficient money to live a frivolous life if he so cared, even to marry the social-climbing Kirkland woman, but Marjorie, Lady Fortescue, would be in charge.

And now, all were dead, except Marjorie and Bunty, and Bernard Fortescue had never signed the final document. He wished that Bunty was dead as well.

He dismissed the thought from his mind, poured himself a glass of red wine, and sat back on his chair, reflecting on when he had met his wife, the two of them children.

She had been a horror back then, always wanting to play with him and Bernard, throwing a tantrum if she

The Horse's Mouth

didn't get her way, and then during their teens, she changed, blossoming out into a fine-looking woman, although not beautiful as Marjorie was when he first met her.

As Bernard had said when he had been at the house one day, the two men in their twenties, Claude the elder by three months, 'Marry Bunty. She's not a bad sort, and she's one of us. If you marry someone else, who knows where it'll lead, and let's be honest, Claude, you may well be bright, but you're no mover and shaker.'

It was a true statement, Claude had known. It was the quiet life that he craved, to be one with his books and his writing, to study as he wanted. And that had been his life since then, Bunty by his side, she frustrated by his indifference and he, by her passionless frigidity. She found horses; he found tranquillity.

And now when his life was slowing down, the added complication of satisfying his wife's wishes, not sure how to. He had made it clear that he would not act in that manner, the reason she was not talking to him again, a situation that pleased him.

In the other office the ever-loyal Mrs Ruxton, a woman whose life was calm and ordered, with a husband who brought home a minimal salary, and at the estate, the maturing Marjorie, her beauty still intact. And what did his wife offer, apart from a cold shoulder, a bare acknowledgement of his presence, not even a son or a daughter?

Claude turned the page on the document and struck through three lines. It would be another five to six days before it was to his satisfaction; five to six days where he could stay late in the office, avoiding the inquisition at home. He poured himself another glass of wine, saw that the bottle was nearly empty. It wouldn't be the last one, not that night.

***

Les Daniels had spent his last few years in a room at the top of two flights of stairs, living on his own, enjoying the occasional cigarette to the bane of the landlady, and drinking himself into a stupor most nights.

'What more can I tell you?' Daniels' landlady said to Tremayne.

After a few days dealing with the upper echelons of society, Tremayne, whose views were more socialist than he cared to admit, relished the opportunity to be with people who called a spade a spade and didn't judge people by a preconception of class and entitlement.

'He had a lot of money in his bank account,' Tremayne said.

'He didn't waste it if that's what you mean,' the old woman, not even up to his shoulders, said.

'It was more than that. He had enough to have moved out of here, bought himself a place.'

'Maybe he was happy here, or couldn't have been bothered. Owning a place is a millstone around your neck. You'd know that, Inspector.'

Tremayne did, especially after Jean had moved out all those years past. He had managed to hold on to the place, and now it was paid off, and Jean, back with him and staying, took responsibility for dealing with the bills and the maintenance. He knew that if it hadn't been for her, he would have considered selling it, finding somewhere quiet and cheap, just paying the rent, no one to pass his legacy on to when his time came.

'I do,' Tremayne said. 'You manage well.'

'If I didn't, who else would?'

'Family?'

'When I die, they'll be here.'

'You're not close?'

'A sister who looks down on me, a son who doesn't even remember my birthday, but then his wife's a stuck-up bitch, on this committee and that, always attempting to speak posh, sounding as if she had a plum in her mouth.'

'You've maintained your humour,' Tremayne said. 'What about Daniels' room?'

'I'll not rent it out again, bad vibes.'

'Do you believe in ghosts, the supernatural, that sort of thing?'

'Not me, but people talk. I'd have to tell whoever's interested that someone died in the room. What sort of tenant do you think I'd get?'

'The ghoulish.'

'Les wasn't a bad man, just rough around the edges and he was a drinker, as well as a smoker, neither of which I approve of, and he knew the rules.'

'He ignored them?'

'He conveniently forgot, but he'd been here for a long time, paid his rent, helped me to put the rubbish out, that sort of thing. I can't say I ever knew him that well, but he came to be a friend.'

'The day he died,' Tremayne asked. 'What can you remember?'

'I was out when it happened.'

'Anything unusual in Daniels, in the time leading up to his death?'

'He seemed sort of vague, but I gave no thought to it.'

'Any visitors?'

'I saw someone outside a couple of days before he died. Les didn't seem happy to see him.'

'You keep a watch on the street?'

'I'm not a busybody if that's what you're thinking. It was a Friday, and if he's around, I make a meal for him, not any other day, though.'

'What did you see?' Tremayne said.

'This person, you've not mentioned him before.'

'I probably forgot. Sometimes I do.'

The woman, whereas her speech was lively, was slow in her movements, and Tremayne remembered that his mother had become forgetful at that age. What was important now was to find out who she had seen.

'Do you know who the man was?'

'I watch him on the television, not that I understand much of what he's saying.'

'Ian Swift?'

'Yes, Ian. He was in the year above my son at school, and look where he is now.'

'Your son?'

'Not him. Left school, barely literate, ended up in an engineering company down in Southampton.'

'That's a few years back. What about now?'

'At least he had the good sense to marry the boss's daughter, get her pregnant, or if you ask me, she was that way before the marriage.'

'Your son has done well for himself,' Tremayne said. It wasn't only the aristocracy who bettered themselves by suitable marriages.

'She keeps him under control.'

Tremayne could tell that the mother and the daughter-in-law didn't get on, the reason her son kept away.

'Did you ask Les afterwards about Swift?'

'I don't pry. And besides, he wouldn't have told me, and as for Ian Swift...'

'What about him?'

'Charming to your face, a total bastard otherwise.'

Tremayne was shocked by the woman's opinion, but he had to agree with her summation of the local celebrity, a man who remained on the periphery but was smarter than all the other players. Why he was in the street face-to-face with Daniels was a mystery that would need to be addressed.

Ian Swift had more questions to answer.

Chapter 26

Gwen Fairweather was upset when Tremayne and Clare walked into her office. 'Ian's not pleased that I've been speaking to you,' she said.

'We've some questions for him,' Tremayne's reply. The last thing on his mind was whether Swift was upset or not, although he had a preference for the former.

'You did nothing wrong,' Clare said.

'I didn't think so, and I've had a chat with Chris.'

Ian Swift was in the adjoining office, but for the present, Gwen Fairweather was of more interest.

'What did he say?' Tremayne said as he took a seat.

'He was vague, spoke to me about how complicated hacking was, and even if he could, which I know he can, covering up his tracks was even harder, and as to moving money from one place to another without their knowledge, he didn't have the skill.'

'Do you believe him?'

'On the money, never interested him. As long as he can get by, and he leaves the bill paying to me, he doesn't bother.'

'If he was?' Clare asked.

'He'd have no trouble. There's no point in my lying to you, is there?'

'None at all,' Tremayne said.

The door from the other office burst open, a red-faced man walking through.

'Inspector Tremayne, either you've got a warrant or you're out of order,' Swift said.

The Horse's Mouth

'That's a mighty fine temper you've got there, Swift,' Tremayne said.

'Your scurrilous accusations are not appreciated.'

Gwen buried her face behind the large monitor on her desk; Clare stayed neutral, taking note of the two men, watching a battle of the titans, interested in the outcome, sure that Tremayne wouldn't accept a losing position.

'I suggest we relocate to your office,' Tremayne said.

'Here's as fine as anywhere else.' The initial fire in Swift had been quenched, although his hands were shaking, and there were beads of sweat on his forehead.

'Suit yourself,' Tremayne said. 'If you'd checked, you would know that we have not accused you of any crime. Conjecture on our part, a need to understand if you or anyone else has been playing a dangerous game, attempting to cheat people, good or criminal, out of their money.'

'Why would I be bothered? I've got enough.'

'Greed is a great motivator. The wealthy always want more, a way of keeping score. You should know that better than anyone else.'

'Very well, my office.'

'A wise move,' Tremayne said.

Clare went over to Gwen, put an arm around her shoulder. 'It'll be fine,' she said.

Gwen looked up, a tear in her eye. 'Will it? Chris could be involved.'

'His involvement may not be with criminal intent, although if your boss is involved, then you'll be looking for another job.'

'I hope he isn't.'

'Not so easy, is it? The man you love not seeing you for your worth; a brother who impacts on your life.'

'Life wasn't meant to be easy. I'm not sure who said it, but it's true.'

Clare had known difficulties in her life, the same as everyone else, but she wasn't about to tell the woman. She had told Kim, Clive's daughter, as she had wanted to, but the violent death of someone she had loved, yet who had given his life for hers, was not a story she wanted to recount again or to remember.

'We take the good with the bad,' Clare said.

'Not if Chris is in prison.'

'I don't think it would be a custodial sentence for him.'

'An institution. That would be worse,' Gwen said.

Clare left the weeping Gwen and joined Tremayne and Swift. An uneasy peace had settled over the room,

'Tremayne knows my position,' Swift said to Clare.

'Do I?' Tremayne looked back at Swift.

'I have a reputation to maintain. Even now, guilt by association is causing concern for the television station where I have my fortnightly thirty minutes, and some of the syndicated radio stations that pick up my radio broadcast are rescheduling.'

'It would be better if you help us wrap this up,' Clare said.

'I don't see how. You badgered Gwen, and she has enough to deal with, what with Chris.'

'And you?' Tremayne said.

'We've been together for a long time; she knows what I need. Invaluable, that's what she is.'

The Horse's Mouth

'Two days before Les Daniels died, you met him not far from where he lived, had a heated exchange,' Tremayne said.

'That's true,' Swift said.

'Why?'

'Is this relevant?'

'Swift, you know it is.'

'Daniels?'

'He had no reason to kill Sally Kirkland, although he liked her, nothing he could do about it,' Tremayne said.

'That old tale about a horse maiming him. The man had more than his fair share of drinks on that, and he could tell it well, make you want to cross your legs and cringe,' Swift said.

'You don't believe it was true?'

'No one did.'

'We obtained his medical records, and an autopsy confirmed it,' Clare said.

'Then he was entitled to those drinks. Not much fun going through life seeing something you wanted, not able to have it.'

'Why did you confront Daniels?' Tremayne asked.

Swift stood up, walked around the room. Neither Tremayne nor Clare spoke.

Swift went to the door, opened it, and said to Gwen, 'Three teas if you can.'

'You upset her,' Clare said after Swift returned and sat at his desk.

'Gwen's tougher than that. We're like an old married couple, can't live with each other, can't live without.'

Clare didn't appreciate the analogy. Besides, Gwen's affection for the man was known, but he had not reciprocated and was unlikely to, even though he could be involving her brother in a dangerous pursuit, the type that makes some very rich, others very dead.

'Gwen's brother?'

'Obsessed, a computer nerd, more interested in women on a screen than cleaning himself up and finding the real thing.'

'Swift,' Tremayne said, 'we've been through this once before.'

'Twice,' Swift replied.

'How many times doesn't matter. We asked Gwen to find out from her brother, whether he's been hacking for someone, accessing information.'

'She'll not tell you.'

'Why?' Clare said.

'She'll protect him.'

'And you?'

'That's what loyalty does. You look out for the person.'

'Even if their criminal actions are responsible for people dying?'

'If – and you're stretching a long bow.'

'We keep coming back to you,' Tremayne said.

'If, and I'm not admitting to anything, I was involved, would I be so visible?'

'That's for you to answer.'

Clare looked for the signs that Swift was either lying or embarrassed or just being evasive.

'Whether it's criminal or not is open to debate. Online gambling, the more reputable companies, those registered in the UK and a couple of other countries, are transparent. But there are a lot more, and God knows where they're based.'

'Hazard a guess.'

'Russia, China, the Middle East, for starters, but nobody would know for sure. Chris Fairweather would know better than me, but they would be hidden in plain sight, concealed behind firewalls and internet protocols, websites registered in another country.'

'Hidden here in the UK, in Salisbury?'

'Do you believe that I, smart enough to understand the concept, smart enough to understand the complexity of what you're suggesting, and a sad, unshaven computer nerd would be able to pull this off?'

'You've checked this out?'

'I have.'

'You never mentioned this before.'

'I'll send you a copy of a radio broadcast I did last year.'

'We've heard a few,' Clare said.

'Not this one. The pitfalls of get-rich-quick schemes, playing the commodities market, pressing the buttons on a slot machine, betting on horses and greyhounds. Even without crime, the percentages are stacked, and in most jurisdictions by the government. Gamble for pleasure with money you can afford to lose, but that's it. It's a mug's game, suited to the desperate, not the astute.'

'Les Daniels?' Tremayne had heard enough of Swift's diatribe. The man could talk ad infinitum, boring anyone listening into mental apathy.

'I blamed him for Sally Kirkland's death.'

'Proof?'

'It seemed that you and your sergeant were missing the point, and Sally hadn't deserved to die. I wanted him to confess.'

'Your evidence?'

'Sally had to be involved. She was horse mad. And you know what happens to retired racehorses, those that don't make the grade?'

'I do,' Clare said.

'You accused him of killing her.'

'Whether by his hand or not, it doesn't excuse Daniels' culpability.'

'What you're saying is that Daniels had placed her in danger.'

'She was protecting the horse.'

'Could Barton Kirkland have been involved?' Clare asked.

'He would have known,' Swift said.

The Horse's Mouth

Chapter 27

At twenty years of age, Jack Doyle was a seasoned jockey, a veteran of over four hundred races in two and a half years.

To Clare, the young man would have passed for fourteen. He was slender, short, almost emaciated, the necessary rigour of keeping the weight off.

'Never touch the stuff,' Doyle said as he and Clare sat down in a pub.

'Cigarettes?'

'Not at all. I need to keep myself fit. A big race this week. I've ridden the horse before, placed third behind Brooklyn Boy.'

'You came second in the Derby last year,' Clare said. 'That's one of the most prestigious races in the country. It was a good result.'

'Not good enough. It was my fault; I'll admit to it. I was on the inside; shouldn't have been there, and on the home straight, I'm boxed in, unable to give my horse the space it needed. It was a dent to my career, that's why I'm back at the regionals.'

'I lost money on that race,' Tremayne said.

'You bet on my horse?'

'Mine limped in behind yours.'

'A fan of horse racing?' Doyle asked.

'I follow it, have the occasional bet. That's why I was at Salisbury racecourse that day.'

'You were riding Red Rose. What did you think?' Clare said.

'I didn't overthink it. I rode the horse a couple of times last year. I won one of the races, came third in the other, but the course wasn't to the horse's liking.'

'Salisbury?'

'Red Rose was fine, ran well, and it was a good win, but then…'

'A stewards' enquiry. Were you asked to give evidence?'

'I was, not that I had anything to say. To me, I was riding Red Rose, not Scarlet Soleil.'

'You must have known,' Clare said.

'I arrived late at the racecourse, only had time to put on my colours, talk to Mr Kirkland, say hello to his daughter, and then mount the animal.'

'When Sally Kirkland died?'

'Straight after the race, long enough for a shower and a change of clothes, I was off. I wasn't there when they found her.'

'Off where?' Clare asked.

A broad smile came over Doyle's face. 'You're only young once, that's what my father used to say.'

'Worthwhile?' Tremayne asked as he drank his beer. Clare had a glass of wine, Doyle kept to orange juice.

'You bet it was. It was later that night that I heard about Sally.'

'How?'

'One of the stewards phoned me up, got the number from her father.'

'I know they found no case against you,' Tremayne said. 'However, we're still struggling to find a reason why the horse was changed.'

'They cautioned about my excessive use of the whip, but I did my job, made sure of a win, which was what Kirkland wanted.'

'Les Daniels told me to bet on you.'

'I couldn't have done it if the horse hadn't been willing.'

'You could have lost, though, if you had wanted.'

'I'd not do that. A few more good wins and I'll have another crack at the Derby or maybe another major race at Epsom, even Ascot.'

'And now?'

'It depends on what you find out, but I did nothing wrong, won the race, even if it was the wrong horse.'

'Why the substitution, Jack?' Clare said.

'Maybe the horse had to run, a lot of money staked on it. What about Red Rose? In good health, when you found him?'

'It was, the same as Scarlet Soleil, and now both of them are dead.'

'Do you know jockeys who would throw a win?' Tremayne asked.

'Not too many, but it's easier at the regional meetings.'

'Would you if your career doesn't work out?'

'Not me,' Doyle said.

'Good money?' Clare asked.

'If you win a major race, it can be. If you don't, it's a living, enough to get by, but I'm not extravagant. A little house in the country, a few acres, and I'll be fine.'

***

Grim, dark and grey, that was how Tremayne summed up the day. An ultimatum from Superintendent Moulton to wrap up the case – pressure from above – or he would bring in help from outside of the area to supplement the Homicide team.

Clare understood the sentiment, if not in agreement with how Moulton had presented himself in Homicide and given the facts to Tremayne, a man intimidated by very few. Yet the threat of retirement or being side-lined filled the man with dread.

'We can still do this,' Clare said after Moulton had left.

'With what?' Tremayne's reaction had a negative undertone to it which Clare didn't like. 'He's given us three days to arrest someone, or else.'

'Anyone we know?'

'I've heard of him. A chief inspector from Exeter, not someone you'd warm to, and besides, you're in line to take over from me. The last thing we need is some high-flying, lick-your-boots type.'

'Is he?' Clare asked. 'Or is it that you're just tired of the superintendent and the internal politics?'

'Policing is still about being out there on the street, using experience and dogged determination to follow through on every angle, leaving no stone unturned. And as for their team-building exercises, leave me out.'

'I'll agree with the team-building exercises,' Clare said. 'But a lot can be done in the office, behind a computer screen, and you know it.'

'You've made your point, but what are we going to do about these murders?'

'Double our efforts, push harder, make someone sweat.'

'Swift's a tough nut to crack, and he'll not bend under pressure, nor will Marjorie Fortescue, and she's still in the race.'

'A pun?'

'It could be. Who have we got? There's Barry Vincent, holding back, Ian Swift on the outside, not far behind Marjorie Fortescue, Chris Fairweather barely out of the stalls, his sister applying the whip to his mount.'

'Bunty Fortescue, where is she?'

'On the inside, trying for the lead, doing a Les Daniels, losing at the last hurdle.'

'What hurdle?'

'Who's the underdog, or in this case, the under horse?'

'Claude Fortescue, Bunty's husband and her ladyship's lawyer. What about him? Does he have the strength of character of either his wife or his sister-in-law? Is he as competent as everyone says he is? After all, he's not made his mark, a country lawyer dealing in conveyancing and minor disputes, the occasional youth in trouble.'

'Sharper than he appears?'

'Or duller.'

'Chris Fairweather wouldn't present too much of a problem, not if we removed him from his comfort zone,' Clare said.

'He might point the finger at Ian Swift, bring us closer to the truth, but Fairweather hasn't murdered anyone. And Swift confronted Daniels, accused him of being instrumental in Sally's death.'

'Not convincing.'

'A pack of lies, that's Swift. He wasn't remonstrating with Daniels over Sally Kirkland; more likely because Daniels had erred, lost him a bundle of money.'

'Or winnings? You got your bet back from Blakely.'

'I did, but I had to hound him for it. It didn't stay with me for long. I put it on another sure-fire winner.'

'Barely lit,' Clare said. Tremayne was back to his old self. His mind was working overtime, weighing up the pros and cons, coming to a conclusion, a way forward.

'At least I had the satisfaction of seeing it run around the course.'

'Who do we talk to first?'

'Bunty's husband, but we need him alone. If she's there, she'll attempt to monopolise the situation.'

***

'Do you intend to involve my brother?' Gwen Fairweather said. The location, Ian Swift's office; the time, nine in the evening.

In the office that day, apart from a couple of phone calls, Swift had disconnected from the outside world. A script to prepare for his next television programme; the subject, the perils of negative gearing.

Gwen had helped him prepare it, typing it up, correcting the grammar, recommending changes. She felt that she had worked for him for so long, knew how he thought, his presentation style, and the general subject matter, that she could have prepared the script without his input. Apart from a personal account, she had access to his business accounts. The man had plenty of money, no need for any more, but he was still hungry, she knew that.

The Horse's Mouth

That was why she had pondered for a couple of days after Tremayne and Clare had put forward the possibility of Swift implicating her brother in crime. She got a bland response from Chris when she had confronted him, and then after the two police officers had spent time with Ian in his office, accusing the man directly, she saw him become angry.

'Chris may have his problems, but he's not a criminal, neither am I,' Swift had said.

'Explain the money in your account.'

'Gwen, you may have been with me for a long time, but you've no right to question me.'

'Ian, I know you're walking a tightrope, taking advantage of tax loopholes, putting your money in offshore accounts to avoid taxation.'

'A man is entitled to minimise his liabilities, maximise his assets. Everyone does it or should, even you.'

'I'll not deny that, and you did help me to secure a loan on my place after Chris took the house.'

'Why did you give it to him? It was large enough for the two of you. He could have lived with his squalor downstairs, and you could have lived upstairs in sublime solitude.'

'Are you accusing me of being a recluse? Do you think I like living on my own, not even a cat?'

'I'm not criticising. It's just unusual and unnecessary. The place is yours, not Chris's.'

'On the proviso of my parents that I would look after him.'

'The internet, the bane of personal interaction. It's not the same, talking to someone through a camera and a computer screen.'

'The money in your account?'

'It's not the first time,' Swift said. 'Large amounts come in sometimes, go out on others.'

'Tell me it's not Chris,' Gwen said.

'The police have this notion that Sally Kirkland's death and the others are somehow related to illicit gambling, fixing of horse races. They're clutching at straws, putting two and two together, coming up with the wrong answer. No doubt, someone smart…'

'As smart as Chris?'

'He's smart enough to deal with the technical side, but calculating the odds would require someone smarter.'

'You, for instance.'

'Believe me, I've not spoken to Chris about it, nor do I intend to.'

It was the first time in all the years that Gwen had worked for the man that she didn't trust him. Not that she was under any illusions about him. The man was no saint, nor did he willingly declare all his income, but then, that was his profession, advising others how to make themselves financially viable.

But to Gwen, her brother was sacrosanct, the reason she had given him the house to live in, the realisation that Chris's behaviour had a disregard for his well-being, and that it had only been computers that calmed him.

'The money?'

'I moved some money from one account to another, closed one of them down, a change in the country's banking regulations. I didn't see a reason to discuss it with you.'

'If you ever–'

'If I ever involve your brother, you'll do something.'

'I'm not sure what I mean. Chris is all I have.'

'I've never done anything contrary to his well-being, and you know it, Gwen. Why won't you believe me?'

'I do. It's just that I'm worried.'

'For Chris?' Swift said.

'For the two of you. Ian, you're dealing with the police and Inspector Tremayne's no dummy. The man's record is flawless, a dog with a bone, never gives up, and you were associated with the dead woman.'

'Don't think I haven't given it some thought. Sally meant no harm, and as for Andrew Fortescue, good to share a pint with occasionally, but not much use otherwise. But Jeremy Liston, he's capable of anything.'

'Who killed who?'

'Fortescue killed Sally, but he's dead.'

'Why haven't you told the police?'

'Tell them what? They must have figured that out; after all, the man committed suicide soon after.'

'Les Daniels?'

'He hated Barton Kirkland.'

'How do you know this?'

'Daniels liked to talk sometimes, and Kirkland told me once that he revelled in keeping his stable hand underfoot.'

'A sadistic nature?'

'Something from the past, that would be my bet, but we'll never know. No one alive to tell the tale.'

'Are you sure, cross your heart sure, that my brother isn't involved in what you're up to?' Gwen said.

'If it makes you feel any better, then I'll give you my word.'

'I hope he's not, for your sake.'

'Now, Gwen, can we get back to work. I need you to finish off the script, make sure my accounts are in order, and then how about dinner, a bottle of wine?'

The relationship with her boss had always been polite and professional, sometimes mildly flirtatious, but never crossing the line to familiarity, the promise of something else.

'Yes, I would like that,' she said, knowing full well that the man was rattled.

Chapter 28

Claude Fortescue hurried along the street, unaware that two police officers were observing him. Not only had he to deal with his usual business but that afternoon, at two, he was to meet with Marjorie and Bunty at the Fortescue mansion.

'Not an impressive man to look at,' Clare said as she drank a takeaway latte.

'We'll soon find out,' Tremayne said, taking the opportunity to smoke a cigarette.

It was a sunny morning, and Tremayne's mood had improved. However, Moulton's ultimatum of the previous day still held. If his job were up for grabs, there would be plenty vying for the position. Junior detectives, politically adept, devoid of any sense of responsibility, caring little, only seeing it as a way to advancement, a hefty salary, and with luck, not a lot of work.

Clare knew that Tremayne was correct about some. However, she had checked out DCI Hector Forsyth, the new man to head Homicide if she and Tremayne didn't wrap up the murder investigations. Despite a harsh voice and bullying style of leadership, he was admired by his team, especially one of his female officers with whom he was having a clandestine affair.

He was not sycophantic or incompetent, quite the contrary, and Clare knew that if the man claimed Tremayne's seat, he wouldn't be vacating it, and no doubt elevating his mistress to sergeant and moving Clare out of Homicide.

In that event, Clare knew it would be easier for her to decide whether to forego a police career for children. She felt more for Tremayne, a man with no interests outside of policing and horse racing, as he would feel the alienation, the grinding drag towards finality, a place in the graveyard.

For her, there was ambivalence. The years with Tremayne had been good, the best years of her life, and she couldn't imagine working with anyone else.

'Fortescue,' Tremayne shouted out as the man came out from the building, he had entered ten minutes earlier.

'Yes, what do you want?'

'Detective Inspector Tremayne, Sergeant Yarwood. We have a few questions for you.'

Clare opened her warrant card, showed it to Fortescue. He didn't check it.

'We've met, briefly,' Fortescue said to Tremayne. 'An arrogance on your part in believing that we're all waiting to be waylaid by the police.'

'Lady Fortescue said that she trusts you, that you're honourable,' Tremayne said. 'Insulting us doesn't bode well for you or her.'

'My apologies. It's just that I've got a lot on today, and your being here doesn't help.'

'We need to clear up a few issues,' Clare said.

'Such as who pushed Andrew out of the window.'

'That's one. Do you believe it was murder?'

'Not with Andrew. Pleasant company, but no drive in the man, an unwillingness to work.'

'A Fortescue trait?' Tremayne said.

'The Fortescue family have a long history of service to this country, one or two villains amongst them, a few black sheep who'd rather squander the money.'

'Andrew, a squanderer?'

'His father tried to get him to focus, to take his responsibilities seriously, to give thought to his position in society, but with Andrew, a pretty girl, an expensive car, and he'd be there.'

'He was serious about Sally Kirkland.'

'Was he?'

The previously important business of Fortescue had taken a back seat. It was, to Clare, not an unusual situation. The meek and timid husband of a forceful woman, deeming it not appropriate to say much if she was around, but only dwelling on what was, observing all, thinking it through, daydreaming even. But given the chance and a willing ear, then the person was transformed.

The three of them were sitting at a wooden table in the park on one side of the street. Neither Tremayne nor Clare was willing to take Fortescue away from his comfort zone. To relocate to somewhere warmer, somewhere more comfortable, might have proved to be an unwise decision.

It was only a small city, no more than a large village, although it had a surfeit of pubs and shops; picturesque if Tremayne had bothered to look, which he hadn't. Clare thought the place charming, the type of place where everyone knows everyone else, full of intrigue and secrets, and the park gave the best opportunity to be undisturbed.

'We believe he was in love with Sally, the reason he committed suicide,' Clare said. 'Are you saying otherwise?'

'Andrew was a romantic, notions of eternal love, but as for her, I wouldn't think so.'

Tremayne wanted to light up a cigarette but decided not to. After all, Fortescue might prove to be a killjoy, a man who disapproved of almost everything, even love, and he neither wanted to offend the man nor make him reticent.

'Bunty thought he was in love with Sally,' Claude Fortescue said, 'but then she watches too many soap operas, the mushy ones where boy meets girl, marries and rears a brood of children.'

'You seem a remarkably balanced man,' Clare said.

'I keep myself to myself if that's what you mean.'

'And observe,' Tremayne added. 'Is that it?'

'I deal in the law, not in people's emotions or peccadilloes. If Andrew had wanted to marry the woman, then fine; he wasn't a driven person, not like his mother.'

'Your opinion of her?'

'A remarkable woman. I admire her greatly.'

'Why?'

'She had it rough as a child, and then when she blossomed in her twenties, she's there educating herself, meeting the right people, making herself indispensable.'

'And sleeping around,' Clare said.

'As you say, but what does that matter?' Fortescue said. 'She was maximising her assets, something we all do in life. I don't blame her, nor do I condone it. She was what she was, what she became.'

'She slept her way to the top?'

'Bernard wasn't the top, the incumbent lord of an estate in Wiltshire, bereft of any real influence. The man lived on his legacy, never made his mark in industry or the law. He was entitled to sit in the House of Lords, but how many times did he do that?'

The Horse's Mouth

'You're about to tell us,' Tremayne said. The cigarette was weighing on his mind as he fumbled in his pocket for the packet.

'Twice, I'm telling you, twice. And then he condemned the burden placed on the aristocracy and the wealthy, the inequitable burden of the crippling death duty that was in force.'

'It's still here,' Clare said.

'It is, but it's open to loopholes, offshore accounts, transferral of assets. Bernard would have been smart enough before his death to have considered it, but he couldn't trust his son.'

'The relationship between father and son?'

'Bernard, not that he had any right, despised Andrew.'

'Did Andrew reciprocate?'

'As a child shipped off to boarding school?'

'You've not answered the question.'

'Andrew was weak, looking to his father for guidance and support, receiving neither. As he matured, Andrew grew to hate his father, which was remarkable as Andrew wasn't a man of strong feelings, other than a fleeting lust for a woman, a belief in love, but not for long. However, the hatred for his father was a constant.'

'He told you this?'

'I hadn't seen him for several years before he died. And no, he didn't tell me, not in so many words, but I observed, watched the interactions of father and son.'

'According to your wife, she had not been to the Fortescue estate for a long time,' Clare said.

'She hadn't. I still maintained a working relationship with Lord and Lady Fortescue. It wasn't often that I went there, but Bernard trusted me, blood being thicker than water, and I had known the man since we were infants.'

'Could you be trusted?'

'Always. You're aware of the conflict between Marjorie and my wife?'

'Your wife believes she's entitled to some recompense on her brother's passing.'

'In the past, she wouldn't have had a chance; the right of inheritance would have been clear, father to the eldest son. However, Bunty does have some claim, although not as much as she would like.'

'Will Marjorie Fortescue use her position wisely?'

'She will, but if Andrew had been alive, legally she wouldn't have had a say.'

'She's a forceful woman, more than capable of advising her son.'

'She would have made him do what she wanted. That wasn't the issue, was it?' Fortescue said as he drew a cigarette packet from the right-hand pocket of his jacket and offered one of its contents to Tremayne. 'You look in need of one of these,' he said.

The two men lit up, savoured the first puff; Clare looked over at Fortescue, realised the man had hidden depths. He professed to be a humble lawyer, but behind the quiet demeanour was a determined man, more of a worthy successor to Bernard Fortescue than his Andrew had ever been.

'What was the issue?' Clare said.

'Andrew had found someone as equally strong as his mother.'

'Sally Kirkland.'

'Andrew, whether he was madly in love with her or not, not that I believe that he was, knew that he needed someone to take control. If it was his mother, then what had changed, and Sally could have given him children, maintained the line, ensured the title.'

'Are you crediting Andrew Fortescue with some wisdom?' Tremayne asked, calmer now with a cigarette in his mouth.

'A weak personality up against an overbearing father, a controlling mother. He didn't want either, and Bernard wasn't long for this world. His mother was still there, but Sally would have dealt with her.'

'Sally would have controlled him.'

'Andrew had had a lifetime of Bernard and Marjorie. They were known quantities, whereas Sally would have given him peace, probably not cared if he continued with his inconsequential lifestyle. After all, it was the title that she and her father, the social-climbing parasite, wanted.'

'Barton Kirkland, you knew him?'

'I came into contact with him.'

'We've not been told of this before,' Tremayne said.

'It's not something Kirkland would have wanted spoken about.'

'But you're about to tell us,' Clare said.

'As you're asking and because it's a homicide, I feel duty-bound to tell you.'

'In your own time,' Tremayne said.

'It wasn't the first time that Kirkland tried to get his daughter married into nobility.'

'Are you saying it was Barton, not the daughter, who pursued Andrew Fortescue?'

'Sally was the palatable face of social climbing, in much the same way as Marjorie had been. Kirkland was a grubby hustler and street fighter from a long time back.'

'You know of his history?'

'Lord and Lady Morris, one son, the Honourable Rufus, as inept a fool as you'll ever meet. That's his father's opinion of Rufus, but Lord Morris wasn't a Bernard, and her ladyship was the daughter of a duke in the north of England. Pure, undiluted blue blood, but Rufus was a hopeless case.'

'And Sally wanted to marry him?'

'It was Kirkland who set it up, Sally nominally agreeing to it.'

'Why?'

'I would have said ask her, but that's not possible, and even if her father were alive today, he'd have a different account of the events.'

'Your view's important for now,' Clare said.

'Lord and Lady Morris are both old, although his lordship is faring better. In his day, Morris had been a man of influence, and he wasn't financially encumbered, no need to sell off any land or assets to survive.'

'But the son was to remain a bachelor, is that what you are saying?'

'Lord and Lady Morris were terrible snobs.'

'Then why consider Sally Kirkland as a suitable bride for the son?'

'Desperation. The Honourable Rufus had epilepsy; he could barely speak without stammering, a poor specimen.'

'Which means?'

'Family history. I checked it out when Kirkland tried to make the love match. The Morrises go back centuries, back to a time when marriage for strategic reasons and financial gain was more important than love and compatibility.'

'Genetically impure?'

'I'm not saying he was, but the man wasn't about to find a suitable woman. Barton Kirkland's offer was manna from heaven for them, not that they liked him, although they approved of Sally.'

'You met her?'

'A few times. Andrew would have done well with her.'

'What happened with the Morrises?'

'A prenuptial agreement was drawn up by me.'

'Kirkland didn't like it?'

'On the lord's death, Rufus would become Lord Morris and Sally, as his wife, would become Lady Morris.'

'Which is what Kirkland had wanted.'

'That wasn't all. All the assets, including the stately home and its lands, would be handed over to Rufus, although there would be restrictions on the money.'

'Not total control?'

'Rufus's mother, while she lived, would continue to stay in the house. It was sufficiently large for her not to need to interact with Rufus and Sally.'

'She had control?'

'Not in itself. A group of eminent and trusted financial advisers would be appointed, who Lord Morris had used over the years. They would have had to agree to any expenditure of over one hundred thousand pounds, not that this would have worried Rufus. He cared for little other than his room and a blaring television in the corner. It would hardly have impacted on Sally either, or Barton for that matter. She could have an expensive car, holidays in the Caribbean, whatever she wanted, but go above the agreed money, and she needed permission.

'It doesn't seem restrictive,' Tremayne said.

'That was one part of the agreement. The second part was what Kirkland objected to.'

'Which was?'

'In the event of Rufus's death, and he was unlikely to live to a ripe old age, Sally would retain the title, and the use of the house and sufficient money to maintain her lifestyle.'

'That sounds acceptable,' Clare said.

'It was; however, Rufus had a first cousin, the Honourable Jordan, the son of his father's sister. And let me tell you that he is an impressive individual. Hardworking, articulate, someone to be proud of.'

'But no title.'

'No chance, either. The agreement stated that in the event of Rufus's death, full administrative control of the Morrises' assets would be placed in Jordan's hands, for him to do as he saw fit.'

'Sally?'

'If she had borne children, a male heir, and that child was of suitable stock, not the same as the father, then Sally, Lady Morris, would be provided for until the child came of age. However, and here's the problem, if she had not had children, male or female, then she would be required to leave the house within twelve months.'

'The title would have come to an end, the same as with the Fortescues.'

'It would have, but Jordan would have taken full control, not only as an administrator but as the holder of those assets. He would inherit it all.'

'Barton Kirkland wouldn't want that.'

'In the end, a compromise couldn't be reached, and Sally Kirkland did not marry Rufus, not that it would have made a difference.'

'Why?' Clare asked.

'Three months afterwards, Rufus died, having never fathered a child, a virgin. Kirkland wouldn't have achieved his dream. He is, as I said, a social-climbing parasite.'

'A dead social-climbing parasite,' Tremayne said. 'However, your opinion doesn't alter the fact that someone murdered him.'

Chapter 29

A clandestine meeting of two people. An out of the area location, a small restaurant discreetly hidden down a side street.

As Ian Swift said at their meeting. 'We're both innocent.'

Marjorie Fortescue had dressed casually; Swift wore a suit. Neither wanted to be there, but as Swift's mother, a stern, uncaring disciplinarian, had said. 'If a person fails in life, chooses their friends unwisely, makes enemies with less thought, then it's that person's problem, not yours'.

Ian Swift needed a tactical advantage; he needed the woman sitting opposite him.

'I am. I don't know about you,' Marjorie said as she perused the menu.

'The police are closing in. Soon they will have their murderer.'

'You said it was important, the only reason I'm here.'

The waiter came and went. Swift ordered a steak well done; Marjorie chose fish and asked for a bottle of their best wine. She wouldn't be paying, not that evening.

'I told Tremayne and his sergeant that you were a bitch.'

'Grantley's wife, that's who you mean?'

'The man's holding me back from becoming the mayor.'

'Why would you want it? It seems a lot of hard work just for a pittance.'

'Power. You and Liston need a friend if you're going to get approval for your venture.'

'It's not a venture; it's a business plan,' Marjorie said, intrigued to hear what the man had to say.

'Speculative then. If your sister-in-law or a group of concerned citizens decide to oppose, you won't have much chance of getting it approved, and then where will you and your paramour be?'

'If that means what I think it does, you can go and wash your mouth, or go and put your face in the gutter where it belongs.'

'You are a bitch, aren't you?' Swift said. 'That's a compliment, not a criticism.'

'Are you one of those female-hating fools who believe a woman should be subservient, there for a man's whim and favour.'

'You ruled your husband, and your son was barely able to do anything without your approval. It was you, wasn't it?'

'You'll need to be more specific,' Marjorie said as she drank her wine, looked down at the fish, realised Swift's choice of the restaurant had not been ideal. The fish looked bland, the salad to one side old and soggy, and as for the best wine in the place, it would have made a good vinegar.

'Why did you encourage Andrew to marry Sally?'

'He was mad for her. It was his decision.'

'Andrew never had a thought in his head that made any sense. Converting the stables to luxury accommodation, renting out your house for wedding receptions, pie in the sky. None of them would have gone anywhere near to paying the annual costs on the estate, let alone the renovation costs of the main house.'

'My husband believed in fate, and that something would change in our favour.'

'Your husband, Marjorie, a fine example of an outdated institution, was out of touch with reality.'

'I loved him, and I would appreciate it if you maintained a civil tongue. And besides, I'm here for a reason, not that I've heard it yet.'

Swift pushed his plate to one side, leant over the table and whispered, 'If I'm the mayor, I can push the planning approval, make sure it goes smoothly for you.'

'Does that mean you want a cut? Is this your attempt, albeit clumsy, at obtaining money from me?'

'I don't want money, not from you.'

'Why? It makes no sense,' Marjorie Fortescue said.

It's the prestige I want. I want Grantley's job. The wife of a dead lord, a son that committed suicide, a member of the aristocracy. Use your contacts wisely, and I'll make sure of the approval.'

'The good life, the women on your arm and in your bed, not enough?'

'Politics appeal. I'm young enough to make my mark. I need prominence and respectability.'

'You'll need a wife. I don't think I'd be suitable.'

'I've someone else in mind. I've not considered you, although it's not a bad idea. Are you interested?' Swift said.

'I might be a bitch, but not that much that I'd consider joining with you in your delusion.'

'Why?'

'I told Tremayne and Grantley's wife, so I may as well tell you. After Jeremy Liston has dealt with the land development, I intend to take off, ask my sister-in-law and her husband to look after the Fortescue estate.'

'Where to?'

'I've still got enough life in me; I still want to get laid, not by a middle-aged lothario with illusions of grandeur, but by a young stud oozing testosterone.'

'In the meantime, while you're obtaining approval, what are you going to do? If, as you said, and you are a bitch in the nicest possible way, you intend to find a young lover, you'll need to do it now, not later. Even you, the beautiful and alluring Lady Fortescue, are ageing. Another few years and the young stud might not be of interest.'

'Is that you, Ian? Age is taking its toll, has finally caught up with you? Mortality, an illness, a need to leave your mark, a child?'

'Jeremy Liston? Have you slept with him yet?'

'That's an impertinence, not the sort of question to ask me.'

'Marjorie, don't come that with me. You might look down on the peasants, but I used my brain to get where I am; you used your body. We've both been successful up till now, but I want something more, as do you. Scratch my back; I'll scratch yours.'

'I want my son.'

'Why did he commit suicide?'

'He didn't. He might have contemplated it, but he didn't jump; it was murder.'

'And you know by who?'

'I have my suspicions.'

'You've told the police?'

'That it was murder, yes.'

'Did you tell them who you suspect?'

'I'm not sure if I want to.'

'Are you capable of murder? Have you killed? Will you kill again?'

'It's been a surprisingly unpleasant evening,' Marjorie Fortescue said as she got up from the table. 'I hope we won't be doing it again.'

'My offer?'

'I'll consider using my influence. If it's a bitch you want, I'm the person. Marry whoever you want, but rule me out.'

'You still need a man,' Swift said.

***

Joe Blakely did not feel comfortable. At the racecourse on his pedestal, taking bets, calling out to the milling crowd, pointing to the sign above him proclaiming that Honest Joe Blakely wasn't just there for effect, that he offered better odds than the others, he felt at ease. And in his home, a place of serenity, somewhere to enjoy the tranquillity of family life. But in the interview room at the police station, he felt trepidation.

'I need answers,' Tremayne said

'Am I accused of any crime?' Blakely said, his voice low. 'This is intimidating.'

'Good. I need answers to specific questions.'

Clare could see the bookmaker was fidgeting in his seat, a man out of his comfort zone.

'I'll help if I can.'

'Let's start with an easy one. Do you know of horses being tampered with, performing below par, jockeys who hold back a horse, people who manipulate the odds?'

'I'll not give specifics, but yes.'

'At Salisbury?'

'It's not endemic, but it does occur.'

The Horse's Mouth

'Have you, Joe Blakely, at any time indulged in behaviour contrary to the rules laid down for horseracing in this country?'

'If that means nobbling a horse, swapping one out for another, then no.'

'Have you known in advance of a race that the outcome was predetermined? And if you had, did you take advantage of that knowledge?'

'I'd be a fool not to.'

'That's a yes,' Clare said. She wasn't sure where Tremayne was heading with the interview. Blakely, they already knew, would have been privy to privileged information. That did not make him guilty of a crime, certainly not of murder.

'It is, but I'm not involved.'

'You never made an official complaint.'

'Where's the proof, and besides, I've got a living to make. It's alright to be sanctimonious from a distance. The police force is not uniquely one hundred per cent without wrongdoing.'

'That's not the point,' Tremayne said. 'We're not after you and a few fiddles; what we're after are the big fish, those who call the shots.'

'I don't know of anyone.'

'But you must have heard rumours.'

'A racecourse is full of them, but I don't give them much credence. That's a good way to get into trouble.'

'Violent men?'

'Influential. People who'd cause you a lot of trouble if you crossed them. Fixing races requires subtlety, not strength.'

'How much could a smart person make on a regional meeting in Salisbury?' Clare asked.

'At the course, a few thousand pounds if you're lucky; online, upwards of ten thousand pounds, but there's a limit, and if you have more wins than you should, you'll find it increasingly difficult to place a bet.'

'Bookmakers don't mind a mug punter,' Clare said, 'but if it's paying out money, then they're not so keen.'

'There are people I don't accept bets from.'

'A good record of wins?'

'I'm not saying that they've done anything illegal. It's still possible by studying the form, checking the course, talking to the jockey.'

'How?' Tremayne asked. 'I've been trying for years with not a lot of success.'

'That's the difference. These people, one of them is a woman, analyse a horse and a jockey, use complex software programming. They lose a few, win a few, but they know the odds, the statistical advantage of one animal over another. To them, it's not criminal, just astute.'

'Can you do it?'

'I'm not that good on a computer.'

'So, if someone's out to make a significant amount of money, they aren't going to achieve that at a racecourse or online.'

'Small bets, try to keep below the radar, and even then, it's only a matter of time before you're blacklisted.'

'Does the bookmaker have the right of refusal?' Clare asked.

'Yes.'

'Online?'

'The reputable ones might take the bets, but they'll have limits on how much. If you want big money, then there's overseas. They'll take a bet on anything, two flies walking up a wall, anything. Whether they'll pay is another matter.'

'If they don't?'

'Money lost. Only a fool would place more money than he could afford with them.'

'Have you?'

'Daily, but I keep my bets low, make sure I get paid. As I said, the reputable companies based in the UK are controlled by legislation, subject to audit if they cheat.'

'Why was Red Rose switched?' Tremayne asked, changing the subject.

'There was a rumour that Kirkland was in financial trouble, and if the horse won, then he would give it to someone else as payment of a debt.'

'That's illogical,' Clare said. 'Why give up a winning horse, when alive it was worth more.'

'It depends how long those owed the money were willing to wait.'

'It still doesn't make sense,' Tremayne said. 'Scarlet Soleil ended up dead on the day, and not long after that, Red Rose.'

'Have you found Scarlet Soleil's owner?'

'The trainer, yes, but the owner, not a chance.'

'Look further, go through Kirkland's papers.'

'Why?'

'No forwarding address or a phone number, not even an email. It's suspicious.'

'Are you suggesting that Kirkland was the owner?'

'It's probable. Sacrifice one horse to save another.'

'Red Rose was kept for Sally, which would mean that Sue Nixon is involved in the conspiracy?'

'Kirkland was at the racecourse. He would have known the difference between the two horses, white paint or no white paint.'

'Not if he wasn't looking.'

'Anyway, that's the rumour. As for me, I've not committed a crime, and the rumour came about after Sally Kirkland and her father died, after Les Daniels.'

'It doesn't explain how Red Rose came to die,' Clare said.

'A defenceless animal, innocent of any crime.'

'Do you like horses, Mr Blakely?' Clare asked.

'I've done well by them.'

'Why did one of the horses die at the racecourse? Surely, it would have been better to wait, away from prying eyes?' Tremayne said.

'If the person or persons intended to claim the horse after the race, and after a few days the paint starts to flake off, better to kill it there and then,' Blakely said.

'But they wouldn't have the horse.'

'They'd have the insurance for the animal's untimely death. Either way, they would have got the money.'

'It was Les Daniels who picked up the deception, told me at the time.'

'Either he wasn't involved, or you were too close.'

'My presence wouldn't have made a difference. I wasn't interested in the horse, not until Sally Kirkland died,' Tremayne said.

Chapter 30

The first flurry of snow, the warning of a long and cold winter, and Tremayne's bones ached as he and Clare stood in the doorway at Barton Kirkland's house.

'I've got a key,' Clare said.

'Yarwood, what are you waiting for, an invite?' Tremayne said as he stubbed out his cigarette.

Clare flicked the light switch to the right of the door on entering – nothing.

'Try the switch box,' Tremayne said.

'No one's paid the bill.'

'It's not important. We know what we're looking for.'

'Do we? If the man had owned Scarlet Soleil as well as Red Rose, what does it prove? Owning another animal through a shell company could have been a tax advantage.'

Tremayne opened the door to the room where Barton Kirkland had died. It had been closed up for weeks; there was a distinctive odour, the smell of death, of dried blood, rising damp and mould. With the heavy curtains closed, it was, to Clare, a scene out of a horror movie, a hand about to reach out and to grab the hapless victim by the throat.

She walked over to the window, careful to walk around where Kirkland had lain, and opened one of the curtains, jumping back in fright.

'What is it?' Tremayne said.

'Someone's outside, looking in.'

'You'd better grab whoever it is. I can't help you there.'

Clare opened the window and jumped out, treading where the solitary footprint of the murderer had once been. She gave it no thought as she headed over to where a young boy was standing.

'You've no right being in there,' the youth, no more than twelve years of age, said. 'Mr Kirkland wouldn't have liked it.'

'I'm Clare Yarwood, Sergeant Clare Yarwood. You are?'

'Oscar Howard. I used to help around the place, look after the horses, sometimes get to ride one or two of them.'

'Red Rose?'

'I've ridden him.'

'Why haven't we heard of you before?' Clare said. The young boy was still wary, not willing to come too close.

'I wasn't here, overseas with my parents. We came back yesterday.'

'Mr Kirkland didn't mention you, nor did Les Daniels. We've got a few questions for you. Would that be okay?'

'Am I in trouble?'

'I don't see why. You've not caused any trouble, vandalised anything.'

'It's the first time since we came back, and then I saw you and the old man go into the house.'

'I'd suggest you don't refer to Inspector Tremayne as the old man,' Clare said. 'He can be sensitive about it.'

'I saw who it was.'

'How?'

'It was the night before we left. I didn't think much about it at the time. Mr Kirkland, he didn't mind me with the horses, but up at the house, he didn't like it.'

'Any reason?'

'It's cold,' Oscar said. 'Where we've been, it was hot every day.'

Clare knew the way to a young boy's heart. 'McDonald's?' she said.

'If you're sure I'm not in trouble.'

'We need you to tell us what you know. Did you like Sally?'

'I kept away after she died, not sure if I should have, but my father, he says it's best to mind your own business if you've done nothing wrong.'

'Your father may have said it for your benefit, but it wasn't good advice,' Clare said.

***

Clare phoned young Oscar's mother to let her know she was taking the boy to McDonald's in Winchester Street. At McDonald's, a fifteen-minute drive, she paid for a cheeseburger with extra chips and a dessert.

'My mother doesn't approve, says it's not good for my health, and if I'm going to be a jockey, I need to think about these sorts of things.'

'Once in a while doesn't matter,' Clare said, although she kept to a coffee.

Oscar Howard was short enough and light enough to be a jockey, but Clare remembered that at his age she had been no taller; later she had shot up, taller by a head than her mother, taller than her father. The boy's ambition could well be thwarted by nature.

Tremayne remained at the house on his own. The smell of death didn't concern him, and as for things that go bump in the night, he did not believe in them. However, he believed that somewhere in the house he would find evidence to confirm Blakely's story; which he thought was very plausible.

The decision for Clare to deal with Oscar on her own was well-founded. A young boy on the cusp of manhood, enamoured by the attention of an older woman, would be more inclined to speak openly.

'She was always friendly, was Sally,' Oscar said as he munched on his cheeseburger.

'Red Rose was her favourite,' Clare said.

'Mine too.'

'You said you used to ride the horses.'

'Les would let me sometimes, not when they were fresh. Racehorses can be temperamental, not easy to control.'

'I rode horses when I was younger.'

'Is it true? You're married to the mayor?'

'I am. Do you know him?'

'Not me, not personally, although I've seen him around. He gets to wear those fancy robes, the chain around his neck?'

'On ceremonial occasions.'

'He must be loaded.'

'As a councillor, as the mayor, he receives a modest salary. He doesn't do it for the money.'

'I didn't mean…'

'That's fine. Good money as a jockey?'

'It can be. Les was good, but then he had an accident, trampled under a horse.'

The Horse's Mouth

'You don't become a jockey to become rich, nor do you join the police. You do it because it's what you love.'

'My father thinks I should focus more on school than daydreaming.'

'He's right. You don't know what the future holds.'

'I read the book. It said you have to believe in what you want, to ignore the negatives, focus on the goal. That's me. I'll make it.'

'Good for you, Oscar,' Clare said. 'We're not here for that, are we? To talk about your dreams.'

'You want to know what I saw?'

'That's it. In your own time.'

'It was the night before we went away. I knew about Sally, but I never came over to the house before that night, and I kept away from the stables. I knew Les wasn't there, and Mr Kirkland, he preferred that I wasn't with the horses on my own.'

'Trevor Lawless would have been there.'

'He didn't like me at the stables, thought I was after his job, not that I was.'

'An unusual person,' Clare said.

'I can't blame him. It's a dog eat dog world out there, or so my father says. With Les it was great, and Mr Kirkland, he could get upset sometimes, and Sally, well, you know about her.'

'Do you? Aren't you a bit young to know about such things?'

'Les, he used to tell me tales, make me laugh.'

'He spoke about Sally?'

'Never unkind. He liked her a lot, and she was always friendly to him. Les told me about his accident, how the mind was willing, but the body let him down.'

'Did your parents approve of him telling you this?'

'I never told them. That was our secret.'

'What other secrets?'

'He saw a man killed once, but I wasn't sure if it was true.'

'Oscar, it was.'

'Is there any more?'

'Sally was going out with more than one man, putting it about something dreadful.'

'For someone as young as you are, you seem to know a lot about the world.'

'It was Les. He loved to talk. You'd be surprised what he knew about, who was with you, who was a crook, who wasn't.'

'Was Barton Kirkland a crook?'

'Les said, not sure why he did with me, that Mr Kirkland was, and that he knew more about crime than he let on, and that some of his friends were dangerous people, kill you in a flash if you crossed them. I think he was just trying to frighten me; thought I was a child.'

'But you aren't, are you, Oscar?'

'I checked up on Mr Kirkland, found out something about his past. He was a nobody, made something of himself, the same as I will.'

'Honestly, I hope.'

'Les told me that after the accident and money was tight, he'd hold back a horse, make sure it was on the inside boxed in, no chance of a win.'

'More money to do that than with a jockey's pay.'

'That's what he said.'

'The person at the window, who was it?'

'It was the man on the television.'

'Ian Swift?'

'Not him, I know who he is. My father watches his programme. The other one, the hero.'

'Jeremy Liston?'

'He was around a few times at the house with Sally, spent the night with her. It used to upset Les when Liston was there; he didn't like him, reckoned he was a snake.'

'Do you know why?'

'Les fancied Sally, not that she would have been interested in him, a woman like that.'

'No accounting for taste, and why not?'

'The other thing, Les wasn't any good for that,' Oscar said.

***

Tremayne, aware of what Oscar Howard had said to Clare, continued to move around Kirkland's house. He had found the switch box, flicked the Mains breaker and restored electricity to the house.

He had been in the house for over two hours, time enough to make himself a coffee, a carton of long-life milk in a cupboard, coffee in a tin on the window sill. He took out his phone, phoned Moulton to let him know of developments.

The revelation that Jeremy Liston had been at the window that night did not surprise Tremayne. Heroes, reluctant or otherwise, rich and famous, even titled – it made little difference where a murder was concerned.

Tremayne had long ago concluded that the line between good and righteous and heinous was narrow and that anyone, given enough provocation, usually passion or a lack of it, was capable of killing another person. But

Liston had been a killer, albeit under orders, and the disgust after the act would not be likely to affect him.

Neither he nor Clare was intent on bringing Liston in yet. After all, the word of a boy who had opened up to Clare wasn't proof. No evidence to corroborate the boy's story, no reason why Liston would want to murder Kirkland.

If the two men were involved in crime or disagreed about Sally, then why? The woman had been dead by the time her father died, and if anyone were to commit murder, it would be the grieving father, not the woman's lover, the last man to have seen her alive, the last man to have made love to her.

Tremayne finished his drink, warmed his hands on the electric kettle, and continued his search. The room where the man had died proved fruitless. He headed up the stairs towards Kirkland's bedroom, passing by Sally's on the way.

Hers was bright and breezy with floral curtains, a king-size bed, the previously white sheets and pillows dulling with the dust and the time left unchanged. In one corner of the room, a dressing table adorned with make-up and cleansing cream, a wilted single-stemmed flower in a slender vase. A television was attached to a wall, tuned to a movie channel, found out after he had pressed the switch on the remote.

The woman had been a reader, judging by the extensive collection of books in a bookcase, some romances, others were crime thrillers.

Tremayne didn't feel that what he wanted was in the room, although what he was searching for, he wasn't sure. Increasingly frustrated and with an empty stomach, its rumbling letting him know, he walked into Barton Kirkland's room. It was the room of a man who slept alone. The curtains were dark, the bedsheets were crumpled, and there was an odour of tobacco. It was how his room had looked before Jean had re-entered his life.

It wasn't the first time Tremayne had been in the room, although that had been in the days after the incumbent had died, and then just a cursory glance.

On a bedside cabinet, a copy of the racing guide that he always read, a brochure for an upcoming auction of thoroughbred horses. Near to the window, a horse's head carved in stone, although Tremayne didn't reckon much to the sculptor.

In the en suite adjoining the main bedroom, not the assortment he had found in Sally's room. A razor in a glass, a toothbrush and toothpaste in another. A towel hung on a heated rail, now getting warm with the electricity on in the house.

He put a chair in the middle of the room and stood on its seat. The chair was neither stable nor suitable for the purpose, but up above he'd seen an anomaly, a slight gap in the ceiling stretching for twelve inches and in a straight line. He touched the edge, felt it give. He pushed a little more, found that it was hinged. Kirkland, savvy, as Tremayne was, had realised that a safe was too obvious; a locked drawer in a desk too easy to force, but a small compartment in the bathroom ceiling was the last place that anyone would look, except for a curious police inspector.

Thrusting his hand in, Tremayne felt a folder. He withdrew it and eased himself back to ground level.

Barton Kirkland's house wasn't the place to check its contents. He then took photos of the room and where he had found the folder. Before leaving the house he remembered to switch the electricity off.

Jeremy Liston had a lot of explaining to do.

Chapter 31

In the interview room, Liston waited. Even though he had been punctual, Tremayne had no intention of following suit. Liston riled and agitated was what he wanted.

At eighteen minutes after the hour, Tremayne entered the interview room with its bare table in the middle, two chairs on each side, the recording equipment, the camera in the corner of the room, mounted up high.

'Mr Liston, it's good of you to come,' Tremayne said as he shook the man's hand.

'Time is money, or haven't you heard?' Liston said.

Clare sat to one side of the inspector, observing the interaction between the sparring partners.

'We had to confirm some facts.'

'About me?'

'We have a credible witness that you were at Barton Kirkland's house on the day he died. Or to be more precise, an hour before,' Clare said.

'Why would I be there? I barely knew the man.'

'Murder's a serious crime,' Tremayne said.

'Inspector, I'm more than willing to assist, but implicating me in this sordid affair does you no credit.'

'Is that it? Sordid, nothing more,' Tremayne said. 'A woman, who we believe had strong feelings for you, is murdered.'

'We've been over this before. Sally knew the rules.'

'The romantic tryst in the stable,' Clare said.

The Horse's Mouth

'I thought it would help to ease the burden for her.'

'Liston, you're full of it,' Tremayne said. 'On the one hand, you tell us you're an emotional vacuum, and now you expect us to believe that you wanted to make it easier for her. That indicates some emotion, even if it's low-level.'

'Love is indefinable. You either love someone, or you don't, but it doesn't stop me regarding a person as a friend, someone you can go out with, have a bit of fun with, and then leave at their door. That's how it had been with Sally, and she wasn't a saint. I owed her no favours.'

'Let me elucidate on your reason for being in the interview room,' Tremayne said.

'I wish you would. I've got an appointment in forty-five minutes, and I don't want to miss it.'

Tremayne took no notice of the man's urgency nor of his appointment. Some questions needed answering or else the hero, the man who'd had a medal pinned to his chest by the Queen, would be in the cells at the station.

'A footprint was found outside Kirkland's window. We have a cast of it, your size shoe.'

'How many people have the same size shoe? Thousands, I'd venture.'

'Based on the evidence against you, we're obtaining a search warrant for your house.'

'What evidence, and why me?'

'Two reasons. You were outside Kirkland's window on the day of his death, and we have a witness to that fact. The second, and the most damning, is that, regardless of you insisting that you barely knew Kirkland, there is a folder full of papers that I found in Kirkland's house that has your fingerprints on.'

263

'None of this is proof.'

'Mr Liston, Jeremy, either you admit to a crime, or we'll hold you on suspicion of murder,' Clare said.

'I'm not sure how you got hold of those papers. Kirkland was clear they would remain hidden.'

'Would you like to explain what you and Kirkland had hatched, or do you need us to go through it in detail, bring in an auditor to check the figures, the fraud squad?'

'It wasn't fraud; it was business, and if it offends your delicate sensibilities, that can't be helped. Kirkland was a manipulator, a man who used whatever tools were in his arsenal. The poor and deprived street urchin image came in handy at times.'

'As does the hero with you.'

'I did my bit,' Liston said. 'To you, one act, no matter that it's not illegal, and the person's damned.'

'Have you told her ladyship?'

'Let her have her illusion.'

'Explain how it came about.'

'His lordship was broke, unable to pay the bills, too proud to ask a bank for money.'

'He asked you?'

'It was over twelve months ago. I was taking out Sally on occasions, as was Andrew Fortescue. The man's father knew that Andrew would be putty in Sally's hands.'

'You and Lord Fortescue hatched a plan?' Tremayne asked.

'It was clear that once Sally was Lady Fortescue and Marjorie was the dowager, that Sally, or more correctly, Barton, would be in charge of the estate and the house. Fortescue loved his wife, had great admiration for her, and he didn't want her disadvantaged.'

'Would that have happened?'

The Horse's Mouth

'Two strong-willed women, a weak man sandwiched in the middle, and one of those women sharing his bed, bearing his children. What do you think?'

'Marjorie would be out on the street,' Clare said.

'Her husband didn't want that, so he asked me to help. A Victoria Cross pinned on the chest lends credibility.'

'He judged wrong,' Tremayne said.

'He misjudged me. I had no intention of committing a crime, but I wasn't about to be charitable. The golden egg was in my clutch; I already had the goose.'

'That was how you saw Lord Fortescue?'

'Not in such disparaging terms, but yes, I did.'

'The idea to sell off the land was his?'

'Marjorie knew nothing about it, not then. His lordship could see it, sell the land, pay off all the debts, secure the place for Marjorie.'

'And your part in this tawdry affair?'

'I was to deal with Sally.'

'To kill her?'

'Nothing as melodramatic. I knew how she felt about me. On the one hand, she's got her father in her ear urging her to marry Andrew, and on the other, I'm there, the possibility of a love match.'

'If you married her?'

'I'm damning myself,' Liston said. 'If I continue, I'll have given you a motive.'

'And if you don't, I'll have you charged,' Tremayne said.

'If you have the papers, then you know what the deal with Kirkland was.'

'It's your story that we need. So far, you've only mentioned the Fortescues.'

'If Andrew hadn't married, or had chosen the daughter of a chinless wonder, then Marjorie would have been able to control her son. That was imperative in the father's plan.'

'But you said you were ending the romance with Sally. And where does her father come into this?'

'Fortescue had offered me the job of dealing with the land at the back, twenty per cent of the nett profit, as well as a hundred thousand pounds. But then that fool takes a jump out of a window.'

'There's an issue here,' Clare said. 'Why were you breaking the romance with Sally if Andrew and his father were still alive?'

'Lord Fortescue's health took a turn for the worse. The land development could have taken three, possibly four years to complete, and by then, my agreement with Fortescue would be dead and buried.'

'You offered the deal to someone else?'

'I approached Sally's father. I knew he was a man with a dubious past, a shady reputation, and Sally had already told me her father was a social climber, always sucking up to the elite. I knew he'd go for my plan. That's why we met in secret, not even Sally knew, the reason I was outside his window that night.'

'The night he died?'

'It was, but I didn't kill him.'

'Why the window?' Sally was dead. You could have gone in the front door.'

'Someone else was in the house.'

'Who?'

'I don't know, never asked. The murderer, I suppose.'

You said you changed directions, involved Barton Kirkland,' Clare said.

The Horse's Mouth

'I had done a lot of work on the land, knew the issues, the profit margins, the fact that it would have cleared the estate of debts, allowed Andrew to convert the house for weddings or whatever nonsense he had in mind. I put it to Kirkland that if Sally married Andrew, he could have the house.'

'How?'

'I'd bankrupt Andrew, a botched job on the land, force him to sell up.'

'And Sally?'

'She could live in the house with Andrew, but her father would own the place, and in the event of his death, it would belong to his daughter.'

'Andrew?'

'What did I care? He could wrap himself around a lamppost in a car accident, drink himself to death…'

'Take a jump out of a window,' Tremayne said.

'That was unexpected, his dying like that.'

'Then you offered it to Marjorie?'

'I had no option. I didn't intend to lose out on the deal. I'd have the money one way or the other, and then there were the fringe benefits.'

'Marjorie Fortescue?' Clare said.

'Alright for a bit of fun, but I wouldn't have married either woman.'

'You're right,' Tremayne said. 'You've given us the motive for the death of one, if not two persons. However, there are more to consider.'

'I didn't kill either Sally or Barton, no reason. I was interested in the money, still am, nothing's changed there.'

'Lady Fortescue will know the truth at some stage.'

'I'll tell her when the time is right. She was always going to be the winner.'

'Not if you had completed the deal with Kirkland.'

'She could have married Barton, kept the title and then she'd have the house. No one else is going to inherit it, not after her.'

'Bunty Fortescue?' Clare said.

'Yes, there's her, and she's tough. But time would have resolved that issue, although Marjorie wanted to give her a cut of the profits.'

'You agreed?'

'Tentatively. But there's a long time between now and then. Things change, and besides, if you want a percentage of the profit, you need to incur your proportion of the ongoing costs. Her husband doesn't have that sort of money; they would have sold out for a pittance.'

'You've thought this through.'

'Military training. Weigh up the options, anticipate how one action will impact on another, make a contingency plan. Discipline and training come in useful in doing deals.'

'As you were so friendly with Kirkland,' Tremayne said, 'what can you tell us about the horses?' Do you believe he was fixing the races?'

'If it was the grey area between criminal and purely unethical, he might have. He cared for nobody, apart from Sally. Your threat of a night in the cells? Intimidation, was that it?' Liston said.

There was something about the man that didn't ring true, Tremayne sensed it, but for the life of him he didn't know what it was, and it troubled him.

Whatever was to happen to Liston, free or in jail for murder, it was Marjorie, Lady Fortescue, who would suffer.

Chapter 32

Chris Fairweather, who rarely ventured far from his house, apart from the supermarket to stock up on frozen pizzas, bars of chocolates and packets of crisps, spent the night in the cells.

It was a sad and forlorn man that sat in Tremayne's office the next day. Being drunk and disorderly in a public place, namely, the market square in the centre of Salisbury wasn't a serious crime, just unusual for the obese and unclean Fairweather.

One advantage of the man's night in the cells was an insistence from his sister, Gwen, summoned at eleven in the evening to the police station, that he took a shower and changed his clothes, the shirt covered in vomit.

'He looks all the better,' Gwen said as she sat alongside her brother.

Clare, who occupied the fourth chair, could only agree. A thirty-three-year-old man-child, unsophisticated in his manner, incapable of holding down a regular job, but extremely intelligent, sat calmly, saying little.

'Chris, why get drunk, make a fool of yourself?' Tremayne said. 'According to your sister, it's out of character.'

'Sometimes he gets down,' Gwen said.

'Gwen, please. We need Chris to answer, not you,' Clare said.

Gwen placed her arm on Chris's sleeve. 'It'll be alright. They just want to talk to you.'

'A friendly chat, nothing more,' Tremayne said. He was trying the softly-softly approach, knowing full well that Fairweather's response wouldn't be predictable. However, there would be no loss of temper, no grandstanding as to his innocence, no accusation of police victimisation.'

Gwen Fairweather, or was it Ian Swift, Tremayne couldn't remember which of the two it had been, had said that the man was low-level autistic.

'I think it would be better if you told the inspector,' Gwen said.

'It was Ian; he asked me to hack this company.'

'When?'

'It was a few months ago. I'd just finished hacking a technology company, a company that sells its services to those who'll pay, those who worry about the integrity of their data. I never did it for gain, just out of interest. There's a group of us, we set each other challenges, see who succeeds.'

'Who are these people?' Tremayne asked.

'I wouldn't know.'

'Online, fictitious names, hidden,' Clare said.

'We give each other silly names, don't even know where they live, although I could find out if I wanted to.'

'You're better than them?'

'I'm better than anyone. Spend more time at it, I suppose, and I've got the best equipment.'

'The company you were hacking?' Tremayne asked.

'I got through. Nobody else would have.'

'If you wanted to hack a government database, the police? Could you?'

'They would never know.'

'How and why?'

'How, that's my secret.'

'Have you hacked us here?' Clare asked.

'I check up on everyone. I've read your file and Inspector Tremayne's.'

'That's criminal, punishable by a prison sentence. You do know this, don't you, Chris?'

'I'd not admit to it outside of this office, and you'll not be able to prove it.'

'If we got the best in the country to try, what then?'

'I'm the best.'

'Chris is incapable of boasting,' Gwen said. 'If he said he is the best, then we have to believe him.'

'His medical condition?' Tremayne said.

'Maybe they're right,' Chris said. 'Nobody can do what I can, and that's why I'm here. You and your sergeant, friendly, trying to ask me about Ian and what I might have done for him.'

'You're perceptive.'

'Perception is not needed. You, Inspector, are the archetypal police officer, Sergeant Yarwood, the trusty sidekick. Both of you want me to spill the dirt on Ian, but I won't.'

'Because you can't, or because he's guilty?'

'He asked me to hack a company, something to do with gambling, said it was one of his.'

'Is that it?'

'I had a good look around, where they banked the money, how the business was structured.'

'How long did that take?'

'On and off, about three weeks.'

'What did you give to Ian Swift?'

'I sent him a report, told him what he needed to know.'

'Is that it? You knew it wasn't Ian's company.'

'He paid me for my time.'

The Horse's Mouth

'This report, enough for Swift to get in?'

'He paid the money; I gave him everything.'

'It's not Chris's fault if Ian uses it for something illegal,' Gwen said.

'If proven, hacking is a criminal offence, although I doubt if an offshore-based company will take it to the police.'

'Why?'

'It's the reason they're offshore, hidden from view.'

'They didn't place the bets with other companies, kept it to themselves,' Chris said. 'If Ian was to start up a company, he could make a lot of money, but he'd need me to do it for him.'

'Which you would?'

'If I was interested.'

'Would you be?'

'It's complex, a high level of skill needed.'

'With what you gave Ian Swift, could he have accessed their bank accounts, withdrawn money, falsified bets and pay outs?'

'If they found out?' Gwen asked.

'People could die,' Clare said.

'I hope not. I wouldn't want anything to happen to him.'

'Even though he barely acknowledges your presence?'

'He does, not in that way though.'

'Gwen's keen on Ian,' Chris said. 'And I like him.'

'Who else have you hacked?' Tremayne said. Chris Fairweather, low-level autistic or certified genius, Tremayne didn't care. He knew this man, who never ventured far, rarely interacted with anyone other than his sister and Ian Swift, could reach into places that others couldn't.

'I've followed your investigation, checked out Barton Kirkland, his daughter, and Jeremy Liston.'

'Andrew Fortescue, Les Daniels?'

'I never bothered with Les Daniels. I need a website or a database, a company name; otherwise, I can't do it. I could have hacked Daniels' bank, but he wasn't important.'

'Why not?'

It was like pulling hen's teeth, Tremayne felt, but with Chris Fairweather, anything other than keeping the conversation low key and non-threatening wasn't going to work.

'He used to fix the races, pay the jockeys to lose, place bets for Kirkland.'

'How do you know this? Why haven't you told us before?'

'I told you that I'm not interested. I only want to be at home.'

'Last night, you weren't.'

Chris looked over at Gwen. 'It's time to go,' he said. 'I'm tired, and I want to sleep.'

So near, yet so far, Tremayne knew. Fairweather was close to locking up again. Tremayne changed tack.

'Chris, let's not worry about last night,' Tremayne said. 'However, your assistance would be invaluable, see it as a community service, ridding the streets of evil-doers, the same as in one of your games.'

'I think the inspector's right,' Chris's sister said, putting her arm around his shoulders.

'If you say so, Gwen.'

The Horse's Mouth

'I do. It's all for the best. I don't want Ian in trouble, and if he's done something wrong, I don't want him harmed.'

'I saw emails that Kirkland had sent to Daniels, outlining the bets and the races to fix, where to place the bets, how to collect the winnings.'

'Daniels was his bagman?' Clare said.

'Kirkland was in for big money.'

'Daniels wasn't an ambitious man, just enough money to get by,' Tremayne said.

'The same as me. I don't want for much, only for Gwen to be there.' Chris said.

'If Barton Kirkland was playing the edges, verging on the criminal, then so was Daniels. Is there more?'

'Kirkland was betting, not to win just a few hundred pounds. It was bigger than that, and the bets became progressively larger.'

'Why didn't we find this out?' Tremayne said. 'We've enough experts in the station.'

'You're the police. You follow procedures; I don't.'

Chris Fairweather started to shuffle in his seat. At best, Clare could see another two or three questions, and the man would be gone.

'Chris, what else did you find out about Barton Kirkland?' Clare asked.

'He had a girlfriend.'

'That we didn't know. Who?'

'Sue Nixon.'

'What about her, their relationship?' Tremayne asked.

'They weren't coy judging by the photos she sent him.'

'We've had her down as not involved,' Clare said.

'Not her. She knew about the substitution. If you want to send incriminating emails, you should encrypt them, but nobody does.'

'I wouldn't,' Tremayne said.

'It doesn't matter anyway. I would have broken the code.'

'Either Sue Nixon is a possible target, or she's guilty of a crime.'

'It could be both,' Clare said. 'Chris, we need you to help us, give us what you have.'

'Why did you tell us now, not before?' Tremayne asked.

'You never asked the right questions.'

'Will you tell us now?' Clare asked.

'I have to, don't I?'

'I'm afraid that you do,' Tremayne said. 'We're sorry that you're involved.'

'I found an email from Sally Kirkland to Jeremy Liston, telling him that her father was in trouble and he was going to use Red Rose as part payment against a debt.'

'A debt with who?'

'She didn't know, but it was Liston. The man was playing both the daughter and the father.'

'Clare, go with Gwen and Chris, stay with them until you have everything that Chris can give you.'

'After that?' Clare said.

'It's obvious.'

'Sue Nixon first, then Liston.'

Chris, finally tired of the station, and in need of a fix of internet porn and a frozen pizza, got up from his chair, shook Tremayne's hand and then Clare's. He then left, Gwen's arm in his.

'We're getting close,' Tremayne said.

Clare wasn't so sure. She could see more twists and turns yet.

***

Bunty Fortescue was adamant; Marjorie Fortescue was circumspect, but basically in agreement with her sister-in-law. Only Jeremy Liston, who sat to one side of Marjorie in Claude Fortescue's office, did not agree.

Fortescue's office was not of Liston's choosing. A location on his turf would have been better, a psychological advantage, bring the enemy to you, not take the battle to them.

He had condescended to meet in Claude Fortescue's pokey and airless office in response to a last-minute request from Marjorie, a chance for her to show that she harboured no ill will towards Claude or Bunty. However, due to a conflict of interest, Claude had advised another lawyer for Marjorie.

To Marjorie, this was a severe blow. She trusted Claude, the only person that she could. As for Jeremy Liston, his recommendation of a lawyer friend of his didn't bode well.

'Bunty,' Claude said after his wife had quietened, 'I don't believe any more has to be said. Marjorie's in agreement, and Liston, clearly opposed, is willing to accede to her on this. We just need to draw up the papers, get them signed.'

Liston managed a weak smile, a nod of the head. He looked at Claude, saw an honest man, a man who would have acted in the best interests of both the women. It was good that he had turned down one of the two women, but he had chosen incorrectly. It was Marjorie who would be needing a competent lawyer, and with the money involved, even the most resolute could be swayed.

'I want ten per cent,' Bunty said, ignoring her husband.

'It's the least I can do, out of respect for Bernard and Andrew,' Marjorie said.

'Could we agree and I'll be off,' Liston said.

'You would prefer for me not to be involved,' Bunty said.

'From a commercial perspective. You are with all due respect the type of person to want to be involved if you're part of it, to cause trouble if you're not. We need committed people, not someone with their hand out, expecting to receive more than they are entitled to, which in this instance is precisely nothing.'

'How dare you?' Bunty exploded.

Liston sat calmly. 'In the military, it was often the least powerful who used insult and abuse. Legally you don't have any rights in this matter. That is what is of interest to me.'

'I have the family name,' Bunty said.

'The title ends with Marjorie, not with you and your husband.'

'In the event of her death, the estate would fall to me. Isn't that true, Claude?' Bunty said, looking over at her husband.'

'That is correct.'

Liston recognised the need to appease Claude Fortescue. The agreement that would have kept the estate under the control of the Fortescues was one hundred and twenty years old. It could be challenged if Marjorie decided to bequeath the estate to someone else or to give the money to charity, or if she wanted to sell the place and move on.

The Horse's Mouth

And Claude Fortescue, a man Liston could see as someone who wanted a quiet life, not to be scolded by his wife.

Liston recognised a tactical advantage: Claude's disdain, probably hatred of his wife, and the admiration of his sister-in-law.

'Bunty, let's not debate this further,' Marjorie said. 'You will receive your money in time, rest assured. I've given my word, and Claude will deal with the details. Now, if you don't mind, I need to go.'

'With Jeremy?'

'We came together, the same car. He's been a dear, taking this on.'

'Sweet words from you,' Bunty said.

Neither Marjorie nor Liston reacted. They bade their farewells and left.

Outside, Liston spoke. 'Your sister-in-law will cause trouble. Are you sure about this?'

'Get the development approved and then Bunty and I will meet again,' Marjorie said.

'On the battlefield?'

'There will be no fighting. She'll accept surrender before it starts.'

'Marjorie, you're not as soft-hearted as I thought you were,' Liston said.

'Jeremy, never underestimate me. Cross me, and you'll regret it.'

It was either a threat in jest or something more serious, Liston couldn't be sure. Whatever it was, it gave him a newfound respect for his partner in the development. Never again would he regard her as a pushover. It caused him to wonder about events past, about the deaths.

He thought of Sun Tzu, the fifth century BC general and strategist: 'Keep your friends close, but your enemies closer'.

'Jeremy, I don't want to go home, not yet,' Marjorie said. 'Find somewhere discreet.'

Chapter 33

Sue Nixon sat as Clare outlined what they had learnt from Chris Fairweather. Not only had he snooped into everyone's business, but he had also backed up the information, a copy now with Homicide.

Tremayne had always regarded Moulton as a worthy adversary, a man who was firm yet decent. However, Chris Fairweather had uncovered information that the man intended to bring in the DCI from Exeter and to transfer Tremayne to another department, force his retirement, and promote Yarwood to detective inspector.

Apart from the retirement revelation, Fairweather had handed over details of previously unknown facts.

Sue Nixon, a previous bit player in the saga, was looking increasingly vulnerable.

Tremayne and Clare had discussed the case on the way down to Devon, Clare driving, Tremayne taking the opportunity to catch up on sleep, to ask her opinion on which horse she fancied for the 3.30 at Newmarket; her reply, non-committal, although more interested than before Sally Kirkland's death.

'Why didn't you tell us about you and Barton Kirkland?' Tremayne said as he warmed his hands on a heater in Sue Nixon's house.

'You were here about Red Rose.'

'And you didn't think it relevant?' Clare said. 'The horse that belonged to your lover appears at your door, payment in full from a third party who you've never heard of.'

The first time they had met Sue Nixon, she had had a healthy glow about her, with red cheeks and a cheery smile, but now, as Tremayne read out some of the exchanges between her and Kirkland, the glow dulled to a sheen, the red cheeks to white, and as for the smile, gone.

'Sometimes we'd go out for a meal, nothing more,' Sue Nixon said.

'Sue, you've been caught with your hand in the cookie jar,' Clare said.

'I don't appreciate this.'

'We don't appreciate your lying to us. We now know of your relationship with Barton Kirkland, and you didn't think it relevant to tell us?'

'It wasn't anything serious.'

'Serious or not, it raises questions,' Tremayne said. He moved away from the heater, stood with his back to an open hearth, the logs still glowing red in it.

'You knew the horse was Red Rose when it arrived,' Clare said. She felt sorry for the woman, involved in what had been criminal on Kirkland's part, but was now murder.

'Is there any point denying?' Sue Nixon said.

Tremayne cautioned the woman again, reminded her that what she said could be used in evidence. They were heading into unknown territory and with a woman who had been innocent but was now far more.

"Barton was in trouble; I know that. Something to do with a deal that had gone wrong,' Sue Nixon continued.

'Did it concern you?' Tremayne said.

'The deal or him sending the horse to me?'

'Both. Start with the deal that had soured.'

'I'd known Barton for a few years, and he used to place his horses here from time to time. He wasn't a man who wanted another wife, and I certainly didn't need a man on a full-time basis.'

'From time to time, you'd meet up with him, a few drinks and into bed,' Tremayne said.

'You make it sound dirty. We got on well, and I knew what Barton was. After all, it was casual, nothing more. I had gone through a nasty divorce, only just managed to hold onto this place. Barton helped me out, dealt with some of the creditors who were trying to take advantage of a defenceless woman.'

'You don't look defenceless.'

'Intimidation, threats of unpleasantness.'

'If you didn't sell the place to them?' Clare said.

'We had a good business, my husband and I, a joint partnership.'

'You said the divorce was acrimonious.'

'It was after I found out that he'd been sleeping with my best friend; moved in with her now, although he's having trouble with her, something he never had with me.'

'Better the devil you know,' Tremayne said.

'I wasn't the devil. Anyway, I may have been partly to blame. We were working hard, seven days a week, fifteen hours a day, not that I'm complaining.'

'Inspector Tremayne and I could agree with you on that,' Clare said.

'I thought he was fine, but a man's a man. And there's my friend, available and easy, and he's over there with her.'

'No longer your friend?'

'I thought my husband was impervious to her charms. After all, she didn't care for horses or the land, preferred to be in town, meeting up with friends, dining out every other night, getting laid as often as possible.'

'Are you in touch with her? Could your husband have set up the creditors to take you on?'

'I see her occasionally. I see no reason to hold a grudge, not long term, too much wasted effort.'

'The creditors?'

'After the divorce, he tried to get back with me, apologetic about what he had done, what a mistake it had been. I wasn't interested, but we agreed to put the past behind us and move on. What with Barton helping me out, and my husband referring clients and their horses to me, I survived.'

'Your husband, do you see him?' Clare asked.

'We meet once a month, neutral territory.'

'For what reason?'

'He has a twenty per cent interest in the place. That way, he can survive. His newfound lady is high maintenance. He needs an income, and I need an impartial adviser; someone I can trust.'

'After he cheated on you?'

'What's in his trousers did, but that's men, isn't it?'

Clare offered no comment. An embittered woman, putting on a brave face as if she didn't care. But deep down, Clare knew, the woman was a romantic, in need of a man, and Barton Kirkland, rogue, racehorse owner and not fit, was that substitute.

'You've not explained how Red Rose came to be here through a third party,' Tremayne said.

'I didn't at the time. I hadn't seen the horse for one thing, although Young Bob had.'

'He would have recognised the horse,' Clare said.

'Do you suspect him?' Sue asked.

The two officers left Sue Nixon at the house and walked down the gravelled track to find Young Bob. Over to one side, two horses trotting, riders mounted; on the right-hand side of the track, an old tractor, a barn containing hay, and the main stables.

'Inspector Tremayne, Sergeant Yarwood, come back to see us again,' Young Bob said as he came out from one of the stables. Grabbing Tremayne's hand firmly and then Clare's, he was effusive in his welcome.

'We have a few questions,' Tremayne said.

'Anything to help.'

'You were here when Red Rose arrived, weren't you?'

'I was, helped to settle the horse down, ensured he got a feed, a gentle exercise. Racehorses can be temperamental, especially after a long journey.'

'Was Red Rose?'

'Better than most, worse than some others.'

'You've been around horses for a long time?'

'Since I was nine or ten, used to help muck out at a stable near where I grew up. My father wanted me to study law or medicine, but he was wasting his time.'

'You knew what you wanted,' Clare said.

'I did.'

'Can you remember the first horses you worked with?' Tremayne asked.

'It was a riding stable, pay your money for an hour or two. Easy to deal with, calm temperaments, trustworthy with children.'

'Not racehorses?'

'Not at all. As I said, suitable for a mild gallop, nothing more.'

'And you remember them, could still name them, tell me how many hands they were, what treats they liked.'

'I don't always remember people, but I never forget a horse.'

'Then here's the problem,' Tremayne said. 'We've checked the records. Red Rose has spelled here before.'

'He was,' Young Bob said. Clare could see the man shying away, not as chirpy as before.

'If you can remember your first horses, over forty-five years ago, how come you couldn't remember Red Rose? It's not as if the name wasn't known. And you knew Barton Kirkland, probably his daughter.'

'But, but…'

'There are no buts,' Clare said. 'Inspector Tremayne's right. You knew the horse, and you knew the Kirklands. Why?'

'Why didn't I tell Sue?'

'Yes.'

'But I did, the same day. Ask her, she'll tell you.'

'Either you're lying, or she is,' Tremayne said. 'Which of you is it? Barton Kirkland was still alive then. As for this cock and bull story about an unknown person or persons sending the horse here, that's a load of rubbish. Where was it?'

'He was here all the time, in another stable.'

'Why?'

'We wanted to protect the animal. We knew what had happened to the other horse, and then with Sally murdered, we were confused.'

'So confused that you lie to the police,' Tremayne said. 'You and your boss are involved in a conspiracy, a crime, murder.'

'Honestly, I didn't know anything. I was just protecting the horse, no more. I didn't think we were doing anything wrong, and as Sue said, "It's Barton, we've got to protect him".'

'At all cost? Is that what she said?'

The Horse's Mouth

'I knew that Sue and Kirkland were friendly, not that she ever told me, but I keep my eyes open; I saw the occasional rubbing up against each other, the whisper in the ear.'

From up the track, a loud voice. 'Say no more, Bob.' It was Sue, and she was running.

'You heard?' Clare said on the woman's arrival.

'Young Bob doesn't understand the complexity of the situation.'

Tremayne was tired of the deception, of the woman, even of Young Bob. One of the two or both was guilty of a crime, but he didn't know what crime yet. But he would before he left the stables.

Clare made a phone call, asked the local station to send over an inspector. A matter of courtesy if there was to be an arrest.

The four relocated to the main house. An air of civility; Clare hoped the woman was innocent.

Tremayne stood close to the heater again, while Young Bob stoked the log fire. Sue Nixon sat on a sofa, Clare on a leather chair, and once the fire was blazing, Young Bob found himself a wooden chair by the window. He looked uncomfortable as though he didn't come into the house that often.

Outside, a car drew up, a woman in uniform, a man wearing a suit.

The two entered into the house, introducing themselves as Inspector McGill and Constable Jenny Hardcastle. Tremayne explained the situation. They were to observe and to transport Sue Nixon and Young Bob to the nearest police station if it was needed.

'We've done nothing wrong, either of us,' Sue said.

'We'll be the judge of that,' Tremayne said.

'Bob, you're first,' Clare said. 'The horse is here for protection, but someone else knew it was here.'

'I never told anyone. It was only Sue and me who knew the truth.'

'The other staff?'

'There are three other full time,' Sue said, 'and a couple of locals, teenagers both of them, but they're casual, after school, at the weekends. Apart from Bob, no one else would have known the horse.'

'But someone did. It's either you two or someone had told someone else, which leads us back to Barton,' Tremayne said. 'Why would he want to kill his horse?'

'I'd say, best if you ask him, but we can't.'

'Sue, the horse was here all along. How did it get from Salisbury to here?'

'Bob picked it up.'

'Which means you knew about the switch.'

'Les Daniels phoned me up, told me it was a matter of the utmost urgency.'

'On Barton Kirkland's instruction?'

'He said it was.'

'Did you bother to check? After all, removing a horse before a race makes no sense.'

'Les Daniels had the authority to make decisions on Barton's behalf. I had no reason to doubt the veracity of his instruction, none at all. Nor did Bob when the horse arrived.'

'You knew the horse was racing?'

'I did,' Sue said.

'Daniels asks you to pick up the horse at Salisbury Racecourse. Wasn't this unusual?'

'I was following instructions. How Barton structured his business was his concern, not mine.'

'Even if it was criminal?'

'Who said it was criminal? The horse could have developed a sickness, a tightness in a muscle. Any number of reasons could be put forward as to why Red Rose wasn't going to run.'

'But it did. Weren't you surprised when you heard?'

'I phoned Barton, asked him what was going on.'

'His reply?'

'Sally had just been found. He wasn't communicative.'

'That we can understand,' Clare said.

The female constable excused herself and left the room; the local inspector watched and listened, transfixed.

'I met with Kirkland on several occasions after his daughter's death,' Tremayne said. 'Why didn't you phone him up afterwards?'

'I did.'

'His reply?'

'He told me he would explain it to me another time.'

'And you accepted that?'

'Inspector Tremayne, the man's daughter's been murdered. His horse is here. What more do you expect me to say to him?'

'Did you spend the night with him after his daughter died?'

'No. My personal affairs are not important.'

'I knew,' Young Bob said. 'None of my business.'

'Kirkland came down here, took it back to Salisbury. What did you talk about while he was here?' Tremayne said.

'He was in trouble.'

'What sort of trouble?'

'With Barton? Money, what else?'

'Barton had fallen foul of someone,' Tremayne said. 'You were never under any illusion about the man.'

'He told me about his past.'

'Did he mention a Billy Shripton?'

'He said he was a snivelling little toad. I don't know why, but he hated that man.'

'Barton Kirkland killed him.'

'The horse that died? Scarlet Soleil?'

'It wasn't Sally's horse. It was expendable,' Sue said. 'Don't think me heartless, but I wasn't judging Barton. He'd done right by me; I would do right by him. And I wasn't about to report him for God knows what. The police need a crime, proof, and I had neither.'

'If you had?' Clare asked.

'Whatever it was that he was up to, whatever crimes, it killed him and his daughter.'

'Les Daniels, as well,' Tremayne said.

Clare looked over at the local inspector. 'Thanks for coming, but there'll be no arrests today.'

'That means you believe us?' Young Bob said.

'It means we don't have any proof,' Tremayne said. 'You are both guilty of criminal negligence, an unwillingness to contact the police, condoning a crime. If we do find evidence linking back to here, evidence that you've perjured yourselves, you'll both find yourselves locked up tight.'

Chapter 34

It was, Tremayne thought, an auspicious start to the day. Superintendent Moulton was in the office, and although he was berating him for no arrests, he felt a certainty that had been building since the interview with Sue Dixon and Young Bob, that by the end of another long day there would be an arrest.

Tremayne could feel it in his bones, the sixth sense. It wasn't mystical or psychological, not even a mental attribute, but a result of years of experience.

Clare could see how her boss held himself that day, the years rolling away, his posture upright, his face bright and alert, no bags under the eyes, no need to be fiddling in his pocket for a cigarette.

'Tremayne, I've given you long enough on this. I've got people to answer to, the same as you, and even if you think I'm the devil incarnate, you should try having to answer to them,' Moulton said.

'Superintendent, we're at an important juncture in the investigation. I believe we've solved the case,' Tremayne said. It was a false statement, he knew that, but one that he felt soon would be true.

'Cases. You've more than one murder.'

'Three that we're certain of, another one a probability, and if we don't wrap it up soon, one more.'

'Who's at risk?'

'Marjorie Fortescue.'

'Why her? I thought she was able to look after herself.'

'She is, but she's all that stands between Lady Fortescue's sister-in-law and the Fortescue estate, and Bunty Fortescue's no pushover, hard as nails.'

'Capable of murder?'

'She wouldn't see it like that. It's her birthright, the place where she was born. She's careful not to let it show, but she didn't like me.'

'That, Inspector Tremayne, is not so hard,' Moulton said.

Clare could hear the conversation from her desk. It caused her to smile, a look from Tremayne telling her to get back to work and not to be enjoying a joke at his expense.

It was a look in jest from her senior and a humorous retort from the superintendent. That day the man was not gunning for his inspector, but looking for information.

'Andrew Fortescue?' Moulton continued.

'He would have been the logical first step. Easy enough to fake the suicide of a man known to be emotionally fragile, and who had seen his intended in flagrante delicto with Jeremy Liston.

'Is that proven? Had he seen her? And if he had, was it him that killed her?"

'He was at the racecourse, left soon after.'

'Not conclusive, purely conjecture on your part.'

'There's a secret entrance into the bedroom, and someone could have snuck up, given the man a push, although he may have been teetering on ending it all. We'll never know from him.'

'How many in the act of despair don't write something down, the chance to unburden themselves, to lay the blame for their wretched life on someone else?' Moulton asked.

The Horse's Mouth

'Not many, but Andrew wanted to marry Sally Kirkland, and then if he saw her with Liston. Fortescue was a weak man in need of a backbone and she needed a title, not only for herself but for her father, a grubby lowlife made good.'

'Barton Kirkland kept Daniels close.'

'Daniels had a hold over Kirkland, proof that the man had killed Billy Shripton.'

'That was over thirty years ago. What kind of proof? A cold case, corroborating witnesses either dead or old, and the investigating officers at the time put out to pasture.'

'Barton Kirkland hadn't given crime up. He was betting heavily, getting himself deep in a financial quagmire.'

'One of your reports said that the man was interested in the Fortescue estate, hardly the act of a man with no money.'

'Kirkland was a man who lived on the edge, skirting bankruptcy, looking for a better time, an opportunity. The Fortescue estate was ripe for redevelopment, not just a sliver of land at the back, but he could have planned to keep the house, enough land to keep the peasants at bay, and with him and Liston, they could have made a fortune.'

And that was it, Tremayne realised. With a start, he got up from his chair, grabbed his jacket and his phone off the desk. 'Sorry,' he said to his superintendent. 'Today, you'll have something to report to your superiors.'

***

As they drove away from the station, Clare turned to Tremayne. 'What was that about, you and Superintendent Moulton?'

'This is not about two horses, nor is it about a love triangle. It's to do with the Fortescue estate.'

'Two horses died.'

'Deal with one at a time. We know from the folder I retrieved at Kirkland's house that he wanted to marry off his daughter to Andrew Fortescue and then bankrupt the hapless fool one way or another.

'If Kirkland's plan to wrest control of the Fortescue estate had come to fruition, he would have made a fortune, and Sally would have had control of her husband.'

'The one fact we've always been certain of,' Clare said. 'Barton Kirkland's love for his daughter. He would have done anything for her; she for him.'

'But someone gets wind of it, attempts to stop it.'

'Sally died, a crime of violence. Yet he never showed it, not the emotional outburst that you'd expect.'

'Don't read too much into that, Yarwood,' Tremayne said. 'The man was stoic. On his own in that house of his, he would have mourned; I'm sure of that now.'

'And if Sally thought she could have Andrew as a husband, and Jeremy Liston on the side, Lady Chatterley, not with the gardener but an estate agent, then she'd play the dutiful wife.'

'Liston was party to all this. He wasn't saying goodbye to the woman, only au revoir, distancing himself for the time being. Sally, a domineering woman, in life and love, was about to embrace the title and the aristocracy.'

'Would Lady Fortescue have suspected?'

'She would have.'

The Horse's Mouth

As Tremayne and Clare turned into the Fortescue estate, another vehicle eased in front of them from the other direction. In the front seats, Jeremy Liston and Marjorie Fortescue.

'One at a time,' Tremayne said. 'We deal with her ladyship first, serve notice on Liston to make himself available for later in the day.'

'He's not guilty of any crime.'

'None at all, not unless you regard an affront against common decency and honesty as crimes.'

'Whatever happens, he'll come out of this badly. A dented reputation, maybe.'

'Yarwood, your naivety, yet again. The man will come out of this smelling of roses, mark my words.'

Clare pulled in behind Liston's vehicle, Liston going around the car and opening the door for his passenger.

'If we weren't here?' Clare said.

'They're playing it cool, putting on an act.'

'The man's incorrigible.'

'You must admit to a sneaking admiration.'

'You might, not me. He uses people, Lady Fortescue now, and then throws them out. If Barton Kirkland wasn't able to achieve his dream, that doesn't mean Liston won't. The man has no morals.'

'Survival of the fittest, the jungle where the most savage and cunning triumph. Who knows what he was like before he killed on active duty, but those experiences must have honed him, made him capable of putting them to good use. He'll throw her to one side when it suits him.'

Liston looked back at Tremayne and Clare, acknowledged their presence and drove off.

Marjorie Fortescue came over to the car as Clare got out of the driver's seat. 'I'm surprised to see you here,' she said.

'We know the truth,' Clare said. 'We need to talk.'

'Jeremy showed me around the land we're subdividing.'

Clare said nothing, only observed. The land was covered in waist-high weeds and soggy underfoot, yet her ladyship was still wearing high heels.

Inside the house, cold and dark on entry, but soon bright as Marjorie Fortescue put on the lights.

'No one to help?' Clare said.

'After Bernard died, I kept the staff for a while, but now I've dispensed with them. I have a company on contract, comes in every three days, checks the place out, does routine maintenance and cleaning.'

'Somewhere warm,' Tremayne said.

'I assume this is official,' her ladyship replied, not commenting on the inspector's sternness.

'Lady Fortescue, I advise you to be careful in what you say here today.'

'An error of judgement is not a crime.'

'We're not here about you and Liston,' Clare said. 'If you're involved in a personal relationship with him, that's not our concern.'

'More of a celebration after I secured a deal with my sister-in-law, removed an impediment to developing the land.'

'It's not that simple,' Tremayne said.

'It is to me. It will release capital, allow me to keep this place, and Bunty and her husband can have one of the cottages on the estate, live in the house if they want.'

The Horse's Mouth

'That's what she would want, not necessarily him. He's not an ambitious or greedy man, just willing to let life pass him by.'

'He's your kind of person, isn't he, Inspector?'

'He is. He may well prove to be the only person in this sorry saga who is.'

'Even me?'

Clare could see that regardless of Marjorie Fortescue's claim that the previous night had only been a distraction, a one-night stand, she was supremely content. Clare couldn't blame her, but very soon her world would come crashing down.

'Lady Fortescue, I will outline specific facts to you. Some you will know of, others, more disturbing, you won't,' Tremayne said.

'Very well, but I'm sure I know most of them.'

'The most significant is that while your husband and son were alive, Jeremy Liston and Barton Kirkland were cohorts.'

'If they were?'

'I obtained certain documents at Kirkland's house. They outlined a plan to bankrupt Andrew when he became Lord Fortescue, the upshot of that was that Kirkland would buy Andrew out and then sell off a large part of the estate, keeping the ownership of the house for himself.'

'But Sally, his daughter, was to be here, married to Andrew.'

'From notes with the documents, Sally would have the title, her father, the house. Jeremy Liston has always been involved, looking for one angle or another.'

'I can't believe this.'

'The documents are available,' Clare said, 'as evidence.'

'Do you, Lady Fortescue, believe that Jeremy Liston will honour any agreement you strike with him?' Tremayne said.

'Jeremy's only interested in what's good for him.'

'Those words that he would have said last night to you, he would have said to Sally,' Clare said. 'Two women, so alike, tough and resourceful, but a charmer such as Jeremy Liston, and you're putty in his hands.'

'If Sally was as tough as me, and I admit that she was, she wouldn't have been fooled any more than me.'

'You were, initially. Somehow, you came to know of Kirkland's and Liston's plans. That's when you decided to act.'

'I don't like where this is heading. I should have a legal adviser with me.'

'Claude Fortescue?'

'I can trust him.'

'His wife?'

'She would have sold out her part of the agreement that we agreed to yesterday.'

'Did Liston suggest that?'

'I'm afraid that I did. You, Inspector Tremayne, are incorrect. Whatever happened, I was never going to be the loser.'

'How did you intend to cheat Liston? A clause in your agreement with him?'

'Marjorie, it would be better to be truthful with us,' Clare said. 'You do not care for Liston. No doubt he was a good lay, and after such a long time with a sick man, a welcome relief, but you had nothing to gain from him.'

'Am I under suspicion?'

'You have known all along what Kirkland and his daughter intended, what Liston intended. We have the proof,' Tremayne said.

The Horse's Mouth

'How?'

'Sally kept a diary. In it, she said you had overheard her and her father speaking.'

'The truth will damn me, but yes, he was here one day. It was the father of the bride and the groom's parents meeting, nothing more. But later, Sally was in another room, and I heard them discussing their plans.'

'The options were limited,' Clare said. 'You couldn't hope to convince your son to give up Sally, to find himself a woman with no spark and vitality.'

'Andrew was infatuated with her, saw it as love.'

'You had to stop it at all costs. Your husband?'

'I never told him. He was close to death. He wouldn't have been able to do anything about it.'

'The only way was to remove their instrument of success: to kill your son.'

'How dare you? I loved my son.'

Clare took hold of Marjorie's arm and lifted her from the chair she had sunk into. 'Take a deep breath. Inspector Tremayne needs the truth. You can't maintain this pretence for any longer.'

'He came home that day, distraught, confined himself to his room. I left him alone for three days, thought that he would get over the woman and what had happened to her. But he told me on the day he died, that he had seen her with Liston in that stable. I tried to console him, but it wasn't possible. I left him for a minute, and he jumped.'

'That's why Jim Hughes and his CSIs couldn't find any proof. It was your house; your prints and your presence were all over the place. Lady Fortescue, you murdered your son, not out of hatred, but out of love.'

'Andrew confessed to me; I could see that the truth would come out eventually.'

'He killed Sally?'

'He saw her with Liston, the two of them, making a fool of him.'

'He took no action against Liston.'

'How could he? My son and Jeremy, hardly a match, and besides, he wasn't the guilty party, only a man taking advantage.'

'As you did, last night,' Clare said.

'To my regret now.'

'Andrew was light of foot, hardly see him in passing, and he was always meticulously tidy. That's why you couldn't find any evidence.'

'And you, Lady Fortescue, realised that he would be sentenced to prison for a long time; to a place where the men are hard and in need of a pliant and weak man, and would have mistreated him, subjected him to all kinds of abuse, violent and sexual. You could not allow that.

'It was love, not ambivalence or hatred for my son. I did what I had to; I had to end it.'

'You pushed him,' Clare said.

'It was the right thing to do.'

'It's still murder,' Tremayne said.

'At least Bunty and Claude will look after the house,' Marjorie Fortescue whispered.

Chapter 35

Agamemnon had sacrificed his daughter Iphigenia for a favourable wind to sail to Troy to reclaim Helen from Paris, and to return her to his brother, Menelaus, the king of Sparta, Clare remembered from Greek studies at school.

Was Marjorie Fortescue's crime any worse, Clare wondered. Agamemnon's motives had been honourable on the one hand, heinous on the other. Was that one act, however wrong, justified?

Clare knew it was not, so did Tremayne, as did society in general, the law in particular. The house and the estate, the proud name of the Fortescues, dashed through a set of circumstances not of Marjorie's making, but she sat in her cell at the police station unrepentant, in mourning for her late son.

It was a contradiction of emotions that Clare felt. She had liked Marjorie Fortescue, still did, yet the woman had confessed to killing her son, an act of selfishness, to save him from a fate worse than death. Agamemnon had acted similarly, an inviolate commitment to his brother to right the wrongs committed against him. Then on his return, Helen reunited with Menelaus, Agamemnon killed by his wife, Clytemnestra.

Whichever was the greater evil, Clare knew that the battle had not raged in Lady Fortescue's mind for long. The woman was decisive, able to reason through the alternatives. Yet the law of the land would not doubt her punishment, nor would public sentiment. Condemned for the murder of her son, life in prison would be hard for her, harder than it would have been for Andrew.

Tremayne affected the manner of a police officer after a successful investigation, the solving of two murders, so much so that late that night, long after Marjorie Fortescue had been charged and put in a cell, he and Clare were at a pub.

'Two down, two more to go,' Tremayne said. He had a pint of his favourite beer in his hand.

Clare knew the smug look of complacency belied the truth. She knew that Tremayne, for all his bravado, would feel remorse and sadness at Marjorie Fortescue's fate.

The man could stand emotionless at a murder scene, looking down at a body, mutilated by a savage killer, but a soppy film on the television, the young lovers dying, would bring a tear to his eye, a lump to the throat.

He was, she knew, sorry that Marjorie Fortescue, a woman of noble intentions, of nobility, was in jail, while villains still walked the street, impervious to the killing of one person or many.

'Unexpected,' Clare said. After such a day, she would have preferred to be at home with her husband, to talk through her emotions with him, but Tremayne was on a roll, and it wouldn't be long before a clarity would appear before him, a set of clues that would lead to the next murderer.

'Logical on reflection. The reason the CSIs couldn't find anything. Could they have missed something else?'

'Les Daniels and Ian Swift, meeting near to where Daniels lived. What was Swift's explanation, remonstrating with Daniels for Sally Kirkland's death? Why would he do that? Swift is no fool.'

The Horse's Mouth

'Marjorie Fortescue was willing to keep her secrets. Why not him?'

'Are you suggesting he was keen on Sally?'

'Did you know the woman?'

'I never met her,' Clare said.

'I did on a couple of occasions. She had something about her. Not a great beauty, but a pleasant face, a little overweight, bound to have put on more in time, but charming. Her father listened to her advice at the racecourse, which horse looked the most likely to win, whether the odds were favourable.'

Moulton had been congratulatory in the station and had soon hurried away to divert the new member of Homicide from setting foot in the police station.

'I was in training with DCI Forsyth,' the superintendent had confessed. 'He's good, but a pain in the rear end; always seems to make you feel inadequate. That's the reason he's a DCI, and I'm a superintendent. If he were here, he'd be casting aspersions about the place, as to how he was the better officer, and what he would do if he were in charge.'

'Is he?' Tremayne had asked.

'There's more to policing than higher grade marks, filling in reports, sucking up to your superiors. You know that, so do I, so does your sergeant, but those up above, they don't care, only interested in runs on the board.'

'And he has them?'

'He's an office man, always makes sure he's got a good team around him; no sycophants, no friends, or if they are, they still have to prove themselves.'

'If they don't?'

'He's made plenty of enemies out of his friends, but if you've got the best people, drive them hard, reward them if they deliver, then it's the results that count. You, Tremayne, wouldn't get on with him, and your sergeant would have struggled, too long with you.'

'Change is coming,' Tremayne said.

'Not today, not tomorrow, but it's not long off.'

'It's not something I want to think about.'

'An old warhorse, never knowing when to quit. I don't want you taken out of here in a pine box.'

Tremayne felt mortality, more than he had in a long time, and for once the acknowledgement by his superintendent for a job well done had had a hollowness about it, not that the man hadn't been sincere.

'I'll know when it's time to hand in my whistle and truncheon,' Tremayne said.

Clare brought over another pint for Tremayne, forcing him to cease reflecting back to his conversation with Moulton.

'Arresting Marjorie will throw Liston's plans to the wind. What's next for him?' Tremayne said

'We'll not get much out of him, and even if Marjorie Fortescue's guilty of murder, diminished responsibility, her mind disturbed on account of her son's confession, she'll still have control of the estate.'

'She'll be notorious, but, in time, she'll be accepted by some. Destroyed by others at the altar of public opinion.'

'Are you suggesting that once the dust has settled, Liston and her will continue with their plans?' Clare said.

'It would need Bunty's and Claude Fortescue's assistance. Left unchecked, Liston would cheat Marjorie, raze the house if he could.'

'Claude Fortescue's the linchpin, the man who'll keep it together.'

The Horse's Mouth

'Hidden behind the veil of respectability, the humble country lawyer, a devious man?'

'I don't believe it,' Clare said.

'You believed her ladyship wasn't guilty.'

'Exceptional circumstance that may happen to any of us. The woman had the provocation; she acted.'

'At 6 a.m. sharp, pick me up on the way through,' Tremayne said as he downed his beer in one gulp. 'Claude Fortescue first, then Bunty.'

'After that Jeremy Liston,' Clare said, pleased to be going home. Clive, she knew, would want to talk, to hear about her day, but that night, she had nothing to say, only the need to sleep and to forget. It had been a trying day, charged with emotion: a mother who had committed prolicide, the killing of her son.

***

It hadn't been a conversation on Clive's mind that night, but romance. Clare realised that he had sensed her mood as she walked in the door, planting a kiss on him and holding him tight.

'Rough day,' he said.

'It could have been better,' Clare's response. 'I'll tell you tomorrow.'

And with that, the two had climbed the stairs to their bedroom, the light soon off.

In the morning, she told him about the events of the day before.

'She'll get off with a light sentence, assuming she has a good lawyer,' Clive said. 'The tragedy of learning that her son had murdered Sally Kirkland, her desire to protect him from becoming someone's bitch in prison.'

'If you were defending her?'

'Seven years, probably less.'

'People wouldn't understand.'

'Why should they? And besides, how do you rationalise what she did? Nobody will ever forgive her or forget, nor will she. Is she emotional, sobbing uncontrollably, unable to constrain herself?'

'On the contrary. Calm and collected, a belief that she took the only course open to her.'

'It may have unhinged her. You better keep a suicide watch on her.'

'We've followed procedures. I wish it could be different.'

'As for Liston, be careful with the man, slippery as a snake, twice as dangerous.'

'He's admitted that,' Clare said as she kissed her husband, another warm embrace, and then walked out of the door. It was fifteen minutes before six in the morning, another long day.

It was seven twenty in the morning when they arrived at the Fortescues' home, delayed due to Jean insisting that Clare came in for a quick cup of tea and a chat.

Tremayne was upstairs, as Jean quickly spoke. 'It's his right leg, arthritis. He won't tell you, but keep a watch out for him. He's not up to these early starts.'

'I've seen it,' Clare said. 'I'll cover for him as much as I can.'

'I know you will. He thinks the world of you.'

'Don't ask him to admit it.'

'Never, but that's Tremayne, not willing to give up, not able to continue. I want him here with me, not out chasing murderers, and now he tells me you've arrested Lady Fortescue.'

'She confessed, killed her son.'

'I should be shocked, but I'm not. Too used to life and death, although Tremayne doesn't talk about it much.'

'It's left a sour taste,' Clare admitted. 'What we had to do yesterday.'

'The woman?'

'It's too early to say. She acts normally, takes the murder of her son in her stride, her incarceration in the same manner. Who knows what goes through the minds of people when faced with impossible situations?'

'Our lives seem uncomplicated compared to hers. All that money and respectability; it counts for nothing in the end.'

Clare could only agree, but as Tremayne came down from upstairs, the conversation between the two women returned to the mundane. Tremayne acknowledged Clare's presence, took hold of the sandwiches on a plate that Jean had given to him with one hand, the other holding a flask of hot tea.

'You'll be driving, Yarwood,' Tremayne said. Clare knew that for someone who thought the world of her, his manner was abrupt, but then she wouldn't have it any other way.

Claude Fortescue sat across the room from Tremayne and Clare. Even though it was just after eight in the morning, and he wasn't due in the office for another hour, he was wearing a navy suit, a white shirt and a black tie. Bunty, casually dressed in an old jumper and a pair of jeans that had seen better days, stood by his side.

'I still don't believe it,' Bunty said.

'We have a signed confession,' Tremayne said.

'I visited her last night,' Claude said. 'I will contend that your questioning of her was prejudicial, an attempt at getting Marjorie to confess.'

'That's for the defence to put forward at her trial, the woman pressured into admitting her guilt. What do you hope to gain from that?'

'A reduction of the sentence if found guilty.'

'Do you believe in her guilt?'

'If I am to be her defence or instructing lawyer, then I don't believe I am in a position to answer that question.'

'Lady Fortescue will want the best lawyer that money can buy,' Clare said.

'According to her, she doesn't. She intends to plead guilty; to throw herself on the mercy of the court.'

Tremayne disregarded Claude, focussed on Bunty. 'Why don't you believe it?' he said. 'After all, you and she weren't the best of friends, animosity existed.'

Bunty squirmed, not sure what to say, which to Clare who was watching the interchange a sure sign that the woman was measuring her response, not willing to speak candidly but to say what fitted the situation. Clare was convinced that behind closed doors, with her husband, Bunty would be disparaging of Marjorie, pejorative words laced with bad language.

'Her son, my nephew. How could she?' Bunty eventually said.

It wasn't a heartfelt utterance from the woman, Clare knew. One thing that Bunty Fortescue wasn't was a sentimentalist, someone who felt strongly for another human being, even her husband. She was, Clare had already realised on their previous encounters with the woman, cold-hearted, bitter at the treatment meted out by her brother, willing to blame his wife, the upstart usurper, the power behind the throne.

'Andrew had murdered Sally Kirkland, a crime of passion, the woman who was to bear the next generation,'

The Horse's Mouth

Tremayne said, attempting to draw the woman into a corner from which there was no escape.

'He was emotional, soft-hearted, but he would have got over her, found himself someone more suitable,' Bunty said.

'Someone more aristocratic, someone more to your taste?'

'If you like. Inspector Tremayne, you might not like me, obvious in your line of questioning, but it was our forebears that made this country something to be proud of.'

Clare knew that Tremayne had no firm views on politics, although he voted. He was a small 'l' labour man, not a cloth-capped, banner-waving believer.

'They made this country. I'll grant you that,' Tremayne said. 'But at what cost? The subjugation of the populace, kept in ignorance, shipped off to the colonies for a minor infraction, condemned to servitude by a corrupt and repugnant minority, your minority.'

'Bunty, Inspector Tremayne, this serves no purpose.' Claude Fortescue attempted to intervene. Neither of the two took any notice of him.

Tremayne wanted the woman riled; he was succeeding.

'The minority, as you put it, did what was necessary. Look at what we have now: decadence, the rights of the common man, apathy and decay.'

'Marjorie was common. You never approved of her, the great unwashed.'

'I wouldn't be surprised…' Bunty attempted to finish the sentence, interrupted by Tremayne.

'If she put a pillow over Bernard Fortescue's face, helped him along to his maker. Is that what you were about to say?'

'Why not? You'd not know, and then she could go and screw Jeremy Liston, make a fool of Claude and me, cheat me at the first opportunity,' Bunty said.

'As you intended to do with her, but how?'

'I would have acted honourably,' Claude said.

'There's a conflict of interest, and you know it. Did Marjorie?' Clare said.

'Marjorie would have taken independent legal advice. And why was Liston so involved? He was there discussing it with Lord Fortescue while he was alive, with Barton Kirkland, attempting to rid the place of the Fortescue's. Then he's here with you and your wife, professing to agree, secretly plotting.'

'My wife does not like the man, nor do I, although he has an admirable record of service to this country, made something of himself.'

'Whereas you, Claude Fortescue, have squandered the opportunities, accepted the role of being decent and honest, a good neighbour. Does that sit comfortably with your wife?'

'It does,' Bunty said.

'How can it?' Clare said. 'From what we can see, it was Bernard, a man seduced by an easy woman of notoriety, a woman who had slept around, who inherited the title and the estate, leaving you, the worthy successor, a person with the strength of character and purpose, floundering, cut off from society, cut off from the wealth.'

'Bernard was weak, not as weak as his son. If it's equality of the sexes that you're looking for, don't look for it in the Fortescue family.'

'Marjorie proved to be more capable than him,' Tremayne said. 'More capable than you. Is that why you plotted against her?'

The Horse's Mouth

'How?'

'Jeremy Liston was covering his bases all the time. His plans with Bernard hadn't come to fruition, and Andrew with Sally at his side would have made it more difficult. That's three people that needed isolating.'

'Are you suggesting that he killed them?'

'It's an interesting thought,' Tremayne said. 'It raises the possibility.'

'Of what?' Claude said. He had maintained a passive stance, willing to let his wife slug it out with the police inspector.

'Liston, it has been said, is a snake. Nobody's under any illusion about that, not even him.'

'In this room, we can all admit that Jeremy Liston has not come off well in this investigation. However, it does not make him a murderer,' Clare said.

'As my sergeant succinctly put it, he's not come off well,' Tremayne said. 'There is still the possibility that he engineered his discovery with the unfortunate Sally. And now Marjorie's involved with him.'

'It didn't take her long,' Bunty said scathingly. 'Who else?'

'Are there others?' Clare asked.

'With her? Why not? She was always a tart, always will be, although I doubt if she'll get much satisfaction where she's going.'

'Where you'd prefer her to be?'

'Claude and I will make a success of it, ensure the legacy remains.'

'It's more than that. Liston would have razed the place or turned the house into a hotel or something equally obscene,' Tremayne said.

'He would have kept the house for Kirkland, attempted to cheat him, but Barton Kirkland wasn't such a fool to fall for his tricks, and he'd killed a man once, could have done it again with provocation. He would have been Liston's match, and now he's dead,' Claude said.

'And that's the problem. One or both of you are holding back, not for reasons of murder, but something else. What is it?'

'We don't know what you're talking about,' Bunty said.

'Bunty,' Claude said, looking over at his wife, 'we've done nothing wrong. We must tell the two officers the truth.'

'I don't agree, but go ahead.'

'Inspector Tremayne, Sergeant Yarwood,' Claude said. 'I was aware of Liston's plans with Kirkland.'

'How?'

'Barton Kirkland asked for my advice.'

'As a Fortescue?'

'As a lawyer.'

'Personally?'

'I could not agree. However, I gave him my legal opinion, the difficulties, the need to ensure that not only I but another lawyer skilled in such complex matters, check any contract with Liston, before signing.'

'It would only have occurred on Sally marrying Andrew.'

'It was a long-term plan, years in the making. Andrew would have made a mess of it, but Sally would have saved the day. Bernard was a fool, and Andrew was even worse. It's often the way that the women are stronger.'

'If Sally had bred a son, you wouldn't have wanted her father to buy the place.'

'That's not entirely true. Kirkland wouldn't have sold off the estate, only select pieces of it. As for the house, if Sally had a son, he would inherit from either her or her father. It would still have remained with the Fortescues.'

'You had no reason to want Andrew dead?'

'Jeremy Liston may have been up-and-coming, but he wasn't a wily old fox, not like Kirkland and me. He would have fallen at the first hurdle, excessive belief in himself, unable to see the fine print.'

'He would have taken legal advice?'

'There's legal advice, and there's legal advice. Mine would be from the highest authority, a place he could never reach.'

'As you can see,' Bunty said, 'we needed Andrew alive; Marjorie was expendable.'

'Did Liston know of the double bluff?'

'Unlikely,' Claude said. 'Sally and her father needed Andrew; Liston didn't.'

Chapter 36

Jeremy Liston remained the prime candidate for the murder of Barton Kirkland on account of his presence outside the house. But Liston had continued to insist that Kirkland wasn't alone.

It was a weak defence, but impossible to prove to the contrary.

Tremayne remained fixated on the horses that had died. They were to him the crux in the final stages of the murder enquiries. The deaths of Sally Kirkland and Andrew Fortescue were not directly related, although that of Les Daniels, a minor player, clearly was.

Clare found herself on the street where he had lived. It was early in the morning, the promise of a cloudless day, although the temperature was below average for the time of the year, and she had worn a heavy jacket, a woollen cap on her head. It was hardly de rigueur for a serving police officer, but she was damned if she was going to freeze to death, and besides, she hadn't been feeling well the last few days.

Clive had advised her to take it easy, to take a couple of days off, but he had known it was wasted advice. He knew his wife, the reason that he loved her: dogged in her pursuit, and, as with her senior, she wouldn't relax until the job was done.

The night before at the police station, she and Tremayne had agreed on a sink or swim strategy, to do whatever was necessary to scare whoever, until someone cracked.

The Horse's Mouth

The plan had been great, but on reflection, what did they have? Tremayne was sure that Liston was up to no good, but that wasn't necessarily a crime, and Bunty and Claude Fortescue were, on the face of it, honourable people, but then so was Marjorie Fortescue.

'It's like this,' Tremayne had said, stifling a yawn, looking over at his sergeant, 'of those who know the truth of the horses up at the racecourse, Sally is dead, so is her father, as is Les Daniels.'

'If Daniels had known Sally's murderer?'

'He would have told me.'

'You're placing faith in a man who didn't deserve it.'

And that was why Clare found herself talking to a woman in her seventies, a small dog on a lead that she held firmly.

'I remember him, a little man,' she said.

The street had been canvassed several times before, people interviewed, one or two not wanting the experience, attempting to duck and dive, to swiftly turn around or open a garden gate. All of them had been collared, given a stern warning about their responsibilities, reminded that it was a murder investigation.

It had only been the landlady who identified Ian Swift on the street with Daniels; Swift's defence as to why was weak and not believed. However, he was not the sort of person who would be able to keep a low profile, sneak into Daniels' house and up the stairs, murder him and then slip out without being noticed.

In the city, Swift was a celebrity, Salisbury's own, imparting his wisdom to a grateful populace, or as it happened, sixty-five thousand viewers on the regional television station, the ratings dropping fast.

As Ben Carstairs, the station manager said when Clare had spoken to him two weeks previously, 'What with their smartphones and their iPads, they can source whatever they want. Ian might know his stuff, but he's not a get-rich-overnight person. How many of them are there on the internet, offering you a million-dollar income, only twenty pounds a month?'

'Hundreds, if not thousands,' Clare had said.

'People want the quick fix, that's the message they want to hear. Of course, the easy fortune con artists don't know how to do it, unless they find a couple of hundred thousand mugs to send them twenty pounds. Who wants to listen to Ian talk about fiscal responsibility, which bank is the best for you, when all you need is twenty pounds to find the secret?'

'Does Swift know?'

'He knows it wouldn't last for much longer.'

'Would it have worried him?' Clare had asked.

'You've met him. What do you think?'

'He would have found something else.'

As Clare spoke to the woman, Carstairs' words kept coming back to her.

'Les Daniels had been a jockey, won a few races in his time,' Clare said.

'Sometimes, he'd come home drunk, fall over the dustbin, bang hard on the door for *her* to open it.'

'His landlady?'

'Always complaining about this and that, sticking her nose in where it's not wanted. Doesn't miss a thing, that one.'

'You don't like her.'

'*Like*? Unable to mind her own business, complaining if Wee Jock makes a call of nature on the grass in front of her house, and I always clear up after him.'

The dog, which Clare had glanced at initially but looked at again, was a Scottish terrier.

'If she was as you say, how could she have not noticed who entered the house, killed her lodger?'

'You'd better ask her.'

If the landlady was a busybody and a troublemaker, it was the first time that Clare had heard it mentioned. However, it was enough for her to knock on the woman's door. One thing was clear; the lady on the street with the little black dog was trouble with a capital T, the type of person you'd not want as a neighbour.

'*Her*, that Jenkins woman,' Daniels' landlady said as Clare settled down in front of an imitation log fire. It wasn't a good attempt at authenticity, cheap and nasty, but it radiated heat at a fast rate, so much so that after five minutes, Clare moved away and sat on the other side of the small living room.

'Her opinion of you was similar. Why?' Clare asked.

'You don't want to know.'

'According to her, you don't miss anything, and you're not telling us the full truth.'

'I wasn't here the day he died. It was me that found him, phoned for an ambulance.'

'We've been over this before, but how could someone get in here, up those stairs, kill your lodger and then disappear?'

'How would I know? All I know is that he paid his rent, gave me no trouble.'

'He came home drunk?'

'Did she say that?'

'It's a question.'

'Her, then. And, yes, Les came home drunk occasionally. Not that I hold with strong liquor, a Methodist upbringing. After all, he was a man disappointed with life.'

'A sad man?'

'Not happy, not sad, just Les.'

Clare wasn't sure where they were heading. It had been intended to be a day of action, not a day of rehashing, attempting to glean a sliver of the unknown from something hitherto unrevealed.

'What is your background?' Clare asked. 'After all, you live here all alone, no friends.'

'I don't need anyone. I have enough money to survive.'

'But you took in Les. Why?'

'Only him. He was kind to me. I met him outside one day. He was looking for somewhere to stay, and he helped me home with my shopping. After that, he became a fixture, nothing more. He preferred to be on his own, so did I. Symbiotic, each needing the other.'

'Since your marriage, anyone?'

'Once or twice, but nothing more. You get used to it in time, find other ways to amuse yourself. Les used to tell me about horses that were going to win.'

'He knew, or he believed they would?'

'They always did, although I didn't get my winnings on Red Rose.'

'Neither did Inspector Tremayne. He was there when the horse died; when Sally Kirkland died.'

'Handy for him.'

'What does that mean?'

'Nothing in itself, just an old woman talking.'

'Did Les talk about the horse?'

'Only that it would win.'

'Nothing to do with him switching the horse for another? If he had?'

'I don't follow the horses that much, and maybe I shouldn't place money on them, but Les was always right. I asked him how once, but he wouldn't say, just to believe in him.'

'And you did?'

'Sometimes he'd talk about his past, his days as a jockey, that accident.'

'And what did you say about your life?'

'Nothing to say. Born and raised here, never been anywhere, other than a two-day trip from Southampton to France and back.'

'Regrets?'

'Why? Why waste my time looking at the past? It's gone, Les has gone, my life soon will be. No reason to be morbid.'

Clare could see the day slipping away. She had better things to do that day than try to draw blood from a stone. The woman knew more, although why she kept it to herself, she didn't know.

'Ian Swift, out on the road with Les? What else can you remember?'

'Swift was angry, that's what I remember, and Les said it was nothing, just a tip that the man had bet on heavily, lost a lot of money.'

'Is there any more?'

'Apart from the papers that Les gave the man.'

'You never mentioned that before.'

'It must have slipped my mind, getting old, forgetful.'

An argument over lost money was one thing, but documents were tangible; they were proof of good or bad, criminal or not.

***

Jeremy Liston's appearance at the police station was not unexpected.

'Liston, I can't let you see Marjorie Fortescue, not now,' Tremayne said. 'She's confessed to murder.'

'Five minutes, no more. What harm can there be?'

'Plenty,' Tremayne said. 'Enough time to pass a message, to give advice, what to say if questioned further.'

Liston was trying to save his skin, Tremayne realised. A man who was devoid of a moral position, only interested in self by his admission. Wherever the investigation took the two police officers, Ian Swift and Jeremy Liston were looking back at them.

One of them was sitting with Tremayne; the other was to receive a visit from his sergeant. Neither man was expected to be pleased with the situation.

'Liston, you're coming out of this badly,' Tremayne said.

'I don't see how. Marjorie still owns the place, and even if she's not at the house, she'll need to pay the bills.'

'Claude Fortescue might try to forestall you. Is the financial situation that precarious?'

'The debts are enough to cripple you and me. Marjorie needed cash fast, and a bank needs collateral if they are to lend money, something she couldn't give.'

'With your help?'

'I wasn't about to put my money in, but if Barton had bought it, he could have raised the money, enough to complete the project.'

'And make you rich,' Tremayne said.

'I would have earned it.'

'How much money?'

The Horse's Mouth

'There are a lot of costs upfront, sweeteners that need to be paid.'

'Sweeteners, to who?'

'Government officials, local and national, the heritage council, the environmental lobby, difficult neighbours.'

Tremayne wasn't surprised by the answer, only the man's honesty.

'How much to Marjorie or Barton before? To you?'

'Allowing for five to six million upfront, I'd reckon close to twenty million, divided down the middle, fifty-fifty.'

'More to you if you can cheat.'

'An ugly word, Inspector. It's business at the sharp end. Marjorie, if she were free, would be trying to cheat me.'

'Bunty Fortescue?'

'Why worry about her? Marjorie certainly didn't, only paying the woman lip service. She fooled me on that one. I thought she was seriously interested in looking after her sister-in-law, but it was a pretence, to keep the woman off our backs while I dealt with the hard work.'

'The greasing of grasping palms,' Tremayne said. All his life he had been frugal, sitting down of a Friday night to balance the books, to pay the bills, to leave some for his pleasures, and here was a man talking in the millions with reckless abandon. The only question that Tremayne could muster was why he had lived such a restrictive life. After all, he wasn't a stupid man, and he should have had the nerve to do more. But he knew he was a creature of circumstance, a child of parents from a different time when food was sparse, when borrowing money was avoided.

Tremayne had seen tough times; his father had seen the Great Depression, starving families living in unheated accommodation, huddled under blankets. Liston had not seen any of that. He had been born in the early seventies when England was becoming wealthy, people were travelling overseas, and optimism abounded.

'Nothing illegal,' Liston said. He had ultimate faith in himself. Tremayne knew that Marjorie, in prison or not, as long as she could control Liston's excesses, tie him up so tight that he wouldn't steal all the money, would one day be released and go back to her house and its grounds.

'There are two people involved in all that's happened, but I don't know where to place them,' Tremayne said.

'Do you need to? Marjorie's admitted to killing Andrew, and he killed Sally.'

'On her say-so.'

'Do you doubt it?'

'My problem is that there are two of you, both men who play the edge, risk-takers, and apparently neither of you has committed a crime. I just don't believe it.'

'Ian Swift?' Liston said.

'Yes.'

'He doesn't take risks, neither do I.'

'What next, work with Claude Fortescue to cheat Marjorie?'

'If it works out that way.'

'Bunty?'

'A formidable woman, but powerless. Claude is the strength.'

'Why do you say that?'

'A lawyer, a man who understands a contract. Bunty might be the driving force behind her husband,

and, no doubt, the man will acquiesce, but he could still be there with the fine print, manipulating the unwary, his wife. Never trust him,' Liston said.

'You've had discussions with him?'

'He despises his wife, but with Marjorie, it's different.'

'Admiration?'

'Possibly love, but he'd never admit to it. He keeps his cards close to him, but if Bunty wasn't there, who knows?'

'Hardly the great lover.'

'Marjorie's not far off the age to slow down, and she respects decency above all else.'

If Liston regarded Marjorie as ageing, then how did he see him, a dinosaur, extinct or soon to be, Tremayne thought.

'Liston, I've still got you down for Barton Kirkland's murder, a distinct possibility for Daniels'. What have you got to say to that?' Tremayne said, knowing that he was crossing the Rubicon, serving notice on the man, aware that his reaction could be averse.

Instead of anger, Liston laughed out loud. 'Inspector Tremayne, you're a blunt man. Short on facts, clutching at straws. I'm no murderer, no reason to.'

'Who else could have got into Daniels' house, past his landlady?'

'I could have done it, shimmied up a drainpipe, come over the roof, but I've put on weight since my army days, not as fit and agile as I once was.'

'Friendly with Ian Swift?'

'In passing. Swift's cerebral; I'm more practical.'

'You seem to have figured out how much money you could make from the Fortescues. That takes a degree of intelligence.'

'Not that much, just enough to set up a spreadsheet, best-case or worst-case scenario. As long as the worst-case makes a small profit, that's enough to be getting on with.'

'After that?'

'Squeeze the margins.'

'You could be wasting your time with the Fortescues.'

'If approval isn't forthcoming, I could be. There's a lot of money upfront, preparation of the proposal, approval from the various government departments, environmental checks, hope there's no endangered newts or butterflies. They can be a nuisance, jeopardise the whole plan.'

'Is that likely?'

'I'll deal with it if it is.'

'Remove the offending creatures?'

'That's one way.'

'Why do you want to see Marjorie? Pangs of guilt, a kindred spirit, love even?'

'I've nothing against the woman, and besides, after the last few days…'

'We know you spent the night with her. She told us that much.'

'An honest woman, although we were discreet. There was no need for her to tell you.'

'No more than there is for you to be so open with me. The two of you protesting your innocence, diverting us with minor infractions, concealing the major one. Is that how it is?'

'Not with me. Why did she confess?'

'Even she, as hard as she can be, could not conceal that from us, not under interview.'

The Horse's Mouth

'You'll waste your time with me. Trained to deal with more ruthless people than you. You're not about to beat a confession out of me.'

Which to Tremayne seemed a good idea; however, it wasn't going to occur. Without irrefutable proof, there was no crime. The man's arrogance, his smugness, his disregard for others had served him well, so far. Tremayne wasn't sure if it was going to be enough to keep him out of prison.

Chapter 37

Jeremy Liston was on a short leash. He knew that, so did Tremayne, and as it turned out, so did Ian Swift.

Clare sat in Swift's office, Gwen outside. It was a subtle plan, agreed with Tremayne, as neither Liston nor Swift was going to confess, both too smart.

'Clare, I don't see the reason for your being here,' Swift said,

'With Marjorie in jail, a confession signed, and with Andrew now known to be Sally's murderer, it lessens the odds.'

'Does it? Gambling's not my thing, only calculated risk, and it seems that you're going out on a limb to bait me, as well as Liston.'

'Here's what we have,' Clare said. 'Two murders solved, two to go, four if you include the horses.'

'Two; let's be precise with this.'

'Very well, two, and it was you who argued with Les Daniels.'

'Remonstrated, accused him of dereliction of duty, failing to protect Sally. I was upset, justifiably so, or shouldn't I have been? Does that make me a murderer?'

'I've not accused you yet.'

'You're working your way there. Tremayne's behind this, send a pretty face, hope that I'll lower my guard.'

'I'm a police sergeant, not one of your easy women,' Clare responded, more indignantly than she should have.

The Horse's Mouth

'Don't worry; I know my place. After all, you're one of Salisbury's leading citizens by marriage, and I'll not cross swords with your husband. Marriage going well?'

Clare took a deep breath, bit her tongue, literally. The man was putting her on edge, and she wasn't going to let him win. If she were to become a detective inspector, in charge of Homicide, she'd have to learn how to control difficult men, violent or clever, on her own.

It was a baptism of fire, taking on Swift, raising the tempo, seeing how far the man could be pushed.

'My husband isn't here, and I don't need you to remind me of my position in the city. I've one question for you, an important one.'

'What is it?'

'When you met with Les Daniels, close to where he lived, the two of you engaged in a heated debate.'

'That's already been mentioned.'

'We know now that he handed you some papers, hardly expected if you and he were at loggerheads, about to come to blows.'

'I don't know where you get this from, although his landlady's a nosey old bat.'

'You knew her?'

'Les told me she was; I assume he told me the truth.'

'How did you get into the house?' Clare said. It was straight out of Tremayne's book of tricks, a direct accusation, wait for the reaction, push the point.

Swift sat silent, said nothing. It was clear he hadn't liked her question. It was a dangerous moment, a leap into the unknown, a place from where there was no return, no retraction.

After what seemed like an eternity, Swift shouted out to the next room. 'Gwen, get in here, bring a notepad or your laptop.'

He then looked back at Clare, focussed his eyes on her and pointed a finger. 'You, Sergeant Yarwood, have accused me of a crime without evidence. I cannot allow this to go unrecorded.'

Inwardly, she was nervous, her body heating. She wasn't going to let Swift have the satisfaction of knowing it. 'Mr Swift, you lied about meeting with Daniels the first time we questioned you, made out that it was anger at Sally Kirkland's death, but it wasn't that, we know that now.'

Gwen Fairweather came in, looked at Clare, smiled at her, a slight nod of the head, which Clare interpreted as 'be careful'. She accepted it in the spirit given.

'Gwen, take down what is said here,' Swift said.

'Don't worry, Ian,' Clare said. 'My phone is on your desk. I'll record what is said, make sure you get a copy. I don't want any evidence that I gain here to be misconstrued. Are you in agreement?'

'I am. Tremayne will get a piece of my mind when I see him, and if he hesitates, I'll phone your Superintendent Moulton, make a formal complaint.'

'That's your prerogative, as is terminating this interview. But I should remind you that two murders need one or two murderers. We've got you and Jeremy Liston. One's more than capable of killing; the other, you, seems unlikely, but you're holding back.'

'Why would I do that? I've nothing to hide.'

'Everyone's holding back. It's when we push that we get the truth, and before I leave here today, you will tell me what you were doing with Les Daniels, what those papers were.'

'Gwen, go and get the file,' Swift said. 'You are right, Sergeant, he did give me some papers, but not what you're thinking.'

'What am I thinking?'

'You're trying to tie me in with the two horses. Believe me; you couldn't be farther from the truth.'

Gwen, who had excused herself, soon returned and placed a brown folder in the middle of the table.

'I'll allow you to open it,' Swift said.

Clare picked up the folder and opened it. Inside four sheets of hand-written scrawl and bad spelling.

'Not the smartest of men, Daniels, but he knew horses.'

'What does it say?' Clare said.

'Les Daniels was interested in purchasing a stable, training racehorses. He came to me, asked for my advice.'

'Were you willing to give it?'

'It was a good proposition. He had twenty per cent of the money. I would arrange the remaining eighty per cent, some of it my own, some from the bank and a few select investors. Owning a racehorse gives a man prestige.'

'Do you need the prestige?'

'I know a few who do.'

'Barton Kirkland craved prestige. Was he one of them?'

'Kirkland never knew, too risky. The man had had Daniels under his foot for a long time.'

'Daniels had a hold on the man.'

'He might have had, but Daniels was loyal, a believer in the goodness of man, which hardly seems feasible seeing that he worked with Kirkland, a rogue unhung.'

'If you were helping him, then why were the two of you arguing?'

'Never mix business with friendship. Daniels understood that, so did I. I was angry about Sally, also about his jeopardising our plans. After all, who else could have swapped the horses?'

'Daniels?'

'You must have realised that by now.'

'We have, but no proof; no one alive to corroborate or deny it.'

'He told me that day outside his place. That's when I became irate. Before that, I had been upset; after all, Sally deserved better.'

'Why didn't she know about Red Rose?'

'She did. Her father was playing with the wrong crowd. He was in trouble, so much so that the horse was security for an unpaid debt, and if he didn't come up with the money, then the horse would have been forfeit, given to someone else to train.'

'Who are these people?'

'I never knew. Daniels knew where Kirkland was heading, and he didn't want Red Rose taken, and Sally was aghast, willing to do anything to save it. Barton Kirkland was a soft man with his daughter; he'd do anything for her, go along with any hair-brained scheme, and it was. If you're playing with fire, don't put your hand in, and that's what he was doing.'

'Who killed Scarlet Soleil?' Clare asked.

'Isn't it obvious?'

'Not to me.'

'Barry Vincent under instructions. It was your inspector who made it easy.'

'Inspector Tremayne wouldn't have been involved.'

'Daniels was in a quandary, your inspector was his alibi, and with him, there with a dead horse, those involved with Kirkland made themselves scarce.'

'Are you saying that Inspector Tremayne was set up?'

'Daniels told me. Red Rose was safe, and Kirkland was off the hook.'

'Vincent was part of the conspiracy?'

'He would have been paid plenty to deal with it.'

'If Tremayne hadn't been there?'

'Nobody would have known that the horse had been euthanised.'

'Would you have helped Daniels, knowing that?'

'I didn't like it, couldn't do it myself, but Daniels would have made a good trainer, and as I said, with a racehorse comes prestige. And now, if you don't mind, leave me alone, and I'll forget your accusatory questioning.'

Clare left the place, a lot wiser as to why Daniels had died, a victim of a cover-up, and Kirkland equally guilty. Overall, she reckoned that she had acquitted herself well.

***

Barry Vincent looked ripe for the picking. Hauled in at short notice after a ride in the back of a police car, the man sat in the interview room, a legal aid lawyer to one side. Nervous, and giving off a smell of bleach, Vincent sat with his arms folded, his face worried.

Tremayne had commenced the interview in line with procedures, advised the man of his rights, that the interview would be recorded. He had said it so many times to so many villains, that he could have said it in his sleep.

'My client understands,' a young woman in her late twenties said. Fresh out of law school, no more than a few months practising law, Tremayne reckoned.

The case file was vague, the killing of a horse. It wasn't necessarily a custodial sentence that Vincent was up for, although the truth would destroy his veterinary practice, relegated back to parrots off their food, neutering dogs and cats.

'Barry Vincent,' Tremayne said, looking over at the man. 'An allegation of the utmost seriousness has been levelled against you.'

'It wasn't me. I didn't do it,' Vincent's reply, his voice cracking.

'Didn't do what?'

'It's documented in the file,' the young legal aid said. She was no slouch, Tremayne had to concede.

'Vincent, what didn't you do?' Tremayne repeated the question.

'I didn't kill Sally; no one will ever make me admit that.'

'Mr Vincent, unless you've been out of the city, or flat out with work, you should know that we do not believe you are guilty of that crime. You are here for another reason, and as your lawyer has stated, she knows what it is, no doubt told you, explained what is to happen here.'

'It wasn't a crime, not that I wanted to, but Barton, he was insistent.'

'When and where?'

The Horse's Mouth

'I knew about it a couple of days before. I never knew the details as to why; he wouldn't tell me that, nor would I ask.'

'What did you suspect? Did Les Daniels tell you? Was he involved?'

'You're badgering my client,' the legal aid said. 'He will be full and frank with you, answer all your questions in due course.'

'That's the problem,' Tremayne said. 'Your client has had sufficient opportunity to come forward before this, and what has he done? I'll tell you – precisely nothing, hoping we'd go away.'

'Who told you?' Vincent asked.

'Les Daniels, in a heated confrontation with a third party, blurted it out.'

'He was in on it, pleased in some way.'

'Vincent, you are in the middle of this, so I suggest you start talking soon before you're found hanging from a hook.'

'That's threatening,' the legal aid said. The woman was tenacious, not about to be curtailed by a seasoned police inspector, a man who had made villains cower through the strength of his personality and his voice, his fists on occasion.

'Madam,' Tremayne said, 'it's a fact. Each time we get closer to the truth, another element is revealed, and we have to re-evaluate. Your client may not be guilty of a crime, not with us, but there are others, as I've said, unseen, lurking in the shadows, looking for whoever acted against their interests. And now, who's left for them to blame?'

'Not me,' Vincent said.

'It will be you,' Clare said. 'Barton Kirkland probably pulled off more than he could handle, and Red

Rose was Sally's favourite. He kept the horse alive for her, sacrificed another.'

Vincent sat back on his chair, looked into space, played with his hands, started picking at a fingernail. No one spoke, only watched. The man was broken.

The legal aid looked across at her client and then back at Tremayne. 'Fifteen minutes,' she said.

'Fifteen minutes, it is,' Tremayne said. 'Take longer if you want, but the truth if we're to save your client.'

Outside, the two police officers stood by a vending machine that supplied coffee and tea with milk or without, sugar or no sugar. Whatever it gave, it tasted awful, but neither was going far, not now. Vincent was about to spill the beans, and they needed to be near.

The fifteen minutes stretched to thirty, then to forty-five. Vincent, who hadn't been charged with any crime, walked out of the interview room with his legal aid.

'We're going for lunch,' the legal aid said.

Tremayne felt that he could have objected, but didn't.

Neither Tremayne nor Clare left the police station, and they returned to Homicide, ordering in a pizza.

After Clare had finished her slice of pizza, Tremayne ate the rest.

After one hour and thirty-six minutes, the interview of Barry Vincent recommenced. Clare sat quietly, sucking on a strong mint, sipping a cup of black coffee, feeling awful, wanting to go home and lie down, but doing neither. Tremayne was full of himself; energy reinvigorating him. There was nothing he liked more than the satisfaction of a job well done, a crime solved.

The Horse's Mouth

'My client will make a statement,' the legal aid said.

Vincent stood up, cleared his voice, as if he was Mark Antony about to give praise to Caesar – *Friends, Romans, countrymen* – but then he sat down.

Clare noticed the legal aid's hand on the man's sleeve. An attempt to pass the blame, to overemphasise his innocence, wasn't going to work. Neither she nor Tremayne was interested in speeches eloquently delivered, and Vincent was no orator.

'Take it easy, Vincent,' Tremayne said. 'Clear and concise.'

'I had worked for Barton Kirkland for close to three years,' Vincent said. 'In that time, I came to observe the man. I wouldn't say that I knew him, as he wasn't open with me or with anyone else, although Les Daniels would occasionally tell me something about him, how they had known each other for a long time. Not that it seemed to matter, as Kirkland was abrupt, treated him as an employee, not as a friend. Why he did, and why Daniels accepted the status quo, I never knew.

'I did my job, always received my money on time. I did occasionally observe that Kirkland was disturbed, but he was a man who thrived on adversity.'

Tremayne had heard it before, the verbiage, the lead up to the main act. It was only a matter of time before Vincent tired of the fancy words and got to the meat, to something that would give him another arrest. It wasn't a time for him to interrupt, only to listen.

'Barton cared for the horses, but he was a businessman, selling one, buying another. But Red Rose was the exception. For whatever reason, and it wasn't as if the horse was better than others that he owned, it was Sally's favourite, a friend. And one thing that Barton would always consider was his daughter. The two of them were exceptionally close, and even though he didn't like her behaviour, it didn't detract from his love for her.'

'You were involved with the woman,' Tremayne said, unable to contain himself.

'The man was in trouble; a deal had gone wrong. I knew from Daniels that the man was betting heavily, winning most times, sometimes losing. It was, Daniels said, a necessary ploy if you didn't want to raise suspicion or get yourself banned by the bookmakers. But Daniels told me on another occasion, a week before Sally died, that Kirkland had been careless, had become greedy, and the bets were progressively higher, and he never lost. Daniels never admitted to it, but I knew he was fixing the races; a whisper in someone's ear, money in a back pocket, one horse in peak condition, the other not at its best. Easy enough to do, hard to prove.'

'It was the day before Sally died. Kirkland invites me out to his house, outlines the plan, tells me that either I'm with him or I'm not. I protested. A perfectly good animal euthanised was contrary to my profession, but I had to agree.'

'Why?' Clare asked.

Vincent put down the paper he had been reading from, folded his arms and rested them on the table. 'It was Barton. He said that if he went down, I'd go down with him.'

'You rigged races,' Tremayne said.

'Sometimes, I'd make sure that one of the horses ran better than the others.'

'The reason I don't win that often.'

'The reason no one does. How can you analyse the outcome of a race if one variable is not defined? It's impossible, but Barton was beating the odds.'

'Why?' Clare asked. 'He had enough money, a good life.'

'Why would he spend a lot of money on a horse, and then quibble over the price of a pint of beer? The rich don't like to throw their money around, not unless it's for them.'

'And their daughters.'

'He warned me off her, not that he had needed to. She was tarred with the same brush, determined to marry Fortescue. Ian Swift knew that, so did Jeremy Liston.'

'Anyone else we don't know about?' Tremayne asked.

'If there was, I don't know them.'

'Why was Kirkland getting greedy?'

'I was in the stables at his place once. He was there, not on his own. They were talking, ignoring me.'

'What did you hear?'

'A scheme that the two men had hatched, a plan to take control of Fortescue's mansion and the land around it. Kirkland was keen on the idea.'

'Were you keen on Sally?'

'A man wants someone he can trust. And besides, it was immaterial. It wasn't to be.'

'The other man?'

'Jeremy Liston. I got the impression that it was his idea, and with Sally spending time with Andrew Fortescue, determined to marry him, Kirkland agreed.'

'Were you in the house on the night that Barton Kirkland died?' Clare asked.

'I didn't kill him.'

'That wasn't the question,' Tremayne said.

'He wanted to talk, although he and I didn't have much in common.'

'What about?'

'He seemed lonely. After all, his daughter was dead.'

'Let's run through this from the start,' Tremayne said. 'From when you arrived at the house until you left.'

'I arrived there just after eight in the evening. Barton opened the door, showed me to the room where he died, asked me to take a seat.'

'For how long were you in that seat?'

'We got to talking about horses, about Sally, about Andrew Fortescue.'

'If you weren't a friend of his, then why?'

'Maybe I'm a good listener, not there to judge, a priest in the confessional.'

'Was it that? A confession?'

'I was speaking figuratively. You got the gist of what I was saying. I wasn't a friend, not an enemy, and I certainly had no axe to grind. He didn't need to impress me or to belittle me. It's the same as an owner talking to their dog, telling them about their day.'

Clare could understand the sentiment. After a previous love of hers had died, she had spent hours talking to her cat, an animal that still perilously clung to life.

'He wasn't his usual self,' Vincent continued. 'I didn't like it, made me feel uncomfortable, and besides, I had better things to do with my time.'

'Such as?' Tremayne asked.

'A girlfriend, someone I've known for a long time.'

'On the rebound from Sally?'

'There was never any rebound, as you put it. My girlfriend, her name's Amy, before you ask, we work together at my surgery.'

'We'll disregard Amy for now.'

'She's nothing to do with this. She never met either of the Kirklands. She deals with the smaller animals; I focus on horses. Getting back to why I was dragged in here as a common criminal.'

'There is nothing common about you,' Tremayne said. 'You did, by your admission, euthanise Scarlet Soleil. But we have Red Rose to discuss. An attempt made on the animal in Devon, someone coming up through the rear of the property, dropping a bag as he or she made a run for it. Where were you at that time?'

'How long ago was this?'

'Three weeks, a Thursday, late at night, no moon.'

'I wasn't in Devon, and I certainly did not attempt to kill Red Rose.'

'Why was Jeremy Liston in that stable with her? Why was Fortescue watching?'

'Inspector Tremayne, I'm a veterinary surgeon, very competent at what I do, but I'm not a police officer. How would I know?'

'Vincent, I'll level with you,' Tremayne said. 'You killed Scarlet Soleil, you repeated the exercise with Red Rose, and you were in Devon. We'll prove the last two in time even if we have to place you in a cell for twenty-four hours, go through the evidence again, ask Young Bob to see if you are the person, he saw that night.'

'I'm–'

'It'll go easier on you if you're truthful,' Clare said.

'Barton Kirkland lost interest in Red Rose after Sally had died. He didn't care one way or the other what happened to it.'

'You euthanised Red Rose?'

'He's a complex man,' Vincent said. 'He was involved in something, not that I knew what it was. He just sat there, talking to himself, to me, regretting his life and the love he had felt for his daughter. He told me about her and her men, the plans he had for the Fortescue estate, the former Marjorie Buxton out on the street.'

'He hated her?'

'He said she would have been a thorn in his side, the one person who could control her son, make him see reason, choose someone of his social status.'

'Which Sally, by birth, wasn't,' Tremayne said.

'How long were you at Kirkland's house?'

'I left his house just after ten in the evening.'

'How can you be precise about the time?'

'In the hallway of the house, a grandfather clock. It chimed ten times before Kirkland snapped out of it and told me not to mention the conversation we'd just had.'

'And yet you, along with everyone else, choose not to bring forward relevant information until forced.'

'It was a conversation.'

'Did you move at any time during those two hours?'

'Not once.'

***

'There are inconsistencies in your previous statements we need to examine,' Tremayne said to the man sitting opposite with his lawyer, not legal aid, but highly competent and expensive.

Jeremy Liston said nothing, only looked at the detective inspector and his sergeant, at his lawyer.

The Horse's Mouth

It was mid-morning of the following day. Vincent had returned to his surgery and Amy. Whether criminal action would be taken against him was for others to decide. He hadn't committed murder, although Sue Nixon and Young Bob were on their way to Salisbury for a line-up of Vincent and others, to bring clarity as to whether it had been him who had attempted to sneak in to Sue Nixon's place. Trespass would be a crime, at least.

Whatever the outcome, the facts of Vincent's actions would become public knowledge, his veterinary practice ostracised.

'My client should not be here,' Liston's lawyer said.

'Let me go over the facts,' Tremayne said. 'Your client has admitted to being at Kirkland's window, and he was sure another person was in the house, but not in the room with Kirkland.'

'There was,' Liston said.

'But where?'

'He was with someone, a couple of glasses on the desk, an open door.'

'We can now prove, based on his statement, and as a result of a further detailed check of the room and the house, that Barry Vincent was with Kirkland from 8 p.m. to just after 10 p.m.'

'How?'

'Based on his statement and his phone records. He messaged his girlfriend on arriving, phoned her on leaving, the location of the phone correlating with Kirkland's house. According to you, you were at that window at 9.30 p.m., and we also have another witness who will testify to the time. Barry Vincent entered through the front door of the house, sat on one chair for his time there. He neither left the room, nor did he visit the bathroom.'

'He wasn't there when I looked in.'

'The house has been checked. There is proof that corroborates his story, and besides, he had no motive, whereas you did.'

'How do you figure that?' Liston said. The lawyer said nothing, just took notes.

'You weren't saying goodbye to Sally Kirkland in that stable, were you?' Clare said. 'You were there to check that everything had worked out. How long have you had this problem?'

'We've checked your military record, found out that your actions had had a detrimental effect on you, post-traumatic stress,' Tremayne said.

'A lot of us suffered from it. It's not so easy to see a friend, his guts splayed out of him, another with half his head missing. I've nothing to be ashamed of.'

'Nothing at all. Your heroism is not in question, but you went through a period of depression, held a gun to your head, and then with the therapy you slowly recovered, involving Kirkland, a man with big ambitions.'

'It will need more than this,' the lawyer said. 'My client is a national hero; people will not take kindly to an inspector, no matter how zealous and determined to wrap up a homicide before retirement, pursuing him.'

'Sally wasn't in that stable to break up with you, even if Andrew Fortescue thought it. You intended to see her from time to time, even after she was married,' Tremayne said.

'That's Fortescue's problem, not mine.'
'Why did you make love to her?'
'She was an ardent woman.'

'Not so brave now,' Tremayne said. 'You're not in the field, illiterate peasants with machine guns.'

'This is a witch hunt,' the lawyer said.

'Either way, whether it was you who put the idea to Kirkland or not is not the issue. Kirkland wanted prestige, and for that, he needed money. You, Jeremy Liston, are not so altruistic. Your motivator was pure unabashed greed. In Kirkland, the ideal partner; in Daniels, the ideal stooge.'

'Can you prove this?' Liston said.

'Based on what we now know about your and Vincent's time at Kirkland's place, we have obtained the necessary warrants to conduct searches of your office, your house and your car. Also, any bank accounts in your name and that of your business.'

Liston leant over to his lawyer, whispered in his ear. The lawyer nodded.

'I'll admit to the partnership with Kirkland and the arrangement with Sally,' Liston said.

'Your gambling?' Tremayne said.

'Not compulsive. Daniels would ensure the odds were in our favour, and we weren't greedy. Online, nothing fancy, placing large bets at the regionals. It all adds up.'

'We believe that Kirkland was under financial pressure. And Daniels was working with Joe Blakely as well, explains why he had so much money.'

'Kirkland wanted more, started to get greedy, placed a few bets without my knowledge. Either you follow the system, or you get fried.'

'Red Rose?'

'We had a float of money. It was our way of keeping each other honest, but the man became desperate. That's when I made a deal with him. Give the horse to me, no hurry as to when.'

'Let the heat die down?'

'Sally, she was upset when she found out about it. That's why I was with her in the stable, told her that I wouldn't take the horse if her father replaced the money he'd taken.'

'She was appreciative?'

'She and that horse had an unshakable bond.'

'But it died?'

'After Sally had died, and that must have been Fortescue, Barton was distraught. Not that he'd show it in public.'

'He wanted the horse dead?'

'He did, but with Sally gone and Kirkland disintegrating, I wanted it. Legally it was mine; I intended to race it.'

'You're guilty of a crime.'

'Minor. Fraud, deceiving the public? I don't think so, and besides, I was the silent partner, figuratively. It was Daniels who paid out the money, made sure the horse won, and Kirkland who placed the bets. As I said, small, a few hundred here and there, a thousand or two if he gets it placed.'

'That's for another department at the station; they'll deal with that.'

'I've been honest, as I have all along,' Liston said. 'When have I ever hidden my nature from you?'

'Never,' Clare said.

'You see, Tremayne, your sergeant agrees with me.'

'With the additional information that we received from Barry Vincent and the fact that you lied about your visit to Kirkland's house, the CSIs have conducted a further investigation inside and out. At eight forty-five, this morning, a knife was found twenty yards from the house. It was in a weighted plastic bag and had been thrown into a small stream. It wasn't the first time a search had been conducted in the area, but then the water was high, the result of rain. However, with no rain for ten days, the level has dropped. The bag was in the reeds on the bank of the stream. Forensics have confirmed your fingerprints, and the blood found on it is under analysis.'

'But—'

'I suggest you say no more,' the lawyer said.

'It's murder,' Tremayne said. 'A full confession will go in your favour. As for how you killed Daniels, that we will find out in due course, but the case against you for the murder of Barton Kirkland is conclusive.'

Faced with the truth, the realisation that his position was impossible, Liston did what so many others had, he started to talk.

'It was Kirkland, even though you wouldn't have known it, but with his daughter dead, he had lost the will to live, only interested in restitution, to tell the police about the horses, about me, about the money we had garnered from fools. About what we had planned for the Fortescue estate. With that revelation, Marjorie would never have agreed to continue with my plan.'

'Daniels?'

'He wouldn't have kept quiet, not if Kirkland said anything or if he was dead.'

Moulton was full of praise, but for Clare, it was a hollow victory. Marjorie, who she liked, would go to prison; Liston, who she did not, would also. He had killed two men, whereas Marjorie had murdered her son to save him from what others would have done to him. She would suffer the most.

Although life had just thrown another reality check; Clare was pregnant. The future, whatever it would be in Homicide, would not be the same as before. As for now, all she wanted to do was to go home and to be with Clive.

The End

ALSO BY THE AUTHOR

DI Tremayne Thriller Series

Death Unholy – A DI Tremayne Thriller – Book 1

All that remained were the man's two legs and a chair full of greasy and fetid ash. Little did DI Keith Tremayne know that it was the beginning of a journey into the murky world of paganism and its ancient rituals. And it was going to get very dangerous.

'Do you believe in spontaneous human combustion?' Detective Inspector Keith Tremayne asked.

'Not me. I've read about it. Who hasn't?' Sergeant Clare Yarwood answered.

'I haven't,' Tremayne replied, which did not surprise his young sergeant. In the months they had been working together, she had come to realise that he was a man who had little interest in the world. When he had a cigarette in his mouth, a beer in his hand, and a murder to solve he was about the happiest she ever saw him, but even then he could hardly be regarded as one of life's most sociable people. And as for reading? The most he managed was an occasional police report, an early-morning newspaper, turning first to the back pages for the racing results.

Death and the Assassin's Blade – A DI Tremayne Thriller – Book 2

It was meant to be high drama, not murder, but someone's switched the daggers. The man's death took place in plain view of two serving police officers.

He was not meant to die; the daggers were only theatrical props, plastic and harmless. A summer's night, a production of Julius Caesar amongst the ruins of an Anglo-Saxon fort. Detective Inspector Tremayne is there with his sergeant, Clare Yarwood. In the assassination scene, Caesar collapses to the ground. Brutus defends his actions; Mark Antony rebukes him.

They're a disparate group, the amateur actors. One's an estate agent, another an accountant. And then there is the teenage school student, the gay man, the funeral director. And what about the women? They could be involved.

They've each got a secret, but which of those on the stage wanted Gordon Mason, the actor who had portrayed Caesar, dead?

Death and the Lucky Man – A DI Tremayne Thriller – Book 3

Sixty-eight million pounds and dead. Hardly the outcome expected for the luckiest man in England the day his lottery ticket was drawn out of the barrel. But then, Alan Winters' rags-to-riches story had never been conventional, and some had benefited, but others hadn't.

Death at Coombe Farm – A DI Tremayne Thriller – Book 4

A warring family. A disputed inheritance. A recipe for death.

If it hadn't been for the circumstances, Detective Inspector Keith Tremayne would have said the view was outstanding. Up high, overlooking the farmhouse in the valley below, the panoramic vista of Salisbury Plain stretching out beyond. The only problem was that near where he stood with his sergeant, Clare Yarwood, there was a body, and it wasn't a pleasant sight.

Death by a Dead Man's Hand – A DI Tremayne Thriller – Book 5

A flawed heist of forty gold bars from a security van late at night. One of the perpetrators is killed by his brother as they argue over what they have stolen.

Eighteen years later, the murderer, released after serving his sentence for his brother's murder, waits in a church for a man purporting to be the brother he killed. And then he too is killed.

The threads stretch back a long way, and now more people are dying in the search for the missing gold bars.

Detective Inspector Tremayne, his health causing him concern, and Sergeant Clare Yarwood, still seeking romance, are pushed to the limit solving the murder, attempting to prevent any more.

Death in the Village – A DI Tremayne Thriller – Book 6

Nobody liked Gloria Wiggins, a woman who regarded anyone who did not acquiesce to her jaundiced view of the world with disdain. James Baxter, the previous vicar, had been one of those, and her scurrilous outburst in the church one Sunday had hastened his death.

And now, years later, the woman was dead, hanging from a beam in her garage. Detective Inspector Tremayne and Sergeant Clare Yarwood had seen the body, interviewed the woman's acquaintances, and those who had hated her.

Burial Mound – A DI Tremayne Thriller – Book 7

A Bronze-Age burial mound close to Stonehenge. An archaeological excavation. What they were looking for was an ancient body and historical artefacts. They found the ancient body, but then they found a modern-day body too. And then the police became interested.

It's another case for Detective Inspector Tremayne and Sergeant Yarwood. The more recent body was the brother of the mayor of Salisbury.

Everything seems to point to the victim's brother, the mayor, the upright and serious-minded Clive Grantley. Tremayne's sure that it's him, but Clare Yarwood's not so sure.

But is her belief based on evidence or personal hope?

The Body in the Ditch – A DI Tremayne Thriller – Book 8

The Horse's Mouth

A group of children play. Not far away, in the ditch on the other side of the farmyard, the body of a troubled young woman.

The nearby village hides as many secrets as the community at the farm, a disparate group of people looking for an alternative to their previous torturous lives. Their leader, idealistic and benevolent, espouses love and kindness, and clearly, somebody's not following his dictate.

The second death, an old woman, seems unrelated to the first, but is it? Is it part of the tangled web that connects the farm to the village?

The village, Detective Inspector Tremayne and Sergeant Clare Yarwood find out soon enough, is anything, but charming and picturesque. It's an incestuous hotbed of intrigue and wrongdoing, and what of the farm and those who live there. None of them can be ruled out, not yet.

The Horse's Mouth – A DI Tremayne Thriller – Book 9

A day at the races for Detective Inspector Tremayne, idyllic at the outset, soon changes. A horse is dead, and then the owner's daughter is found murdered, and Tremayne's there when the body is discovered.

The question is, was Tremayne set up, in the wrong place at the right time? He's the cast-iron alibi for one of the suspects, and he knows that one murder leads to two, and more often than not, to three.

The dead woman had a chequered history, not as much as her father, and then a man commits suicide. Is he the murderer, or was he the unfortunate consequence of a tragic love affair? And who was it in the stable with the woman just before she died? There is more than one person who could have killed her, and all of them have secrets they would rather not be known.

Tremayne's health is troubling him. Is what they are saying correct? Is it time for him to retire, to take it easy and to put his feet up? But that's not his style, and he'll not give up on solving the murder.

DCI Isaac Cook Thriller Series

Murder is a Tricky Business – A DCI Cook Thriller – Book 1

A television actress is missing, and DCI Isaac Cook, the Senior Investigation Officer of the Murder Investigation Team at Challis Street Police Station in London, is searching for her.

Why has he been taken away from more important crimes to search for the woman? It's not the first time she's gone missing, so why does everyone assume she's been murdered?

There's a secret, that much is certain, but who knows it? The missing woman? The executive producer? His eavesdropping assistant? Or the actor who portrayed her fictional brother in the TV soap opera?

Murder House – A DCI Cook Thriller – Book 2

A corpse in the fireplace of an old house. It's been there for thirty years, but who is it?

It's murder, but who is the victim and what connection does the body have to the previous owners of the house. What is the motive? And why is the body in a fireplace? It was bound to be discovered eventually but was that what the murderer wanted? The main suspects are all old and dying, or already dead.

Isaac Cook and his team have their work cut out, trying to put the pieces together. Those who know are not talking because of an old-fashioned belief that a family's dirty laundry should not be aired in public, and never to a policeman – even if that means the murderer is never brought to justice!

Murder is Only a Number – A DCI Cook Thriller – Book 3

Before she left, she carved a number in blood on his chest. But why the number 2, if this was her first murder?

The woman prowls the streets of London. Her targets are men who have wronged her. Or have they? And why is she keeping count?

DCI Cook and his team finally know who she is, but not before she's murdered four men. The whole team are looking for her, but the woman keeps disappearing in plain sight. The pressure's on to stop her, but she's always one step ahead.

And this time, DCS Goddard can't protect his protégé, Isaac Cook, from the wrath of the new commissioner at the Met.

Murder in Little Venice – A DCI Cook Thriller – Book 4

A dismembered corpse floats in the canal in Little Venice, an upmarket tourist haven in London. Its identity is unknown, but what is its significance?

DCI Isaac Cook is baffled about why it's there. Is it gang-related, or is it something more?

Whatever the reason, it's clearly a warning, and Isaac and his team are sure it's not the last body that they'll have to deal with.

Murder is the Only Option – A DCI Cook Thriller – Book 5

A man thought to be long dead returns to exact revenge against those who had blighted his life. His only concern is to protect his wife and daughter. He will stop at nothing to achieve his aim.

'Big Greg, I never expected to see you around here at this time of night.'

'I've told you enough times.'

'I've no idea what you're talking about,' Robertson replied. He looked up at the man, only to see a metal pole coming down at him. Robertson fell down, cracking his head against a concrete kerb.

Two vagrants, no more than twenty feet away, did not stir and did not even look in the direction of the noise. If they had, they would have seen a dead body, another man walking away.

Murder in Notting Hill – A DCI Cook Thriller – Book 6

One murderer, two bodies, two locations, and the murders have been committed within an hour of each other.

They're separated by a couple of miles, and neither woman has anything in common with the other. One is young and wealthy, the daughter of a famous man; the other is poor, hardworking and unknown.

Isaac Cook and his team at Challis Street Police Station are baffled about why they've been killed. There must be a connection, but what is it?

Murder in Room 346 – A DCI Cook Thriller – Book 7

'Coitus interruptus, that's what it is,' Detective Chief Inspector Isaac Cook said. On the bed, in a downmarket hotel in Bayswater, lay the naked bodies of a man and a woman.

'Bullet in the head's not the way to go,' Larry Hill, Isaac Cook's detective inspector, said. He had not expected such a flippant comment from his senior, not when they were standing near to two people who had, apparently in the final throes of passion, succumbed to what appeared to be a professional assassination.

'You know this will be all over the media within the hour,' Isaac said.

'James Holden, moral crusader, a proponent of the sanctity of the marital bed, man and wife. It's bound to be.'

Murder of a Silent Man – A DCI Cook Thriller – Book 8

A murdered recluse. A property empire. A disinherited family. All the ingredients for murder.

No one gave much credence to the man when he was alive. In fact, most people never knew who he was, although those who had lived in the area for many years recognised the tired-looking and shabbily-dressed man as he shuffled along, regular as clockwork on a Thursday afternoon at seven in the evening to the local off-licence.

It was always the same: a bottle of whisky, premium brand, and a packet of cigarettes. He paid his money over the counter, took hold of his plastic bag containing his purchases, and then walked back down the road with the same rhythmic shuffle. He said not one word to anyone on the street or in the shop.

Murder has no Guilt – A DCI Cook Thriller – Book 9

The Horse's Mouth

No one knows who the target was or why, but there are eight dead. The men seem the most likely perpetrators, or could have it been one of the two women, the attractive Gillian Dickenson, or even the celebrity-obsessed Sal Maynard?

There's a gang war brewing, and if there are deaths, it doesn't matter to them as long as it's not their death. But to Detective Chief Inspector Isaac Cook, it's his area of London, and it does matter.

It's dirty and unpredictable. Initially it had been the West Indian gangs, but then a more vicious Romanian gangster had usurped them. And now he's being marginalised by the Russians. And the leader of the most vicious Russian mafia organisation is in London, and he's got money and influence, the ear of those in power.

Murder in Hyde Park – A DCI Cook Thriller – Book 10

An early morning jogger is murdered in Hyde Park. It's the centre of London, but no one saw him enter the park, no one saw him die.

He carries no identification, only a water-logged phone. As the pieces unravel, it's clear that the dead man had a history of deception.

Is the murderer one of those that loved him? Or was it someone with a vengeance?

It's proving difficult for DCI Isaac Cook and his team at Challis Street Homicide to find the guilty person – not that they'll cease to search for the truth, not even after one suspect confesses.

Six Years Too Late – A DCI Cook Thriller – Book 11

Always the same questions for Detective Chief Inspector Isaac Cook — Why was Marcus Matthews in that room? And why did he share a bottle of wine with his killer?

It wasn't as if the man had amounted to much in life, apart from the fact that he was the son-in-law of a notorious gangster, the father of the man's grandchildren. Yet, one thing that Hamish McIntyre, feared in London for his violence, rated above anything else, it was his family, especially Samantha, his daughter; although he had never cared for Marcus, her husband.

And then Marcus disappears, only for his body to be found six years later by a couple of young boys who decide that exploring an abandoned house is preferable to school.

Grave Passion – A DCI Cook Thriller – Book 12

Two young lovers out for a night of romance. A short cut through a cemetery. They witness a murder, but there has been no struggle, only a knife to the heart.

It has all the hallmarks of an assassination, but who is the woman? And why was she alongside a grave at night? Did she know the person who killed her?

Soon after, other deaths, seemingly unconnected, but tied to the family of one of the young lovers.

It's a case for Detective Chief Inspector Cook and his team, and they're baffled on this one.

Murder Without Reason – A DCI Cook Thriller – Book 13

DCI Cook faces his greatest challenge. The Islamic State is waging war in England, and they are winning.

Not only does Isaac Cook have to contend with finding the perpetrators, but he is also being forced to commit actions contrary to his mandate as a police officer.

And then there is Anne Argento, the prime minister's deputy. The prime minister has shown himself to be a pacifist and is not up to the task. She needs to take his job if the country is to fight back against the Islamists.

Vane and Martin have provided the solution. Will DCI Cook and Anne Argento be willing to follow it through? Are they able to act for the good of England, knowing that a criminal and murderous action is about to take place? Do they have an option?

Standalone Novels

The Haberman Virus

Phillip Strang

A remote and isolated village in the Hindu Kush mountain range in North Eastern Afghanistan is wiped out by a virus unlike any seen before.

A mysterious visitor clad in a spacesuit checks his handiwork, a female American doctor succumbs to the disease, and the woman sent to trap the person responsible falls in love with him – the man who would cause the deaths of millions.

Hostage of Islam

Three are to die at the Mission in Nigeria: the pastor and his wife in a blazing chapel; another gunned down while trying to defend them from the Islamist fighters.

Kate McDonald, an American, grieving over her boyfriend's death and Helen Campbell, whose life had been troubled by drugs and prostitution, are taken by the attackers.

Kate is sold to a slave trader who intends to sell her virginity to an Arab Prince. Helen, to ensure their survival, gives herself to the murderer of her friends.

Malika's Revenge

Malika, a drug-addicted prostitute, waits in a smugglers' village for the next Afghan tribesman or Tajik gangster to pay her price, a few scraps of heroin.

Yusup Baroyev, a drug lord, enjoys a lifestyle many would envy. An Afghan warlord sees the resurgence of the

Taliban. A Russian white-collar criminal portrays himself as a good and honest citizen in Moscow.

All of them are linked to an audacious plan to increase the quantity of heroin shipped out of Afghanistan and into Russia and ultimately the West.

Some will succeed, some will die, some will be rescued from their plight and others will rue the day they became involved.

Prelude to War

Russia and America face each other across the northern border of Afghanistan. World War 3 is about to break out and no one is backing off.

And all because a team of academics in New York postulated how to extract the vast untapped mineral wealth of Afghanistan.

Steve Case is in the middle of it, and his position is looking very precarious. Will the Taliban find him before the Americans get him out? Or is he doomed, as is the rest of the world?

ABOUT THE AUTHOR

Phillip Strang was born in England in the late forties. He was an avid reader of science fiction in his teenage years: Isaac Asimov, Frank Herbert, the masters of the genre. Still an avid reader, the author now mainly reads thrillers.

In his early twenties, the author, with a degree in electronics engineering and a desire to see the world, left England for Sydney, Australia. Now, forty years later, he still resides in Australia, although many intervening years were spent in a myriad of countries, some calm and safe, others no more than war zones.

Printed in Great Britain
by Amazon